RAVES FOR RISING STAR, JENNIFER ARCHER!

"Body & Soul is a fun romp that readers who enjoy an amusing romance with a serious undertone will relish. . . . Jennifer Archer scores a bulls-eye with her warm debut novel."

—*Painted Rock*

"For every woman who has ever wanted to trade lives with someone else, Jennifer Archer's *Body & Soul* is a must read. You'll laugh, you'll cry, you'll relate, but most importantly, you'll count your blessings."

—Ronda Thompson, author of *Cougar's Woman*

"Body & Soul, Jennifer Archer's first book, sets a fast-pace, offers a delicious story, and introduces unique characters, which mark this novel with excellence, and promises readers new and exciting things in the future from this gifted author."

—*Calico Trails*

"Body & Soul is a charmer of a debut and a MUST for fans who love humor that makes you laugh out loud with sassy dialogue and sizzling sensuality. Jennifer Archer is definitely an author to watch."

—Dia Hunter, author of *The Beholding*

"Body & Soul has a fresh plot, delightful characters . . . Ms. Archer has done a great job!"

—*Under the Covers*

"Lighthearted, funny, a delight to read."

—Jodi Thomas, bestselling author of *To Kiss A Texan*

BETRAYED BY A KISS

The first brush of lips was a whisper of warm silk that whisked away all rationality. With her back pressed to the cold car and Michael molded warm against her front, Lisa opened to his kiss, welcoming the intrusion of his tongue, urging him on when gentle persuasion turned to greedy demand.

How she'd missed the eager touch of his hands, the hard insistent feel of his body next to hers. Like a starving beggar she devoured every sensation—the texture of skin beneath her fingers, his taste, his scent.

After several long seconds, Michael eased back and drew in a noisy breath. Forehead to forehead, nose to nose, their mouths lingered only a fraction of an inch apart. He twisted his fingers in her hair and closed his eyes. "Tory," he whispered.

Tory. If he'd punched her in the stomach, the jolt would've been less jarring. Lisa drew back an arm, then slapped Michael's face.

BODY & SOUL

JENNIFER ARCHER

LOVE SPELL BOOKS NEW YORK CITY

LOVE SPELL®

September 1999

Published by

Dorchester Publishing Co., Inc.
276 Fifth Avenue
New York, NY 10001

Copyright © 1999 by Jennifer Archer

ISBN 0-505-52334-5

The name "Love Spell" and its logo are trademarks of Dorchester Publishing Co., Inc.

Printed in the United States of America.

To my husband, Jeff,
for all the years of love, laughter and support;
and to my sons, Ryan and Jason,
for making me smile and keeping life interesting.
You three are my wishes come true.

And finally,
to the girl in the old red Volkswagen . . .
whoever you were.

ACKNOWLEDGMENTS

Too many people helped me during the writing of this book to mention here. I appreciate all of you—you know who you are!

I wouldn't have made it past chapter one without the following talented writers and cherished friends who not only read and re-read, but went the extra mile for me. Thanks to: Charlotte Goebel, for assuring me of my abilities even when the writing stunk, for the numerous fun "therapy" sessions, and for always insisting we have dessert; Kimberly Willis Holt, for her honest feedback, her encouragement, and for showing me what can happen when you reach for the moon; Ronda Thompson, for the hours spent brainstorming, and for sharing her humorous insight, her shoulder and her Hot Tamales; Deborah Elliott Upton, for being with me from the start, teaching me about angst, and helping me bring the story full circle.

Special thanks to my editor, Alicia Condon, for taking a chance on me, to Jean Price and DeWanna Pace for standing in my corner, to Jodi Koumalats for letting me pick her brain, and to Micki for taking the time and effort to make *Body & Soul* a better book.

BODY &
SOUL

Chapter One

Today your wish will come true.

"Right." Lisa O'Conner crumpled the scrap of paper in her hand, then stuffed it into her skirt pocket. She picked up the fortune cookie, broke off a piece, and popped it into her mouth.

"I'm sorry, did you say something?"

Lisa looked across the table at her husband's serious, amber eyes, the firm angle of his jaw. She and Michael had just spent an entire lunch hour together without exchanging a single sentence. "Never mind. Did I tell you Jake's teacher called yesterday? He's falling behind in math. She told me . . . " Lisa stopped abruptly. Michael hadn't heard a word she'd spoken. He glanced at his watch, then up at her, his eyes preoccupied with worries separate and far removed from their son's schoolwork, far removed from her.

She propped an elbow on the table and nibbled her thumbnail, watching him. "Do you like me?" she asked, startling herself with the question, startling Michael, too, judging by his expression.

"What kind of question is that?"

"A simple one," Lisa answered, her voice thick with an odd sense of loss she couldn't explain, a feeling she'd been aware of and holding inside for too long. "Do you like me?"

Michael's answering laugh was nerve-tinged, confused. He pinched his earlobe. "I love you. You know I do."

"That's not what I asked."

A memory surfaced, bobbing clear and vivid. For days it had haunted her, struggled to rise from the clouded depths of her mind, where she'd anchored it safely away years before.

It was Michael's third year of college, her second. He'd transferred to a four-year university; she had another year to complete at the two-year junior college where they'd met. Two hundred and ten miles separated them. Three hours by car. At the beginning of his fourth week away, she surprised him by driving down on a Sunday to spend the day.

As if it were yesterday, Lisa could see herself there, waiting for Michael in a dormitory lobby filled with curious, lounging men. Men wearing tank tops and athletic shorts, with running shoes or flip-flops on their feet. She could still smell the odor of stale pizza, could still hear the buzzing drone of the fan. She'd felt exposed, self-conscious. But she'd called from the front desk for Michael, and her desire to see him was stronger than her embarrassment, so she'd stood erect and feigned an air of confidence, willing herself not to blush.

"Lisa . . . " Michael said now, tugging her back to the present. The muscle in his jaw twitched, as it always did when he was tense.

Like she had that day in the dormitory, Lisa suddenly felt exposed, caught in the center of a spotlight. Distracted by the feeling, she glanced over Michael's shoulder and spotted an elderly Chinese man in the corner, studying her. Their eyes locked for a moment, and an odd sensation drifted over her. A feather-light dusting of snowflakes on the surface of her skin. Pleasantly chilly, but unsettling.

Lisa licked her lips and forced herself to look away. She leaned across the table and brushed a crumb from Michael's tie, unable to fathom the unsettled feeling inside her. She wanted out of here. Now. She'd get no answers from Michael today anyway. The timing was wrong. When was it ever right?

"Are you ready to go?" she asked, and watched relief rush through him like water through a faucet, washing away his discomfort, returning him to his confident, businesslike self.

"Yeah." Michael undraped his suit jacket from the chair beside him and stood. "I'm interviewing a college student at one-thirty for the part-time runner job. She's pre-law at the university and looking for some hands-on experience in a law firm." He shook his head. "If I'd known all the administrative decisions would fall on my shoulders, I might have thought twice about opening a law firm with Jarrod."

As she followed him from the restaurant, Lisa almost choked on the last of the fortune cookie. "You know it wouldn't have mattered. Being in business for yourself has been your top priority ever since you graduated from law school."

"Well, so much for prestige." He sighed. "But, seriously, I don't get paid for taking care of office business. Gotta get in those billable hours, ya know. I'm short of my goal this month."

Michael stood beside Lisa's minivan while she fumbled with the lock. "What's on your agenda this afternoon?" he asked.

"The usual. Grocery store, dry cleaners, post office, bank. Then pick up Kat and Jacob at three." She opened the door of the van and climbed inside.

Michael leaned over and pecked her on the cheek. "I'd better run." As he headed across the parking lot toward his car, the breeze barely ruffled his stylishly short auburn hair.

With an aching sadness that never seemed to leave her these days, Lisa remembered again that bygone time when he'd worn his hair a little too shaggy, when old, faded jeans and rumpled chambray shirts had been his standard attire . . . when his eyes had often been more teasing than serious.

"See you tonight," Michael shouted over his shoulder. "Don't hold dinner; I might be late."

Lisa closed the door and scowled. "I love you, too, Michael. I really do."

"That's mine!" Kat jerked a sucker from her brother's hand. "We got 'em in class today from the teacher."

Jake grabbed Kat's fist, then gave it a hard twist. "So did we, and that one's mine. You better give it back right now, you little butthead!"

"Jacob O'Conner! Quit calling your sister names." Lisa turned toward the backseat. She hadn't finished her other errands in time to make it to the bank before picking up the kids. The cleaners had ruined her newest blouse, and at the grocery store she'd dropped a dozen eggs, the evidence of which now lay splattered in dry, scablike droplets across her panty hose.

Arms and legs flailed in the air behind her and banged against the side of the van as her children battled.

"Ouch! You're hurting my arm."

"Get outta' my seat, you stupid . . . "

"Katherine O'Conner!" Turning, Lisa reached between the bucket seats, grasped Kat's bony arm with one hand and Jake's shoulder with the other. "You two stop it right now!" she hissed between clenched teeth. She glanced toward the bank teller's window and forced a stilted smile before returning her attention to her offspring. "One more word out of either of you and you're both grounded for the rest of your lives."

Weary, she sank back in her seat and looked across the street, where a woman dressed in an elegant suit, briefcase in hand, entered an office building. *That's supposed to be me.* Lisa laughed silently at herself, remembering a time when she had imagined a life quite different from the one she now lived. She'd believed she could pull it all off—marriage, family, career. She'd give her all to each, 100 percent. Wonder Woman—minus the conical breasts.

The van began to jostle and whine, and Lisa smelled a whiff of smoke. *Great, the damn thing's overheated again. Just what I need.* She glanced at the rearview mirror in time to see Jake stick out his tongue and aim it at Katherine. Kat returned the gesture.

Before she could comment, Lisa caught sight of her own reflection. Her hair looked as frazzled as her nerves. And dull. Dishwater blond. Mousey.

How long had it been since she last highlighted it? Running her fingers through the limp locks, a nail snagged. She lowered her hand and groaned. Not a single nail without chipped polish. *What wouldn't I give to have time for a professional manicure?* Imagining her fingers soaking in heated oil, she sighed. *What a luxury! Heaven.*

In the next lane, a candy-apple red Volkswagen pulled up. Music blared from the radio through the open windows. The driver, apparently oblivious to the crisp November air, sang along with the tune, her hair flowing soft and wild and free around her shoulders in spiraling tendrils of burnished copper.

Lisa watched the girl reach out the window for the money carrier. *Long, flamingo-pink fingernails. Perfectly manicured. Easy enough to have at age twenty.*

When the male teller greeted the driver over the intercom, the young woman turned toward the window and grinned, her eyes bright as the winter sun. "Hi. I need to cash this check, please."

Feeling ancient and dowdy beyond words, Lisa observed and listened. The girl's voice radiated energy, a lust for life, as she resumed singing, tapping her squared-off nails against the dashboard to the beat of the song, shoulders swaying to the rhythm.

The jab of a foot through the seat behind Lisa brought her back to reality. Still, she kept her eyes focused on the girl.

"Ouch! Mo-oom! Kat bit me."

With a whoosh and a clatter, the carrier fell into the slot beside Lisa's window. She retrieved her deposit slip, then looked toward the Volkswagen. "Oh, to be twenty again," Lisa muttered under her breath. "On days like today, I wish I had your life." The van vibrated and rattled. "Oh, how I wish I had your life."

Silence. Weightless, Lisa floated at the bottom of a deep, black, water-filled tunnel. Far above, a pinpoint of light speared the darkness. Mustering every ounce of energy in her body, she made a desperate struggle toward it.

As she neared the top, the light grew larger, brighter. Sounds swirled in her head. Intense ringing. The hum of a motor. Words. Voices. Music.

All at once, the melody of an unfamiliar song blasted around her, and it crossed Lisa's mind that someone must have fiddled with the radio dial. *This definitely isn't the classic rock station. It's that new junk. Nothing but a bunch of noise.*

Lisa closed her eyes against the glaring light, pressed her fingers to her throbbing temples. She felt dizzy, disoriented. Her head pounded. *A migraine. I must be having a migraine.*

She heard Kat and Jacob arguing and remembered she was at the bank. Opening her eyes, she looked into the backseat to quiet the kids and check for buckled seat belts before she drove away. The seat was empty.

"Mom, let's go! What's the matter, Mom?"

Jake called to her. Lisa heard him clearly, though he sounded far away. She turned toward his voice.

A blue minivan sat in the drive-up lane beside her. *Her* blue minivan. Through the side window, she saw Kat and Jacob. They leaned toward the front of the vehicle, talking in worried voices to a woman in the driver's seat. The woman pressed a hand to her head, then slowly lowered it to her lap.

Lisa gasped. *Dear God, it's impossible!* The woman with Jake and Kat might've been her own twin if she'd had one, her carbon copy, her clone. A shiver skittered down Lisa's spine, then traveled up again. A wave of nausea clutched her stomach. Her head fell back against the seat. She closed her eyes.

After several steadying breaths, she gathered the courage to look around. The hood stretching beyond the front window of the car in which she sat was short, round, and candy-apple red. Her hand shook like a gypsy's tambourine as she reached for the mirror. Fingernails—long, flamingo pink, and filed in flawless squares— flashed before her eyes. Terrified, Lisa tilted the mirror toward her face.

The image of a young woman with wide hazel eyes and a curly halo of long, copper hair stared back at her.

Ten minutes later, Lisa pulled the Volkswagen to the curb across the street from her house, then cut the engine. She'd been horrified to see her van drive away from the bank before she could climb out of the Volkswagen and get to it. In a panic, terrified for her children, she'd thrown the tiny car into gear and followed.

Now, she rolled the window down and watched through tear-ravaged eyes as her minivan came to a stop in the driveway. The back door slid open and Kat and Jacob emerged.

Jake walked to the driver's side and opened the door. "Quit crying, Mom," he said, his troubled voice adding a new layer to Lisa's increasing panic. He reached out a hand toward the vehicle as Kat moved tentatively up behind him. "Come inside."

"Are you gonna call Dad and tell him Mom didn't know the way home?" Kat asked.

"Shut up, Kat. You're just makin' her cry harder. She'll be okay in a minute."

With shocked disbelief, Lisa watched the woman take hold of Jake's hand and step from the van. The woman's shoulders shook as she allowed herself to be led toward the house. "I'm sorry. I . . . I'm just so confused," the woman sobbed. "I have this pounding headache and . . . " She glanced down at the dried egg stuck to her legs. "And . . . ohhh!"

When the threesome disappeared inside the house, Lisa tried to pull herself together. Unable to locate a tissue, she wiped her eyes and nose with the sleeve of the blouse adorning her current body. The material slid across her skin. *Silk.*

She glanced down to survey the new Lisa O'Conner. *Definitely a new and improved version. No wonder the body thief's crying. No question about it—the poor girl got the raw end of the deal with this trade.*

At thirty-five and after two babies, Lisa knew her old figure wasn't anything to complain about too loudly, despite an added few pounds here and there. Nevertheless, the old her couldn't begin to compare with the lithe, smoothly toned, athletic build she'd somehow jumped into.

Lisa nibbled the immaculate nail of one index finger while considering her predicament. How could she drive away and leave her children with a stranger? And an hysterical stranger at that? But if she went inside, the girl who now occupied her body might recognize herself and become even more distraught. The kids were already frightened enough without that happening.

If she called Michael and tried to explain things, he would never believe her. Why should he? She didn't believe this herself.

Then again, if she didn't go inside, where would she go? She couldn't just sit here the rest of the day . . . the rest of the night . . . forever.

She leaned her forehead against the steering wheel and gave in to a fresh wave of tears. *This is a dream . . . a nightmare. I'll wake up soon. All I have to do is wait.*

So she waited, head down, eyes closed, hands grasping the wheel, as time ticked by. The silver bracelet watch she wore on her new slender wrist proclaimed each passing minute. And nothing happened.

With a sniff, Lisa reached for the handbag in the passenger seat and sat up. "I can't leave Kat and Jacob with that woman," she said, jumping at the sound of the voice that wasn't her own. "Not until I know they're okay."

She opened the car door with a determined shove, stepped outside, then made her way up the walk toward her house. Jake appeared after the second ring of the bell.

"Hi, I . . . uh, work for the city," Lisa stammered. "I'm a census taker." She looked past her son to the weeping form huddled on the living room sofa. "Could I speak to your mother?"

"She can't talk to anybody right now." Jake turned toward the woman he assumed was his mother. "You'll have to come back."

When he started to close the door, Lisa reached out a hand. "Your mother seems upset. Can I help?"

Jake shook his head. "Thanks anyway."

"Have you called your father?" Lisa asked, bracing a palm against the door.

"Yeah, but he wasn't in the office."

Jake pulled off his wire-framed glasses and stepped back. He chewed on the end of one earpiece, studying her. The tense, controlled look on his face slowly fell away, revealing a vulnerable fright that shifted Lisa's maternal instincts to high gear. She wanted to grab him, hold him, comfort him.

Despite his initial reluctance to talk to her, he suddenly seemed relieved to have someone to confide in. Even if that someone was a stranger. "I . . . I don't know what to do."

"Why don't you ask a neighbor to come see about your mom until your dad returns to his office?" *Sandy Northrup, Jake. Get Sandy. I saw her going inside her house when I drove up. She won't leave you alone with me . . . that woman . . . in such an emotional state.*

"Uh, I guess I could see if Mrs. Northrup is home next door." He put on his glasses. "She baby-sits us sometimes."

Lisa blew out a long, slow breath. "Good idea. I'll come back when your mom's feeling better."

As she returned to the Volkswagen, Jake yelled something to Kat, then ran next door. Lisa waited inside the car until Sandy Northrup came out, her pregnant belly bouncing like a dropped bowling ball as she hurried across the lawn with Jake at her side.

Lisa knew the kids were in competent hands until Michael arrived. She rummaged inside the purse in her lap and drew out a wallet, then flipped through it until she located a driver's license.

"Tory Beecham," she read aloud, noting the Oklahoma City address underneath. "Maybe I have to go with the flow . . . follow this dream through before it can end."

After replacing the wallet inside the bag, she started the engine. "Okay, Tory Beecham, let's see where you live."

23

* * *

Lisa found Unit 510 (E) on the second floor of a tan brick building much like any number of apartment buildings in the city. She stood in front of the door trying every key on the silver key ring that had dangled from the car ignition, amazed by how Tory's body climbed stairs, two at a time, without becoming the least bit winded.

The final key slid in and the knob turned with ease. Lisa stepped over the threshold.

Closed miniblinds covering a sliding glass door darkened the room, but Lisa could see well enough to make out a standard apartment den. Easing the door shut behind her, she went to open the blinds.

Beyond the sliding door, a fenced patio extended approximately five feet from the building. A small grill sat between two lawn chairs. Wind chimes dangled from the overhanging roof and tinkled in the breeze.

Lisa turned and noticed a threadbare couch along the length of one wall. Another wall displayed a cheaply built entertainment center housing a television set, VCR, and Nintendo game player. Two beanbag chairs, one navy and one white, adorned two opposite corners of the floor. Remembering the bright orange beanbag from her own college days, she smiled. *Must be the return of an old fad.*

The living room opened onto a small kitchen cluttered with dishes. Lisa peeked down a tiny hallway leading away from the kitchen to what she supposed was the bedroom. She walked toward the closed door, twisted the knob, then stepped inside.

The room was dark. She couldn't see much of anything other than shadows. Fumbling along the wall, Lisa located the light switch and flipped it on.

Light flooded the room. A room dominated by a king-sized water bed. An unmade, rumpled, king-sized water bed with a sleeping young man sprawled naked in the center.

He opened one groggy eye, lifted his head from the pillow, and pushed strands of long, sleek, dark hair from his face.

"Hi, babe," he said in a hoarse, lazy voice. A voice that shot her temperature so high, her internal smoke alarm screeched. He reached out and grabbed Lisa's arm, then pulled her onto the bed beside him. "Come here."

Chapter Two

Lisa rolled, face first, into the young man's smooth, bare chest as the waterbed swayed around them. He ran a hand down her spine to her bottom and pressed her gently against him, nibbling at the spot just beneath her ear.

"Mmmm, what a way to wake up. I think I like this arrangement. I'm glad I moved in."

Lisa's pulse skyrocketed. She pushed away and scrambled to stand. Heat crept up her neck, her face, scorched her skin to the roots of her hair. In an attempt to hold back her lurching heart, she flattened a palm to her chest. "I . . . "

He propped up on one elbow. "What's with you?"

With trembling hands, she smoothed the silk blouse she wore, then adjusted the short emerald-colored skirt covering her hips and thighs. "I . . . you . . . you're getting me wrinkled." Mortified by his state of undress, she lowered her eyes.

He yawned, rolled out of bed, and stretched. "Wow! Look at you. New outfit for the interview?"

She couldn't move. He faced her, one specific part of his body in direct line with her lowered gaze. Lisa's mouth fell open and, try as she might, she couldn't tear her attention away from the view.

"Pretty amazing, isn't it?"

"Um . . . what?" She blinked and looked up, focusing on his dark, hooded eyes. His grin was more of a leer than a smile, suggestive and full of arrogant male pride.

"Take off those new duds and I'll astound you even more."

Lisa stepped back. *Men. Young, old, or somewhere in-between—they're all the same.* "I . . . can't. I'm, uh . . . busy."

He gave her a puzzled frown, then looked at the clock radio on the nightstand. "I gotta get to work anyway."

Lisa decided that in addition to losing her old body, she must have misplaced the part of her brain that controlled speech and body movement. Though her mind told her to do something, say something—anything—she could only stand frozen in place, silently staring, as he crossed to a dresser, pulled out a pair of underwear, then walked to the closet for jeans and a shirt.

His eyes, black as a raven's wing, had a curious slant, his skin an olive hue. Gleaming, ebony hair, straight and parted down the middle, brushed the tops of his shoulders, and though those shoulders were broad, the body beneath was whip-thin and tall. He had a strange appeal, this young man.

This young man! Good grief! I'm alone in an apartment with a naked kid! A kid who thinks I'm his girlfriend!

Despite the awkwardness of the situation, Lisa couldn't help comparing him to Michael. How could she *not* be curious? After all, she'd been with her husband forever, it seemed. Except for in movies and a magazine or two, she'd never seen another man naked. Her one other complete close encounter with the opposite sex had occurred during her high school dating years. One night of awkwardly consummated groping in the backseat of a pitch-dark Trans Am.

At five-foot-eleven, Michael was shorter than this kid, but every bit as trim. And though the years had softened him some, Michael still possessed the body of an athlete, the legs of a runner.

In contrast, this guy's well-toned, graceful physique was less compact than Michael's, but equally as masculine. The muscles running along his shoulders, thighs, and calves were long and rippling, rather than bunched and bulging, as Michael's were when he went on a workout binge.

"Are you sure you're feeling okay?" he asked, opening the miniblinds on the room's single window, then pausing at the entrance to the bathroom.

Lisa opened her mouth to speak. Instead, she only managed a nod.

"You're acting strange, Tory. If I didn't know you were a teetotaler, I'd think you had one too many margaritas last night."

He swung back his hair, and sunlight from the window reflected off the diamond embedded in his left ear.

"How did the interview go?" he asked.

She shrugged.

He made a face, then disappeared behind the bathroom wall. "You coming up to the club tonight?" he shouted.

Lisa sank to the edge of the bed and took a deep breath. "No. I think I'll just stay home and rest."

"Sounds like a good idea. Maybe by the time my shift ends you'll feel better. Don't be wearing anything that wrinkles when I get home." He poked his head around the corner and grinned, narrowing his eyes. "On second thought, don't be wearing anything."

When he was out of sight again, Lisa slapped a hand to her forehead and groaned. The shower came on in the next room and the guy began to sing. *Alternative rock?* She pushed to her feet, praying her shock-weakened legs would hold her weight and follow her commands.

She hurried to a corner of the bedroom, where a pile of discarded clothes lay on the floor. Kneeling, she searched the pockets of a pair of wide-legged, dirty men's jeans for identification. Nothing.

After a frantic survey of the room, she finally spotted a wallet lying next to a computer on a cluttered desk. Inside, she found what she had hoped for—a driver's license. She pulled it out and scanned the information.

Dillon Todd. From the birthdate, she calculated his age at twenty-one—*barely.* Eyes black—*and expressive.* Height six-foot-two—*every inch impressive.* Sex male—*definitely.*

Twenty minutes later, Dillon answered the ringing phone. "Hello?" He paused. "Just a sec."

He handed the receiver to Lisa, where she still sat at the edge of the bed. "For you." Brushing a kiss across the top of her head, Dillon stepped back, then raised and lowered his brows. "See ya tonight, babe."

Lisa waited until she heard the front door open and close before pressing the receiver to her ear. She fell back onto the bed, smelled Dillon Todd's musky scent on the sheets, then quickly sat up again. "Hello," she said, her voice weak.

"Ms. Beecham?"

That depends. Do you wish to speak to her body or her soul? "Yes?"

"This is Michael O'Conner with Wilder and O'Conner Attorneys."

"Michael . . . " Lisa whispered. Her heart hammered faster than a woodpecker on diet pills. This dream was getting crazier by the second.

"Excuse me?" Michael said.

Dream or not, she was curious as to why her husband might be calling Tory Beecham. Lisa decided to play along. "Oh, nothing. I was just telling my boyfriend good-bye." She placed a palm over the mouthpiece to muffle her words. "See you later!" she shouted, then talked back into the receiver. "He's gone now. What can I do for you, Mi . . . Mr. O'Conner?"

"I'm calling in regard to the runner position with my firm we spoke about this afternoon. My partner and I want to hire you, if you're still interested."

Good grief! Tory Beecham was Michael's one-thirty interview! In a matter of seconds, Lisa considered her options. She could accept the job and be close to Michael every day. By doing so, maybe she would summon the nerve to tell him the truth. If this wasn't a dream, she needed his help now more than she had at any other time during their lives together. Or, she could avoid making an already awkward and unbelievable situation all the more difficult by declining the offer. *And then what?*

"That's wonderful," Lisa heard Tory's voice answer. "Of course I'm still interested. When do I start?"

"Let's see. You said you have classes until noon every day for the remainder of this semester, right?"

How should I know? "Right."

"And if I remember correctly, next semester's the same?"

Lisa bit down on the corner of Tory's fingernail. "Uh-huh." The nail snapped in two.

"Fine. We would like you to work from one until five while you're in school. Would it be possible for you to work full-time during your winter break? I noticed from your résumé that you have word processing skills. My secretary requested vacation time around the holidays. We could use your help to fill in."

"Umm." She wiped beads of perspiration from her upper lip with the back of one hand. "Uh, that would be great."

Across town, Michael frowned. *And could you get those umms and uhs under control and work on your speaking skills?* he wanted to ask. "Can you start day after tomorrow?" he asked instead.

"Sure."

"Good. I'll see you Wednesday, then, at one o'clock. Oh, and dress casual. You might be doing anything from running errands to filling out a deposit to digging around in the storage room for old files. Jeans are fine."

"Great. I'll be there day after tomorrow. In jeans."

Immediately after Michael hung up, his secretary buzzed. "Jacob's on line one, Michael. He called while you were out, too, but I didn't have a

31

chance to tell you before you got on the phone. He seems rather upset."

Punching line one, Michael grabbed the receiver. "Hi, son. Is something wrong?"

"It's Mom."

Michael's pulse jumped and he gripped the receiver tighter. "Is she hurt?"

"I don't think so," Jake answered, his voice uncertain. "She's just . . . well, she's been crying for a long time, and I don't know why."

"Call her to the phone."

"I don't think she'll talk, Dad. Mrs. Northrup is here, but will you come home?"

"I'll be right there."

Michael hung up. He wondered what could be wrong with Lisa. She'd seemed okay at lunch.

Her odd question popped to mind. *Do you like me?*

Gathering his jacket and briefcase as he made his way out the door, Michael shouted over his shoulder to his secretary, "Nan, I need to leave early today. I'll be at home if you need to reach me."

Hours later, Lisa awoke with a start, the sound of her heart thudding in her ears. She lay still, listening to the steady beat, trying to figure out where she was.

Remembering brought a possibility she couldn't fathom. Now she would discover whether it had only been a dream, or if the impossible had really taken place after all.

She opened her eyes and squinted, waiting to adjust to the darkness. Disbelief filtered in. The bedroom she occupied was not her own. It belonged to Tory Beecham.

Lisa glanced toward the only distinguishable light—the soft green glow of the clock. *Just after midnight. I must have fallen asleep after Michael's call.* She still wore the same skirt and silk blouse she'd arrived in. *So much for avoiding wrinkles.*

The thought brought Dillon Todd to mind. *Good grief, what am I going to do about him?* Panicked, Lisa stood and flipped on the light. He might be home any minute. She desperately wanted a shower before he returned. She had to be asleep, or at least pretend to be, when he arrived.

Rushing to the dresser, Lisa made a frantic search of every drawer until she found one filled with nightgowns and underwear. *Cotton nightshirt—too short.* She tossed it aside. *Black satin teddy—absolutely not.* She pushed it to the back of the drawer. *Mickey Mouse T-shirt—too cute.*

Finally she found it. *Pink, long-sleeved flannel. Ankle-length, buttons to the neck. Perfect.* She tucked the gown beneath one arm, shut the bureau drawer, ran into the bathroom, then closed the door behind her. *No lock. Great!*

She remembered Dillon's earlier question. *"You coming up to the club tonight?"* Relief washed over her, relaxing every muscle, stilling her pulse. *He works at a club. Bars don't usually close until two in the morning. Still a couple of hours left.*

While surveying the small, cluttered bathroom, Lisa noticed a giant plastic bottle of bubble bath on the floor beside the tub. After what she'd been through today, she decided she deserved some relaxation, or at least an attempt at it. At this point, she wasn't sure anything less potent than an elephant tranquilizer could calm her nerves.

She turned the water on full force, letting it beat against her hand until it felt warm enough. After closing the drain, she poured a generous amount of gooey, iridescent-pink liquid under the faucet. Fluffy, white bubbles billowed atop the water. A delicious floral fragrance permeated the air.

As the tub filled, Lisa unzipped her skirt and let it fall past her amazingly slender hips to the floor. She peeled off panty hose, unbuttoned the cuffs of her blouse, then started to work on the others down the front of the garment. The silk slid from her arms, floating to the floor to join the skirt in a heap.

With a glance toward the bathtub, which was now almost full, Lisa reached between her breasts and released the hook on her bra. She pulled it off and dropped it, then turned toward a cabinet to look for a washcloth and towel.

Tory's image in the mirror caught her eye. "Oh, my God!" she shrieked. The bathroom door flew open as Lisa's chin fell to her chest.

"Tory! What's the matter?" Dillon gasped. "You scared the crap outta me!"

"I have breasts," Lisa whispered, gazing down.

Dillon leaned against the doorframe sucking in air. "I certainly hope so."

"But they're so . . . so . . . *big.*"

"You don't have to convince me."

Brought back to reality by the suggestive inflection in his voice, Lisa glanced up. He was smiling that smile again. That *leer*. She looked down at her new body, then back up at him, her arms quickly crossing in front of her, palms covering her very full, very exposed breasts. "What are you doing here?"

"It's after midnight." He looked toward the tub, then down at her skimpy lace panties. "I see you're waiting for me. And wearing wrinkle-resistant clothing." Dillon stepped forward.

Lisa stepped back. The sink counter jabbed into her spine, and she was vaguely aware of water and bubbles trickling over the side of the tub.

Arms still crossed, she stooped, lowered one hand, scooped the blouse from the floor, then held it in front of her. "Dillon," she said, watching anticipation turn to disappointment on his face, "we need to talk."

Michael sat in a rocker in his bedroom studying Lisa while she slept in their bed. His wife had rocked many a mile in this chair when Jake and Kat were babies. He'd rocked a few miles himself, though not nearly enough, he guessed, recalling his conversation with Lisa's best friend, Valerie Potter, when he'd talked to her earlier on the phone.

"Jake called me at the office, Val. He and Kat said Lisa started crying at the bank and didn't stop until she fell asleep just before I got home." Confused and more than slightly concerned, Michael blew out a long, slow breath. "That's another thing: They said she didn't know how to get here. They had to give her directions, for pete's sake!"

"They had to give her directions? You're kidding! How is she now?"

"She's asleep. I don't want to wake her. Maybe she's just exhausted. Has she mentioned that anything's been bothering her?" The long silence at the other end of the line insinuated that Val was considering the consequences of spilling her guts to her best friend's husband.

"Well, Michael," Val finally said, "normally I wouldn't betray Lisa's confidence, but under the circumstances, maybe it's necessary."

"I need to know. Get on with it, Val."

"Last week Lisa and I had lunch. She's . . . she's worried about your marriage. I think she's having an identity crisis, Michael. Her life revolves around you and the children. There's no time left for her other needs and wants."

Michael went still, both inside and out. He pictured Val at the other end of the line; her dark, glossy cap of hair, her professional, sleek appearance. Could Lisa's friendship with divorced, childless, career-woman Val have her questioning the path she'd chosen? He'd known Valerie Potter since college and liked her. It bothered him to think that she might encourage doubts in Lisa about her own lifestyle. "Which are . . . ?" he asked.

"You mean her needs and wants? Who knows?" Val's chewing gum popped. "I don't think Lisa even knows. She's so wrapped up in satisfying everyone else's, I think she's forgotten her own. Don't get me wrong: She's crazy about you and the kids. Wouldn't trade you for the world. But maybe you guys need to think of her for a change. Fend for yourselves some."

"And our marriage?" Michael asked, trying not to sound as defensive as he felt. "What did she say about it?"

"I feel funny talking to you about this, Michael, but if it will help Lisa get back to normal . . . " Val blew out a noisy breath. "She said that the two of you never talk about anything important. That you both avoid any topic that might raise a conflict—so nothing gets resolved."

Though he resented Val's lecture, Michael had hung up unable to soothe the guilt gnawing at his conscience. *Do you like me?* Lisa had asked him. But they hadn't discussed what prompted such a question. They'd changed the subject to a safer one instead. Maybe that was what this episode, so unlike Lisa, was all about.

But why now? Michael wondered. Why would Lisa suddenly be upset over a way of dealing with issues that had been the norm throughout their marriage? Changing the subject was nothing new. After spending his childhood with parents who cooked up conflict for breakfast, lunch, and dinner, seven days per week, he'd made a conscious effort to steer clear of it in his own marriage and family life. Past experience had convinced him that hashing things out didn't necessarily solve anything. And since Lisa never prodded, he'd assumed she agreed. She'd seemed content to keep things smooth and unemotional. Until now.

She was the only woman for him, Michael thought as he gazed across at her sleeping form. When had he last told her so? While other men seemed to complain constantly about their wives, he honestly couldn't do the same about Lisa. He admired her caring, giving nature. It warmed his heart to see her with their children. He was attracted to everything about Lisa, inside and out. And though he admitted to himself that maybe he'd begun to take her for granted, he loved her as much as ever. More.

Was she going to sleep all night? Michael had wanted to talk to her ever since he came home. Wanted to be assured that everything was okay; to make everything okay if necessary. He wouldn't sleep until he did.

He stood and crossed to the bedside, then brushed the hair from Lisa's face. *So soft.* He loved the color. So what if it came from a bottle? She'd chosen well. She looked completely peaceful. Had she been worn out lately? He hadn't noticed. Hadn't taken the time, Michael realized with another stab of guilt.

Lisa stirred beneath his touch. Her eyelids fluttered open to reveal the intense blue eyes that had stolen his soul so many years before. They were swollen now, and in them, to his amazement, he saw fear. She jerked away from him.

"Who are you?" she rasped.

"What?"

She sat up and scooted against the headboard, clasping her knees to her body with trembling arms. "I said, who are you?"

"Lisa," Michael groaned. "You've got to be kidding. It's me. Michael." When recognition didn't register, he added, "Your husband."

Her eyes roamed his face. She squinted. "My husband? Michael. Lisa. I'm Lisa?"

"Of course you're Lisa. What's wrong, honey?" He sat at the edge of the bed, frowning. "Tell me what's wrong."

"I . . . I don't know who I am." Gentle sobs shook her body. "I mean, I don't remember anything. Not a single thing."

Fear clutched his heart, then just as quickly transformed to uncertainty. Was she trying to prove a point? If she was anyone other than his wife, he'd think so. In fact, he'd be certain she was lying. But this was Lisa. It wasn't in her to manipulate. She'd never jerk his emotions around.

Again, he recalled his earlier conversation with Val. If Lisa had reached a breaking point, if she felt desperate to change things between them, would she try a new tactic to get through to him? Would she go this far? Would she?

Frustrated irritation swept through him, momentarily overwhelming his concern. So, maybe he hadn't thanked Lisa lately for clean socks and underwear. *Big deal.*

Did she ever express even an ounce of gratitude every morning when he dragged himself from bed to make the staggering climb up the ladder of success? *No.*

True, he neglected to tell her what a wonderful job she did balancing the checkbook every month, how he appreciated the fact that she always kept milk in the fridge. *So what?*

He couldn't remember a single time when she'd given him the credit he deserved for his regular paycheck or admired his lawn-mowing abilities.

As though to further his annoyance, Michael's jaw began to twitch. "If this is a game, Lisa, I don't want to play. If you're mad at me about something, then, damn it to hell, just say so and get it over with. We're not getting anywhere like this."

The stricken look on her face had concern taking precedence again. He softened his voice. "Let's talk about it. I know it's not easy for either of us, but please, please talk to me, honey. No changing the subject. I promise."

She shrank away from him, trembling like a terrified child. "I don't know what you're talking about," she choked out between sobs.

Michael's anxiety returned full force. He ran a hand through his hair, stood and paced, uncertain how he should handle the situation. "You're scaring me. Why don't you take a shower? It'll probably make you feel better. We'll see how you're doing in the morning."

After rolling off the opposite side of the bed, she walked a wide berth around the room, avoiding Michael on her way to the bathroom. Once inside, she closed the door. The lock clicked.

Michael folded down the comforter and sheets, then stripped to his boxers and climbed beneath the covers. What could've gotten into Lisa? She was acting like a stranger.

He turned to one side, then the other, then onto his back, unable to find a comfortable position. Pushing to sit up, he grabbed the pillow and fluffed it, then stuffed it behind his neck.

He finally settled in just as an agonized shriek filled the air. Lisa's shriek. Tossing back the covers, he jumped out of bed, then ran to the bathroom door. "Lisa!" he shouted, jiggling the doorknob to dislodge the faulty lock. "Are you okay?"

His efforts finally worked. The door swung open.

She stood naked before the mirror, a look of horror on her face. "This can't be my body!"

Michael fell back against the wall to catch his breath. She'd scared him out of three years of life. "What's wrong with it?"

"It's just . . . not what I expected."

He scanned his wife's familiar naked body from head to toe and frowned. He liked her figure—her small, firm breasts, the soft curve of her waist, even her slightly rounded belly—evidence she'd carried his children. Okay, so she'd gained a pound or two in the hips and thighs. He wasn't complaining. Yet, there she stood, gaping at herself with displeasure, as if owning her figure was a fate worse than death.

"You have a beautiful body, Lisa. Have I ever led you to believe otherwise?" Michael reached out a hand to her as a dread-filled anxiety spread through him.

Something was wrong with Lisa. Something serious.

Chapter Three

Lisa sat on Tory's couch and watched Dillon lift the last box of his meager possessions, then head dejectedly toward the front door. Last night, she'd learned those boxes hadn't rested long in the recesses of the closet. Dillon had moved in last week.

She was probably missing Tory's classes at the university this morning. That possibility made Lisa's feelings of guilt all the more aggravating. Not only was Tory about to lose her boyfriend, if this went on for very long, she'd be behind in school, as well.

When Dillon left the apartment to add the final load to his over-filled old Jeep, Lisa sighed. She had her own problems to worry about without fretting over Tory, but she couldn't help herself. It had been a horrible night. The worst. Under the circumstances, she didn't know how she could possibly feel blameworthy for telling Dillon they couldn't live together, but she did. What if Tory Beecham loved him? It was obvious he loved her. From what he'd told her, they'd even talked of marriage.

She inspected the jagged fingernail on the index finger of her left hand and scowled. When this whole crazy fantasy ended and she and Tory were back where they belonged, what if Dillon and the girl were lost to each other forever because of her?

Still, what other choice did she have? She couldn't go home and face Michael with everything until she talked to Tory and they figured out a way to convince him. And she couldn't live with a healthy, twenty-one-year-old, red-blooded American male, either.

Upon reentering the apartment, Dillon stood in the middle of the room and stared at her. A myriad of emotions darkened his face like a brooding storm cloud. Confusion . . . hurt . . . anger. As much as she wished she could, Lisa couldn't think of anything to say to ease his mood or make him understand.

"Well, I guess this is it." With a jerk of his head, Dillon tossed back the hair from his eyes. "I don't understand you, Tory. It was your idea for me to move in. I broke the lease on my place; even lost the damn deposit. Where am I supposed to go now?"

"I told you, you can stay here. I'll find another place."

"This is your apartment. If anyone's leaving, it'll be me."

"In that case, I'm sure one of your friends would let you move in for a while." Lisa hugged Dillon's pillow to her chest. He'd spent the night on the couch, and from the feel of the lumpy cushion beneath her thighs, she realized it must've been misery. "Besides," she continued, scrambling for a reason to give him, "I didn't say this was forever. We just rushed into it too fast, I guess. I need some time."

"Rushed into it too fast? We've been together two years. What's with you, Tory? It's like you've turned into a different person in the last twenty-four hours. Next thing I know, you'll be joining a sorority and wearing your hair in a bob."

His laugh was quick, humorless. "If you think I'm gonna set myself up for this to happen again, you're crazy," he said. "When I walk out of here, that's it for us. I told you so last night. I meant it."

For a few tense, silent moments he stood there, scowling through narrowed bloodshot eyes, as if waiting for her to change her mind and ask him to stay. When she didn't, he turned and left. The door slammed shut behind him, the sound echoing through the apartment with terrible finality.

Michael sat across from the family doctor. A sleepless night on the couch had strengthened his conclusion that something was horribly wrong with Lisa. She really *had* lost her memory. Earlier, he'd called Nan, his secretary, and canceled his morning appointments.

"What's going on with her, Doc?" he asked now, rubbing his gritty eyes.

Dr. Piaro tapped the earpiece of his glasses, then scratched his shiny, bald head. "To tell you the truth, Mr. O'Conner, I'm not sure. I can't find anything physically wrong with Lisa. You've said that, as far as you know, she hasn't suffered a recent head injury, and I don't see any signs to contradict that." He steepled his hands on the desk and leaned forward. "Are you having any marital problems?"

"Just the usual spats now and then. Like all married couples," Michael added, pinching his earlobe.

The following prolonged silence, along with the physician's shrewd gaze, had him feeling like a witness under interrogation. Michael cleared his throat. *Better come clean.* "I talked to Lisa's best friend last night. She said Lisa's concerned about our marriage, that she's going through an identity crisis. Apparently she's not as happy with our life together as I thought."

"Well, I don't believe discontent is enough to trigger amnesia. Sometimes a severe shock can cause something like this to occur. It's the body's way of protecting the mind from incidents too difficult to face. Has your wife received any bad news lately? A death in the family, perhaps?"

"No."

"What about her past? Did she suffer any significant trauma as a child? I'm referring to physical or emotional abuse, or possibly a terrifying experience she never forgot."

"Not that I'm aware of."

"This type of condition doesn't usually last long. I think she should just continue in her usual routine the best she can. On your way out, tell the receptionist I'd like to see Lisa again in a week. If she's not getting any better by then, I could refer you to a psychiatrist."

The doctor stood and ushered Michael down the hallway. "Your wife should be dressed by now and waiting in the reception area. Call me if any new problems or questions arise."

After scheduling Lisa's next appointment, Michael stood at the entrance to the waiting room and watched her before she noticed his presence. Her eyes were red and puffy, her face pale. Last night, after her shower, Lisa had refused to sleep with him. Curled around her pillow, she cried miserably until she finally drifted off.

This morning, though still disoriented and distant, she'd been somewhat calmer. He convinced her to see the doctor, but now, watching her sit despondently in the waiting room, he wasn't certain it had accomplished anything in the way of providing answers or solutions.

When Lisa lifted her hopeless eyes to his, Michael walked toward her, extending his hand. "Let's go home." Her hesitance wounded him more than he would've imagined. "Please, Lisa. Trust me." After a moment, she took his hand and followed him out of the office to the car.

On the way home, he drove to the children's school and parked at the curb. "As much as I hate to, I need to go into work for at least a short while this afternoon. Do you think you can pick up the kids at three?" He motioned toward the building. "This is their school. I'll show you the route from here to the house. Will you be able to remember the way?"

"I'll try."

"I could make arrangements for someone else to get them."

"The doctor told me the fastest way to regain my memory is to do familiar things. If picking the kids up at three is what I always do every day, then that's what I'll do. I mean . . . I guess I should."

"Fine." Michael shifted the car into drive and headed for home. "We don't live far from here. I'll write down my office number before I leave. Keep it in your pocket. If you have any problems, honey, stop somewhere along the way and give me a call."

She leaned her head back against the seat and stared through the window at the scenery whizzing by. "What else do I do every day?"

Michael cast her a sideward glance. "Let's see. You take care of the house. You know, the cleaning and laundry and everything. You do errands. The banking, grocery shopping, the cleaners and all of that." Pausing, he realized he wasn't entirely sure how Lisa filled her days. "You pay the bills. And you take care of the kids, of course. And me." When she faced him, he saw Lisa blink back fresh tears.

"That's my life? I mean, that's what I do every single day?"

"If you ask me, that's a lot for one person to handle."

"For some reason, I imagined myself with a job or something. A career."

"You went back to work in pharmaceutical sales last year when Kat started first grade, remember?" He reached across and briefly touched her hand, more worried than ever by the change in her. She didn't even *speak* like herself. "Of course, you had to start at the bottom of the ladder again, you'd been out of the job market so long. After a while, we decided what you earned wasn't worth the stress. Coping with the demands of a job and running a household were just too much."

"Did you offer to pick up some of the slack?" she asked, her tone accusing now instead of distressed.

Michael stopped at a red light. He felt a rising sense of doom at the turn of the conversation. "You mean around the house?"

She nodded. "And with the kids. Did you take on some extra responsibilities and stuff with them, too?"

"You never asked me to." From the corner of his eye, he saw her nostrils flare.

"I shouldn't have to ask."

"I suggested we hire a housekeeper. You said you'd just be working to pay her."

"That didn't answer my question. Did you, or did you not, start helping out more at home?"

The light turned green. Michael stepped on the accelerator and stared ahead, wondering how he would ever squirm out of this one. "Well . . . no, not really. It's not as if I don't already mow the lawn and everything."

With a huff, she turned away from him to glare back out the window. "So what you're telling me is, my entire purpose in life is to keep other people's lives running smoothly, right?"

Anticipating another crying jag, Michael reached across the seat and clasped his wife's hand. "No, no, there's more," he assured her as he confronted the desperate hope in Lisa's expression. "You handle the bookkeeping for the law firm."

"Am I paid?"

"Well . . . no."

With that, the first heartbreaking sobs began. Michael hurriedly checked traffic before glancing back at her. "You also do some volunteer work at the school." As the first tears fell, he quickly added, "And you're on the PTA board."

Her eyes widened. "PTA! I'm in the PTA?" Tears ran down her cheeks unchecked.

Confused and frustrated, Michael pulled into the driveway. "What's wrong with that?"

"I . . . I don't know." She accepted the handkerchief he pulled from his pocket. "I mean, somehow I just can't imagine myself in the PTA."

How many times had Lisa lamented that she just wasn't PTA mom material? Over and over, he'd encouraged her to quit, but she always signed up again the following year, intent on staying involved and keeping a finger on the pulse of their children's education. He'd always admired her for it, though he couldn't recall ever telling her so. Still, crazy as it sometimes drove her, she'd never become hysterical over the matter, as she seemed to be doing now.

She blew her nose and wiped her eyes before peering over at him, the hope in her expression flickering. "I'm not in the Junior League, am I?"

Michael shook his head. "No."

She squeezed her eyes shut, clutching the well-used hanky between her fist. "Oh, thank God!"

To avoid a crowd, Lisa arrived at *Confucius Says* after the lunch rush.

Earlier, when Dillon left the apartment, Lisa had spent the remainder of the morning mulling over her circumstances, desperate to determine how something so incredible could've happened to her. Thinking back from the time of the body switch, she retraced the events of her day, and finally remembered her lunch with Michael at the Chinese restaurant and the fortune cookie's prediction, *Today your wish will come true.*

When she saw Tory at the bank afterward, she'd wished for the girl's life, even said it aloud. The fortune cookie was the answer to her dilemma. She had to grasp onto that hope, had to believe it was true. Because if the fortune cookie wasn't the answer, where would she turn? She'd be lost. Alone. Helpless. Hopeless.

Determined to re-create yesterday's scenario as precisely as possible, Lisa sat at the same table, in the same chair. She ordered the same food hoping, maybe . . . just maybe, by some twist of fate

. . . she'd be granted the same fortune. Or possibly another that would indicate the course of action she should pursue to pop back into her own body and resume her old life.

A short time later, her meal finished and lodged in her nervous stomach like a rock, Lisa waited as the waitress took her plate from the table. She replaced it with a tiny plastic tray with three crescent-shaped cookies in the center.

"Three?" Lisa asked. Her heart pounded wildly as she glanced from the tray to the waitress.

"You must read them all," the woman answered, her dark eyes gentle, her voice melodic.

A strangely familiar sensation fell over Lisa—the same one she'd experienced during her lunch with Michael the day before. Snowflakes dancing across her skin . . . the certainty that she was being watched. She turned and spotted the elderly Chinese man. He stood in a far corner of the restaurant, staring at her with wise, old eyes . . . mystical eyes that seemed to read her thoughts. Something told Lisa that behind those black eyes lived a mind filled with the answers to all the questions of time.

Goose bumps scampered up her spine as the waitress left the table. The aged gentleman nodded his head, then slowly turned and disappeared into the kitchen.

For a minute, Lisa remained focused on the spot where he'd stood. Then, shaking off the surreal feelings he generated, she shifted her attention to the cookies.

Which one? Which one first? So much counted on the words inside those golden wafers; her life with her children, her marriage, her very identity. Left to right seemed a logical order, so she lifted the cookie at the tray's far left with an unsteady hand, then gently broke it apart.

Pulling out the sliver of paper, Lisa held her breath. Her trembling hands, coupled with the nervous tears in her eyes, made for difficult reading of the words printed neatly side-by-side.

Look at your life.

Lisa blinked. She reread the message before placing it on the table.

The second wafer beckoned. She balanced it in her palm, half expecting to feel some magical flow of energy from its core. After a moment, she carefully cracked it open, freed the paper inside, and read.

Open your heart. Look inside for the answers you seek.

Lisa shook all over now, from head to toe. "What does this mean?" she whispered. How could she possibly find her way back by looking at her life? By looking inside her own heart?

Perspiration beaded between her breasts. Forty-five degrees outside, yet she was sweating. *The last cookie.* The solution rested inside. It had to. With mounting anxiety, Lisa broke the last cookie in half.

Watch for the sun before the last quarter moon. Talk to the one you love. The truth will set you free.

Sniffing, Lisa scanned the message a second time. "So, does this mean this won't last forever?" she whispered. She reread all three slips again in order, a slow smile creeping across her face. "This won't last forever," she stated aloud, then laughed.

She slipped all the strips into Tory's wallet, then fumbled inside her purse and retrieved a pocket calendar she'd run across before. She found the current date, November 28, then searched the days ahead. *November 29, first quarter moon.* "Tomorrow," she said quietly, then read *December 6, full moon,* and finally, *December 14, last quarter moon.*

Lisa counted forward, feeling hopeful again. With the promise of returning to her real life soon, she just might enjoy being twenty again for a while. In only seventeen days she would change back, return to the two kids she loved dearly and couldn't imagine living without. And Michael . . . their marriage. An imperfect marriage perhaps, but a union she cherished and hoped to revive, despite the flaws.

Two weeks and three days. Michael, Jake, and Kat could survive without her for that long. And she could keep tabs on them by working in Michael's office.

Tory . . . she'd have to meet with the girl and tell her about the last quarter moon. The two of them could pull this off for seventeen days. "If I knew how to make it happen faster, I would," Lisa whispered. But she didn't have the vaguest idea how to accomplish such a feat. And besides, this was a fate, a time frame, she could deal with and accept.

Giddy with relief and excitement, Lisa paid her check and started to leave the restaurant. The knowledge that she'd soon return to her old life changed everything.

At the door she felt them again. *Snowflakes.* She turned. The Chinese man stood behind her. "First two fortunes important as third," he said in a voice that crackled like old parchment. Then he nodded and walked away.

For several moments, Lisa stared after him, trembling. Outside, she slid behind the wheel of the Volkswagen, rolled down the windows to take in some much-needed air, then started the engine and pulled out of the parking lot. The old man's words weighed heavy on her mind. She thought of the first two fortunes.

Look at your life. Open your heart. Look inside for the answers you seek.

So she had some soul-searching to do in the next seventeen days. Simple enough. Then she'd tell Michael what had happened. It wouldn't matter if he believed her or not. The fortune had clearly stated that the truth would free her. She had no other choice than to believe it.

Crisp November air whipped her hair about her head. She welcomed the biting chill, was energized by it. Maneuvering through the streets, Lisa headed toward Tory's apartment—her home for the next seventeen days. She turned the radio dial to the classic rock station, then, on impulse, pumped up the volume until Steppenwolf's "Born To Be Wild" throbbed around her.

At a red light, she eased to a stop, drumming her palms against the steering wheel to the rhythm of the music and singing along with the words.

The light turned green. Still singing, Lisa shifted her attention to the next lane, where a fortyish woman in a Suburban shook her head and stared back, a condescending smirk on her face.

Just for effect, Lisa gunned the engine. Then, grinning, she waved at the woman before taking off.

"Born to be wi-iiild . . . !"

Chapter Four

When Lisa arrived at Tory's apartment, she checked out every nook and cranny. For the next seventeen days, there'd be no one to dictate her time, nobody's messes to clean up but her own. If she wanted, she could read a novel straight through without interruption. She could sleep late on Saturdays without being pestered to scrounge up breakfast. And she'd have total custody of the TV remote control. No kids' cartoons. None of Michael's "Monday Night Football" or Discovery Channel documentaries on everything you never wanted to know about the sex life of dung beetles.

A closer inspection of her temporary home had Lisa frowning. The place obviously hadn't seen a dust rag or a vacuum cleaner in weeks. No dishes sat on the cabinet shelves because they were all in the kitchen sink—dirty. But that could be easily remedied.

The furniture was another matter. Lisa scrutinized the navy and white beanbags. Dillon had asked if he might leave them until he knew where he'd be staying. As she returned to the kitchen to clean up the dishes, Lisa guessed she should at least be grateful he didn't own a lava lamp.

After a quick spruce up of the quarters, she studied her new face in the bedroom mirror. "Smooth as a baby's butt," she muttered. Tory's complexion was flawless, her coloring vibrant. Lisa smiled, then relaxed. "No crow's feet at the corners of my eyes!"

The wide eyes staring back at Lisa were a poet's inspiration. *Sparkling emeralds. Deep. Sultry.* Tory's nose was small and pert, the lips below, full—made for kissing. It was the type of mouth to arouse wicked fantasies in even the most puritanical man.

Motivated by that thought, Lisa tilted her chin and puckered up. "If you want me, all you have to do is whistle," she crooned in the huskiest Lauren Bacall she could muster. Then she slid her hands beneath her hair, lifted it from her shoulders, and ran her tongue suggestively across her upper lip.

She collapsed on the bed in a fit of giggles before pushing up to her elbows and coming face-to-face with the full-length mirror on the bathroom door. In her hurry to dress that morning, she'd grabbed Tory's rumpled, emerald-green suit and blouse and put it on. Now, she slid the jacket from her shoulders and stood, studying the reflection of the figure she'd had little time to inspect before.

It was the body of a goddess. A head-turning, jaw-dropping, va-va-voom kind of body. The type Lisa had not possessed at age twenty—or any other age. A figure she would never achieve, she knew, even if she spent thousands of dollars and a few choice hours at the mercy of a surgeon's knife.

Lisa gave a low whistle as she turned from side to side, then, unable to resist, unbuttoned her blouse until an abundance of cleavage showed. She leaned forward at the waist and pressed her upper arms against the sides of her breasts, posing like a calendar girl.

Standing tall again, she turned and walked away from the mirror, looking over her shoulder at the image of her backside. For effect, she exaggerated the swing of her tight, round bottom. "This could be fun," she said, turning and propping a fist on one hip, pointing the toe beneath one shapely leg. "I could really learn to like this."

At one o'clock the next afternoon, Lisa entered the lobby of the Wilder and O'Conner law firm. Janice Waterman, the receptionist, sat behind the front desk staring into a compact mirror, checking her makeup. Early on, Michael's partner, Jarrod, had hired Ms. Waterman for her physical attributes rather than her work skills. Or, to be precise, Lisa thought, *despite* the woman's *lack* of work skills.

Janice lowered the compact, looked up, and smiled when Lisa approached the desk.

"Hi," Lisa said. "I'm Tory Beecham, the new runner." It seemed awkward and strange to tell this woman she'd known for so long that she was someone other than who she really was. It seemed strange to tell anyone her name was Tory Beecham, and she found herself waiting for Janice to point a finger at her and scream, "Liar! Imposter!"

But Janice didn't scream. Janice didn't even speak. Instead, her smile vanished. Her eyes went

55

cold as they moved from Lisa's wild copper curls, down her hourglass figure, settling on her high-top tennis shoes. When the receptionist finally looked up again, Lisa wasn't sure what to make of the woman's expression. Hatred? Disapproval? Jealousy? Maybe a touch of all three, she decided, realizing that Janice, who was always on the make, regarded her as competition.

Annoyed, Lisa decided to give the woman a dose of her own medicine. She threw back her shoulders and lowered her long, naturally curved lashes. "I'm supposed to report to Michael . . . oops, I mean Mr. O'Conner, at one."

"I'll buzz him," the receptionist said in a stilted tone. She picked up the telephone receiver, then punched a button. "The new runner's here, Michael." After a moment, she lowered the receiver to its cradle. "His secretary will be right out."

Yearning for spiked heels and a red leather skirt, Lisa fluffed her hair with polished nails. "Michael . . . I mean Mr. O'Conner, is just *so* nice. I can't wait to meet his partner, Mr. Wilder. He's single, isn't he?"

Janice, who often jumped at the chance to decorate Jarrod Wilder's arm when it suited his fancy, narrowed her eyes. "He's divorced."

"Hmmm." Lisa winked. "And lonely, I'm sure."

When Michael's secretary, Nan Jones, appeared in the doorway, for the briefest of seconds Lisa expected the attractive silver-haired woman to display her customary warmth, to ask how she was, to, as usual, inquire about the kids. Instead, Nan was friendly but businesslike as she introduced herself and led the way toward Michael's office.

"I hope I'm dressed okay," Lisa said. Other than Tory's emerald-colored suit, the oversized, Army-green sweater she now wore was the closest thing she could find to conventional in Tory's closet. She wondered why a young woman with a knockout figure wore mostly baggy, unattractive clothing.

Heat burned her cheeks as she glanced down at the bell bottoms and red high-top tennies she'd reluctantly chosen. Lisa had heard about "retro" dressing—the return of '70s fashion—being a fad among many of the younger generation but hadn't paid much attention to it. Obviously, Tory Beecham had paid *close* attention. "Mr. O'Conner told me to wear jeans."

Nan chuckled. "You're dressed fine. Different, mind you, but fine." She pointed to a chair on the far side of a desk just beside the doorway to Michael's office. "Have a seat. I need to run and use the fax. Michael knows you're here. I'm sure he won't be long."

Nan left, and Lisa settled into the chair. The door to Michael's office was ajar, so she heard the conversation going on inside. She recognized Jarrod Wilder's laugh and cringed. *He sounds like a hyena in heat.* Leaning closer, she strained to listen.

"It's not funny," Michael said. "This is serious."

"Don't let her pull one over on you, Mikey. You don't really believe Lisa lost her memory, do you?"

Lisa frowned. She wondered if Tory had really lost her memory.

"She's playing a game," Jarrod continued. "Trying to prove a point. Wives do that sort of thing. Which is one of the many reasons why I got rid of mine."

That laugh again. Lisa imagined herself rushing into the office, delivering a fist right smack to the middle of Jarrod's overindulged face. Despite the wall separating them, she swore she smelled the sweet stench of his cologne.

"I should've known better than to bring this up with you," Michael said, sounding disgusted. "Lisa and I don't have that kind of marriage. We don't play hurtful games with each other. We never have."

Lisa slumped in her chair. *He sounds exhausted.* She could only imagine what he'd been through in the last couple of days.

"So you've told me before," Jarrod said, "but somehow I knew Lisa would come around. They always do."

"Shut up, Wilder. You don't know what you're talking about. I think she's really sick. I'm worried about her."

"Well, Mikey, if you're going to fall into her little trap, then you might as well enjoy it. You're due some time off, aren't you? Why don't the two of you take a vacation over the holidays?"

"We already told Nan she could take off a week, remember?"

"With the new runner helping out, Janice and I can hold down the fort. Here's an idea: Leave the kids at home and fly to the Cayman Islands. There's something about that island. During the middle of our divorce negotiations, I talked Kate into going to lunch with me one afternoon to discuss some financial matters. We got totally blitzed and ended up taking my plane to Cayman on the spur of the moment. I paid a friend to fly us down. Pissed as she was when she finally sobered up, I couldn't keep Kate off me."

Yeah, right. It took a monumental effort for Lisa not to laugh out loud. *In your dreams.*

"Kate flew home alone on standby," Jarrod went on. "I stayed. It was worth it. You wouldn't believe this doll I hooked up with. A real no-strings type. One look at me and she was ready. I bet she'd love to hear from the old wild man again. If only I'd asked her name."

Lisa rolled her eyes at Jarrod's self-designated nickname. *Spare me.*

"You know, that isn't a bad idea, Wilder," Michael said. "Time away together might be just what Lisa and I need. We could leave the day after Christmas."

"There's only one problem," Jarrod said. "They book up fast this time of year. Better move fast."

"I'll call my travel agent today."

Lisa's heart pounded with exhilaration. Val had vacationed at Cayman once and loved it. Michael was right; they desperately needed some time alone together. She'd be her old self again long before Christmas, and she'd always wanted to go to the Caymans, especially after hearing her friend's description of the islands. Though Val's overall experience had differed significantly from Jarrod's, one particular aspect had been the same. She could still hear Val's dreamy voice when she returned.

That place is seductive as hell. Fifty percent of the time we spent on the beach; the rest of the time we stayed in bed. I don't know what it was . . . the man I met is no knockout. But I'm telling you, Lisa, he might be the one I've been searching for. I think I could love the guy.

Minutes later, Lisa looked up to see Michael following Wilder through the doorway.

"Miss Beecham!" Michael glanced at his watch. "I'm sorry I kept you waiting. I guess I lost track of time." He turned to Wilder. "Jarrod, this is Tory Beecham, our new runner. Tory, Jarrod Wilder, my partner."

The skin at the back of Lisa's neck prickled as Wilder's beady, bespectacled eyes roamed slowly over her body. Willing self-control, she stood and extended her hand with all the dignity she could muster. "Glad to meet you Mr. Wilder."

He clasped her fingers a moment longer than necessary, giving them a gentle, yet meaningful, squeeze before letting go. "You, too, Tory. You, too. Call me Jarrod. We're on a first-name basis around here." He straightened his tie, then hiked his pants over a protruding beer belly. "I hope you're ready to go to work. I've got plenty to keep you busy."

I'll just bet you do. Lisa had heard many a story about Wilder's slave-driving tendencies with the office personnel. The man turned into the original male-chauvinist porker when it came to his work.

Often, she'd asked Michael what enticed him to go into business with Jarrod. He always reminded her that, underneath it all, Jarrod Wilder was a good person—and he brought a lot of money into the firm. Whatever else he might be, Lisa thought, Wilder was a tough-as-nails attorney who knew his stuff.

Lisa noticed that Jarrod's sandy hair was even curlier than usual. *Good grief. He must've had it permed.* She forced a smile, hoping it looked genuine. "Where do I start?"

Wilder clapped his hand across Michael's back, grinned, then started off down the hallway. "Mikey'll show you the ropes," he said over his shoulder. "I have an appointment."

Michael cleared his throat, then tugged at his earlobe. "Jarrod takes some getting used to." He lowered his hand to his side. "Come into my office and have a seat. We'll go over a few things."

Lisa sank into the chair beside his desk as he closed the door. *This is it. Can I pull this off? Maybe I should just tell him the truth right now and see how he reacts. If he believes me, we could enjoy my new youthfulness together.*

She bit down on her thumbnail, wondering if her previous thought might qualify as overly kinky. Kinky or not, she worried about telling Michael too soon about the switch. What if she couldn't convince him that her story was true? Before yesterday, would she have swallowed it if someone came to her with this crazy tale? The answer was an undeniable no. She would've thought the person crazy—just as Michael would think Tory was crazy if she suddenly informed him that she was his wife. And where might that leave her? *In the unemployment line, without a doubt.*

Questions Dillon had posed that morning—questions about how she intended to pay the rent without his contribution and how she'd afford the utilities and groceries now that both he and her previous roommate were gone—led Lisa to believe Tory didn't get much financial help, if any, from her parents. Lisa could relate to that situation. When they changed back to their old selves, Tory would need this job.

And the fact of the matter was, Lisa herself couldn't afford to lose the job. The check Tory cashed two days before was almost gone, and the balance in her bank account was practically nil. Michael and Jarrod paid their part-time help by the week, and she found herself looking forward to payday.

Losing this job also would mean losing her only link to Michael and the children for the next two weeks and two days, and, fun or not, she intended to make sure her life—her *real* life—ran as smoothly as possible while she was away. No sense in coming home to utter chaos.

And then there were the fortunes. She'd better not regard them lightly and foul things up. She hadn't had a chance to look at her life yet, or to open up her heart and look inside . . . whatever the heck that meant. And the last quarter moon wouldn't be around for a while.

The truth might set her free . . . but not today.

To Lisa's amazement, her heart accelerated as she watched Michael cross the room and sit down. He looked worn out and tense—the lines around his eyes deeper than usual, his face pale and drawn.

She recalled, again, the time she'd surprised him by driving two hundred and ten miles and showing up in his dormitory lobby. He'd looked tired then, too, his face sleep-lined and wonderfully familiar. But his eyes came alive when he saw her—they always did back then. He'd walked her outside onto the porch and pulled her against him, and she'd felt whole again for the first time in weeks. "I want to be alone with you," she'd told him, and he eased back to look at her, his eyes sparked by desire and a hint of teasing mischief. Oh, how she missed that look.

Lisa blinked, brought back to the present by Michael's failed attempt to stifle a yawn. He smiled as his gaze settled on her, but the old spark didn't flare in his eyes.

"We're a young firm, Tory," he said. "I'll be honest with you; we have to pinch pennies and cut corners whenever possible. That doesn't mean we aren't every bit as professional and capable as the most prestigious firms in the city. We just do things somewhat differently behind the scenes."

He lifted a hand and gestured around the room. "As you can see, we're not extravagant. We're not stuffy, either. I like it that way. It's one of the reasons Jarrod and I chose to go out on our own, to avoid the pretentiousness typical of some of the larger firms. . . ."

Michael stopped in midspeech. Lisa had barely heard a word he'd spoken and, apparently, he'd noticed. She couldn't keep herself from staring at him, her thoughts sixteen years in the past.

"Tory? Miss Beecham?"

Lisa blinked back unexpected tears. "I'm sorry. It's just that . . . you remind me of someone. Someone I miss very much."

Michael looked as though he might pass out. He drew in a sharp breath when she reached out her hand and scraped a bright pink fingernail across his tie. "You have a speck of mustard . . . "

He shrank back, and Lisa realized the horrible blunder she'd made. "I'm sorry," she stammered.

The look on Michael's face made her want to giggle and cry at the same time. For a split second, she'd forgotten that he didn't know she was his wife. Touching his tie had been a simple, ingrained gesture. Something she did instinctively. Routine. Thinking quickly, she said, "My boyfriend always seems to carry his lunch around on his tie. I'm constantly cleaning him up. It's a . . . um . . . a habit of mine, I guess."

Michael reached for his ear. "Uh . . . n-no problem." His laugh was nervous, self-conscious. "My wife does the same thing."

Easing back into her chair, Lisa took a deep breath and struggled for composure. "You must be having second thoughts about hiring me right now. I wouldn't blame you." She swallowed.

"Give me a second chance, Mr. O'Conner. Nothing like this will happen again. I promise."

Michael stared at her for several long seconds, then coughed and cleared his throat. "Okay, Tory. Let's start over."

Before today, she would never have believed a meeting with her own husband could be so awkward. It was as though they were strangers—and to him, she realized, they were.

Lisa wasn't certain what she'd expected from this first meeting with Michael, face-to-face. Questions, maybe. An inkling of suspicion. But, of course, such an expectation was ridiculous. How could he ever suspect something like this? Something like this was unthinkable. Something like this would never cross a sane person's mind.

Still, amnesia or not, surely the woman occupying Lisa's body had said things to, at the very least, raise questions in Michael's mind about Tory Beecham, his new employee. What had gone on at their house last night? What did Tory tell him? They couldn't have possibly spent a normal evening at home—dinner, homework, television. Obviously, Michael hadn't slept much, if at all. Hard to do, she supposed, with a stranger in your bed.

The realization stung her like a slap in the face. *Tory in his bed! My bed!*

Though Michael handed her documents to deliver, a deposit to make at the bank, Lisa barely heard his instructions. Her emotions vacillated between helplessness, frustration, and anger. The fantasy of a lifetime had come true and, since she couldn't change it, she planned to make the most of it while it lasted. But what if Tory was doing the same? Making the most of a fantasy she couldn't change . . . with Michael.

Lisa left the building and headed for the nearest convenience store to buy a bag of chocolates. They were her weakness, her one addiction, and though she'd sworn off them only last week, today she badly needed a fix.

Despite her state of mind, she somehow managed all the necessary errands without a mistake. Later, when she returned to Wilder and O'Conner, she helped Nan pull outdated files and took them, in boxes, to storage. Shortly before five o'clock, Michael called her into his office.

"How did everything go today?"

"I think everything went okay."

"Good. Do you have any questions?"

Before she could answer, the receptionist buzzed Michael's intercom. "Your son is on line two."

"Thanks, Janice." Michael reached for the receiver. "Hi, Jake."

Every possible apprehension a mother's brain could conjure ran through Lisa's mind when she noted the concerned expression on Michael's face. She stepped toward his desk.

"Slow down, Jake," Michael said. "What's the matter?" His brows drew together. His jaw began to twitch. Lisa's anxiety grew.

"When's the test?" Michael tapped his fingers on a file that lay on his desk. "Tomorrow? And you're just now studying?"

The annoyance flashing across his face quickly faded to frustration. "I'll help you when I get home. . . . I know, I know, I'm no good at math, but I passed fourth grade. I'll give it my best shot. How much does this test count toward your final grade?" He paused. "That much? Maybe Mom will feel up to it later. How is she?"

Michael ran a hand through his hair and sighed. "She is? When did that start?" He closed his eyes. "Okay, Jake. We'll work it out. I'll be home soon. Good-bye."

Lisa had never felt more powerless. She always helped Jake with his math homework. The subject was a struggle for her son and his grade was suffering. Though she knew Michael was capable, he often lost patience with the kids when it came to their homework.

"I'm sorry for the interruption," Michael said, his voice weary. "Why don't we call it a day?"

The idea came suddenly. Not only could she help Jacob, but also get into the house to determine Tory's condition and survey her family's situation. "It sounds as though your son's in a bind." When Michael looked up at her, she grinned. "I always make an A in math. I love kids, and I don't have plans for the evening. I could tutor him, if you'd like."

She saw the apprehension in his eyes. Undoubtedly, he sensed that it would be a mistake to allow Tory Beecham into his home, to let her become involved with his children. Earlier, when she'd scraped the mustard speck from his tie, he'd clearly thought she was coming on to him.

Lisa held her breath until the tense lines around Michael's mouth finally softened. "Maybe that's not a bad idea," he said. "My wife's not feeling well. She usually helps our son, Jacob, with his math." He shot a quick look at the open file on his desk. "This case I'm working on . . . my clients are coming in tomorrow morning. I have a lot of papers to go over tonight at home." He gave her a wary smile. "Why don't we give it a try? I'll pay you, of course."

Despite every effort not to, Lisa laughed. She'd started to object to any compensation, but something stopped her. For once she could actually be paid for the work she did at home. Think of it! Money for tutoring her own son! "I don't charge much," she said.

Chapter Five

Not even five o'clock traffic could wreck Lisa's mood. Things were turning out better than she'd hoped; a trip to Cayman Island awaited her when she awoke, and, in the meantime, she could spend time with her family by helping Jake with his math.

She turned into the parking lot of a fast-food restaurant, taking her place in the line of vehicles inching toward the drive-through window. When she'd left the law firm a few minutes earlier, Michael was preparing to leave, as well. She'd give him time to reach the house ahead of her so he could explain the tutoring plan to Jake before she arrived.

Ten minutes later, soft drink in hand, she steered back onto the street and headed for home. At first, she barely noticed the canary yellow Mustang in the lane beside her. But when she stopped at a red light, a movement inside the yellow car caught her eye. A young, blond barbarian stared across at her. He motioned toward the curb with one hand and a nod of his head, then mouthed words she couldn't decipher.

What? Lisa mouthed back, squinting.

Again, he nodded toward the curb and mouthed, *"Pull over."*

The light turned green. Lisa frowned. *Maybe I have a flat tire. Why else would he ask me to pull to the side of the road?* Tapping her blinker, she puttered into a nearby grocery store parking lot.

Once outside, Lisa gave each tire a quick inspection, only to find nothing wrong. Just to be sure, she kicked the right rear tire as the Mustang pulled alongside her and stopped.

A car door slammed. Lisa looked up to see the barbarian coming toward her. "What are you doing?" he asked in a smooth baritone. He placed his hands on his knees, then leaned forward to look at the tire she'd just kicked.

Val always said that the difference between a good-looking man and a "fine" one was the way his butt looked in a pair of jeans. Well, this guy was definitely fine, Lisa noted, though he wasn't wearing jeans. He wore flimsy jogging shorts and a tank top that barely covered his chest—a chest chiseled from solid, golden granite.

She blinked once, then looked into his shimmering blue eyes when he turned his head toward her. His hair, like his skin, was golden and damp. "Um . . . is something wrong with my car?" she asked.

He grinned and stood tall again. "I don't know, is there?"

"But, I thought . . . " She opened an arm toward the street. "It's just that you . . . " As understanding dawned, Lisa lowered her arm to her side. How could she have forgotten? She was no longer Lisa, frazzled housewife. She was Tory, gorgeous college student.

"Do you want something?" she asked. *Good grief. Of course he wants something. Whatever you do, don't ask what.*

His baby blues slinked over her from head to toe, then back again. "What's your name?"

"Lisa," she blurted. *Tory, stupid. Your name is Tory.*

"Lisa who?"

"Lisa who?" she repeated.

He chuckled. "What's your last name?"

"I . . . um . . ." Lisa hadn't felt this awkward since age sixteen, and she'd handled it better back then. She took a deep breath. *Now, wait just one minute. Who has the upper hand here? This is part of the fantasy. Live it.*

"What's your last name?" he repeated.

Lisa smiled. She remembered the game, now . . . sort of. She remembered how it was played . . . barely. "Who wants to know?" she asked, trying to appear confident and coy as she shifted her stance, tilted her head, and tucked a strand of hair behind one ear.

His eyes met hers and held. "I want to know."

"And you are?"

"Chad Reynolds."

"My last name is Beecham," she said, "and I'm late for an appointment."

He followed her around the car. "I haven't seen you around here before."

"I'm not usually in this part of the city." Hoping he wouldn't notice her scrutiny, Lisa allowed herself a quick glance at his pumped-up biceps and muscular thighs. He noticed. When her eyes

70

returned to his, his amused gaze told her so. "Aren't you cold?" she asked, striving to sound unimpressed.

"I've been working out."

She opened her car door, climbed in, then slammed it.

He tapped on the window. Lisa rolled it down. "I'd like to call you," he said. "What's your number?"

Lisa grinned up at him and started the engine. "I'm in the book. Nice to meet you Chad Reynolds."

As she took off, she glanced into the rearview mirror and saw him standing where she'd left him, staring after her, smiling. Dizzy laughter bubbled up from deep inside her. "I could get used to this," Lisa mumbled. She didn't stop giggling until she reached her own driveway.

"You're doing great, Jake," Lisa said over an hour later. She pulled a pencil from behind her ear and propped her elbows on the kitchen table. After checking the final answer on the homework paper in front of her, she admitted to herself that it felt wonderful being at home. Only the day before yesterday she'd left to run errands and meet Michael for lunch. It seemed like weeks.

"You know all the answers," she continued. "If you'll just slow down and take your time, you'll ace that test tomorrow." She knocked gently against his forehead with her fist. "Use your noggin. Think."

Jake wrinkled his nose and gave her a curious frown. "My mom always does that. She always says that, too." Behind his glasses, Jake's blue eyes darted in the direction of the sunroom just off the kitchen, where the woman he assumed was his mother pumped the pedals of an exercise bike. "She used to, anyway."

Things were worse than Lisa had imagined. Jacob's sad face made her want to cry . . . made her long to pull him onto her lap and rock him against her bosom as she'd done when he was a baby. But Jake wasn't a baby anymore, Lisa realized with a pang. She looked down at her chest. *And this definitely isn't my bosom.*

She blew out a sigh. Sometime over the years, her son had turned into the independent young boy sitting next to her. A boy with his father's willful determination and her own quiet sensitivity. Jake was on the brink of becoming a young man. In the chaotic whirlwind that had become her life, she'd somehow failed to notice his transformation before now. When had it happened? How had she missed the event?

Lisa gave in to the twisting of her heart and placed a hand on Jake's shoulder. "Your dad told me your mom isn't feeling well. I'm sure she'll be better soon and things will return to normal. Be patient with her, Jake."

When he looked back at her, tears of bewilderment clouded Jake's eyes. He pulled off his glasses, blinking back the emotion with an embarrassed duck of his head. "I hope so."

After returning his glasses to his nose, Jake folded his homework paper and slipped it into the math book. His face lit up. "I remember where I saw you before! You came to the door the other day. You were taking the sin . . . " He frowned, apparently trying to come up with the correct word.

Lisa nibbled her cuticle. She had hoped he wouldn't remember. "Census. Now that you mention it, I do seem to remember stopping at this house. Since I went to work at the law firm, I'm not a census-taker anymore."

"I'm glad you're working for Dad. And I'm glad you're helping me. Thanks."

Jake mustered a crooked smile, and Lisa concentrated on the tiny dimples in his cheeks, the two beaverlike front teeth so typical of nine-year-old boys. Her heart strings stretched tighter, and she fought an urge to hug him. "Anytime, Jake. Just call me."

The door leading from the garage opened. Michael entered with Kat trailing behind him. The sight of her daughter brought a whole new surge of emotion. Lisa found it difficult to differentiate between the freckles smudging Katherine's face and the remains of a fudge pop she'd seen her eating earlier. The tufts of hair poking out from beneath Kat's ball cap had never darkened to a soft auburn brown as Jake's had. She was a skinny little tow-headed tomboy—all smiles and silliness.

Michael stopped midway into the kitchen. "Everything okay in here?"

Lisa stood. "Everything's great." She cleared her throat but failed to dislodge the knot of emotion there. "Jacob has his math down pat."

Pulling a check from the pocket of his jeans, Michael handed it to her. "Thanks a lot, Tory."

He turned his back on her and looked toward the monotonous whizzing noise of the exercise bike. Lisa saw the flush of crimson creeping up his neck. She saw, too, as her attention slipped lower, that Michael ranked "fine" by Val's scoring method. The thought surprised her, but not nearly as much as the realization of how long it had been since she'd noticed him in such a physical way.

"Like I said," Michael muttered, "Lisa's not herself lately."

Lisa nodded. *You don't know the half of it.*

The doorbell rang, and Michael sent Kat off to answer it, then ushered Tory in the same direction, with Jacob walking alongside her. "I really appreciate your help," Michael said.

"You're more than welcome." Lisa looked across at Jake. "If you need me again, I'm available." She reached across and tapped his forehead with her fist. "Don't forget what I said about using that noggin."

Unnerved by Tory's action and choice of words, Michael stopped walking and studied her.

Laughing, Jake stopped, too. "That's what Mom always says, isn't it, Dad?"

Her gaze only met his briefly, but Michael saw the startled flash of her eyes before she looked away. An uneasy feeling stole over him. "Mom does say that," he said slowly as Val stepped into the entry hall in front of them. "Hi, Val. Am I ever glad you're here."

He plied his attention away from Tory, gave Val a quick hug, then stepped back. "This is Tory Beecham. She's been tutoring Jake. Tory—Valerie Potter."

As usual, Val looked energetic and pulled-together. Lisa had once told him that Val owned a different pair of shoes for every outfit. Michael believed it.

She extended a hand. "Glad to meet you, Tory. You're certainly a brave soul to tackle this one." Ruffling Jake's hair with her free hand, Val winked at him. In turn, he made a face at her, then followed his sister into the den.

With mounting curiosity, Michael took measure of Tory's responses. Wide-eyed, the girl stared at Val while clutching her fingers like a lifeline.

Val winced, then gave her a dubious grin. "Wow! What a grip!" She eased her hand away, shaking it as if to revive the circulation.

"Well," Michael said, stepping around them to the door. "I'll see you tomorrow at the office, Tory." He pulled the door open wider when she didn't respond.

She glanced outside, then looked from him to Val, then back to him again. "I guess I'll be going now."

"Thanks again," Michael said. He closed the door when she finally stepped outside, and he and Val exchanged perplexed glances.

"Interesting girl, Michael," Val said, laughing. "Very interesting."

When the door closed behind her, Lisa turned to face it, an odd sensation creeping over her at being dismissed from her own house.

Val. She was the solution—the person to approach with the truth. Michael would never be convinced of a tale as wild as the one Lisa had to tell. With Michael, things were either black or white, right or wrong, possible or impossible. And, Lisa had to admit, this did sound impossible.

Val, on the other hand, had been known to consider the unconventional. Hadn't they once gone together, on a whim, to have their palms read, their pasts prodded, their futures predicted? Val even admitted to believing a ghostly presence might reside in her vintage Victorian home. How else to explain the disappearing shoes, the glowing lamps when she returned from work in the evening—lamps she *knew* she'd turned off that morning—the floors that creaked every night just as she dropped off to sleep? Val might be convinced and, if so, she could sure help out.

Lisa trudged down the walk toward the Volkswagen that, in a very short time, had started to feel like her own. Michael might tell Val things he wouldn't confide to an employee. Like, whether or not he and his wife were sleeping together. And her best friend could help keep the family running smoothly for the next couple of weeks, until everything returned to normal. Besides, this fantasy would be more fun if she had someone to share it with. Yes, she'd make it a point to talk to her friend soon. But first things first . . .

Minutes later, after parking the car at the end of the block, Lisa sneaked down the alley and crept quietly around to the side of the house. With a nervous glance behind her, she surveyed the surrounding neighborhood for anyone who might spot her. Finding no one, she eased behind a hedge, then crouched, ignoring the brisk November wind and the scratchy, jabbing twigs that scraped against her clothing.

Slowly, she raised up to eye level with the bottom of the kitchen window and peeked inside. From her vantage point, the offset sunroom lay in full view.

Val stood alongside Tory, who was now using her legs to push mercilessly on the elongated, narrow pedals of a thigh-thinning machine. *The woman's a fanatic!* Lisa's exercise equipment hadn't seen so much action in the two years she'd owned it, much less in just one day.

Val propped knotted fists on her slender hips, her long legs extending from beneath the knee-length skirt of her ecru-colored designer suit. One matching ecru shoe rapped impatiently against the floor.

Lisa wished like crazy she could hear her friend's words. If anyone could hold her own and get to the bottom of things, Valerie Potter could. Val was a woman used to maneuvering in a male-dominated world—a cattle-brokering dynamo in high-heeled pumps.

As Lisa watched, Tory finally halted her routine and stepped away from the torturous apparatus, perspiration glistening on her skin. She shot Val a hesitant glance, then followed her from the sunroom.

Lisa changed her position at the window to gain access to a better view. As she watched, the two women entered the master bedroom, closing the door behind them.

She inched along the side of the house and made her way to the next window. She peered through the slatted shutters. Kat and Jacob sat on the floor in front of the television, intent on a video game. At his desk in the same room, Michael sat with one hand supporting his forehead, the other grasping a pen, work spread out in front of him.

If she could sneak inside without making too much noise, she could slip past them down the hallway to the guest bathroom—the one no one ever used. The room shared a wall with the master bedroom, and Lisa knew from experience that if people in the bedroom spoke in a normal tone of voice—anything above a whisper—occupants of the bathroom could overhear the conversation. Around Christmas time, she often took advantage of this feature of her house when Michael made his yearly call to Val for gift ideas.

With a quick look around, Lisa left the cover of the bushes and walked casually through the yard and across the front porch. Holding her breath, she slowly twisted the doorknob as far as possible to the right, then paused. Maybe this was a mistake. If Michael caught her, how would she explain? He'd given her a second chance after what he probably considered a come-on in his office earlier. Knowing Michael, he wouldn't grant her a third. He'd fire her on the spot for sneaking into his house and eavesdropping on Tory and Val. He'd think she was a stalker!

Despite her apprehensions, Lisa gave the door a gentle push. It opened into the entry hall without so much as a squeak. Familiar fast-paced music, the perfect accompaniment for karate-kicking, crime-fighting animated characters, drifted to her ears from the television set. She stepped inside, easing the door closed behind her.

Risky or not, she needed to find out just exactly what was going on with Tory. If she got caught, she'd make up something. An emergency . . . that might work. She could say she needed to go to the restroom and couldn't wait. She could say she rang the bell but no one answered, that the television must've been so loud they never heard. She could say she forgot something. Her pen . . . her jacket . . . her purse.

On tiptoe, Lisa crossed the tiled floor, the pounding of her heart a drumbeat in her ears. Though the entrance to the den was only six or so feet ahead of her, a connecting wall hid Michael and the kids from her sight—and her from theirs.

With relief, she turned right onto the carpeted hallway leading past Kat's and Jacob's bedrooms and into the guest bath. Once inside, she secured the lock.

Pressing her ear against the shared wall, Lisa listened. Val's voice, not prone to softness in the best of circumstances, came through loud and clear, her concern evident.

"Okay, Lisa. You've had a good cry. Every woman needs one now and then. Now dry your eyes and please tell me what's wrong."

Tory sniffed. "Just look at me! I'm a middle-aged housewife with a husband, two kids, and dishpan hands!"

"Hold on just a minute!" Val exclaimed. "I'm the same age you are. Thirty-five is hardly middle-aged."

"Close enough. I don't *feel* thirty-five. I mean, not inside, anyway. Where did the years go? It's like . . . my husband's a stranger. A stranger who'll probably have one of those spare tire things around his gut before I know it."

"Michael's a very attractive man. You know that as well as I do."

"He *is* good-looking for an older guy. His eyes are beautiful. And he has great legs. And broad shoulders. I like broad shoulders."

"His butt's not anything to complain about, either," Val said, sounding amused. "As a matter of fact, I've always thought it was great."

Behind the wall, Lisa's eyes widened. Not once in the past had Val admitted to an admiration of Michael's backside. She'd have to talk to her about that.

Tory sighed. "But he seems so . . . I don't know, mature to me. I mean, I'd sort of like a younger man."

"Wouldn't we all," Val said in a dreamy voice.

"And my kids," Tory continued. "They're nine and six. Is that possible? I gave birth *nine and six years ago!* You'd think I'd remember something like that."

"They say you forget the pain once it's over."

Tory didn't respond to Val's comment. "Look at

my body," she continued. "It's . . . it's a *disaster!*" she sobbed. "I'm even starting to wrinkle! It's just *too* weird!"

Lisa felt her hackles rise. She bit back a defensive retort.

"Didn't we have a similar conversation last week?" Val asked. "I had no idea, at the time, that you were so upset. When I told you that you should do something to get Michael's attention, I never dreamed you were this bad off."

Over Tory's weeping, Lisa heard the crackle of what sounded like a paper sack.

Val sighed. "Here," she said. "I brought you some chocolate to soothe your nerves."

When she heard Val's gum pop, Lisa winced, imagining a giant pink bubble protruding between her friend's pursed lips. Whenever Lisa complained about the habit, as she often did, Val defended herself, declaring that it was better than her old vice—cigarettes.

"I'm worried sick about you, Lisa. Michael is, too. Maybe you should seek professional help."

"Michael took me to a doctor."

"I'm talking about a shrink. Don't you think you should see one before this gets any worse? We're talking amnesia here." After a long silence, Val sighed again. "If you won't talk to a psychiatrist, then talk to me. Tell me every little thing that's on your mind. *Everything.* Come on. This is Val. You can't shock me; I know you too well."

"Happy to meet you, Val," Tory said sarcastically. "But I *don't* know *you.*"

"Trust me," Val said sounding more frustrated than ever. "You *do* know me. Better than anyone else does. How do you expect me to help you if you won't talk to me?"

"Who says I expect anything from you?"

"You and Michael aren't sleeping together, are you?" Val asked after several tense, silent seconds. Her tone of voice was gentle and sympathetic, coaxing. "I noticed the blankets and pillow on the couch."

"I just can't bring myself to sleep with him. I mean, it doesn't seem right."

Lisa went limp with relief.

"It doesn't seem right confiding all this to me, either, does it?" Val asked.

"No."

"I was afraid of that. Well, I'll just leave you alone for a while to sort through your feelings. I'll be available when you're ready to talk. You know where to find me."

Lisa heard a shuffling sound, then, "Aren't you even going to thank me for the chocolate?" Val asked in a lighter tone.

"Chocolate?" Tory said with disgust. "I never touch the stuff. . . . Do I?"

Val gave a short, baffled laugh. "Only when you're alone or with somebody."

The bedroom door slammed shut. Lisa waited until she heard Val yell out to Michael, "I'll call you later!" then opened the bathroom door just a crack. At the far end of the hall, she saw Michael staring toward the entry, scratching his head. Lisa didn't have to see it to know that his jaw was clenched and jerking to beat the band.

When he returned to the den, Lisa escaped down the hallway. Halfway to the door, it hit her. Something was wrong. Something was missing. The music had stopped. *The kids aren't playing video games anymore!*

Overwhelmed by panic, she halted, frozen in place. Then, forcing her feet to move, Lisa fled to her exit. When she reached for the doorknob, it turned. The door flew open and Kat stood before her.

"I forgot my purse," Lisa whispered. She winked at Kat, a shaky grin plastered across her face. Then, without looking back, she bolted toward the end of the block.

Chapter Six

Michael pressed the receiver to his ear and counted the rings. " . . . nineteen . . . twenty . . . twenty-one." Sooner or later, Val would have to get home and answer. It irritated him, the way she'd left the house without so much as a word about her conversation with Lisa.

He'd almost decided to give up when the shrill ringing ceased and Val's out-of-breath "Hello!" sounded across the line.

"It's about time," Michael grumbled.

"Well, *excuse me!* Michael, I presume?"

Michael propped an elbow on the desk, leaned his forehead against the clenched fist of his free hand, and closed his eyes. "Sorry I snapped at you. It's just that I've had about all I can take. Lisa's locked herself in the bedroom and won't come out. What did the two of you talk about while you were here, anyway?"

"She locked herself in the bedroom?" He understood, all too well, the exasperation in Val's sigh. "You were right, Michael," she said. "This is serious. I don't know what to think." She gave a humorless chuckle. "Maybe I deserve some of the blame for all this. Last week, Lisa reached out to me. She needed my help, and what did I do? I told her that she should do something to get your attention. Some friend I am. I should've seen how troubled she really was. I should've come to you immediately, or insisted she see a doctor."

Michael scrubbed a hand across his face and stretched, easing weary muscles. "Don't blame yourself; I didn't see it, either. I don't know. Maybe she's having a nervous breakdown. It's certainly not Lisa's style to be so out of control. She'll hardly even speak to me."

"I know. She won't say much to me, either. If it were only you, I might understand. But to shut me out too, *really*. If she can't open up to her best friend, then who can she open up to?"

He was silent for a moment, stung by Val's comment, wondering if Lisa felt the same. "Me, that's who," he finally said, his voice quiet.

"Oh." Val cleared her throat. "Well . . . of course Lisa would turn to you first in most situations. But . . . uh . . . there are just some subjects that . . . well, it's a girl thing, Michael. I don't expect you to understand."

Michael raised a brow. "Whatever," he said. "What did Lisa say to you this afternoon? That is, if it's not privileged information. You know, a girl thing."

Val gave a little cough. "She rambled on about the horrors of being middle-aged. Can you believe it? Middle-aged!"

"What exactly did she say?"

"Oh, the typical where-did-the-years-go sort of thing. Yesterday she was young, today she's thirty-five with a deteriorating body, two kids, and a husband with . . . " She stopped short.

"A husband with what?"

Val coughed again. "It was nothing, Michael, really."

"Damn it to hell, Val, don't give me that. Finish what you were about to say."

"Okay, you asked for it. You want honesty, you've got it. Here goes. A husband with the beginnings of a paunch, or a spare tire, or something to that effect. You get the idea."

Heat crept up Michael's neck, settled in his cheeks, then radiated against his skin as though trying to escape. "Unfortunately, I guess I do." He placed one hand against his middle. "She really said that?"

"I'm sorry. You wanted the truth."

Michael lowered his head to check out his stomach. "You know what they say." He sucked in his belly and winced. "The truth hurts."

"If it's any consolation, I think she's full of baloney about that. You look great." Val paused. "Someone's at my door, Michael. I'll be in touch. Call me if you need me. 'Bye."

He stared at the receiver before replacing it in its cradle. Then he slid a palm across his middle and frowned. Not as firm as it had once been, but a long way from a potbelly. "Spare tire, huh?"

Indignant, he remembered Tory Beecham's behavior toward him earlier in the day. After he'd made it past the initial shock, he'd felt flattered by her attention. Then he'd decided he must've gotten the wrong impression. Why on earth would a twenty-year-old girl who looked like

Tory be the least bit interested in him? She was damn good-looking. He'd have to be blind not to notice. But at thirty-six, he must seem ancient to someone her age. Besides, she'd mentioned a boyfriend, hadn't she?

But maybe it had been a come-on after all. Why not?

Michael stood. He pictured the young woman, her expression dreamy as she gazed at him.

Then he thought of Lisa and tightened the muscles in his stomach. "Some people don't have any complaints about my physique," Michael muttered.

Val had never been good at hiding her feelings, and today was no exception. When the door opened and they stood face-to-face, Lisa was aware of Val's surprise, curiosity, and annoyance at finding Tory Beecham on her front porch.

"Hi," Lisa said as she shifted self-consciously from foot to foot.

"Hello," Val answered. "Is there something I can do for you?"

"I'm . . . Tory Beecham. Remember? We met at Michael's a little while ago."

Val crossed her arms over her chest. Her foot began an agitated tap against the polished wood floor. "I remember."

Lisa swallowed hard. This wouldn't be easy. Knowing Val as she did, she should've expected as much. True, there was a better chance of convincing Val of her story than Michael. But the woman standing across from her didn't put up with nonsense. Val had no time for anything or anyone she considered a nuisance. Lisa had the distinct impression that she would soon be placed in that category.

"Could I come in for a few minutes?" Lisa finally asked, hugging her jacket around her to ward off the cold. "I'd like to talk to you about something."

After a quick appraisal of her visitor through narrowed eyes, Val uncrossed her arms and shrugged. "Sure, why not? Just so it doesn't take too long. I need to feed my cats."

As if on cue, Val's white Persian cat, Samantha, slinked between her ankles. "Hello, Sa . . . kitty," Lisa murmured. Her eyes shot up from the cat to meet Val's look of wary suspicion. They stared at each other several long, silent moments before Val turned and led the way to the living room.

Lisa dropped her purse on the floor at her feet, then sat at one end of the sofa while her friend took a place in the opposite chair.

Filled with antiques, expensive rugs, and impressive paintings, Val's house reflected her diverse character. Lisa admired the familiar decor, each carefully chosen piece of furniture, every elegant knickknack.

Less than a week ago, she realized, her emotion would've been envy rather than admiration. And perhaps a bit of envy remained, even now. The time Lisa invested in husband and children, cleaning and car-pooling, Val invested in a career and her home. It had always been easy to look at Val and imagine greener pastures, much too easy to be seduced by a lifestyle so unlike her own.

"Miss Beecham?"

Val's impatient glare snapped Lisa out of her musing. "I'm sorry." She smiled. "You have a beautiful home."

"Thanks. Now . . . what did you want to talk about?"

Lisa straightened her back and drew a steadying breath. "I started working for Michael today.

Not only tutoring Jacob, but as a runner at the law firm, too. I'm a pre-law student at the university, so I only work part-time."

Val crossed her legs, her top foot batting the air in a restless cadence. "Yes?" she prompted, and tossed back her short, dark hair.

"Well," Lisa continued, "Michael told me his . . . wife hasn't been feeling well, and I couldn't help but notice the tension between them while I was at the house. Jake seemed rather upset, too, over his mother's strange behavior."

Val pulled a piece of bubble gum from her pocket. After unwrapping it, she slipped the chunk into her mouth and began to chew. "So you noticed Lisa's weird behavior. I'm sorry, but I really don't see where all this is leading."

A sick sensation settled in the pit of Lisa's stomach. She moved to the edge of the sofa and said a silent prayer. "I know what's wrong with her." She spoke so softly, she almost didn't hear her own words.

"You what?"

"I know what's wrong with Lisa."

"Really? What?"

She leaned forward to emphasize the next statement. "She's not Lisa."

Val widened her eyes derisively. "Then who is she?"

Lisa gulped. "She's Tory Beecham."

"She's Tory Beecham," Val repeated in a mocking whisper. "And who does that make you?"

"*I'm* Lisa."

For a moment, Val didn't move; then the laughter started. At first a slow, quiet chuckle, it quickly escalated to hysterical, gasping shrieks. She clutched her arms across her stomach and fell against the back of the chair. "You are really too much. Poor Michael. What has he gotten himself into?"

"Poor *Michael?*" Lisa frowned. "What about poor me?" Remembering the blond barbarian, she added, "Not that this situation doesn't have its moments; it does. But there are problems I need to handle, and I need your help."

"Miss Beecham," Val said, with an obvious struggle to compose herself, "I'm not sure what it is you're up to, but believe me, it won't work. I don't put much stock in the supernatural claptrap so popular these days, and Michael O'Conner believes in it even less than I do."

Lisa shook her head. She stood, then moved to the front of Val's chair. "This is no joke."

Val pursed her lips. "How on earth did you come up with a crazy story like this?"

"Please listen to me," Lisa pleaded as she began to pace back and forth across the Oriental rug. "I didn't make this up. Day before yesterday I saw Tory at the bank. I didn't even know who she was then, but she seemed so carefree . . . so full of life. I was having a terrible day, and when I looked at her, I remembered how things used to be. I envied her youth, her freedom."

Lisa glanced at her beautifully manicured nails—nine of them, anyway. "I even envied her fingernails. For a moment I wished I was twenty years old again, my life all ahead of me, plenty of time to make whatever I wanted of myself."

She stopped pacing and turned to face Val. "I wished I was her, Val. And the next thing I knew . . . I was."

With the sinking feeling that Val hadn't paid attention to a single word she'd said, Lisa watched insight replace amused distrust on her friend's face.

"I think I'm beginning to get the picture," Val said with a snide smile. "Beautiful young college student, poor and penniless but filled with lofty dreams, goes to work for attractive, thirty-something man—a lawyer, no less. And everyone knows attorneys are loaded, right?" She rolled her eyes.

"In the course of the day, poor student overhears rumors that handsome boss's wife has somehow lost her memory," Val continued. "The man is obviously suffering over the incident, miserable and in desperate need of consolation. Beautiful student decides this is a prime opportunity to turn her dreams into reality. More than willing to offer him comfort on the chance it might get her what she wants, she sets 'Plan A' into motion."

On a roll, Val stood and retraced the path Lisa had trod only moments before. "But it doesn't take long to figure out that thirty-something boss is not the stereotypical full-of-himself, good-looking male she'd guessed him to be. He's not the wandering type, no matter how bad his situation at home. Enter 'Plan B'—which I can only assume is the outrageous story you just told me."

Val chuckled again. "*Really!* Surely you can do better? That plot line wouldn't even make it past a soap opera script editor!"

"Think about it," Lisa pleaded. "If I was Tory and I'd invented this entire scenario in order to get my hooks into Michael, why wouldn't I be trying to convince him I was Lisa right now instead of you?"

"Easy. Michael isn't the kind of man who'd sit still for one second and listen to this phony baloney. He doesn't play games when it comes to people's lives. Especially if it involves his family."

Lisa arched a brow. "But how would *I* know that about him if I was Tory?"

Val lifted the cat from the floor and started out of the room. "This is the most bizarre conversation I've ever had," she said over her shoulder. She stopped just beyond the doorway. "You'd better leave now. I really don't think your joke is very funny. Michael won't either. And by the way, I plan to tell him all about it. If I were you, I'd start looking for another job."

Not willing to give up yet, Lisa grabbed her purse and moved toward Val. When she stood close enough, she reached out a hand to stroke the cat. "Hi there, Samantha. I guess you're getting hungry." Lisa's gaze rose to find Val's expression startled. "I know your other cat's name, too," she said softly. "Where is Tabitha, anyway?"

"You could've found out their names easily enough," Val said, her voice somewhat breathless. "Maybe I've said them since you arrived. I really don't remember." She backed away a step.

"Yes. But you didn't. And you know it."

Val brightened. "You spent the afternoon with Jake. He knows my cats' names. He comes over with his mother to feed them when I'm out of town."

"I know he does. And, as I've told you before, you pay him way too much, considering it's me who drives him over here, me who opens the can of cat food, and me who cleans up the mess he makes."

Val returned the cat to the floor, grasped her visitor's wrist, and dragged her into the entry hall. "I've had enough of this." She released her grip and jerked the front door open. "Good-bye!"

Lisa walked past her, turning outside just in time to see Val pull a fresh piece of gum from her pocket. She stopped. "If I've told you once, Val, I've told you a thousand times, smacking that bubble gum doesn't do a thing for your image. It drives me crazy. I think I liked it better when you smoked."

When Lisa saw the first hint of doubt shadow her friend's eyes, it filled her with urgent hope, causing her heart to beat faster. Val's face suddenly became as pale as the winter sky overhead.

"I know other things, Val. For instance, last summer . . . your vacation . . . " In her desperation for Val to believe her, Lisa's hands began trembling so violently that she dropped her purse, spilling the contents onto the brick porch below. She scrambled to scoop everything up.

Val stooped to lift a piece of chocolate candy from the ground. "Lisa's favorite," she whispered. Her eyes met Lisa's and fused.

After a minute, she stood and grabbed Lisa's arm. "Have I ever been married?" she asked, a wild look darkening her eyes, her voice unsteady.

"Yes. Your husband's name was Ray."

Val's fingers dug deeper into Lisa's arm. "Was Ray buried or cremated?"

Lisa's pulse jumped. "Did Ray die?" She wanted to laugh but was afraid to. She guessed a minuscule chance existed that Ray's death was a very recent development and not just Val trying to trip her up.

Astonishment crossed Val's face, confirming Lisa's suspicion. "Val," Lisa went on, "last I heard, Ray was alive and kicking . . . and living in Arizona since your divorce."

Val dropped her arm and stepped back. "I still don't believe you. You haven't told me a single thing you couldn't have found out by asking the right people the right questions."

"As I was about to say a minute ago . . . your vacation last summer—"

Val covered her ears. "Not another word. I don't believe you." She backed toward the door. "I can't."

Then she went into the house, leaving Lisa outside and alone.

Chapter Seven

Nan faced the computer printer, her back to Lisa. The machine hummed, and paper emerged in a steady stream, falling into a pile on the table below. Gathering a stack, Nan arranged it neatly, then set the pile aside for Lisa to retrieve.

Across the narrow hallway, Lisa sat at her newly appointed desk, folding statements and stuffing them into envelopes. Mindless work. The kind she needed at the moment. Her thoughts revolved around her dilemma and how she proposed to solve it.

Observing the situation at home firsthand had only complicated matters. If only she'd been more successful in swaying Val her way, Lisa thought, pausing to wince over a paper cut on her finger. Val could find out what Michael was thinking. Val could attempt to smooth things over with him and the kids. Then Lisa could enjoy her short-term youth worry-free.

Lisa pulled a pencil from behind her ear and tapped the eraser against her temple as Michael stepped from his office. Her heart tripped at the sight of him.

During their years together, Lisa's opportunities to observe Michael in his work environment had been few. At home, she'd mistaken the extreme focus she saw in him now at the law firm for distraction—boredom with their life together. Before, she had only felt small jolts of the energy that sparked from Michael here. Energy that sent shock waves through the room, through Lisa, as he strode past her desk.

For one brief second he was so close, the side of his leg nearly brushed Lisa's arm as he passed. She smelled the lingering tangy scent of his shaving cream—a scent she'd always loved. It brought a sudden fantasy to mind: the two of them alone in Michael's office, Lisa the sole recipient of his acute focus and all that energy.

Tension built inside her like a pounding drum. Louder, stronger, tighter. Each beat more intense than the one before. Shaken, she glanced across at Nan, wondering if she, too, felt Michael's energy. But Nan remained on task, apparently unaware of his presence.

Lisa drew a calming breath, oddly excited yet terrified, too, by this new response to her husband. Had he always possessed the potential to turn her bones to hot lava? Even in the past few years? Had she just stopped paying attention to him, or to her own feelings? Possibly, she admitted. After all, until today, she'd labeled the single-minded determination she saw in him now as indifference. Disinterest in her.

Look at your life.

She remembered two years before, when Michael and Jarrod first opened their own firm. Despite his typically easygoing nature, Michael had begun to seem preoccupied, and he spent more time than usual at his work even when away from the office.

Still, he'd never completely lost his fun-loving spirit, his warmth and humor. It surfaced most often around Kat and Jacob. When he found time to spend with them, Michael became an overgrown child—a fact that either annoyed or amused Lisa, depending on her mood.

But this focus—this energy . . . Why hadn't she noticed it before for what it was?

Open your heart. Look inside for the answers you seek.

The past two years had been lonely. Did she really want to return to the way things had been? She looked forward to eventually regaining her identity. But did Michael have anything to do with that desire? Did she look forward to returning to their marriage, or were her children the only reason she yearned to go back? And these disturbing erotic feelings Michael suddenly generated inside her—would they disappear along with Tory's body?

She wasn't the only one confused, Lisa realized as she studied her husband. Yesterday and today she'd noticed Michael's uncommonly short temper with clients, the staff, and with Jarrod. It worried her to see him so out of sorts, yet she had no doubt that his behavior stemmed from the circumstances at home—from his bewilderment over his wife's sudden curious condition.

Michael stared at a brochure in his hand. "Nan," he said, his voice raised to be heard over the din of the printer, "I need you to do me a favor." When his secretary turned to him, he handed her the pamphlet. "Call my travel agent and see if she can book two seats to the Cayman Islands and a room at this resort the week after Christmas. If they're full then, the following week will work just as well. It's a surprise gift for Lisa."

Nan scanned the brochure, looked at her boss, and smiled. "What a wonderful present!"

His grin was hesitant. "You think she'll like it? She's been under a lot of stress lately, and she really loves the ocean."

Excitement rushed through Lisa like a sudden gust of wind.

"Lisa will be thrilled!" Nan exclaimed. "I can't think of a better place to relax than on a beautiful tropical island, alone with your husband, away from the kids for a while."

Michael's grin widened as he headed toward his office. Turning under the doorframe, he looked back at Nan. "I hope you're right. We really can't afford a trip now." He scowled at the buzzing printer. "There are so many things we need around here. Like a new laser printer, for instance. But the way Lisa's feeling, I don't think we can afford *not* to take this trip."

Silent for a moment, his gaze wavering, Michael tugged at his ear. "Oh, and Nan, I'm sorry I've been such a bear lately. It doesn't have anything to do with you."

"I understand," Nan said, her voice filled with motherly compassion.

His attention shifted to Lisa. "You deserve an apology, too, Tory."

"Don't worry about it," Lisa answered, trying to remember when she'd last heard a heartfelt "I'm sorry" from Michael . . . and failing.

As he entered his office, Michael added, "Don't

wait too long to make that call, Nan. We'll be lucky to get two seats on a plane or a room this late in the game."

Only minutes before, Lisa had questioned her intention of resuming a life with Michael. If she didn't want him, why did a week alone with him sound so appealing? Surely it wasn't simply the prospect of going to the Cayman Islands that caused her tingle of anticipation.

She stood, then walked over to Nan. "Let me make Michael's reservations for you. I know you're busy. You have documents to work on after these statements are finished, don't you?"

Nan nodded, sighing. "I'm looking at a couple of hours in overtime. After I'm through with this, though, I need to get the November check stubs and receipts together so Michael can take them home to his wife. She does the bookkeeping." She shook her head and handed the Cayman brochure to Lisa. "I should've reminded him not to leave without them. Would you tell him for me?"

Lisa nodded.

"Thanks."

Lisa returned to her desk. *The bookkeeping.* Maybe if Michael tackled it himself for a while, he'd appreciate how time consuming the task really was, and realize how much money she saved the firm by foregoing the salary of a bookkeeper.

She settled into her chair and scanned the travel literature, her heart accelerating at the sight of powdery, white beaches . . . gentle blue waves lapping the shore . . . quaint, cozy bungalows nestled beneath swaying palms. The heady, sweet fragrance of tropical flowers filled her senses. When the scent didn't diminish after several seconds, Lisa realized that what she was smelling was actually Jarrod Wilder's cologne.

She looked up to see Michael's partner towering over her.

"I see Mikey's chosen the most secluded spot on the island," Jarrod said, his voice amused. He peered over her shoulder at the photographs of the hotel, then gave an insinuating wink. Lisa gazed back at the pictures, heat scalding her cheeks.

"Guess he plans on starting out the New Year with a bang." Jarrod started toward the exit to the lobby, cackling like a hen. "I'm leaving for the day. See you ladies in the morning."

Still uncertain about whether she should go on the trip, Lisa watched him walk away.

Open your heart. Look inside for the answers you seek.

With a hesitant glance at the back of Nan's gray head, Lisa set the brochure aside and resumed stuffing envelopes. She knew time was critical in making the reservations, but she decided to give herself a day or so to consider her feelings toward Michael before making the call. If he asked about the reservation, she'd bluff her way out of it—she was becoming an expert at bluffing.

She placed a folder on top of the brochure, hiding it from sight, then went to the door of Michael's office. She poked her head inside to remind him about the check stubs, but he was nowhere in sight. Suddenly, the back of his head appeared above the side of his desk. It lowered again, then popped up a second or two later. When she realized Michael was doing sit-ups, Lisa blinked down at him in astonishment, then cleared her throat.

Startled, Michael jumped up, readjusting his clothing with nervous fingers. "Oh, Tory!" he said, breathless and humiliated. "I was just . . . uh . . . well . . . " He motioned toward the floor.

"Sorry to interrupt," she said, a blush turning her ivory cheeks hot pink. "Nan wanted me to remind you not to leave without the check stubs and receipts for your wife." She turned to leave.

"Tory . . ." Michael ran a hand through his rumpled hair, smoothing back the cowlick that never seemed to want to stay down. At the sound of her name, she turned back to him, cocking her head to the side in a way that brought Lisa to mind. "I thought you'd like to know that Jake made an eighty-nine on the math test you helped him study for. He just called to tell me."

"That's wonderful!"

Her eyes met his, and Michael recognized genuine pleasure there over Jake's success. Then she glanced away, running her hands down the front of her jeans in a nervous gesture. He noticed that her hands were shaking and was surprised.

"Thanks for your help." Michael wondered about this new development in Tory's behavior toward him. From the start, every one of her reactions had been somewhat offbeat. But self-consciousness had never been one of them. Now, she looked as if she couldn't decide between jumping his bones or hiding under his desk. Her uncertain flirtation seemed strangely familiar and made him feel like a kid again.

Michael's own gaze faltered as he considered his next words. So what if Tory had a crush on him? More than likely it would end as quickly as it had started. For Jake's sake, he could handle spending more time around the girl. "I'd like to hire a tutor on a regular basis, at least until Lisa gets back on track. Would you be interested?"

"Oh, yes!" Tory exclaimed with an urgency that

caught him off guard. "I could really use the extra money. Does Jake need me every night?"

Michael chuckled at her enthusiasm. When Tory Beecham walked into Wilder and O'Conner for an interview, it had been his lucky day. Workwise anyway, he thought with a jolt, recalling that Lisa's memory loss had occurred the same afternoon. "I think a couple of times a week should be enough," Michael said. "Let's see; today's Thursday. Could you come again this evening after dinner? Say around seven-thirty?"

"That'll work out great." She cocked her head in that vaguely familiar way again, tucked a copper curl behind one ear, and beamed at him.

"And how about Mondays?" Michael heard himself ask. He realized something in Tory's nature made him like having her around. He told himself it was only because Jake related to her so well, though in his heart he knew it wasn't that simple. "We could make it twice a week on Mondays and Thursdays, if that suits your schedule."

Lisa smiled. "Perfect."

Hours later, Michael scrambled around the den, gathering discarded clothing from the floor. Assorted magazines and several days' worth of newspapers lay scattered across the coffee table, along with numerous glasses and cups, some partially filled with liquid.

Arms and hands full, he headed toward the kitchen, where Jake sat alongside Tory at the table. A quick glance reminded him that things weren't much cleaner in this room. Dinner dishes cluttered the countertop where he'd left them, pots and pans sat on the stove, and the children's school papers were everywhere.

Lisa had never been a spotless housekeeper, but she'd never been a slob, either. Michael wondered how she'd passed the time while he was at work. This evening, as soon as he had arrived home, she'd left to run errands.

As he crossed to the garbage pail, then moved toward the sink, the rubber soles of his running shoes stuck to a substance on the floor that looked like splattered juice. After depositing the glasses and cups in the sink, he cleared the counter while listening to the conversation transpiring between Jake and his newly-hired tutor.

"Keep after it, Jake. You're doing better," she said, closing Jake's math folder as Kat came up beside her.

"Would you read this to me?" Kat asked in a small, uncharacteristically bashful voice. She shoved a book under Tory's nose.

"Sure."

Michael watched Tory take the book and scoot to the side of her chair to allow Kat to sit beside her. "Tory's tired, kitten," he said, forcing a glass inside the already overloaded dishwasher. "I'm sure she's ready to get home."

"I don't mind." Tory smiled at him, and he instantly felt a little less harried. "I'd like to, really," she continued. "No extra charge."

He took one look at the hope in Kat's eyes and gave in. Lisa hadn't spared a moment for either of the kids since she'd become ill. That's how he classified her behavior now—as an illness. She truly suffered from amnesia. Nothing else explained her radical change of character.

"Okay, Kat," he said. "But only one story. Tory has studying of her own to do."

He continued tidying the kitchen while listening to Tory read. Like Lisa's, her voice was soothing yet animated. Kat snuggled up in her lap. Jake leaned against her chair. They seemed so comfortable, so at ease. Michael couldn't explain the instant bond they shared with the girl, but he could relate to it. Her presence in their home added a certain something that had been sorely missing these days, since Lisa's illness. Something warm and cozy and right. He could feel it all around him now, like a thick, soft quilt on a bitter cold night.

Lulled by the peaceful intonation of her voice, Michael leaned against the counter and closed his eyes. It seemed forever since he'd taken the time to really savor a simple moment like this one. It was just that he wanted so much for Lisa, Jake, and Katherine.

He remembered the vow he'd made to himself when he and Lisa married. Her parents had died in an accident her first semester of college, and Michael was determined that she'd never have to struggle again just to make ends meet. But, in his efforts to give her all that she deserved, he'd become too wrapped up in his work. Obsessed by it. So much so, he'd forgotten that the smallest things in life were often the sweetest . . . the most important. Moments like this one.

When had he last listened to Lisa read to the children? Really listened? Her voice took on a different tone and accent for each character, making him smile. When had he last shared quality time with his family? From now on, he'd make more of an effort to be a part of these moments . . . these simple, perfect moments.

Michael's eyes popped open. The moment wasn't perfect. Not quite. It was Tory with his children, Tory's voice filling the room—not Lisa's. He was troubled . . . shocked that he'd needed to remind himself of that fact. He left the room to gather his wits while she finished the story.

Several minutes later, he walked Tory to her car. They stood in the driveway next to the red Volkswagen. The weatherman predicted snowfall later in the night. Frigid air nipped Michael's cheeks, leaving them numb. "I really appreciate what you're doing for Jacob. It means a lot to him." He swallowed as he glanced across at her. "And to me, too. Jake expects so much of himself. If he doesn't do as well as he thinks he should, he's crushed."

Red and green Christmas lights twinkled on the house across the way. Tomorrow was the first day of December, Michael realized with a strange sense of urgency.

"Jake's a good kid," Tory said. She leaned against the side of the car, her arms crossed tightly in front of her. "So is Kat."

"They are, aren't they?"

"They're the best." Her sudden smile erased another chunk of weariness from his heart and, for reasons he couldn't explain, stirred up old memories. As he stared at her, for one crazy second, he half expected to see Lisa's blue eyes gazing back at him instead of Tory's green ones.

"How's your wife?" she asked, breaking the spell, returning the weariness to his heart.

"She's okay." Michael glanced toward the house. He'd turned on the porch light earlier. It glowed in the darkness like a halo. "I'm sorry the place was such a mess. Lisa had some shopping and errands to do. She's not back yet."

"I hope she's feeling better. If there's anything I can do to help—"

"You've done it already," Michael interrupted.

For the second time that day, it occurred to him that he hadn't known what he was getting when he hired Tory Beecham. She was a great girl. She'd taken to the work at the office without much instruction, as though she'd done it for years. Tory was energetic and enthusiastic and capable . . . much like Lisa had been at the same age.

Lisa. He couldn't bear to think of their problems right now. It scared him too much. It hurt too much. And he was so tired . . . so tired.

Before he knew what was happening, Michael lost himself in Tory's wide hazel eyes. Night sounds encircled the two of them, separating them from the rest of the world. The curls fluttering around Tory's face drew his gaze, and he lifted a hand to brush a strand from her mouth, sucking in his stomach and standing a bit taller.

A car horn blared in the distance, bringing reality with it. Jerking back his hand, Michael took a startled breath, embarrassed and more than slightly worried over his actions.

She bit down on the corner of her lower lip, then sighed. "If you need someone to talk to, I'm a very good listener. Just say the word."

"I will."

Aware of a dull pounding in his head, Michael watched Tory climb into the car and back slowly out of the driveway. "Damn it to hell, what am I doing?" he muttered under his breath. "I've got to stay away from that girl."

Tory's apartment seemed cold to Lisa, despite the blowing heat that rattled the vent overhead. She curled into a ball beneath the covers and cried silent tears into a pillow that didn't belong to her. *Tory Beecham's pillow. Tory Beecham's apartment. Tory Beecham's life.*

Heavy, gray fingers of grief seized her, and she couldn't shake free of them. They poked and tortured and tormented until nothing remained but a cold and hollow emptiness, a dull, monotonous ache. A hunger for her children. And for Michael.

Who would have guessed it? Lisa wondered, wiping the streaming wetness from her face. She missed him every bit as much, if not more, than anything or anyone else. It would be different if she was simply away on a trip. But seeing him and the kids so upset, and seeing them through another woman's eyes, was too painful to bear. Not being able to really comfort them, having to pretend she didn't love them, was killing her.

Lisa ran a hand across the unoccupied space beside her in the bed. At first, she'd known a moment's thrill when she left Michael earlier in the evening. All she'd been able to think about was his smile. That quick, ready smile that had first attracted her to him so many years ago. And his eyes . . . she'd forgotten how they changed from amber to brown, depending on his mood. Remembering now, Lisa felt an instant tug that amazed her. She shivered, despite the sudden heat that danced beneath her skin.

When Michael had looked at her in the driveway, she'd felt a familiar stirring deep inside her stomach—and a not-so-familiar clumsiness with him that, until lately, she hadn't experienced in years. Something in his beautiful eyes had made her breath catch. Something she'd seen before, long ago, that had dimmed through the years of their marriage. The excitement of finding it shining bright again held her spirit high halfway back to the apartment.

But all too soon, she came crashing back to

earth with a painful shattering of faith and pride. Michael had gazed into *Tory's* eyes with that wistful look of longing, not hers. *Tory's* gorgeous blowing hair had captured his attention.

The realization brought with it instant jealousy, and an overwhelming, if unreasonable, urge to slap Michael's face . . . hard. She imagined his roving eyeballs bouncing back and forth across his head like the ball in a pin ball machine. *That no good, two-timing, lousy bastard!* It didn't matter if she was the spirit inside the body he admired. In his own mind, it was another woman he looked at with lust in his heart.

A renewed surge of jealous irritation brought Lisa out of bed. She flipped on the light switch, then crossed the floor and grabbed Dillon's guitar from its resting place against the wall. He'd forgotten it when he left the apartment.

She headed for the living room and sprawled in a beanbag on the floor, her legs crossed in front of her, the guitar positioned between her arms. She'd played some during high school and college, and though she never got around to taking a lesson, she hadn't been too bad. But somewhere along the way she'd pushed aside her interest in music—like so many other things she'd cared about way back when.

Lisa strummed the guitar. It took every ounce of self-control she possessed not to call Val. She hadn't talked to her friend since the incident at her house. Always before in times of crisis, Val had willingly offered a sympathetic ear . . . comfort. Lisa needed her now, but she wanted to give Val more time to mull things over.

Struggling with an old, melancholy tune, Lisa

attempted to concentrate on the chords and forget everything else for a while. When the doorbell rang, it took her by surprise, sending her heart to her throat. It could be anyone, anyone at all from Tory's life, and she wouldn't know them or have the faintest idea how to respond to their questions.

She put the guitar aside and moved to the front window, pushing the drapes apart. Her pulse raced faster at the sight of Val's shiny black hair. Lisa rushed to the door and flung it wide.

Val stared, her lips pressed together, her face filled with uncertainty and a touch of fear. For a moment, her attention settled on Lisa's Mickey Mouse T-shirt. "I have two questions," she finally said, the words tumbling out in a jumbled rush. "Lisa O'Conner is the only woman on earth besides myself who knows the answers, and she'd never misplace my trust by telling anyone."

Val licked her lips. "When I went on vacation last year, where did I go, and how did I spend every second that I wasn't on the beach?"

Lisa smiled, her nerves taut as a stretched rubber band. "You went to the Cayman Islands and, as I recall, you spent a lot of time in bed not sleeping."

A flush of red gathered in Val's cheeks. "The man I was with . . . what was his name?"

"That's three questions." Lisa's smile widened. A river of relief washed over her. "I don't know his name."

"Why not?"

"Because you don't know it, either. He never told you and you never asked."

Val's cheeks glowed brighter. She shifted from foot to foot. "Lisa knows something, well, *personal* about this man. Can you tell me what it is?"

Lisa chuckled. "Let's just say you assured me

that good things sometimes *do* come in small packages."

Val touched Lisa's shoulder with tentative fingers. "Lisa?" she whispered.

Chapter Eight

"What am I going to do, Val?" Lisa unwrapped another chocolate, popped it into her mouth, then shook her head. They sat on Dillon's bean-bag chairs facing each other, legs crossed in identical fashion, an ever-growing hill of candy and bubble gum wrappers littering the floor around them.

"Oh, hell." Val spit a large wad of gum into one of the wrappers. She pulled a pack of cigarettes and a lighter from her purse.

"Val! I thought you quit!"

"This is so bizarre. It really is you, isn't it?" With an astonished sigh, Val lit up. "I did quit, but I think I just started again." She took a long drag off the cigarette, blew out a cloud of smoke, made a blissful sound, then frowned at Lisa's reproachful expression. "Do you want me to admit I'm a weak person? Will that make you feel better?

Really! Considering the circumstances we're faced with, bubble gum isn't cutting it. Surely I'm allowed a one-night reprieve."

"You're right." Lisa waved smoke from her face and coughed. "If I eat one more chocolate, I think I'll puke." She stood and walked into the kitchen, throwing open cabinet doors to search inside.

"What are you looking for?"

Lisa scanned the interior of the refrigerator, frowned, then closed the door. She dragged a chair to the counter and stood on the seat to explore the overhead cabinet.

"Aha!" With a triumphant smile, she hoisted a tall bottle into the air. "Little miss perfect body, perfect hair, and perfect fingernails isn't all exercise and health food after all."

She gnawed the corner of her lower lip as she climbed down from the chair, bottle in hand, her smile of moments before dissolving. "Maybe I shouldn't be so happy about that fact." She thought of Michael, then Dillon. "Maybe I'm a lot better off if Tory is prim and proper. But then, I already know she's not prone to old-fashioned morals."

"What on earth are you mumbling about?"

"Nothing." Lisa plopped down beside Val and gave the liquor a closer inspection. "Just my luck. Jim Beam."

"I seem to remember that whiskey's not your best friend."

"It used to give me a whopper of a headache. Who knows what it'll do to this head," she said poking a finger through her mass of curls. "Oh, well, since it's already pounding, why worry?"

Lisa unscrewed the lid and took a swig straight from the bottle. "Whoa!" she gasped, trying to catch her breath. The liquid seared her throat and scorched a pathway through her chest.

"Look at you! If I wasn't already convinced you're Lisa, I'd never believe it now! Boy, are you gonna be sorry. Take it easy; we're not college kids anymore."

"Speak for yourself." Lisa stood and headed back into the kitchen. "Maybe I should find a soft drink to mix this with." She returned with a plastic soda bottle and two glasses, then mixed herself a drink before starting on Val's.

"Make mine heavy on the cola."

"Coward."

"No, just smarter than I used to be." Val reached for the cap of the Jim Beam bottle and tapped her cigarette ashes into it. Her eyes followed the swirling ribbon of smoke rising from her fingers into the air overhead. "Well, a little smarter . . . sort of."

Lisa handed her friend a full glass, then hoisted her own. "I'm only having one of these, so I plan to make the most of it. Drink up."

Val sipped. "So, what's the plan?"

"I don't know. I honestly don't." Lisa stared into the amber liquid clasped between her palms. "This is so crazy! What would you do?"

"Me? I'd take advantage of the situation while it lasts. Which is exactly what you should do. You know you're changing back on the fourteenth, so until then have a good time. Live it up!"

"That's what I was planning to do, but after being at the house a couple of times and seeing the state they're all in . . . "

"Confide in Michael if you feel guilty. You made a believer out of me; why not him, too? After the shock subsides, he might get a kick out of the whole thing."

"I've considered that. But what about the fortunes? They didn't say anything about telling him until the last quarter moon. I'm afraid I'd mess up the spell. Anyway, what if I couldn't convince him? As difficult as you were, Michael would be worse. What if he tossed me out on my ear? I need a job if I'm going to eat for the next couple of weeks." She downed half the whiskey in one woeful gulp.

"Baloney. I'll lend you the money you need. You can pay me back when you're yourself again."

"But I feel bad for Tory. *She* needs the job. I've been there, Val. I know what broke feels like. Besides, I want to continue tutoring Jake so I can keep an eye on things at home."

"I'll help all I can in that department."

"Good. I hoped you would. Michael's sleeping on the couch these days, and I want him to keep right on sleeping there. We have to make sure he and Tory stay together, but not together together. You know what I mean?"

Val frowned. "I guess not."

"I don't want to change back when this is over and find myself in the middle of divorce proceedings."

Val propped one sweat-suited leg over the other. Her ankle sliced through the air—up and down, up and down. The fingers of her free hand drummed restlessly against the carpet. "I hadn't thought of that."

"But I don't want Tory carrying on with my husband, either."

Val patted Lisa's knee. "Don't give up hope. We'll figure something out. We only have to look at this logically." She snorted. "We're dealing with body switches here and I'm talking logic?"

"No, you're absolutely right," Lisa said, then finished off the rest of her drink.

Val lifted her glass and clinked it against Lisa's empty one. "In that case, here's to logical solutions. As opposed to illogical solutions, that is."

The whiskey Lisa had consumed began its liquid massage, loosening her limbs, her nerves and emotions . . . and her tongue. "Did I ever tell you about the time when Michael went off to college and I drove down one Sunday to see him?"

"I don't think so."

"That was the turning point. The fork in the road."

Val blinked, her expression blank. "Excuse me?"

"I should've taken the high road that day. Instead, I took the low road."

"Are you telling me you got lost on your way to see Michael?" Val shook her head. "I don't get it. What does getting lost fifteen or so years ago have to do with anything now?"

"I didn't get lost. Not literally, anyway." Lisa was on to something. She felt it in her bones. The fortune said to look at her life, to look inside her heart. An answer was hidden there. She thought she'd just caught a glimpse of it.

"That was the day I think I first realized something wasn't quite right between Michael and me," she continued. "I could've easily fixed the problem then, but I was too afraid of losing him, so I chose to pretend it didn't exist. And it just got bigger after that. With every year that passed it grew, kind of like a tiny hole in your jeans, ya know?"

She drew a deep breath and hiccupped. "If you stitch it up right away, it doesn't do much damage, but ignore it and it just gets bigger and bigger." She hiccupped again. "It's really started to unravel these past two years."

Val stared at her and blinked again. "Okay. Hmmm. I'm afraid you've lost me."

"Michael said his roommate had the flu. He couldn't boot the poor guy out of the room, so we didn't have any place private to go to be alone. I didn't really care all that much. Just being with Michael anywhere, doing anything, was really enough. But then it all went wrong."

"What happened?"

Lisa shook her head. "Forget it. This is somethin' I need to work out on my own. In the meantime, there must be a reasonable solution to the Tory and Michael situation."

She felt light-headed, but it was a giddy feeling, not a bad one. Lisa grinned. "What do other people do when their souls get promiscuous and go off co . . . cojudicating with strange bodies without so much as a nibble of remorse?"

Val smirked. "I don't think there's such a word as 'cojudicating.' You'd better slow down on the juice, Lisa. You're not used to it. Anyway, get serious. We need to think this through." She stubbed the cigarette out in the Jim Beam lid, then took a draw off her own drink.

Minutes ticked quietly by as the two women sat, lost in thought, tossing around options. Val finally broke their mutual silence. "You could always tell Tory. The three of us together might have a chance with Michael."

Lisa hiccupped. "I've been thinkin' about that. It's a definite possibility; it definitely is. I wanna spend more time around her first, though. When I saw her yesterday she seemed to be walking a really thin line." Lifting an index finger to her temple, Lisa rotated it in a circular motion. "You know what I mean? We wouldn't wanna push her over the edge."

"Good point," Val conceded. "I could feel her out for you—see how she's doing." She ran her fingertip around the rim of her glass, then touched it to her lip. "There's something else to consider here."

"What's that?" Lisa made her way into the kitchen for ice. Her lips felt numb, her tongue thick and cottony. The entire situation seemed funny now. More than funny. Hilarious. She bit the inside of her cheek to suppress a laugh.

"If worse comes to worst, those fortunes might not come true," Val said, "and you might be in Tory's body forever."

Ice cubes clinked against glass as Lisa swayed toward the empty beanbag, which now looked like a large, blurry blue blob. She flopped down, picked up the whiskey bottle for a refill, then peered at Val through bleary eyes. "You really know how to cheer a girl up."

Val reached across and took the bottle from Lisa's hand before she could pour. "Like it or not," she said, "it's something we need to think about. Just in case, maybe you should get close to Michael."

Lisa blinked. "Whatta ya mean?"

"You know—make him fall for you. It's obvious to anyone with eyes that he's been miserable these past few days with the woman he thinks is his wife. If the two of you had an affair and he divorced Lisa—I mean Tory—oh, you know who I mean—then if you never changed back, you'd still have him and get to be around the kids."

"I'd be their stepmother, for God's sake!" Lisa's eyes filled with tears. "I don't wanna be my own kids' stepmother! And what if I do change back, like the fortune says? Then he'll be in love with Tory, not me. Besides, Michael's trying to make things right with Tory—I mean me—I mean, *you* know what I mean!"

Lisa giggled. She wiped the back of one hand across her running nose. "He's taking me to . . . to . . . the C-Cayman Islands!" Hiding her face in her palms, she sobbed again and again. "Isn't he a wonderful husband? I love him, Val. I really, really do. But after what happened tonight, I'm so damn mad at Michael O'Conner, I'd just as soon never see him again." She lowered her hands from her face and stared at her knees. "I won't have an affair with my own husband, Val; it's outta the question."

"Let me get this straight. Michael's wonderful and you love him, but you'd just as soon never see him again? Why? And don't talk in riddles this time. No high roads, low roads, or holey jeans. Agreed?"

Lisa nodded.

"Okay, then. What's the deal?"

"He—he looked into my eyes." With difficulty, Lisa lifted her fuzzy head to focus on Val. "I mean, he *really, really* looked into my eyes, ya know?" she asked with a suggestive rise and fall of her brows.

"And that made you mad? I don't understand."

"My eyes aren't my eyes, they're *her* eyes, and that lousy, no-good cheater looked into them like . . . like . . . *that!*" She flung an angry hand into the air. "All along he thought they belonged to another woman. He didn't know for one single minute that her eyes are mine now."

Despite Val's reproachful scowl, Lisa grabbed the bottle and sipped again. Before she could swallow, she spewed the liquid out in a sudden fit of laughter. "So see, I don't want him to feel that way about me 'cause I'm not in me anymore, I'm in *her*, but at the same time I don't want him to feel that way about her even though she's in me,

117

'cause she's not me, she's . . . " Lisa lowered the bottle to the floor and shoved it away. She grasped her sides and shrieked. "She's *her!*"

"Makes perfect sense to me," Val said between convulsive gasps of laughter.

For several minutes they lay on the floor, snorting and screeching, bodies shaking, tears streaming down their cheeks. Finally gaining control, they sat up, only to dissolve again into hysterical laughter.

"Anyway, none of this matters 'cause I'm changin' back after I tell Michael on the day of the last quarter moon."

"But the fact is," Val choked out, "the way things are right this minute, Michael can either love your body or your soul. You have to make a decision. Which is it?"

Lisa sobered. "Oh, Val! I don't think I can settle for less than both."

Val groaned. "Let's get out of here."

"Great idea. Let's go have some fun and get our minds off this. Maybe it's nickel beer night somewhere. Do nickel beer nights even exist anymore?"

"Who knows? There's only one way to find out." Val grabbed her purse. "I'm still sober so I'll drive."

Pickup trucks seemed to be the vehicle of choice. The lot was so packed with them, Lisa and Val were forced to park in the alley. And it was only a Thursday night. Lisa supposed on weekends people parked miles away and hitchhiked in.

During the drive over, she'd sobered up a bit. Now, she stared at the establishment's entrance with apprehensive eyes. "I don't like country and western music."

Val took hold of Lisa's arm to coax her forward. "This is a hot spot. The singles I cross paths with at work are always talking about it. And more than a few of the married people, too."

"Why don't you ever come here?"

"I'm not into the bar scene. But with you along, it might be fun."

"I don't want to mingle with a bunch of old cowboys. I'm a college student. I want to go where they go."

"This is it, I'm telling you. All ages hang out here. We'll both fit in. Really, would you trust me?"

Lisa stopped a few feet from the front door to give Val the once-over. Before coming to the bar, her friend had changed into a blouse, casual khaki slacks, and loafers. Lisa, on the other hand, put on the outfit she'd worn earlier to work— black polyester bell bottoms, a shiny, satin blouse in putrid green, and shoes that looked like platform combat boots.

"You might fit in, but I'll stand out like a sore thumb. Look at me, Val!"

"At Tory's age and with that body and face, you can get away with anything."

A twenty-something couple wearing cowboy boots and skintight Wranglers opened the door and walked inside. Boot-scootin' music blared, then muted when the door shut behind them.

Lisa shrugged. "Maybe you're right." She thought back to her own partying days and grinned. "I may not like listening to country music, but as I recall, dancing to it is kind of fun. I used to be pretty good." She resumed her course toward the entrance. "Remember the two-step and the waltz?" Her blood began to pulse with the beat of the music. "And the Cotton-Eyed Joe?"

Inside, the mix of music and conversation was deafening. It didn't take Lisa long to discover that Val was right about Tory's funky attire. It didn't cost her a dance partner. They'd no more than approached the bar to order drinks before a Clint Black look-alike, black hat, dimples and all, appeared at Lisa's side.

He cupped his hands around his mouth and leaned toward her. "Would ya like to dance?"

Her attention slid from his glittery, down-slanted eyes to the dance floor. Her ears tuned into the music. A two-step played. A slow one. *I can handle it.* Lisa nibbled her one jagged finger-nail. She shifted her gaze back to Clint, then to Val, then back to Clint again. "Sure, why not?" she yelled.

With a gentle clasp of her arm, he guided her through a maze of people and tables onto the dance floor. They faced each other and he took her right hand in his left while his other hand splayed across the small of her back.

Lisa placed her free arm around his shoulder. Rigidly following his lead, she shuffled backward two steps, then forward. Backward, then forward. Not an easy maneuver in platform combat boots.

Still, she relaxed as it all came back to her—those years she'd frequented the clubs with Michael and their friends. Though it wasn't his favorite pastime, Michael had even learned to dance.

At the corner of the dance floor, they made the turn easily. Apparently satisfied that she wouldn't stomp on his toes, Clint grinned down at her. "You're good at this."

Lisa grinned back. "Thanks. You're not so bad yourself." She'd forgotten how much fun dancing could be, forgotten how nice it felt to be held in a man's arms as she moved to the music.

Clint initiated a spin and she followed without missing a beat. "What's your name, darlin'?"

"Tory. What's yours?"

He spun again. "Melvin."

Melvin. The name conjured images of sagging jowls, baggy overalls, and sweat-stained T-shirts. It didn't fit. "Do you mind if I call you Clint?" *Good grief. That whiskey must've curdled my brain.*

Melvin shot her an injured look. "What's wrong with Melvin?"

"Not a thing. Forget I asked."

An expression of sheepish pride crept over his face. "Clint, huh? I'll bet I know who you think I look like." Before she could respond, he continued, "I hear it all the time. Darlin', you can call me whatever you like."

Melvin pulled her closer. Lisa winced. Because his dimples were so darn cute, she decided to overlook the endearment he'd chosen for her.

"What do you do?" he asked.

Two steps forward.

I'm a homemaker, she started to say. A mother of two. Part-time unpaid bookkeeper. Cook, chauffeur, domestic engineer. She held her tongue. "I'm a student at OU."

Two steps back.

"My alma mater. I graduated a couple of years ago."

Forward. Step, step. Back. Step, step. Another slow spin.

Then the music changed.

"Hang on," Melvin said. He tugged her against him, squeezing the breath from her lungs. Then, in a spiraling frenzy, Melvin took off across the dance floor.

"Wait!" Lisa shrieked. "I can't go this fast."

"Darlin', you're doing fine. Follow along and let me do the work."

Right, Lisa thought. A kaleidoscope of colors swirled around her. Everywhere she looked, other couples spinned, too, miraculously avoiding collisions as they forged their perilous paths. Once or twice when Melvin whisked her around, both of her feet left the floor at the same time. She felt like a limp rag doll.

Holding her by one hand, Melvin swung Lisa away from him, and before she knew what was happening, she was twirling. Around and around and around.

"My ankles!" Lisa yelled. "I'm going to break my ankles in these shoes!" Melvin didn't seem to hear her. Amid a blurry sea of faces on the sidelines, she caught sight of Val. Val's mouth hung wide open, her nose wrinkled, and her eyes stretched wide with startled disbelief. Lisa burst out laughing.

Melvin pulled her to him again and resumed his hurried two-step. Though Lisa was no longer twirling, the room was. Her stomach flip-flopped and the whiskey she'd guzzled earlier rose to her throat.

"Clint." No answer. "Clint!" No answer. "*Melvin!*"

"What's the matter?"

"I don't feel so good."

He took one look at her face and let her go. Dizzy and gasping for air, Lisa stumbled toward the tables. Smoke swirled through the room like mist in a low-budget horror movie. She sucked in two lungs full and immediately coughed it back out. Not an empty chair was in sight, so she wove her way to the bar, then braced her forearms against it, letting her head drop between them.

When the room stopped rotating and she finally caught her breath, Lisa lifted her head to find Melvin standing beside her. "I can't remember when I've had so much fun," she said dryly.

"Glad to hear it, darlin'." He leaned into the bar and looked down at her.

Lisa looked up. He was gazing into her eyes. First Michael, and now this college-educated cowpoke wannabe. Until tonight, it had been years since any man other than her optometrist had gazed into her eyes. Unless she counted the times Michael helped her fish out a stray eyelash. Today it had happened twice, and her lashes were all intact.

Lisa couldn't help herself. She sighed. He was *really* gazing now. As though she was the most desirable female on earth. As though he couldn't tear his attention away from her face. As though he was dying to know everything about her. Her interests, her opinions, her hopes and dreams.

"Wanna take a little walk?" Melvin asked, his voice a low croon.

"Pardon me?"

He twisted a strand of her hair around his finger and winked. "My truck's outside. It won't take long to heat up." His eyes took a leisurely stroll down the length of her body. "Hell, we probably won't even need the heater."

So much for my interests, opinions, hopes and dreams. "I don't think that's such a good idea," Lisa answered. Val approached, and Lisa gestured toward her. "I'm here with a friend. Here she is now."

The glitter in Melvin's eyes dulled as Lisa made introductions. "You two aren't leaving, are you? The night's young."

"You ready to go, Val?" Lisa asked.

"Not unless you are. I ran into a co-worker a second ago. He offered to help me brush up on my Cotton-Eyed Joe."

"Oh." Lisa wiggled her brows at Val as if to say, *watch this*. "I don't know if I can last much longer. Melvin about wore me out on the dance floor. I'm about to suffer a heat stroke and I'm dying of thirst." Eyes wide and adoring, she stared up at him and grinned.

"A cool drink will fix you right up," Melvin said with enthusiasm, his glitter returning. "Let me buy a round for you and your friend."

"Why, thank you. I'd love a drink," Lisa gushed.

"Nothing for me," Val said, "I'm the designated driver tonight."

"Doesn't he look exactly like Clint Black, Val?" Lisa asked just loud enough for Melvin to hear as he moved to the opposite end of the bar to place the order.

Val crossed her arms, then tapped her fingers against her shirtsleeves. She leaned close to Lisa's ear. "Why, Lisa O'Conner, you surprise me," she said. "Tricking that sweet young thing into buying your drink."

"Hey, it's not every day I have this kind of influence over men. I rather like it for a change. Besides, I'm broke, and Melvin owes me. He's called me *darlin'* at least three times in the last twenty minutes, and I refrained from giving him my condescending-male speech."

Lisa stared across to where her dance partner stood conversing with the bartender. "Boy, is he young. He's only a kid, really. And good-looking, too. Show me a better-looking guy than Melvin in this place and I'll eat a cocktail napkin."

"Start eating."

"What?"

"He only has eyes for you and he's headed this way."

"Who?"

"A guy better looking than Melvin." Val fanned her face with her hand. "Be still my heart."

Lisa looked over her shoulder. "Good grief," she whispered. The blond barbarian who'd motioned her to the side of the road yesterday strode toward them, an ever-widening grin on his chiseled, bronze face.

"Lisa, right?" he asked as he sidled up beside her.

Melvin appeared on her other side, holding two drinks. "Lisa?" His eyes narrowed. "I thought your name was Tory."

The room started spinning again. Lisa's stomach rolled. She looked at the barbarian. She looked at Melvin. Then she looked at Val. "I don't feel so good."

Val snickered behind her all the way to the rest room.

Chapter Nine

Michael stood at his office window staring out into the parking lot. During the night the promised snow had arrived. It blanketed the city in a soft layer of white.

Thoughts of the previous evening sent his hand to his ear, and he gave an exasperated tug. Tory Beecham was beautiful, yes, but much too young. Though her body was a woman's, she was still very much a girl. Take the clothes she wore—faddish, sometimes downright silly-looking. *So, why am I obsessing about the way she looks?*

Michael watched cautious traffic maneuver the slushy streets outside, all the while remembering Tory's patience with Jake as she explained math problems. She'd probably stayed up all night afterward with her own schoolwork. Young or not, he reminded himself, Tory was dedicated. And smart. The grades on her college transcript

126

were topnotch. He'd be lying if he said he wasn't impressed with her quick, confident intelligence. But he'd known scores of other intelligent women over the years. *So what makes Tory different than any of them?*

She had a rapport with his kids, there was no denying it. And that impressed him even more than her sharp mind. Tory's compassion, her warm and witty way with the children, were traits Michael appreciated and admired. But Val was all those things, as well. Val took an active interest in his children's lives, and it never gave him any pause for thought. *So why am I standing here feeling Tory is something special?*

Michael swore softly as he turned away from the outside view. Beautiful and young, smart and compassionate. *So what? What is it about her? What is it that has me acting like a pubescent fool?*

He shoved a hand through his hair, then slipped out of his office and down the short hallway to Jarrod's domain. After a quick knock, he stepped inside uninvited and closed the door behind him.

"Come in," Jarrod said sarcastically.

Michael slumped in the chair across from his partner's desk as Jarrod shut the book in front of him.

"What's wrong?" Jarrod asked.

"We, um . . . " Michael averted his eyes. "We have a problem."

"Spit it out, Mikey. I have work to do."

"It's Tory."

Jarrod grinned. "You mean that hot little number you hired? What could possibly be the problem?"

"She's not working out."

127

Jarrod tilted back in his chair, eyeing Michael with open astonishment. "Tell me you're joking. For once, we not only hire someone who doesn't have to be told how to do something twice, but who's also damn fine to look at. That's one gorgeous set of—"

"You can keep your observations to yourself, Wilder. It's not her appearance I came in here to discuss." He cleared his throat. "I . . . I just think we'd be better off with someone else. I want you to fire her."

"I see." Jarrod's eyes thinned to slits. "You want *me* to fire the girl." He pulled off his glasses and polished the lenses with his tie. "Give me one good reason why."

Michael's mind went momentarily blank. "Well, because . . . because she's overqualified. Before you know it, she'll be bored with the job and lose interest."

"I see your point. That makes a hell of a lot of sense, Mikey. Has she had any complaints so far?"

"Well, no, not that I know of."

"So you want to get rid of her before she does, correct?"

"Something like that."

Jarrod chuckled. "One of these days you're going to jerk that ear of yours right off." His laugh escalated as, blushing profusely, Michael lowered his hand to his lap. "There's more to this than what you're telling me. Unless you can give me a better reason than overqualification, you'll have to be the one to give Tory the boot. Personally, I think she's a damn good worker."

Michael stood, flattened both hands on Jarrod's desktop, then leaned toward him. "But I *can't* be the one to do it."

"Why not?"

"Just trust me."

Jarrod returned his glasses to the bridge of his nose. "You have to trust me first. Tell me what the problem is. I'll be happy to help straighten it out."

For a moment Michael considered the consequences of confiding in his partner. No doubt, Wilder would get an enormous kick out of the entire situation. He quickly tossed aside the prospect.

"Forget it." He stormed toward the door, his jaw twitching violently. "I'll do it myself."

Over the slam echoing behind him vibrated the sharp-edged crescendo of Wilder's laugh.

"Ohhh, my head," Lisa groaned. She'd spent the night at Val's house but hadn't slept much. Now, they sat across the table from each other in a shopping mall's food court. Steam from a Styrofoam cup drifted into Lisa's face and she breathed it in deeply.

"Serves you right." Val bit into a huge cinnamon roll, chewed, and swallowed. "I warned you to take it easy on the drinks."

"Other than what we had at the apartment, I only had the one Melvin bought me. This headache must be the after-effect of all that smoke and noise."

"Don't forget about Chad. He bought you a drink, too."

"How could I forget Chad?" Lisa groaned again, remembering the blond barbarian. "He was worse than static cling. He stuck to my side the entire night. But he didn't buy me anything but tonic water and lime. Maybe Tory's body doesn't tolerate alcohol."

"You didn't seem to mind Chad's attentiveness last night. Melvin wasn't too happy about it, though."

Lisa took a sip of coffee, lowered the cup to the table, and smiled. "Okay, I'll admit it was an ego trip, watching the two of them make fools out of themselves trying to win me away from the other. But it got boring after a while. A conversation with your cats is more stimulating than talking to Chad. Melvin, on the other hand, might've been interesting if I could've persuaded him to talk about anything other than going out to his truck. He's a social worker. Has a degree in psychology. And he tried his best to use it on me."

"Poor you. Men only love you for your looks. I should have such a problem."

"Don't give me that. You weren't hurting for attention. That co-worker of yours was good-looking. He seemed nice, too. Why won't you go out with him, Val? He asked you, didn't he?"

"Yes, but I'm not interested."

"Why not? It's the guy you met in Cayman, isn't it? You're mooning over him."

Val looked away, shrugging. "Speaking of Cayman, we'd better get moving. I only took the morning off, and you have to go to work at one o'clock yourself."

The throbbing in her head made Lisa wince as she stood. "Don't remind me. Are you sure you don't mind buying me a few clothes to take on the trip? I'll pay you back as soon as I can."

After the incident with Michael last night, she knew she had to go to Cayman with him. Just the memory of his fingers against her cheek made her fluttery and weak inside. Her marriage was important. Michael was important. They just had some problems to work through.

"I don't mind at all. After you change back, you'll have a lot at home to straighten out. I doubt you'll have time to get all your Christmas shopping done and buy for your trip, too. It's going to take some looking to find hot-weather clothing during the winter."

"That's not all that'll be tricky. I know what size my real body is, but I usually try clothes on before I buy them."

They slid their purses onto their shoulders as they headed into the mall. "While we're at it," Val said, "let's buy you an outfit or two to wear now. I know you're not comfortable with Tory's taste in clothing. Pick out some things you'd buy if you really were built like her."

Because it was December, they didn't have much luck finding shorts, tank tops, sundresses, or swimwear. Lisa decided she might be forced to make do with her clothing from the previous summer. And Val reminded her that she'd spend most of her time wearing a swimsuit on Cayman anyway.

They ended up in a lingerie shop, with Val insisting that Lisa pick out something sexy to wear for Michael on the trip. "After what he's going through with Tory right now, he'll need some special attention."

Lisa shuffled through satin, lace, and silk, then held up a skintight black lace bodysuit with snaps in the crotch and a plunge-inducing bra top.

Val trilled her tongue like a purring cat. "Try it on."

"Get real. The old me would fill this out, but in all the wrong places."

"It'll fit. Look." Val pointed to the tag. "It's one-size-fits-all."

Lisa's lip curled. "Spare me. I've heard that before."

"So your real body doesn't measure up to Tory's. Whose does? You have a good figure, Lisa. Try it on."

Lisa wasn't the least bit interested in trying on underwear. War was being waged inside her skull, and she wanted to go home and sleep it off before work. But she didn't have the energy to argue. "Oh, all right."

Val stood outside the dressing room. When she heard Lisa's startled gasp and nervous giggle, she jiggled the doorknob. "Let me see."

"Wait until you get a load of this!" Lisa let her in.

Val stared bug-eyed at Lisa's protruding bosom. "Those are unreal!"

"Oh, they're real, all right."

"How can you be sure?"

"I checked for scars."

Lisa turned to give Val a rear view. The bodysuit's leg openings were cut high on the sides, almost to the waist, and Tory's thighs didn't contain a single bulge or lump of cellulite. She swung back around. "Now do you really believe the old me could wear this?"

"Of course you could," Val said, gawking. "You just won't plunge as much."

"That's the understatement of the year. I don't want to look foolish."

"You won't. Believe me, Michael will love it."

Lisa couldn't tear her eyes from the mirror. Undeterred by Val's laughter, she struck pose after provocative pose.

"Hang on," Val said. "Turn around again."

"What's wrong?"

"I think there's a bug on your butt."

"Get it off!" Lisa swatted her bottom.

132

"Calm down. It's only a tattoo. There, look," Val said, pointing. "Just under the edge of that lacy elastic."

"A tattoo?" Lisa twisted into an awkward position to see her rear end. "Good grief! It's a butterfly!" Her gaze met Val's in the mirror. They stared at one another for a moment, then burst out laughing. "I have a tattoo on my butt, can you believe it?" Lisa laughed again, then caught her breath. "Go find me something else to try on."

"Like what?"

"Anything. Everything. The sexiest, most outrageous stuff you can find. This is like feast after famine, you know?"

"You're exaggerating again."

"How can you say that? Look at me! I'm built like an underwear model in one of those lingerie catalogs I'm always getting in the mail. The ones Michael flips through more than I do. I've caught Jake peeking, too, when he thinks I'm not looking. Let's have some fun. You try on something, too."

They spent the next hour in everything from leopard-skin garter belts to floor-length, body-hugging satin nightgowns. Once, the salesclerk poked her head into their dressing room to ask them to hold down the noise, they were laughing so loud. But the woman's eyes twinkled with amusement as she made the request.

Lisa finally purchased a see-through, stretch-lace teddy, crotch snaps and all. Then they made a quick visit to a nearby department store, where they chose some less trendy outfits for Lisa to wear to work.

Somehow or another, Lisa managed to avoid Michael all afternoon. Immediately after arriving at work, she'd left again to make a bank deposit and run various business errands. Now, with her back to his office door and her nose in a file cabinet, she felt a delirious, almost embarrassing sense of anticipation at the thought of him seeing her for the first time in her new clothes.

A hangover-induced wave of nausea took hold, replacing her buzz of excitement. Val was right, she decided, shaking off the sick feeling. Confusing or not, jealousy over Michael's attention was ridiculous since it was *her* inside Tory's body, his own wife he was responding to.

Behind her, Lisa heard a low whistle, muted steps on the carpet, and a loud knock.

"It's me," Jarrod said to Michael. "Can I come in?"

"Sure," Michael answered.

Lisa looked over her shoulder in time to catch Jarrod's wink before he entered Michael's office. He left the door wide open, and she didn't hesitate to listen to their conversation.

"When I saw you earlier," Jarrod said, "I forgot to mention that I talked to Bill Perkins over at Packard, Stewart, and Leighton. He just got back from a trip to Cayman. Booked it through an outfit called . . . let me see."

Paper crackled, and Lisa strained to hear over the noise.

"Here it is," Jarrod continued. "Dale Scott at Caribbean Tour Company. This is the number. Bill says Scott has a great package deal, and he supposedly works last-minute miracles. Why don't you give him a call?"

When Jarrod reappeared in the doorway, Lisa busied herself, not anxious to be caught in the act of eavesdropping.

"Bill ended up paying about a fourth less than the travel agents could swing," Jarrod said.

"I'll call now," Michael said. "Thanks."

Jarrod closed the door. "You're looking good today, Tory." He fingered his sandy curls, then hiked up his pants. "Real good." Turning, he sauntered back down the hallway.

Lisa cringed. *Great. Just the man I want to impress.*

Several minutes later, Michael stepped out of his office and called to Nan, who was in her own office. She met him in the hallway. "Cancel those reservations you made with my travel agent," Michael said. "I've found a better deal."

After he returned to his work, Lisa told Nan she'd handle the cancellation. She imagined the rushing roar of the ocean, the scent of tangy salt air, a sultry island breeze filtering through her hair . . . soft as a lover's touch. She pulled the brochure from under the folders where she'd hidden it.

The intercom buzzed, and Michael's voice sounded over the line. "Tory, could you come in here for a minute, please?"

"Sure," she answered. Her heartbeat quickened. Standing, she replaced the brochure, then straightened the sweater and skirt she and Val had purchased that morning. Something to make her appear more "pulled together," Val had said. *Sexier is more like it,* Lisa thought as she glanced at her image in the mirror on the opposite wall. The cream-colored sweater clung to every curve, just low enough at the neckline to offer an enticing hint of Tory's ample cleavage.

She felt awkward beyond words, and her legs quivered like gelatin as she entered Michael's office. *He's your husband, silly. Why should you be nervous?* Still, when he looked up, Lisa felt an annoying flush of self-consciousness. "You wanted to see me?"

His goggle-eyed expression was more intoxicating than the previous night's whiskey. After several silent moments, Lisa walked to the side of his desk. "Is something wrong?"

"No!" Michael picked up a pen and flicked it back and forth between his thumb and forefinger, his gaze darting from her to the desktop.

Lisa drew a deep breath. "I heard you tell Nan to cancel the reservations for the Cayman trip. Did you want the literature back? I can get it for you."

"No," Michael said quickly. "I don't need it anymore."

"Oh. Well, I've heard about the Cayman Islands. Unless you're into diving, there's nothing much to do there. Which is exactly why honeymooners love the island so much, I guess. Is that what you're planning? A second honeymoon?"

The pen flew from Michael's hand and landed with a clatter on the floor at Lisa's feet. They stooped at the same time, but Lisa's hand closed over the pen first. She started to rise, then looked up to find Michael only inches away . . . so close she felt his breath on her face . . . smelled the clean scent of his skin.

For a long moment neither moved, their eyes locked in a wordless exchange that spoke volumes. Then the door to Michael's office flew open.

"Michael! You'll never guess . . . " Jarrod froze, the expression on his face changing slowly from surprise to humor.

Lisa rose quickly.

In his own haste to jump up, Michael stumbled forward, bumping his head on the side of the desk.

Lisa turned toward the bookcase on the back wall. She busied herself pulling leather-bound volumes from the shelves and scrutinizing their titles with unseeing eyes.

"Excuse me," Jarrod said. "Sorry to interrupt." He exited more quietly than he'd entered, not laughing aloud until he'd taken several steps down the hallway.

What on earth had come over her? Lisa wondered, chewing on a hangnail as she slid a book onto the shelf. After a few moments, she stopped her meaningless project and forced herself to turn and face Michael.

He stood across the room, his head bowed. With one hand, he rubbed the rising goose egg on his temple. "Tory, we need to talk." He cleared his throat but didn't look up at her. "I'm afraid this isn't working out."

"I don't know what you mean."

His gaze was dark with worry when he looked at her. He walked around to the outer edge of his desk and leaned against it. "I think it might be best if you didn't tutor Jake anymore."

Lisa stepped toward him. Tears stung the back of her eyelids. "Please, don't punish Jake for my mistake. Nothing like this will happen again. I promise." She recalled making the same vow only days ago. Michael's expression told her he, too, remembered.

"Why does it mean so much to you?" he asked. "You hardly know my son."

"I can't explain it," Lisa said, her voice trembling. "Helping him, well, it . . . it gives me so much satisfaction."

"I'm sorry. I appreciate all you've done, but it's time my wife took over that responsibility again. She's feeling better now."

Michael was a terrible liar. She guessed he was so desperate to stay away from her, he'd say anything to accomplish it. The wife in her admired his efforts, but the mother in her rebelled. Lisa's heart sank. She only managed a nod in response to his statement. She couldn't explain why she felt so upset. She'd be back in her own home with her family soon enough. Yet she knew that if she tried to speak, she'd end up making a scene . . . blubbering and begging and ultimately making things worse.

"And about your job here . . . " Michael continued. He looked at the floor.

Dread reached out and grabbed Lisa by the throat. Unreasonable or not, losing this job suddenly seemed a threat to her own future as well as Tory's. *Don't do it, Michael. Please don't. I need this job. And Tory will need it later.*

Michael moistened his lips and looked up. "About your job," he said again. After a long, tense pause, he continued, "You're doing fine. Keep up the good work."

Lisa almost collapsed with relief. She knew in her heart that he'd intended to fire her. Something had stopped him at the last minute. She was thankful for whatever it was.

Chapter Ten

Lisa tossed her purse on the dresser, kicked off her shoes, and fell backward onto the water bed. She slowly massaged her temples. The ache inside her head hadn't eased at all. If anything, it had only grown stronger.

She rolled, face first, into the pillow, closed her eyes a moment, then turned to the window across the way. Outside, a slowly darkening sky obscured the dense, gray haze that had hung overhead like a frown throughout the afternoon. Rising wind whistled through the cracks of the cheaply built apartment building, causing joints to creak in eerie protest.

She'd almost blown everything, Lisa thought as she curled into a ball, settling in for a lonely night. Because of her stupid behavior, she couldn't see Jacob and Kat anymore. Her heart ached over it.

Only two more weeks. But she and the children had never been apart so long without contact, and with Tory in charge, how could Lisa be certain they'd be properly cared for? After all, Tory was little more than a stranger.

The telephone rang, interrupting Lisa's thoughts. She considered not answering. It would probably be someone calling for Tory, and she didn't want to deal with questions she couldn't answer. But since Val might be at the other end of the line, she reached for the receiver. "Hello."

"Tory? Is that you?"

The young woman's voice was unfamiliar. "Yes. Who is this?"

"It's Kathleen. Are you okay? I've been worried about you. You haven't been to classes all week. Didn't you get all the messages I left on your machine?"

"My answering machine's on the blink," Lisa lied. "I've been a little under the weather. Don't worry; it's nothing serious."

"When you didn't show up for dance class, I was really worried. I know how obsessed you are about staying in shape." Her voice lowered to a confidential tone. "Is it Dillon?"

Lisa hesitated. "What do you mean?"

"You know. He told me the two of you broke up. Is that why you've stayed home all week?"

"That's part of it, I guess," Lisa answered, at a loss to explain.

"Things will work out, Tory. You two are meant to be together, you know?" When she didn't receive a reply, the girl continued, "Well, I just wanted to call and remind you about tonight."

"Tonight?"

"You said you'd fill in for me at the club, remember? My shift starts at seven."

The club. Why did those two words sound an alarm bell in her mind? "What club?"

"You know, *the club*." Kathleen's tone took on an impatient edge. "The place near campus where you used to work."

"Sorry. Your call woke me. I guess I'm kind of groggy." Lisa glanced at the clock. *Five-thirty*. She didn't feel like being out of bed in an hour and a half, much less running her feet off as a waitress at some club, serving drinks or food or whatever the heck it was Kathleen did to earn spending money. "I'm sorry, Kathleen. I forgot. I'm really not up to it."

"But, Tory! My sister's getting married tomorrow. I have to leave right now to make it home in time for the rehearsal dinner. You promised!"

Lisa stared up at the ceiling. It wasn't Tory's fault any more than her own that they'd switched places. She'd already lost the girl a boyfriend and put her a week behind in school. Maybe by doing this one thing, she could at least save a friendship. Besides, she'd never waited on tables before. It might be fun . . . might take her mind off her troubles for a few hours. "Okay, Kathleen," she said. "I'll be there."

After driving from Oklahoma City into Norman, Lisa headed for the university campus in search of a club—any club—nearby.

Something Kathleen had said before ending their earlier telephone conversation nagged at her thoughts.

"Thanks a lot, Tory. I hope things won't be too awkward."

The statement, whatever it meant, filled her with a sense of impending doom.

When she spotted a sign outside a respectable-looking, though trendy, establishment that indicated THE CLUB was the *name* of a restaurant, it took her by surprise.

Several of the staff waved and smiled when Lisa walked in. One girl, a carrot-top redhead with a generous sprinkling of freckles, grabbed her by the arm as she passed.

"Hi, Tory. You're filling in for Kathleen, right?"

"Y-yes," Lisa stammered, as the redhead hustled her past tables filled with laughing, chattering patrons, then through swinging doors to the kitchen at the back.

"Harry wants to see you."

Harry, who Lisa concluded must be the manager, stood around six-foot-four-inches, a heavyset man with receding gray hair and a perfectly matched full beard and mustache. He wore a Hawaiian shirt and a broad, beaming grin.

"Boy, am I glad to see you," he said in a high-pitched voice that contrasted comically with his bulk. "We're short-staffed. I need someone who can do the work of two, and you're it."

"I am?" Lisa took in the behind-the-scenes pandemonium with unconcealed wariness.

"This is the busiest Friday night we've had in ages. You'll need to be on your toes." He nudged her in the side with an elbow and winked. "Hey! Don't look so panicked. You're the best waitress I know."

The blood drained from Lisa's body. *Fantastic.*

"It's the same old routine as when you used to work here," Harry continued, "but if you have any questions, one of the staff will be happy to help out." He turned to the redhead. "Get her started, Kasi."

As Harry disappeared around a corner, fatigue and apprehension battled for dominance in every bone of Lisa's body. But as Kasi showed her the section of tables she'd be serving, a surge of adrenaline kicked in, giving Lisa her second wind.

She balanced a tray filled with water glasses and menus and approached a booth occupied by three teenaged males, trying to act as if she did this every day. "Hi, my name is Tory. I'll be your waitress this evening." Lisa lowered the tray to the table, then distributed the water and menus. "Could I get you something to drink?"

"We'll have a pitcher of beer and three mugs," one of the guys told her.

She squinted, inspecting each of them in turn. *Mere babies.* "I'll have to see some ID, please."

"In that case, make it a pitcher of Coke."

Lisa grinned at them before turning to go. "I'll be back in a minute to take your order."

The kid closest to her touched her arm and gazed up at her from beneath the bill of a ball cap. "What's your hurry, Tory? Why don't you take a break? Sit down and join us. We're not that hungry, are we, guys?"

Affirmative answers came from his companions.

She looked them over. *So cute.* Their interest was endearing and flattering.

"Sorry, guys," Lisa said, grinning wider. "Maybe some other time. Duty calls."

"When's your shift over?" The kid who'd issued the invitation stuck out his lower lip, feigned a pout, then pressed his palms together in front of him as if to beg. "I know this great coffee bar. Let me buy you a cup."

The friend at his side jabbed him in the ribs. "Give it a rest, Luke. She's not interested. You're jailbait to her."

"Shut up," Luke said, jabbing back, his eyes fixed on Lisa.

"Thanks, but when this night's over, I think I'll be too exhausted to do anything but go home." She walked away to turn in their drink order, amused by the quietly issued murmurs of approval that followed her departure.

"Miss, we need more bread," a man at the next table said as she passed by.

"Sure, right away," Lisa answered. His peeved look only added to her sense of inadequacy in this arena.

Kasi brushed up beside her. "Table eight's getting antsy, Tory. Better get a move on."

"Right." Glancing frantically between the guys waiting on their pitcher and the man demanding bread, Lisa shrugged, then headed for table eight.

She positioned an order pad in front of her, pulled a pencil from behind her ear, and forced a smile. "Are you ready to order?"

The elderly couple at the table gave her a rock-piercing stare. "We haven't seen a menu yet," the woman said blandly.

"Oops. Sorry."

The next hour was a chaotic blur. She spilled two drinks, one accidentally, the other on purpose. The latter she poured onto the lap of a potbellied, middle-aged barracuda who pinched her on the butt.

It wasn't until she'd decided things couldn't get crazier that Lisa noticed a familiar face behind the bar. Eyes black as onyx blazed with a mixture of anger and confusion when they met hers. He'd smoothed his gleaming dark hair into a ponytail. *Dillon.*

That's why "The Club" had sounded familiar when Kathleen mentioned it over the telephone, Lisa realized. Dillon had said something about working there on that first afternoon she'd met him. But it hadn't meant anything to her then. She'd been too overcome by his nakedness and the swaying water bed for the information to register. Now, Kathleen's comment about awkwardness made perfect sense.

Her mouth went dry and her heart sank at the sight of him. Lisa tried to smile but managed only a quiver of her lips. Too busy to cross the room and speak, she simply nodded in his direction and returned to work. But as she moved from table to table, she felt him watching her . . . felt his resentment riddling her skin like bullets from a machine gun each time she passed the bar.

Anxious to escape Dillon's scrutiny, Lisa ducked inside the kitchen to pick up an order. She hefted a plate-filled tray into the air as Harry rounded the corner.

"Relax, Tory. You're doing fine. After you finish with that, take a ten-minute break. I'll have one of the other girls cover for you. You can return the favor later."

Lisa welcomed the short reprieve from the high noise level and bustling atmosphere of the restaurant. She exited the back of the building. Outside, she filled her lungs with snow-freshened air, enjoying a moment of uninterrupted silence.

She thought about the last hour or so. To her surprise, she was having a good time. The fast pace of the restaurant appealed to her, and other than a few exceptions, she liked dealing with the patrons.

Low-hanging clouds caught the reflection of parking-lot lights off the snow. One determined star glimmered through the haze. Lisa focused on it, admiring its fierce tenacity.

"You're shivering."

The deep voice behind her caught her off guard. Lisa whirled around, her heart in her throat.

He leaned against the building, his black eyes and hair blending with the shadows. "Dillon! You scared me!"

"Sorry."

Funny, she'd been oblivious to the cold outside before, but the stinging chill in Dillon's deep voice scattered goose bumps across her skin. Lisa rubbed her palms up and down her arms to generate heat. "How've you been?"

"Okay."

He didn't move away from the wall, so she found it difficult to discern his features in the dark. Still, she felt his gaze steadfast upon her. "I'd better get back to work," Lisa said, uncomfortable with his tensely quiet demeanor.

Dillon wrapped a hand around her wrist as she headed for the door. "Wait," he said, his tone softening. "I want to know something. Was it the conversation we had a few weeks back about having kids that freaked you out? Because if that's the problem . . . well, I've been thinkin' about it, and I can live without kids of my own."

Lisa tried to ease away, but he held fast to her arm. "That's not it at all, Dillon." Her heart filled with pity at his confusion. "I just need time. It doesn't necessarily mean forever."

"No, I mean it, Tory. I know how you feel about having kids. Your mom had a hard time raising you alone after your dad died. You had a hard time, too. That's understandable." He paused to catch his breath. "It's not as if I don't have four brothers and sisters. We'll probably have dozens of nieces and nephews to spoil. It won't matter if we don't have kids of our own."

Words wouldn't come. Lisa averted her eyes. "I need to go in," she whispered.

He dropped her arm. "Will you think about what I've said?"

She couldn't bear to hurt him anymore. Lisa nodded. "Just give me a couple more weeks." She started inside.

"Oh, Tory . . . I left my guitar at the apartment. I'll stop by and get it sometime. Okay?"

She nodded again and closed the door behind her, telling herself that the worst was over. At least they'd finally spoken. Maybe the tension between them wouldn't be as strong now. She could make it through the rest of the night.

As she moved through the kitchen, Kasi called out from across the room, "There you are! Thank goodness! I'm swamped. A couple was seated a second ago at table ten. Can you take care of them?"

Lisa grabbed two menus and went out front, her thoughts on Dillon. "Hi, I'm Tory," she said automatically. She placed menus on the table in front of the couple. "I'll be your waitress tonight." She glanced to her right at the woman and smiled, then flinched when she saw her own face . . . her own blue eyes. Michael's startled voice drifted to her ears.

"Tory . . . I didn't know you worked here."

Michael watched Tory walk away from the table. Of all the places they could've had dinner, why did Lisa have to choose the restaurant where Tory Beecham worked nights? Considering the crazy reactions Tory stirred up in him lately, she was the last person he wanted to see tonight—especially with Lisa at his side. He'd hoped this evening might be a first step toward setting his marriage back on track.

After work, when he'd suggested a night out minus the kids, Lisa had hesitated. But then she'd asked if they could go to The Club. The name of the restaurant had simply popped into her mind, she'd explained. A hidden memory she couldn't quite focus in on.

When she'd mentioned the restaurant, an instant change in attitude settled over her. She'd almost seemed frightened, yet lured by the place. Intrigued, Michael had agreed to give it a try.

He studied his wife. "You look . . . nice." His gaze drifted slowly over Lisa's outfit, and he forced a smile, hoping to cover his true opinion as well as his bewilderment. The clothes weren't typical of Lisa's usual style. They were faddish, silly-looking, like something Tory might show up in at work. He swallowed, remembering what Tory had worn today. Nothing faddish or silly-looking about that outfit.

Tory. Annoyed that she'd slipped into his thoughts again, he glanced down at the menu. This afternoon he'd almost fired her, almost made her pay the price for his own foolish feelings and behavior. He was the adult, for pete's sake. Tory was only a kid. He should never have let things get so awkward between the two of them.

"That waitress," Lisa said, bringing his head up. "Isn't she the girl who works at your office? The one who's been helping Jacob with his schoolwork?"

For the first time all week, Michael noticed a glint in his wife's eyes. Jealousy? he wondered. No, it was more along the lines of curiosity, or perhaps suspicion. "Yes, she is. I had no idea she works a night job, too. Must be nice to have so much energy." He reached for his ear, then stopped himself and looked around the restaurant. "What do you remember about this place? Anything?"

She leaned back and idly surveyed her surroundings. "Not really. But, it feels . . . comfortable. I mean, sort of familiar or something."

"Well, as far as I know, you've never been here before. I know I haven't." He watched her face as she scanned the room, and he noticed immediately when her expression changed to one of surprise. Michael shifted his attention across to where she was looking.

A young man stood behind the bar mixing drinks. Lights overhead brought out the dark, gleaming highlights in his long hair and sparked a tiny, dazzling beam in the diamond adorning his left ear. Michael's eyes shifted from the bartender back to Lisa. She stared unabashedly at the guy. Her face flushed, and her chest rose and fell visibly with the rapid pace of her breath.

Michael leaned back. He jammed both hands into the pockets of his jacket, his gaze darting from his wife to the unaware kid and back again. "A friend of yours?"

Her eyes lingered a moment longer on the bartender. "I . . . I don't know. He kind of reminds me of someone I used to know, I guess." She gave a nervous giggle.

Across the way, the bartender stopped mixing drinks. His head jerked toward Lisa, and Michael noticed the expectant look on his face. But the look quickly faded to a frown, and the kid returned to his work.

It was Lisa's laugh, Michael thought as suspicion flared again. *Did the bartender recognize it?*

149

After a moment's consideration, Michael removed his hands from his pockets. He reached across the table to clasp Lisa's fingers. She tensed when they touched, but Michael tried not to let that bother him. "Lisa, I'm not going to pretend I understand any of what's going on with you—your memory loss, your attitude toward the kids, the way you seem to feel . . . " He paused. "I guess I should say, the way you seem *not* to feel about me."

He linked his fingers with hers. "I can't make you remember the way it was, but I want to try and make things right between us. I want to be a family again."

A few feet away, Lisa, carrying a basket of bread and an order pad, approached Michael's table. When she saw the exchange taking place between him and Tory, something compressed inside her at the look on both their faces. The tightness became painful as she drew nearer and heard Tory's words.

"It's just like so *weird* for me, Michael. I know I'm not being fair to you or to Kat and Jacob." Tory glanced down at their joined hands, her voice cracking. "I'm so tired of being depressed. I want my memory back. But even if that never happens, I want to be happy again. I'll try, Michael. I promise."

Lisa forced herself to take a deep breath, drawing air into her lungs in noisy little hitches that finally caught the couple's attention.

"Oh," Michael said, glancing over. "I guess you're ready to take our order."

Somehow, Lisa managed to write down the order, conscious all the while of Tory studying her every move, analyzing every word she spoke.

Though the girl had amnesia, seeing her own face and body, hearing her own voice, must stir up some crumb of recollection. Lisa found it difficult, herself, to see the woman sitting across from Michael—the woman with her own features, her hair, her eyes. Because the experience was unnervingly strange, she avoided eye contact with Tory.

As hard as she tried, though, she couldn't keep from looking at Michael. Awareness whispered through her. When had she stopped really seeing her husband? She loved the strong angle of his jaw, the intensity in his eyes, his sturdy shoulders and slender build. Her fingers itched to touch his hair, to smooth the unruly strands she'd grown so accustomed to seeing over the years.

Though she told herself that she was being stupid, she couldn't suppress her sick fear about what might happen between Tory and Michael after hearing the girl's promise to him. Why should she care if they slept together? Michael would be making love to *her* body, not Tory's. Still, she cared a great deal.

Lisa headed into the kitchen to deliver the order, then back out to the bar to get Michael's and Tory's drinks. "I need a gin and tonic and a club soda and lime," she said mechanically to Dillon.

"Who is he?" Dillon asked, his tone cold, distrustful.

"Who?"

"That man at table ten you can't keep your eyes off of. You've been staring at him ever since he walked in."

"He's my . . . my boss." Lisa had to struggle to push the words through her tightened throat. She left before Dillon could make a comment, making her way to the rest room.

Inside, she leaned over the sink and splashed cold water on her forehead. A thousand thoughts and anxieties ran through her mind, all too puzzling to be of any help.

When she lifted her face to the mirror, she almost screamed at the image behind her. Tory stood there, her eyes suspicious, searching.

"I know you," the girl said.

"Of course you do." Lisa turned, grappling to regain her composure. "I work for your husband. We met the other day at your house."

"No," Tory said. She took a tentative step closer. "Before then. I knew you before."

Chapter Eleven

"I think we did meet once," Lisa said cautiously. "A long time ago."

"You know I have amnesia, don't you?" Tory took another step forward. "Did you really just start working for Michael, or have you known him a long time?"

Shaken by the prospect of Tory's revived memory, Lisa grabbed a paper towel to blot the water from her face. "What are you thinking?"

Tory frowned. "I'm not sure. I mean, maybe something happened between you and my husband before I got sick. Or maybe you wanted something to happen, but Michael wasn't interested. I see the way you keep looking at him all the time."

Disappointment filtered in. So Tory didn't know anything after all. Surprised by her accusations, Lisa shook her head. "You've got it all wrong." It was time, she decided. Time to take a chance and tell the truth, regardless of what trouble it might cause. It was unfair to Tory to leave her so confused. She touched the girl's arm. "Let me explain."

Tory backed away toward the exit. "No way. I'm not interested in hearing your excuses. I mean, just because I'm not myself doesn't mean I'm going to let you take advantage of me. Stay away from my husband."

Three hours later, Lisa climbed the stairs to Tory's apartment. Snow drifted from the sky in plump, downy flakes, clinging to her lashes, coating her hair with a fine layer of frost.

She unlocked the door and turned to stare out at the night. Christmas lights winked in the distance, multicolored sequins against a black satin sky. They symbolized hope, peace, and family, and seemed to mock her sudden desperation and loneliness.

Lisa stepped inside the apartment and slammed the door on the outside world—the steady din of traffic on the highway, the smoky scent of fires burning in cozy households, the bitter desolation of winter. She closed her eyes and leaned back against the door for several minutes, reliving her troubling encounter with Tory.

When she finally made her way to the bedroom, the doorbell rang. "Will this day never end?" she muttered under her breath as she returned to the den.

"Who is it?"

"It's me. Dillon."

"Dillon." Lisa forced back the lock to ease the door open.

He stood with his hands crammed into the pockets of his jeans. His breath formed hazy puffs of white in the frigid night air. "I came for the guitar." He paused. "Can I come in?"

After a moment's hesitation, she stepped aside and motioned for him to enter.

Dillon crossed to where the guitar stood propped against the wall. He stared down at it, then stooped to run a finger across the strings. "Out of tune," he mumbled, lifting his eyes to look at her.

Lisa felt cornered by his dark gaze, and oddly guilty. She was relieved when Dillon finally cleared his throat and looked away. He scanned the candy and gum wrappers that littered the floor from the previous night. "When did you start eating junk food?" Gesturing toward the whiskey bottle on the coffee table, he added, "And drinking?"

Lisa remained by the door, her arms folded in front of her. It didn't seem Dillon had any intention of leaving soon. She couldn't handle another confrontation. "I'm really tired. It's been a long day."

"Are you saying you want me to go?"

She nodded. "I'm sorry."

Dillon picked up the guitar. He walked toward her, stopping only inches away. He'd freed his hair since leaving The Club. It fell to his shoulders and shadowed the contours of his face. "How long have you known your boss? Did you know him before you interviewed at the law firm?"

"Dillon, please."

He reached for her hair, twisted a copper curl around one finger, then let it fall. "You watched him all night. You should've seen your face. He's the problem, isn't he, Tory?"

155

Lisa tried to step back but was stopped by the door.

"He's what broke us up."

"No," she whispered. Dillon's brooding eyes gleamed with a certainty she sensed she couldn't sway. "I didn't ask you to move out because of another man. You're wrong."

"Am I?" His voice was a low rumble. "We'll see. We might've had our differences in the past, but there was one thing we always agreed on."

In one fluid movement, he lowered the guitar to the floor and pulled her against him. She felt determined strength in the long arms that held her, felt urgent insistence in his lean, graceful body. There was no tenderness in his kiss, no gentle persuasion or demonstration of love. Instead, his mouth moved over hers roughly, aching with raw need, demanding she prove his suspicions wrong.

Desperation mingled with the warm, male taste of him. Though his anguish tugged at her compassion, Lisa couldn't respond. Tensing, she placed palms against Dillon's chest and pushed. Then she touched her lips with trembling fingers.

His eyes fired like heated coals. The veins in his neck pulled taut, and his mouth hardened to a rigid line as he stared at her. After what seemed like forever, he reached around Lisa for the doorknob.

When she moved away, he yanked the door open and stepped onto the landing, then faced her again. "We're not finished. When I cool off, I'll be back to talk this out."

Lisa stood before the open door staring at the empty space where he'd stood. Slowly, she looked down at the floor, where he'd left his guitar.

"What did you think of the movie?" With a quick glance over his shoulder at Lisa, Michael draped his jacket on the back of a kitchen chair, then went to the refrigerator for a drink of water.

"It was good. Really funny."

"It was, wasn't it?" After dinner, they'd taken in a late show. It had been a relief to think of something other than his troubles for a while. Better yet was the fact that he'd heard Lisa laugh with joy for the first time since her illness.

Michael scratched his head and frowned. Strange, but something about her laugh bothered him, though he couldn't put his finger on the problem. He thought of the bartender at The Club. The kid had responded to Lisa's laugh, too. He'd looked her way as if he'd expected to see someone he knew.

"Robin Williams really cracks me up." She giggled, ending with a soft snort before catching her breath to start over again.

Michael drank several gulps of water before looking at his wife's reddened face. *That's it! That's what's wrong. Lisa's never snorted like that before when she laughed*

He shoved a hand into his hair and studied her. Lisa's clothes looked like she'd bought them in the young teen department. And the way she talked—the way she curled her hair all tight and wiry lately. Then there was her sudden, all-consuming obsession with physical fitness. Now this. Instead of getting better, if anything, Lisa seemed more and more a stranger with each passing day.

He brushed aside the thought. At least she'd agreed to try to resume their life together. And now Lisa was laughing. Surely he should consider that a good sign.

Michael began to chuckle along with her. "The kids would like that movie. We should take them sometime."

"They could've come along tonight," she said as she headed toward the bedroom, with Michael following behind her.

Michael reached for her arm, pulling her around to face him just short of the bedroom door. "We needed this time alone. Nan was glad to have them spend the night. She misses having her own grandchildren close by."

He cupped her head in his palms, and rubbed the base of her neck with his fingers. "Can I sleep with you tonight?" he asked quietly and quickly, before he lost his nerve. He nodded toward the couch, his pulse quickening at the possibility that she might say no. "That thing's beginning to get uncomfortable." Because of the uncertainty clouding her eyes, he dropped his hands to his sides, afraid to pressure her.

"I . . . guess it would be okay." She gave him a tentative smile. "I haven't been fair to you, making you sleep on the couch. I mean, you've been so understanding."

They walked together into the bedroom. "I know you haven't been feeling well."

"I meant it when I said I want to make things right," she murmured as she headed into the adjoining bath. She looked at him before closing the door. "Try to be patient with me."

While Lisa was gone, Michael turned down the covers and stripped to his underwear. He climbed beneath the sheets, dimmed the lamp, then glanced around the room. Like the rest of the house, it was a horrible mess: clothes strewn everywhere, the furniture covered with dust. He hoped Lisa included a return to housework in her plans for "making things right" again.

He heard the shower turn on and imagined her naked beneath the spraying water, her skin sleek and wet. Desire slammed into him with the force of a bullet. They'd slept apart less than a week, but it seemed longer. Before now, he'd never realized how much he'd miss having her beside him at night—her body, soft and warm, the sweet smell of her hair.

Until recently, sex with Lisa had been unpredictable. Sometimes fast, fevered, and greedy; other times slow, sensual, and giving. And then there were the playful times, with Lisa's throaty laughter a backdrop to their frolic in bed.

"Damn," Michael muttered. The thought of Lisa's laughter brought images of Tory to mind. He'd listened often these past days from the confines of his office, to Tory and Nan working together on the other side of the wall. Tory's deep, husky laughter roused something inside him. *Like Lisa's . . . before she started to snort.*

The bathroom door opened and she emerged, her hair damp from the water's mist, wearing a knee-length sleep shirt. He'd hoped for something sexier for their first night back together. Maybe he'd expected too much. Despite the outfit, she looked fantastic. Though he told himself it was too soon to notice results, he'd swear Lisa's dieting and exercise frenzy had already started to pay off. She slipped under the comforter next to him and gave him a hesitant smile.

Despite her memory loss, for some reason Michael had expected the familiar, uninhibited intimacy of longtime lovers. He never dreamed it would be like the first time, never imagined she'd come to him like a virgin . . . face flushed pink, eyes shy, body quivering with each shaky intake of breath.

Michael pushed back a wet lock of dark blond hair from her face. He leaned forward and brushed a light kiss across her mouth, then stared into the striking blue of her eyes. Though he knew her body better than his own, had memorized every curve, each hollow, the anticipation of touching her seemed new, almost forbidden, filling him with wary excitement.

"You're shivering." He drew her against him and covered her mouth with his own again, deepening the kiss when her lips parted beneath his. Then he moved over her, eased her onto the pillow, explored the sweetness of her mouth with his tongue.

Something was wrong . . . different. He should recognize the way she felt beneath him. After years of marriage, they always fit like a puzzle, moved together in perfect rhythm, blended. But this time the pieces didn't seem to match; the beat was off, the combination awkward.

Still, needs twisted . . . heat sweltered. His fingers traced a pathway down the curve of her neck while his lips followed course to the peak of one breast. She tensed, and Michael held his breath.

"Michael," she gasped, squirming out from under him, "I'm sorry. I mean, I guess I'm not ready for this yet."

Because tears welled in her eyes, he fought to squelch his impatience. "Okay."

He rolled to his back to stare up at the ceiling, the pounding of his heart so loud he could hear it in the room. "When, Lisa?" he asked after a moment. "When will you be ready?"

Her only answer was a quiet series of sobs.

Minutes later, when his pulse finally slowed to a normal beat and desire eased from his body, leaving only frustration, Michael replayed the night's events in his mind. He relived every scene, heard each word. Questions tumbled through his brain. Questions he wasn't sure he wanted answered.

After a while the silence threatened to suffocate him. Tension flowed between them like a living, breathing entity. He swallowed hard, then took a deep breath when he couldn't endure the strain any longer. "That young guy at the restaurant tonight, the exotic-looking one?"

"Yes?" she answered.

Michael turned to look at her. "Is there anything you'd like to tell me about him?"

Briefly, her eyes met his. When she glanced away, something died inside him.

"I'm not sure who he is," she said in a voice barely stronger than a whisper. "But I won't lie to you, Michael. I'm like . . . well . . . *drawn* to him, I guess. I must've known him once. Before the amnesia."

Chapter Twelve

Saturday evening, Val treated Lisa to dinner and a movie. Val had dropped by the O'Conner household that morning and found little changed since her previous visit. Lisa was relieved to hear that the couch was still made up as a makeshift bed.

Val offered to let Lisa move into her spare bedroom for the next couple of weeks, but Lisa wanted Michael to be able to reach her by phone if necessary. She anticipated an awkward explanation if she gave him Val's number. Besides, she'd decided that if she was to fully experience being twenty years old again, she'd have to put up with the negatives along with the positives. And Tory's lonely apartment definitely qualified as a negative. Lisa had quickly come to realize that sharing custody of the TV remote control was preferable to living alone.

On Sunday she spent a couple of hours at a nearby laundromat—something she hadn't done since early in her marriage. To pass the time, she carried along a few of Tory's schoolbooks and notes.

Look at your life.

Lisa flipped through page after page while the clothes washed and dried. By the time everything was folded, stacked into baskets, and loaded into the Volkswagen, she'd reached two conclusions. The first being that, years ago, she and Michael had made a wise investment by saving for a washer and dryer, though they were strapped for cash at the time.

The second—she should hightail it to the university tomorrow and sit through Tory's classes. Startled by the volume of written material Tory accumulated in a week's time, Lisa decided the least she could do was take notes for the girl while taking a look at the campus for herself. She could kill two birds with one stone, as the saying went: do Tory a favor, while satisfying her own curiosity about returning to college.

So early Monday, after a little song and dance with the woman behind the desk at the registrar's office to obtain a copy of Tory's schedule, Lisa walked into a political science class and took a seat.

Across the aisle, a petite bleached-blonde rearranged her tousled curls with quick-moving fingers as she looked Lisa's way. "I was almost afraid you wouldn't show up again," she said. "How did it go at The Club? Did you make up with Dillon?"

The whiny voice brought instant recognition. Lisa was reminded of the phone conversation with Tory's friend on Friday. This must be Kathleen, she decided. The girl she'd filled in for at the restaurant.

Before Lisa could answer Kathleen's question, the professor entered the room and began discussing the previous assignment. Soon, his monotonous voice had Lisa yearning for intravenous caffeine. Her eyelids drooped. Her head suddenly seemed too heavy for her neck to support. It began to bob like the plastic puppy her granddad used to have mounted on the dashboard of his pickup truck. Just before her chin hit her chest, she jerked it up, blinked, then widened her eyes, only to feel them sagging again moments later.

Her head fell forward and her pen slipped from her fingers to the desktop, where it rolled to the edge and fell to the floor with a clatter. The noise snapped Lisa to attention. Bending to the side, she reached for the pen. When she sat up, her elbow knocked a notebook to the floor on the opposite side of her desk. Avoiding eye contact with anyone in the classroom, she gathered it up, then stared down at her lap. She drew a deep breath, then exhaled, desperate to send oxygen to her sluggish brain.

"Are we having problems, Miss Beecham?"

Lisa glanced up. The professor stood beside her desk, his watery, gray eyes condescending.

"No, sir." Someone behind her snickered.

The professor pursed his lips. "We've missed an entire week of classes, haven't we?"

"I, um, haven't been feeling well, sir."

"So sorry to hear that. Perhaps we're not up to returning to class yet."

What's with the "we" bit, Professor? Do you have a frog in your pocket? "I'm okay. I didn't mean to disturb your lecture." More snickers from behind. "It won't happen again."

"Very well."

He returned to the front of the room. Lisa, embarrassed by her sleepiness and irritated at the professor's pompous response, forced herself to concentrate for the rest of the hour. She'd forgotten how boring a classroom lecture could be.

When the class finally ended, she gathered her things and walked with Kathleen and another woman—this one tall, with long, straight hair the color of chestnuts—out into the hallway.

"So, are you going to make Allison and me beg for the juicy details about you and Dillon?" Kathleen asked.

"We aren't back together, yet," Lisa said, choosing her words carefully. "I just need some time. I asked him to give me a couple of weeks."

The tall young woman Kathleen referred to as Allison stopped in the middle of the hallway to place a hand on Lisa's shoulder. "What's really wrong with you, Tory? I've never seen you like this. You know, falling asleep in class and everything."

Lisa shrugged. "Guess I didn't get enough rest this weekend." She glanced from one girl to the other. "I better run."

"You'll be at the game tonight, won't you?" Allison asked. Her expression threatened bodily harm if Lisa gave the wrong answer.

"What game?"

Allison and Kathleen exchanged a concerned look. "The roller hockey game, of course," Kathleen said. "We're counting on you. Be there at seven."

"Better yet, we'll pick you up," Allison interjected. "Just to make sure."

Lisa stepped forward. "But—"

"See you tonight!" The girls walked away, ignoring Lisa's protests.

"Roller hockey." Lisa groaned. "Wait until Val hears this." Deciding she'd worry later about coming up with a way out of the game, Lisa left the building.

But despite her best intentions, she couldn't bring herself to attend the next class. If it went anything like political science, she'd only wind up hurting Tory rather than helping her. So instead, she wandered around campus, inspired by the atmosphere, remembering the freedom and exhilaration of a world filled with options. She wondered what she'd change if she had her college career to plan over again.

Around her, Lisa noticed several students all well beyond their teens and twenties, and for the first time, a liberating thought struck her. There wasn't a rule written anywhere that said she was stuck with the career choice she'd made a decade and a half before. It was a rule she'd imposed on herself. But what would she study if she returned to school? She had enjoyed the business classes she'd taken. *For the most part,* Lisa silently amended, recalling more than her share of boring lectures in the past, much like the one she'd endured moments ago. She'd made good grades while she was in school. Maybe she hadn't chosen the wrong field of study, but had only grown tired of working in sales.

Lisa continued her walk, thinking. She could use her business training in any number of other areas. Areas she hadn't considered before.

She returned to her car, then flipped through a class catalog she'd picked up at the registrar's office earlier in the day.

Open your heart. Look inside for the answers you seek.

"So many things I could do," she mumbled. "What do I really want?" With a sigh, she tossed the catalog into the passenger seat and headed back into the city.

"Can I play goalie?" Lisa asked a few hours later. Beneath Tory's hockey garb—bulky cushioned pants, shoulder pads, knee pads, elbow pads, and an oversized red jersey with TERMINATORS written across the back—she quivered like a cornered animal. She didn't have a clue how to play goalie, but was pretty sure the position didn't require much skating. Maybe with a little luck she could stand in front of the goal without falling flat on her face. Maybe.

The hockey arena loomed beyond the bench where she sat. Nothing ominous about it, she kept telling herself. It was only a roller rink with goals set up at either end. So why did she feel sick to her stomach each time she looked at it?

Allison laughed. "Very funny, Tory. You're not a goalie, you're a center. The best in the league, and you know it."

The look she shot Lisa's way was somewhat perplexed, somewhat worried. "Get ready, already. It's bad enough Kathleen and I practically had to dress you at the apartment. Do we have to put on your skates and helmet, too? Honestly, Tory, I'm beginning to wonder about you."

Lisa was beginning to wonder about *Tory,* too. The *real* Tory. *What self-respecting, feminine girl would involve herself in a tough sport like roller hockey?* She splayed her fingers wide across her lap and looked down at them. *How on earth does she keep from breaking these gorgeous nails? What ever happened to plain old basketball? Or volley-*

ball, for that matter? Not that Lisa could play those games, either. She barely knew a dribble from a serve. But at least they were wheel-free sports.

Visions of junior high school physical education class flashed through Lisa's mind, bringing the old humiliation back with them. She'd always been the last student chosen by the team captains when they divided up sides—the loser the most unfortunate team got stuck with.

As she took in the flurry of activity around her—whoops and whistles, people gliding by clacking hockey sticks against the cement floor, shouts issued back and forth from the sidelines to the players on court—Lisa's head began to swim, her heart to pound. It took twice the effort necessary just to cram her feet into Tory's leather in-line skates and adjust the buckles. Once the task was accomplished, she plopped a helmet—face shield and all—onto her head and, following the lead of those around her, snapped the strap into place.

She jammed her fingers into a pair of padded gloves, then with one hand, gripped the low wall separating the arena from the sidelines and pushed to a standing position. Wobbling, her stomach taking a sharp dive, she swung her other arm around to grab hold of the wall, too, bending over and clinging to it as if it were a life preserver.

Allison, now dressed in full gear and looking like a knight in padded armor, clutched Lisa's shoulder. "Are you okay?"

"Not really. I don't think I can do this. I . . . I don't feel well."

"You've *got* to play. It could mean our losing the championship if you don't. We're counting on you, Tory. Maybe it's nerves. Take a few deep breaths. See if that helps."

"It's nerves, all right. But not because of the championship. It's my butt I'm worried about."

"What's that? I can't hear you; you're mumbling."

"Nothing."

As Allison skated away, Lisa took her advice and sucked in several deep breaths. Slowly, she let go of the wall and stood. She'd skated during childhood and, like climbing onto a bicycle after years of not riding, the basics gradually came back to her. She practiced in the area outside the arena until she felt more confident.

She watched several men and women warm up, hoping for a glimmer of insight into the rules and object of the game. When a shrill whistle sounded, all the players headed off court with the exception of what she assumed was the starting line.

A short, muscular man no older than Dillon whose nose looked like it had been rearranged one time too many, turned to Lisa from his spot at the end of the bench. "What are you waiting for, Tory? Get out there!"

Lisa pressed a hand to her chest. "Me?"

"Yeah, you. They're ready for the face-off."

She flapped her arms to keep balanced as she stumbled toward the entrance to the arena. Once inside, the muscular man, whom she figured must be the Terminator's coach, called to her.

"This is no time to be joking around, Tory. You fall and break a wrist or something and we're in deep shit."

Lisa nodded. A nervous giggle bubbled up at the thought of a broken *anything*.

He reached over the short surrounding wall to hand her a hockey stick. "You might need this."

She gulped. "Thanks."

A referee and a player dressed in yellow from the opposing team, the Sting, stood at center court staring at her. Feeling as graceful as a drunk elephant, Lisa used the stick like a cane and moved toward them. She stopped near the referee, looked at him, then turned to her opponent, and smiled. "Hi."

The Sting's center snarled back at her. *Good grief! He's missing a tooth.*

The referee stood off center between them. He pointed down court at the Terminator goalie. "Goalie ready?" he yelled.

The goalie nodded.

Lisa winced. *What about me? I'm not ready.*

The referee pointed down court in the opposite direction. "Goalie ready?"

The Sting's goalie nodded.

Lisa turned pleading eyes on the man. *Are you going to ask me now?*

"Timekeeper ready?" the referee yelled again.

The timekeeper nodded.

Lisa tried to breathe. *Help.*

The referee raised a round plastic disc about the size of a small bagel into the air. Lisa grasped for a memory of the one ice hockey game she'd attended in her life. *Let's see . . . that little bagel-thing's called a puck, and all I have to do is hit it toward the other team's goal before the toothless wonder beats me to it.*

Mimicking the opposing center, she clenched her teeth, grasped the stick between her trembling fists, and took a stance. Her muscles tensed.

The referee lowered his hand.

The puck didn't drop.

He lifted it into the air again. Lowered it.

On impulse, Lisa swung her stick.

Crack!

The puck flew from the referee's hand. Yelping, he grabbed his knuckles. Lisa placed one palm over the part of her helmet covering her mouth. "Oops. Sorry."

The Sting's players and coach shouted their indignation. The Terminator's coach didn't sound much happier.

The referee massaged his knuckles and turned on her. "You're dismissed to right wing," he bellowed.

"Okay." *Whatever that means.*

A player at side court skated forward to take her place. Lisa guessed she was supposed to fill the girl's position so she cautiously glided in that direction.

The two centers and the referee resumed the face-off. When the puck dropped on three, the Terminator's new center knocked it toward Lisa. Miraculously, it hit her skate. Her heart pounded as she placed her stick behind it and looked up toward the goal. A swarm of yellow jerseys rushed in her direction like giant bees converging on an unsuspecting flower.

Lisa dropped her stick and skated away from the oncoming yellow blur, stumbling and swaying in her effort to flee. Only feet from the Sting's goalie, Lisa realized that she didn't remember how to make a quick stop. "Watch out!" she shrieked just before crashing head-on into the goalie, tumbling the two of them into a heap of arms, legs, and hockey sticks.

While they attempted to untangle themselves, the Sting's defense overtook the puck. Breaking away, they whisked down court for a score. Through the ringing in her ears, Lisa heard a whistle, then the growl of the Terminator's coach.

"Tory! Get over here!"

Grunting and groaning, she pushed to her feet and went to face him.

"What's wrong with you?" he thundered.

She shrugged, her shoulders twitching spasmodically due to the condition of her nerves.

"You're sitting out for two lines; then I want you to cut the crap and get out there and skate your ass off. Understand?"

She felt like kissing him for pulling her out. With a nod, she gratefully sat on the bench. For the next four minutes, she watched the game, absorbing every detail, intrigued by what she saw.

"We're gonna change lines on the fly," the coach said. Seconds passed. "Change it up!" he yelled again.

The players around her stood. Lisa tapped the coach's shoulder. "Is it the fly?"

His eyes sparked fire; his crooked nose turned red. "Are you trying to be funny? Get out there!"

Adrenaline pumped into her as she made her way onto the court. When the puck slid in her direction, panic hit her like a Mack truck. Then, a miracle happened. Tory's reflexes kicked in.

Lisa rushed toward the puck and the on-coming Sting defense. Her stick clashed with several others' as they battled for possession of the puck. Lisa won. She grabbed the puck with her stick and broke away, streaking toward her destination while maneuvering the round disc like a pro.

The goal loomed before her, a light at the end of a tunnel, her pot of gold at the rainbow's tip. She pictured herself in slow motion as she sped toward it, the anticipation of victory drumming through her veins.

While sitting on the bench, she'd noticed that the players often went around back of the goal with the puck, then stopped behind the net to wait for an open player to shoot to. Lisa attempted the same move now, but instantly realized she was on her own. None of her teammates were clear for the shot. Racing around in front of the net, she aimed, took her best shot, and scored.

A roar went up from the crowd. "Yes! I did it!" Lisa tore off her helmet and soared toward the arena's center, her hands raised high, pumping the air like Rocky Balboa.

Triumph tasted sweeter than she'd imagined. She had never felt such a heady sense of power, such excitement. She savored it, wanted to share it with the team. But the congratulatory pats on the back she expected didn't come.

Allison ripped off her own helmet, then threw it to the floor. "Way to go, Tory." She shot a disgusted glare over her shoulder as she skated away.

"You're benched for the rest of this half!" the coach screamed. His nose glowed like a Christmas tree light.

Confused, Lisa turned to Kathleen, who stood beside her shaking her head.

"That was a beautiful goal, Tory," Kathleen said. "Too bad you made it for the other team."

Chapter Thirteen

Friday afternoon, Lisa looked up from her desk to watch Michael usher a client from his office toward the reception area. He didn't acknowledge her presence when he passed. They'd barely exchanged three words all week. Michael wasn't really rude toward her, just businesslike, impersonal.

Michael settled a hand on his client's hunched shoulder when they paused in the reception area doorway. "Things will look up soon."

"They better," the man said. "My family has to eat."

Michael rubbed his chin. "How's your artwork going?"

"Pretty good. It's mostly a hobby, but I sell a painting ever now and then at a craft show."

Michael smiled. "Remember when my wife and I ran into you last Christmas out at the mall? You

174

had your work on display. Are you still painting everything on velvet?"

The man's face brightened. "Sure am."

"Lisa really admired your work. Especially the portrait of Elvis on red. Has it sold yet?"

"Nope. I still got Elvis."

"Why don't we make a trade? My bill for your painting, and we'll call it even. I'll give it to Lisa for Christmas."

Lisa bit her lip to keep from laughing out loud. She remembered the man's work, and Michael knew good and well she considered it gaudy beyond words. Particularly Elvis. He'd never give it to her for Christmas. It would go into storage and probably end up in a garage sale later.

Lisa smiled as another emotion nudged its way into her heart, pushing amusement aside. Obviously Michael, who'd pinched every penny these past two years, was doing a favor for a man in need.

Touched by his caring gesture to his client, she studied him from a fresh perspective as the two men walked into the front lobby. She almost felt as if she was seeing him for the first time. She'd always known Michael was a generous, compassionate man, but when it came to his law practice, she'd assumed he thought business was business. Lisa would've never believed he'd make such a worthless trade if she hadn't heard it with her own ears.

A delivery boy entered through the front door with a large arrangement of daisies in his arms. "Does Tory Beecham work here?" Lisa heard the young man ask. Janice led him back to her desk.

"For you," the receptionist said, then returned to the lobby with the delivery boy behind her.

Nan poked her head out of her office door. "Special occasion?"

"Not that I know of." Ignoring the quizzical smile that deepened the lines around Nan's eyes, Lisa pulled a tiny envelope from the flower arrangement.

"Well, I'm just being nosey," Nan said, then ducked back into her office. "They certainly are lovely," she called.

Lisa slid the card from the envelope and read the inscription aloud. "Love, Dillon." She sighed, glanced up, and jumped. Michael stood at the far side of the desk, watching her.

"We haven't missed your birthday, have we? Jarrod doesn't like to overlook any opportunity to celebrate."

He looked wonderful. Irresistible. Tired and worried, too. Lisa saw the evidence etched clearly in his brown eyes, heard it echo in his voice. She had a sudden, intense longing to coax away the fatigue and make him relax, to massage his rigid shoulders, brush her hand through his tawny hair, touch her lips to the tensed muscle along his jaw. She wanted to reach out to him and enjoy the very things she'd ceased to find time for through the course of their marriage. When had a simple shared pleasure between husband and wife become nothing more than a chore not worth attempting? Why had either of them allowed it to happen?

"It isn't my birthday." Lisa swallowed the lump in her throat. She returned the card to the envelope, then replaced it among the blooms. "I broke up with my boyfriend a while back." When her eyes met Michael's, she nibbled the corner of her lower lip. "I guess these are his way of letting me know he's not cooperating."

Michael crossed his arms and sat on the edge of the desk. "He must think a lot of you."

"I guess he does."

"You don't feel the same?"

Lisa thought of Dillon and the things she'd learned about his and Tory's relationship. She raised a hand to her mouth, remembering the emotion, the despair in his kiss. "I did once."

"But not anymore?"

"No."

Michael shook his head, perplexed. "Women. I hate to sound like an old cliché, but I don't think I'll ever understand any of you. Especially after these last couple of weeks." Embarrassed over the personal turn the conversation had taken, he studied a paperweight on Tory's desk to avoid having to look at her.

"How is she?"

"My wife?" Michael choked down the lie that sprang to his lips. Everyone in the office had been affected lately by the strain he suffered at home. What good would it do to pretend things were fine? "I'm afraid she's not doing any better."

"I'm sorry. The two of you seemed so close Friday at The Club."

His heart twisted as he recalled the look on his wife's face and her admission late Friday night when he'd asked her about the young bartender at the restaurant. Other than trivial necessities, they hadn't spoken since . . . or shared a bed.

He thought he might go insane if he didn't find someone to talk to, someone who'd listen. After several consultations, he finally resolved himself to the fact that the doctor had no answers. There was always Jarrod, but his partner didn't know the meaning of the word compassion. And as for Val, though they saw her often, she'd distanced herself emotionally from Lisa since the onset of the amnesia, and thus from him, as well. Val seemed different these days, uneasy. For the first time in his life, Michael felt totally alone. Alone with a problem he had no idea how to solve.

"Friday . . . " Michael said, his voice drifting off. "You know, I thought things were finally getting back on track, too. I told myself we'd reached a turning point that night."

He looked into Tory's hazel eyes and saw sympathy there. Sympathy and concern that spurred him on. "But nothing has really changed at all since then, except she does seem to find more time to spend with the children. Between the two of us, though . . . " He reached back to rub the crick in his neck, a crick derived from sleeping on the couch.

"How are Kat and Jacob?" she asked.

Michael guessed she had recognized his discomfort with their previous subject and was graciously changing it. "They're okay, considering the circumstances at home."

Heat inflamed his cheeks, then pulsated to an aggravating beat. He couldn't imagine why he'd allowed himself to confide in Tory. For some strange reason, trusting her with his personal life seemed perfectly natural, even comfortable, in a way. Despite that fact, he knew it was wrong. He had to end it. Now.

But the sudden tears he saw in her eyes caught him off guard. "I really miss them," she whispered. "I really miss Kat and Jake."

All of Michael's rational intentions flew out the window. He was touched by Tory's affection for his children, and he forgot his self-imposed rules of etiquette. Suddenly, it didn't matter if she was his employee. He didn't care if she was only twenty years old. The reasons he shouldn't be drawn to her, shouldn't need her, completely slipped his mind. Tory cared. She understood.

"Every year since Lisa and I've been married, she's always put a tree up and decorated the house by the first of December. But this year, she hasn't done anything to prepare for the holiday. Christmas is slightly more than two weeks away." He lifted his hands into the air, then let them fall. "No tree, no decorations, no presents. Nothing. I guess I'll have to get busy this weekend and do it all myself."

Michael stood. He paced the small area in front of Tory's desk. When he glanced at her, she seemed lost in thoughts of her own. He looked at the flowers and sympathized with the sender. Having a girl like Tory and then losing her would be difficult for any man to accept. She'd be worth fighting for, he thought, worth the risk of acting like a fool.

His last thought hit a bit close to home. He was getting too personal. Michael ran a hand through his hair and forced his mind back to business. "I hate to ask this, as busy as you already are, but do you have any experience in bookkeeping?"

She slid a pencil from behind her ear, and a spooky sense of déjà vu clutched Michael by the throat. He recognized the restless expression on her face, the distracted manner in which she drummed the pencil against her temple. He'd observed that same look often enough in the past. Not in Tory, but in Lisa. The old Lisa.

"Michael? Is something wrong?"

"You always have a pencil behind your ear, don't you?"

She laughed. "Either a pencil or a pen. I can't count the number of times I've gone to the grocery store or shopping or even to a movie and found I had one tucked away there."

179

An uncontrollable shudder rippled through him. "Lisa does the same thing." Michael closed his eyes and swiped a hand across his face, as if to whisk away cobwebs. Funny how the mind could play tricks, he thought. For one split second, he'd been stunned by an uncanny resemblance between Tory and Lisa. "Well," he said, stepping away from the desk. "What were we talking about? Oh, yeah, the bookkeeping. Do you have any experience?"

He was staring at her as though she were a murky pool with something sinister hiding beneath the surface. An odd sensation started inside Lisa. The moment after she'd told him about her habit with pencils and pens, she'd realized her mistake. Could he be suspicious about her identity? Impossible, she reminded herself. Such a suspicion would never occur in a sane person's mind.

She tried to remember the issue at hand. Bookkeeping, she thought, suppressing a groan of frustration. "As a matter of fact, I've had some basic accounting," she told him. Though she wished she could lie and say she didn't know a debit from a credit, she realized, in the end, that she'd end up doing it anyway, and have to play catch up in the bargain.

"Good. We'll let Nan take over some of your other duties and have you do the bookkeeping until Lisa's feeling better. That is, if you don't object."

"Not at all." *This just proves you can't hide from those nasty little annoyances in life.*

"I'll show you how to get into the program on the computer. Lisa has the same one at home with a modem. It's fairly simple. I don't think you'll have any problems." He circled around the desk to stand beside her, then flipped the switch on her terminal.

As Michael fumbled his way through the computer's menu, Lisa feigned fascination. Finally, after several minutes passed and he hadn't managed to pull up the appropriate screen, she said, "That's okay, Michael, I'll figure it out."

"Good deal. I'll round up the check stubs for you, then leave you to it." He went into his office.

Lisa hated losing the intimacy they'd shared this afternoon. It had reaffirmed how much she wanted to be with Michael. And she desperately needed to find a way to be with her children again, too. She didn't think she could survive another day without seeing them.

While toying with the computer, she mulled over the previous conversation. It provided her a certain amount of satisfaction to think Michael might finally get a dose of his own medicine after years of letting her tend to the holidays on her own. He'd find out it wasn't an easy task to tackle alone. But that didn't ease her mind about what her children were missing. Or what she was missing, for that matter.

Despite all the hassle, she truly loved the season—the festive decorations and peaceful music, the spicy aromas of delicacies she never baked at any other time. Most of all, she enjoyed the secrets: the children's faces when she teased them about their gifts, their barely concealed anticipation, their laughter.

Lisa sighed. There was always the chance that, despite his best intentions, Michael wouldn't get around to the decorating and shopping. And when she tried to imagine him baking cookies or making fudge, the picture just wouldn't develop in her mind. If he put it all off, she'd be forced to do everything after the quarter moon, when she changed back. That would be difficult, if not impossible. But she couldn't spend Tory's money to buy the family gifts, and she'd already borrowed too much from Val.

Lisa looked away from the computer screen when Michael returned with the check stubs. "I have a proposition for you," she said.

"Crybaby! Poor little crybaby!"

"Shut up! Mo-om! Jake's makin' fun of me! You're a cheater, Jake."

"You're a big wuss."

"Stupid." Kat sobbed, her lower lip trembling. "Mo-om!"

When Michael entered the living room with Lisa at his side, he saw Jake quickly avert his gaze from his sister.

"Tattletale," Jake mumbled out of the corner of his mouth, then busied himself straightening a stack of video games on top of the television.

Kat whimpered with rage. She balled her hands into fists at her side. "You . . . " she sputtered, "you *virgin!*"

The videos fell from Jake's hands onto the floor. His face twisted with laughter and his blue eyes sparkled mischievously as he looked over at Michael. "Did you hear what she called me?"

"Kat!"

Michael jumped higher than Kat at the sound of Lisa's shriek. He watched her as, in three quick strides, she crossed the room and clasped Kat's skinny shoulders. "Where did you hear that word?" she asked.

"He was callin' me names first." Kat's tearstained jaw clamped shut. She lifted her chin a fraction, as though preparing to defend her case.

Michael pressed his lips together to stop his own laughter. "Katherine," he said calmly. He cleared his throat. "Do you know what a virgin is?"

Kat dragged the back of one hand across her freckled nose. "Nope."

"Well, it's a good idea not to use words unless you know what they mean."

Kat tugged on the bill of her cap and turned a glare on her brother. "I know what butthole means. Can I call him that?"

"Kat!" Lisa screeched again. When Michael began to snicker along with Jake, she scowled at them. "You two, cut it out. Especially you, Michael. I mean, you're their father. Do you want them to think it's funny to talk like that?"

Michael scrubbed a hand across his mouth. He coughed, then coughed again, trying his best to compose himself. "Sorry, honey. But let's not make a big deal out of it." When her blue eyes widened, he hastily added, "She could say a lot worse. Why sweat the small stuff?"

"Kat, Jacob, go to your rooms," she ordered.

When the kids were safely out of earshot, she descended on Michael, nostrils flaring. "I'm trying to be a mother to our children. Maybe you don't know how tough that is, considering I can't even remember becoming a parent in the first place. I mean, the very least you could do is back me up when I discipline them."

"You're right, Lisa." His lip twitched. "But you have to admit it was funny. A *virgin*, for pete's sake!"

Michael was relieved to see her give in to a weary grin. "The things they say and do sometimes. I mean, my own kids shock the hell out of me." Her shoulders lifted, then slumped. "I don't know. It's like I missed something along the way.

Something that would prepare me for all of this, so I'd know how to deal with it."

"There's no way to train to be a parent. It's something you learn as you go. Surprises are unavoidable, and so are mistakes. That's just part of it."

"I guess. It's all, like, so foreign to me, though. Yesterday the school called at noon because Kat forgot her lunch. When I went up there, her teacher stopped me outside the classroom to show me a picture Kat had drawn. It was titled 'My Family.' We were all there in living Crayola color, stark naked with appropriate body parts."

"You're kidding!" Michael didn't even try not to laugh this time.

"Her teacher thought it was funny, too. I was horrified. I mean, what are we raising? A pervert?"

"I admit Kat could use a lesson or two in lady-like behavior." Michael placed an arm around her shoulders and squeezed. "Don't worry so much. She's a perfectly normal, curious six-year-old kid. I think it might be time for the infamous mother-daughter talk, though."

She paled. "You want me to explain to a six-year-old about sex?"

"We told Jake at that age, but I guess you don't remember. With everything on television these days, they're exposed to so much more than we were as kids. I want them to know the truth about sex, not all that hype they're fed by the media. I want them to know they can come to us and talk about anything. You used to feel the same way."

"I did?"

Michael nodded.

"Okay. I guess you know what you're doing." She stared at him, her blue eyes wide and mortified. "Will you come and, like, back me up or something? I'm not sure I can handle this alone. I mean, I don't have a clue what to say."

"Sure." Michael chuckled as they started off in the direction of Kat's room for the inevitable conversation. "Oh, by the way, Tory's coming by later on. I gave her a list and my credit card and asked her to pick up a few Christmas gifts for the kids. I hope you don't mind. You haven't seemed to feel up to it lately."

He thought it best not to admit that the idea was Tory's rather than his own. Though he'd hesitated to accept her proposal at first, after consideration, he realized that Tory offered a solution to at least one of his current problems.

"She didn't mind shopping for you after hours?"

"She didn't seem to."

"I'm not surprised."

Michael stopped outside Kat's bedroom door. "What is that supposed to mean?"

"Nothing. Nothing at all. I mean, I'm glad Tory's coming over. I want to talk to her."

"You do?"

"Yeah. Don't you think we should ask if she'll tutor Jake again? He needs her. I'm afraid I'm not much help to him. I just can't get into it." She shrugged. "Sorry."

Unsure of how he felt about her suggestion, Michael opened the door to his daughter's room and stepped inside. "We'll see about that later."

He moved aside to allow Lisa entrance, amused and astounded by her hesitance. After all, she was the one who'd insisted they teach their children the clinical names for body parts rather than the silly substitutes many parents used. "After you," he said, offering her an encouraging grin. "Relax. We'll keep this as scientific as possible."

Chapter Fourteen

Arms loaded with packages, Lisa followed Michael onto the front porch. "That's it except for the bikes," she said. She watched him struggle to open the door. His arms, too, were filled with presents, and she laughed as he juggled everything, wedging a knee between the storm door and its frame. To her amazement, nothing fell. He held the door open with one shoulder and allowed her to enter ahead of him.

"I'll stop by the bicycle shop tomorrow after work and pick them up," he said, following her into the living room. "You don't know what a help you've been to me by doing this. I'll pay you overtime. You deserve it."

Lisa stooped to add her packages to a pile on the floor they'd brought in earlier, then gazed up at him. "You don't have to pay me. I enjoyed it."

Their eyes met and held, and for the first time all season, the warmth of Christmas filled her heart. And the warmth of something entirely different filled every inch of the rest of her body— aching awareness, throbbing need.

Lisa rose slowly. She noticed everything about Michael; the strong, angular features of his face, the shape of his mouth, the honesty in his eyes. A sudden, overwhelming need to touch him . . . hold him . . . taste him, tugged her like a magnet.

Michael didn't attempt to unload the burden in his arms. He simply held it all and looked across at her, and she wondered what was running through his mind while they stood there, joined by an invisible force so strong that she knew he, too, must feel its pull.

"All we need now is a tree."

With a start, Lisa turned to face the woman who'd spoken. Despite the other times they'd come face-to-face, she was still stunned to see her own image and hear her own voice. Shaken by Tory's sudden appearance after the silent exchange with Michael only moments before, she found herself at a loss for words.

Michael lowered his packages to the floor. "I'll get the tree and decorations down from the attic."

Kat and Jacob ran into the room upon hearing their father's comment. "It's about time," Jake said. "Christmas is almost here."

"Look!" Kat pointed at the multicolored gifts stacked high on the floor behind her dad. Then she and Jake raced across the room and began to rattle and shake each shiny paper-covered box.

Michael watched the children check out their packages, then turned to his wife. "Tory did the shopping," he said. "All I have to do is pick up a couple of things tomorrow and we're set."

When he saw the gray veil of detachment drifting over her face, desperation settled like a stone in the pit of his stomach. She was slipping away from him . . . and from the children. He'd never allowed himself to admit it before, but he sensed it now with a dreadful certainty that wrenched his soul.

A time or two over the past week, she'd offered him a sliver of hope—a smile, an offhanded statement that indicated that she was trying—only to snatch it away by sinking back into the black hole of depression that seemed to covet her spirit.

The sound of Kat's and Jacob's enthusiastic banter had him looking toward them. *Somehow I'll survive this, but how will they? It's my fault. I've been married to my work these past two years.*

Funny, Michael thought; Tory seemed to be the one person who could take his mind off his problems with Lisa, if only momentarily. He glanced across at her. When he was around Tory, it was easy to forget other important things, too. Like who he was and what he believed in. He liked watching her—the way she moved; the tilt of her head; the tell-all emotions that played across her face. He liked listening to her—the rhythm of her voice more than the tone; the pattern and emphasis of her words.

His response was quick, almost painful. A swift kick of desire that left him stunned. Being with Tory felt right somehow. They seemed to share an oddly familiar intimacy. Her nearness comforted and aroused him at the same time.

He knew when she caught him watching her. A look of pure frustration crossed her face. "Well, I guess I'll go now," she said, smiling at the children as she started for the door.

Michael followed her as far as the entry hall. "Thanks for everything." Feeling awkward and guilty, he left her there and headed for the attic to put distance between them before he made a total fool of himself.

Lisa stepped out into the brisk night air. Only six more days and she'd be home for good. Her family's torment would end. The anguish on Michael's face when he'd left her a moment ago was almost more than she could stand. She longed to spend time with him and the children, to share in Kat's and Jacob's excitement over the gifts, to soften Michael's pain somehow. But she sensed he'd needed her to leave. What could she do? How could she help them?

When she heard the door open and close behind her, Lisa jerked her head around, hoping to find Michael standing there. More than anything, she wanted to throw herself into his arms, to tell him everything and beg him to believe her. But Tory stood on the porch behind her.

"Don't go," Tory said. "I want to talk to you. I have to ask you something."

Every muscle in Lisa's body tensed, perhaps from the cold, perhaps from fear. She wasn't sure which. "Okay."

"The bartender at The Club, the one with the long dark hair . . . " Tory's voice trailed off, and she closed her eyes on a sigh. "I guess I shouldn't be talking to you about this, but I have to know who he is."

When Tory opened her eyes, Lisa thought she'd never seen such sadness, such misery and confusion. Her heart went out to the girl.

"Ever since I saw him the other night, I can't stop thinking about him," Tory said, her voice trembling. She pursed her lips but failed to halt the quivering of her chin. "I dream about him."

"It's okay. I understand. His name is Dillon." Lisa hesitated as she searched Tory's face for any signs of recognition. "Dillon Todd. He's a college student. He works part-time at the restaurant."

"Dillon Todd," Tory whispered. She stared past Lisa into the night as though probing the jumbled files of her mind for a misplaced memory. Frowning, she finally focused on Lisa again. "The name sounds vaguely familiar, but I'm not sure."

"I'm sorry." Uncertain of what else she should tell the girl, Lisa started again for the driveway.

"Wait," Tory called. "Did Michael tell you that we'd like to hire you again to help Jake with his math?"

Lisa's heart tripped at the prospect. "You would?"

"Yes." Tory gave a hopeless shrug. "I tried, but it's not my thing."

"I'd love to, but are you sure it's okay with Michael?"

Tonight there was no suspicion in Tory's eyes, no threat in her voice as there had been during their confrontation at The Club. Lisa swore she saw resignation in her expression, a sudden indifferent acceptance.

"I'm sure, but you could ask him if you like," Tory said. "I don't feel much like decorating for the holidays tonight. I know that's not fair to Michael and the kids, but it's true. I'd only put a damper on everything. They'd probably enjoy your help . . . and your company."

Surprised, Lisa watched Tory jog around her, then head down the walkway. For the first time, she noticed the black spandex exercise outfit the girl wore. *Good grief! Is that really my body? I must've lost ten pounds!*

"Tell Michael I've gone for a run," Tory yelled.

"Silent Night" drifted softly from the stereo, a pinecone-scented fire crackled in the fireplace, and the tree sparkled with tinsel and jewel-colored lights.

Lisa stood beside Michael admiring their handiwork while tears of sentiment brimmed in her eyes. She felt blessed to have not missed out on this family tradition. Until tonight, she hadn't known how much it meant to her.

Kat and Jacob arranged gifts on the floor beneath the branches. They stopped periodically to speculate on the contents. Lisa looked up at Michael and smiled. "Thanks for letting me help. I really enjoyed it."

Michael smiled back. "Thank *you*," he said, then returned his attention to the tree. "I think it looks better this year than ever before."

"It does," Lisa agreed. When Michael's head jerked in her direction and she saw the puzzled look on his face, her heart jumped to her throat. "It must, because I can't imagine a more beautiful tree."

The front door slammed. Tory came in panting and puffing, cheeks flushed and hair awry. "Wow! You guys do fast work!" She looked around the room, then back toward the enty hall. "Hey, you not only decorated the tree, you did the house, too."

"You've been gone quite a while," Michael mumbled. He glanced at his watch. "Over an hour. You shouldn't run alone after dark, honey. It's dangerous."

"Sorry if I worried you." She headed toward the kitchen. "I lost track of time, but I felt perfectly safe."

Gathering her coat and purse, Lisa seized one last appraising look at the cozy scene in her living room. "Guess I'll be going."

"Don't leave!" Kat crossed the room and tugged at her sleeve. "We can make hot chocolate."

Jake, having stopped the music, turned on the television set and glanced back at her. "Yeah, and look what's on. It's that Christmas movie."

Lisa stared fondly at the familiar face of James Stewart on the screen. "*It's A Wonderful Life*," she murmured.

"Yes, stay," Tory prompted when she returned from the kitchen, a glass of water in hand. She slouched onto the couch and drained the water in several thirsty gulps. "I mean, after doing all the shopping and decorating, the least we can offer is a movie and hot chocolate." She shifted her attention to Michael. "I'll even make it."

Lisa was flustered by Tory's sudden friendly, welcoming attitude after their run-in the previous Friday night. She was tempted to accept the offer but suspected Michael's hesitance. He confirmed it by tugging his ear. "I really shouldn't," she said, shaking her head. "I've intruded on your evening long enough. Besides, the movie's more than half over."

"The end's the best part," Kat argued.

Lisa took a long look at her tiny daughter. Kat's hair stuck up in straw-colored tufts all over her head. It appeared not to have been combed all day. Though bathed and dressed for bed, her mouth was smeared with ice cream. Lisa couldn't recall when she'd last seen anything so adorable. Still, she had to bite back an instinctive urge to tell Kat to go wash her face. God, how she wanted to curl up on the sofa with her children cuddled up beside her. But, right now, she had to think of Michael instead of herself.

"Thanks," she said, "but I'd better go."

Michael was baffled. He studied his wife. She didn't seem to mind having Tory around. In fact, she'd virtually begged the girl to stay.

Out of the corner of his eye, he watched Tory prepare to leave. She seemed so lonely. He wondered if she had any family. Other than the boyfriend she'd recently dumped, Tory never spoke about her private life. Awareness struck him like a punch in the gut with a velvet fist. He needed Tory to leave . . . he wanted her to stay.

"Please stay," he said, giving her a tentative nod.

She was wavering, he could see it in her eyes. Finally she deposited her coat and purse on a nearby chair. "Well, okay," she said. "I guess I can stay for a while." She sat on the couch. "This is one of my favorite movies."

"It's one of Mom's favorites, too. Isn't it, Mom?"

Michael noticed the blankness in his wife's expression as she considered Jake's question. "I guess it is," she answered. She lifted her glass from the coffee table and stood. "I'll make that cocoa now."

Jake plopped down on the couch next to Tory.

"I was gonna sit there!" Kat snapped, moving toward the couch.

"I got here first," Jake snapped back.

"You—"

Before Kat could say another word, Michael took her by the wrist and eased her into the recliner beside him. "Remember this afternoon? Name-calling got the two of you sent to your rooms."

Jake smirked. "You shoulda heard what she called me, Tory," he said in a loud, conspiratorial whisper. "Mom and Dad had to give her the sex talk."

Michael cleared his throat. "I'm sure Tory doesn't want to hear about it, Jake." But the slight smile lifting the corner of Tory's mouth when he glanced her way dissolved his discomfort. If only Lisa could be as relaxed when it came to the kids, he thought, remembering her response to Kat's outburst earlier in the afternoon. Before her amnesia, her reaction would've been closer to Tory's.

And as for Lisa's long, late-night run earlier . . . Michael turned toward the kitchen, where she'd disappeared. What bothered him more than the fact that she'd stayed away so long was the realization that he hadn't really missed her.

Worrying over it, he shifted his attention to the television. On the screen, James Stewart came home to Donna Reed, pulled her into his arms, and smothered her with desperate kisses.

Kat giggled. "He better watch out or he's gonna lose some sperm!" she said, her voice high-pitched and innocent.

The room quieted. Everyone sat motionless, avoiding each other's gaze. Then Jake doubled over, giggling. When Tory joined him, Michael gave in to his own laughter.

"You sure didn't leave anything to the imagination during that father-daughter talk, did you?" she asked.

Michael's laughter stopped abruptly. He frowned and sniffed the air.

"What's wrong, Michael?" she asked.

He sniffed again. "Something's burning."

* * *

A short while later, Lisa made her way down the walk to the red Volkswagen parked outside the house.

"Sorry about that. My wife's never been a gourmet cook," Michael said from behind her, "but I thought she could at least boil a kettle of water without burning down the house."

The night was cold and crisp, the stars vivid in the blue-black sky. To clear away lingering smoky fumes, Lisa took a deep breath of air.

She bit her lip, remembering the cup towel Tory had tossed aside haphazardly while making the hot chocolate. It had landed atop the stove, where she'd left a burner on. "Thank goodness we got to the fire before it caused any damage." She leaned against the side of the car and faced Michael.

"If you hadn't grabbed the extinguisher when you did, things would've been a lot worse." He looked down at her with tired, grateful eyes. "How did you know where to find it?"

"I took a wild guess. It all happened so fast, I really don't remember."

"You're quick in a crisis." He wiped her cheek with his thumb. "Soot," he said, his voice thick and quiet. "From the fire."

To Lisa's surprise, self-consciousness seized her. Fighting the urge to turn away, she met his gaze. "Things still aren't right, are they? Between you two?"

"I wish I could say they were."

"I'm sorry." A fear she'd pushed aside before took hold now, filling her mind with disturbing possibilities. What if things were even worse than she realized? What if Tory and Michael decided to divorce before the spell ended? Where would that leave her?

195

"We had something special," he murmured, a far-off tone to his voice. "In the beginning, it was magic—so new and exciting. We couldn't get enough of each other. I think I spent every waking minute trying to let her know how much she meant to me.

"I'm not sure when that stopped," Michael continued. "Not that I loved her any less. If anything, I've loved her more the longer we've been together. The love just changed somehow. Evolved with time, I guess. I . . . well, quit thinking about us so much. I thought things would stay the same. I assumed Lisa would always be here, happy to share our lives. And I guess I assumed it went without saying how crazy I was about her. It wasn't until I lost it that I realized what I had." He glanced at the ground and gave an ironic laugh. "Typical, right?"

Lisa's throat constricted, but she still managed to smile. She was every bit as guilty as Michael of taking their marriage for granted. Only now, seeing him through another woman's eyes, did she understand the value of what she'd easily cast aside with a careless wish.

Maybe she should be grateful for the upheaval the spell was causing in her marriage. She suspected that if her life had continued as before, she would've never experienced this new awareness of her feelings or of Michael. She might never have looked at him and recognized what she saw in him now.

Lisa remembered falling in love with him over sixteen years ago. It had been a wonderful, heady, all-consuming thing, that love. But she'd been hardly more than a girl then, with a girl's insecurities, a girl's fears and hesitance to explore her own feelings or his. Now she was a woman. And the emotion she felt for him at this very second went deeper than anything she'd ever known. Lisa searched her heart for insecurity or hesitance and found none. And the only fear she recognized was the possibility that she might never get the chance to let him know what he meant to her.

Moonlight shimmered in his hair, sparking the tawny highlights. He placed his palms against the car window at either side of her shoulders. "Sometimes you remind me of Lisa, before . . ." His eyes lowered to her lips, making them tingle. "I shouldn't compare the two of you. I won't again. You're different in as many ways as you're alike."

"It's okay," she said, realizing that she referred to the needs reflected in his eyes as much as the comparison he spoke of.

A snowflake drifted down and landed on his cheek. Another fell as they stood there in silence, then another and another, sifting from the sky like powdered sugar from a sieve.

Lisa laughed. "It's coming down pretty good now. We'll get wet if we stay out too long."

"I don't mind a little water, do you?"

She tilted her head back and looked into the sky. "We could try to dodge them," she said, moving her head right, then left, getting hit nonetheless.

Michael grinned at her, his brow lifted at a teasing angle. "Dodging snowflakes? An activity doomed to failure, I'm afraid."

Lisa planted fists on her hips, an indignant scowl on her face. "I'll have you know I was the champ when I was a kid. And not only at dodging snowflakes—raindrops, too. I ran home from school during a downpour in fifth grade and was dry as a bone when I got there. I have witnesses, if you'd like to call them up."

Michael lifted both hands, laughing. "I believe you, I believe you. How does a champion snowflake and raindrop dodger decide on becoming a lawyer?"

Her heart floated to her stomach, like a leaf drifting down from a tree. For a moment, she'd forgotten she was inside Tory's body. She'd been too caught up in enjoying Michael's company. And now she'd have to resume the lie.

She didn't have the faintest idea what would entice a young woman to the practice of law. Though she respected the profession, a desire to pursue it had never been hers, and she wasn't sure she could fake enthusiasm for the endeavor. "I haven't decided on a law career for certain," she said. "That's one of the reasons I wanted a job in a firm, to find out if the atmosphere suits me before I take the plunge and apply to law school."

Michael nodded. His eyes moved over her face. "Ahh . . . you're cautious. Just like Lisa."

Something in the tone of his voice bothered her. "You don't admire that trait in your wife?"

"Actually, I do. To a point." He paused. "One thing I'll say for her, she seldom walks into any situation blind. She examines every angle, so she's usually prepared to handle anything that might come up unexpectedly. I, on the other hand, sometimes let my ambitions carry me away. I've been known to end up in some tight spots because of it."

"But you said 'to a point.' What does that mean? You have a problem with Lisa being cautious, don't you? I can hear it in your voice."

He shrugged. "Yeah, well, a person can be *too* cautious at times. It can set up unnecessary roadblocks."

Lisa tilted her head, feeling more intrigued than insulted by what he was unknowingly telling her about herself. "Roadblocks. You mean in life?"

"Yeah."

The sudden discomfort in his expression warned her that he wouldn't likely say much more on the subject. He was feeling guilty, she guessed, discussing his wife's shortcomings with another woman.

"What about you?" Lisa asked him. "Why did you choose law?" It amazed her to realize she didn't know. In all the years they'd been together, they'd never discussed his career choice, and she wondered why she'd never asked him before. Michael's career was a major part of what made him tick. She knew that . . . had always known it. As far back as she could remember, he was either a lawyer or preparing to be one. She'd accepted that as a part of who he was. No questions . . . no curiosity about it. That made her feel ashamed.

Michael cleared his throat and shifted from one foot to the other. "The reason's not very interesting."

"I'd like to know."

"You'll think I was silly and idealistic, and you'll be right."

"Don't be so sure." She grinned. "Besides, I won't tell anyone."

"Okay then." He shifted again. "It was the book *To Kill a Mockingbird*. I read it in seventh or eighth grade, and I knew I wanted the power to make a difference in someone's life. You know, to help people who can't help themselves." He gave an awkward grin. "As it turns out, I spend the majority of my time wading through a sea of paperwork and settling petty disputes. See, I told you I was idealistic and silly."

She'd never felt more pride in anyone. Michael's client with the velvet Elvis sprang to mind and, again, she was touched by what he'd offered the man. "You're wrong," Lisa said softly. "You do so much more than you admit. And I can't think of a more important reason to pursue anything than what you just told me."

Snowflakes dusted the air around them. She lifted a hand to his beard-stubbled face, traced the outline of his mouth with one fingertip, tilted her chin in invitation.

The first brush of lips was a whisper of warm silk that whisked away all rationality. With her back pressed to the cold car and Michael molded warm against her front, Lisa opened to his kiss, welcoming the intrusion of his tongue, urging him on when gentle persuasion turned to greedy demand.

How she'd missed the eager touch of his hands, the hard, insistent feel of his body next to hers. Like a starving beggar she devoured every sensation—the texture of skin beneath her fingers, his taste, his scent.

After several long seconds, Michael eased back and drew in a noisy breath. Forehead to forehead, nose to nose, their mouths lingered only a fraction of an inch apart. He twisted his fingers in her hair and closed his eyes. "Tory," he whispered.

Tory. If he'd punched her in the stomach, the jolt would've been less jarring. Lisa drew back an arm, then slapped Michael's face.

Chapter Fifteen

Monday morning, Lisa called Nan to say she was ill and wouldn't be in that afternoon. The excuse wasn't entirely a lie. After a sleepless night, she'd dragged herself from bed feeling nauseous. A result of worrying all weekend over the episode with Michael, she told herself. Just thinking about it made her sick.

As much as she hated doing it, she also asked Nan to give Michael the message that she wanted to postpone Jake's tutoring session. She had some thinking to do before she faced her husband.

Lisa's second call was to Val, who agreed to meet for lunch at their favorite salad bar. They met at one o'clock to avoid the noontime crowds.

"It's what you wanted, isn't it?" Val asked, stabbing an olive with her fork. "Really, Lisa, how can you even complain?"

"Yes, I wanted it." Lisa closed her eyes and sighed. *If you only knew how much,* she thought as she envisioned her initial response to Michael the night before. "But he thought he was kissing Tory."

Val pointed her fork at Lisa. "Would you forget about that? Get over it. It's *you* Michael's reacting to, not her. So what if he doesn't know that himself? It's not as if he's cheating."

"But *he* thinks he's on the verge of cheating, which is the point." When Val glared across at her, she added, "I know, I know. He's as mixed up as I am. More so. It's not his fault."

With a quiet snicker, Val leaned in toward Lisa. "I can't believe you slapped him!"

Heated blood rushed to Lisa's cheeks. "It isn't funny, Val. You should've seen his face." She attacked her salad, finished it, then started on a second bowl of soup the waitress delivered.

"Hungry?" Val asked.

"Starved."

"Maybe Tory's body requires food in a crisis."

At the mention of Tory's name, Lisa lowered the spoon to the table, dropped her head into her hands, and began to cry.

Val glanced uneasily around the restaurant. "What are you doing?"

"What does it look like?" Lisa looked up. "It was great having so much freedom at first, and I love having a young, firm body. Every time a man's head turns my way it's an ego trip. But you know what? They aren't the least bit interested in what I think or feel. Their minds are on sex. Period. I don't blame Tory at all for wearing baggy, weird clothing."

"I'd be willing to bet she likes her clothes. She's

not the only kid who looks like she stepped out of a sixties hallucination."

Lisa sniffed. "You want to know something else? For some reason, I haven't had any more energy these last several days than I had at thirty-five." Tears welled again in her eyes. "I'm so tired of going home to an empty, drab apartment every night after working half the day for minimum wage. The rent's due soon, and I don't have any money. No wonder Tory and Dillon lived together."

Val pulled a tissue from her purse and offered it to Lisa. "I seriously doubt it was only for financial purposes."

"How could I have thought I wanted to be twenty again? I only remembered the positive parts; I forgot everything else."

Val shot a measuring look across the table. "I'm sorry you're in this fix. But, as I recall, you weren't completely satisfied being thirty-five, either. What will have changed when you go back?"

Lisa hiccupped and wiped her nose with the tissue. "What are you saying?"

"Just that I don't understand how returning to the way things were will make you happy when you weren't before." Val stared unflinchingly into Lisa's eyes and shrugged.

The waitress approached and offered hot bread, which Lisa readily accepted. She bit into the roll, savoring the yeasty aroma and taste while considering Val's statement. After some time, she admitted to herself that Val was right. Her previous life hadn't been the perfect picture of happiness. Her marriage had been far from it. She hadn't achieved the success she'd hoped for in either. She'd let the small, often annoying incidents at the surface of her day-to-day existence overshadow the richness that formed the foundation. Her current situation had taught that lesson, if nothing else. Imperfect or not, she was lost without her family and her marriage. Somewhere deep inside, she'd always known she would be.

Something she'd read long ago flashed in Lisa's mind.

Happiness isn't having everything you want, it's wanting everything you have.

When she'd first seen the quotation, she hadn't paid any attention to it. Suddenly the words made perfect sense.

While absently dragging a spoon through lukewarm cheese soup, a sluggish wave of fatigue settled over her, leaving Lisa desperate for a nap. She yawned, abandoned the food, and leaned back in her chair. "I've discovered a lot about myself, and Michael, too, because of this fantasy-come-true. My eyes have been opened to some surprising realities."

Michael's description of her as overly cautious came to mind. "You know, the other night when I drank too much and told you about the time in college when I made a surprise visit to Michael?"

"How could I forget the high road, low road, holey jean story? Sure I remember. Michael's roommate was camped out with the flu in their dorm room."

Lisa nodded. "So Michael said. I didn't care all that much. I just wanted the two of us to be together. You know, to go eat lunch and go for a walk or see a movie . . . whatever. But Michael ruined it."

"What do you mean?"

"He left me out front and went to the room to get his keys. But after he'd gone, I decided it would be fun to have a picnic, so I went after him to tell him to bring a blanket."

Val propped both elbows on the table and leaned forward. "And?"

Lisa took a deep breath. "When I got to the room, the door was ajar. I started to knock, but then I heard a woman's voice. I peeked inside and saw Michael talking to a girl. His roommate wasn't even there."

"You mean to tell me . . . " Val's eyes narrowed. "Michael did that to you?"

"I slipped away before they ever saw me." Lisa shrugged. "Needless to say, the rest of the day was tense. I didn't bring it up at first. I kept hoping Michael would tell me the truth on his own. Finally he asked what was wrong, so I told him."

"What did he say?"

"He told me she was only a friend, that she'd only come over to study. Call me a fool if you want, but I believed him. Besides, it was the lie that bothered me most. The fact that he didn't trust in my love enough to tell me the truth. But when I told him that, he didn't want to talk about it. He'd admitted his lie and explained the situation. He thought that was enough." Lisa shook her head. "When I left that evening to drive home, I was so depressed. I felt more distanced from Michael than ever."

Slumping back in her chair, Val sighed. "I can imagine."

"I should've forced the issue then and there and straightened it out. Instead, we never spoke about it again. To tell you the truth, I was afraid to examine it too closely. I was afraid I'd discover something I didn't want to face."

"I can't believe you've been carrying this

around all these years and you've never mentioned a word about it to Michael. How long have you been married, anyway? It took me less than two weeks of marriage to learn to set Ray straight."

Lisa folded her hands in her lap and stared down at them. She'd been cautious back then . . . just like Michael accused her of being. Overly cautious not to stir up trouble between them. She'd known that the mere thought of conflict in his personal relationships was a source of unbearable discomfort for Michael. So much so, she'd been afraid he might rather walk away from her than admit they had problems that needed working through.

"I haven't been fair to Michael or to myself," she said, meeting Val's gaze. "For instance, Michael's career. It's no wonder he stays late so often at the office or brings work home with him at night. During the day, if he's not answering phone calls, he's seeing clients. It's overwhelming. There's no time to finish anything."

As Val peeled the wrapper off a stick of gum, Lisa admired her friend's dark, glossy cap of hair, reminding herself that Tory's golden tresses were well past due for a trim and a conditioning treatment. The lustrous locks had dimmed since she'd taken possession. *I really should've been a better tenant.*

"So you're accepting all the blame for the problems in your marriage?" Val asked.

"Not at all. Michael's made mistakes, too. Remember when I tried to go back to work? It was easy enough for him to give me verbal support and encouragement, but when it came right down to pitching in and helping out . . . well, that was another matter. But did I call him on it?" She lifted her shoulders, then let them fall. "No."

"You ought to kick his butt," Val said, chewing. "If you can't bring yourself to do it, give me a call."

Lisa laughed. "You have to understand, his parents were arguers. Michael hated their bickering. I think that's why he avoids talking about any unpleasant issues between us. Or even admitting any exist."

"Or maybe he's just a typical man."

"He has more than his share of strong points, Val. But you're right about one thing. When I switch back, changes will have to be made, and I'm the one who'll have to start them rolling. I wish you would've knocked some sense into me a long time ago and told me to take some kind of action to make things right."

Val slipped a second stick of gum into her mouth. "I'm telling you now: Get busy and make things right. After you change back, don't waste any time. Tell Michael how it's going to be, no ifs, and, or buts."

Lisa grinned. "Can I take a nap first?"

Her old bedroom, her old bed, and Michael in it. She'd finally come back!

Lamplight spread a dim radiance throughout the room, the air was warm and fragrant with the scent of burning candles, and the music on the stereo was soft and low.

Lisa gazed across at her husband, every one of her senses intensified. She smelled her own perfume radiating from the heat of her body, felt a tantalizing tremor as the fabric of her robe brushed against her skin, heard the pulsing beat of her own heart.

The eager anticipation in Michael's eyes sent excitement skittering through her body as she crossed the floor to the bed.

She briefly scanned his attire, attempting to hide her opinion of it by keeping her expression neutral. The robe he wore reminded her of a smoking jacket she'd seen in some old Cary Grant movie, the matching slippers on his feet of house shoes her granddad used to wear. Was that a gold chain peeking out from the V at his neck? She gulped. What had come over Michael? Normally, he was a boxer shorts kind of guy. Which suited her just fine. But this . . .

"Like it?" *Michael asked, smoothing a hand down the front of his body.* "I bought this especially for the occasion. I wanted tonight to be special . . . different."

"Well . . . it's certainly different."

She stopped beside him, reached to her waist, and pulled at the tie to her robe, allowing it to fall open in front. "I've missed you. Let me show you how much." *Her eyes never strayed from his as she let the garment fall from her shoulders to the floor.* "Would you like that?"

His gaze swept across her skin like a hot breeze. She watched his eyes wander over the see-through, black lace bodysuit, then down the length of her bare legs.

"I'd like that very much. You do great things for Mickey Mouse."

Mickey Mouse? Lisa glanced at the front of her T-shirt and saw what he meant. She shook her head, as though to sort the contents. She could've sworn she wore lace.

For a moment, neither of them moved. Then, slowly, Lisa pulled the T-shirt over her head and dropped it next to the robe. She stood, not speak-

Get Two Books Totally
FREE —
An $11.48 Value!

▼ Tear Here and Mail Your FREE Book Card Today! ▼

PLEASE RUSH
MY TWO FREE
BOOKS TO ME
RIGHT AWAY!

Love Spell Romance Book Club
P.O. Box 6613
Edison, NJ 08818-6613

AFFIX
STAMP
HERE

ing, knowing the lamplight illuminated the smooth swell of her breasts.

He rose from the bed until he stood in front of her. Gently, he placed his hands upon her as though for the first time. His eyes followed his fingers, watching each leisurely stroke.

A shuddering bolt of sensation shot from her head to her toes and she gasped—a short intake of breath that hovered on the air, stopping time.

"You're so beautiful," he said. "I never dreamed you'd be so beautiful."

Though his words confused her, since he'd seen her hundreds of times, she kissed him, lightly brushing his lips, then outlining them with her tongue.

His hands moved to her shoulders and slid slowly down her back, molding, teasing, testing. Alternately frantic and calm, he nipped her skin with impatient teeth, then soothed with an aching slowness that drove her to the edge. Moving from the hollow of her neck down to her stomach, he showered her with the warm, wet kisses she begged for.

Her fingers trailed the muscles along his back, then maneuvered forward and down to fumble with the tie at his waist. The robe slipped from his shoulders. Beneath it, he was naked except for . . .

"What's this?" she asked, unable to disguise the baffled shock in her voice.

He touched his midriff, where a girdlelike contraption was strapped tightly around him, Michael's jaw twitched hesitantly. "Oh. Guess I forgot to take it off."

Desire vanished like smoke in the wind. Forget it, Lisa told herself, as he unfastened the ridiculous thing and tossed it aside. It's our first night back together. He's understandably nervous. But a girdle?

"You don't need that, Michael." She skimmed her fingers across his stomach and felt the first flames of rekindled passion. They fell together onto the bed. She lay on her back gazing up at him.

"Michael . . . is that . . . what I think it is?" Lisa stared over his shoulder and up. The reflection of her husband's naked backside stretched full across the ceiling.

Michael twisted his head, looked up, then turned back to her. *"Oh that,"* he said, grinning sheepishly. *"It's a mirror. I thought someone your age might get a kick out of it."*

Someone my age? *Lisa thought. What did he mean by that? And a mirror on the ceiling? She didn't know whether to laugh or grab her clothes and run.*

As she squirmed out from under him, she spied her own reflection. The room began to swirl. Tory's image stared back at her.

Lisa closed her eyes. *"No, God!"* she cried. *"This can't be happening. I can't be her anymore! I can't!"*

Hesitantly, she opened her eyes again, her pulse slowing a bit when she saw her own face and body. Relief seeped in. *"It's me! Oh, Michael, it's really me!"* She turned to look at him and instead found Dillon Todd—body flushed with desire, slanted eyes dark and sultry—occupying the space beside her. A renewed jolt of arousal surged through her. *"No! . . ."*

"No!" Lisa shrieked, jerking awake as the water bed jostled around her. Her heart skipped around in her chest as she squinted into the darkness, trying to gain her bearings. After a second she risked a peek overhead, releasing a nervous breath when she found no mirror on the ceiling.

Lisa pressed a hand against her breasts, unnerved by the lingering sensation there. "Wow, what a dream," she whispered.

The leather seats in Val's car seemed a sinful indulgence. She'd grown accustomed to the Volkswagen, Lisa realized, leaning her head against a padded cushion. "Thanks for bringing me to work, Val. The starter must be out on Tory's car. I have no idea how I'll pay to repair it."

"How many times do I have to tell you, I'll lend you whatever you need?"

"I already owe you too much. Besides, it's only two more days until the car is Tory's responsibility again. Maybe she has money tucked away I don't know about."

Lisa stared across the parking lot at her blue minivan. Michael and Tory sat inside, apparently engrossed in a serious conversation, both obviously unaware that they were being observed.

"I'm glad your windows are tinted so they can't see us. What do you think they're talking about?"

"Who knows?" Val answered. "Could be anything. What you need to worry about is what to say to Michael when you go inside. Maybe he deserved it, maybe not, but I think you should apologize for slugging him."

"You're right. As difficult as it is to deal with, I've got to get past this jealousy thing." Lisa glanced down at herself and sighed. "Thank God this is almost over. I don't think I can keep up the charade much longer."

When Michael stepped from the van, Lisa's heart dropped when she saw his forlorn expression.

"Michael's a dedicated husband," Val assured her. "He doesn't look very happy, but he won't give

211

up on the marriage easily. He can last two more days."

Val was right. Michael had sworn to be faithful "for better or for worse." Well, now was definitely the "for worse" part of the deal. But Michael, being a man of his word, would do his damnedest to work through it. And though she knew he had feelings for her as Tory, he'd never break what he considered to be the most important promise of his life to pursue a frivolous fling.

They'd discussed fidelity frequently during their marriage, and agreed it was vital to both of them. Trust meant everything, too. Lisa knew those talks were spurred by the episode they'd never resolved, by the fact that Michael had lied to her all those years ago about the girl in his dorm room.

"I can't help wondering whether or not they've . . . you know . . . been together." Lisa gazed pensively out the window at the back of Michael's head as he talked to Tory through the van window. "Just the thought of it makes me sick to my stomach. Who knows what might've gone on between them? Maybe she's even seen him do that silly dance thing he does." Lisa closed her eyes. "Oh, God, I can't stand to think about it!"

"Dance?"

She opened her eyes. "You know, that routine men feel inclined to perform sometimes when they're naked." Lisa noted Val's puzzled frown. "You were married once. Don't tell me Ray didn't do it?"

"Maybe we weren't together long enough for our relationship to reach that comfort zone," Val teased. "Tell me what I missed."

"Well . . . how can I explain it?" Lisa nibbled the nail on her index finger, then smiled. "It's the same principle as the old bump-and-grind strippers, only from the male perspective."

Val's eyes widened. She cleared her throat.

"I guess it's a Chippendale's fantasy or something," Lisa added.

As a distracted Michael made his way toward the building, Val burst out laughing. "Michael O'Conner does *that?*"

Lisa snickered. "He's been known to. He'd kill me if he found out about this conversation." She scowled at Val's flushed face. "Why are you staring at him?"

"I'm trying to imagine Michael with a tassel—"

"I didn't say anything about tassels!"

Val wiped tears of laughter from her eyes. "Maybe if Ray had been that much fun, we'd still be married."

Lisa went soft inside as she watched Michael enter the building. The door closed behind him. "We've had a lot of fun times. How could I have forgotten that? When I made that stupid wish, we were both so caught up in ourselves—him in his law practice, me in my identity crisis—it had been ages since we spent time relaxing together. You know, acting silly. Laughing. I miss him, Val."

A blaring horn made both women jump. Turning, Lisa spotted Tory outside the window, where she pulled the minivan alongside the car. When Tory motioned for them to roll down a window, Val quickly complied.

Tory looked past Val at Lisa. "I guess I should hate you," she yelled over the rattling of the vehicle. "For some reason, I don't. Maybe I'm kind of jealous of you, though. I mean, you want what I'm *supposed* to want but don't." She frowned. "Am I making sense?"

Baffled by Tory's impromptu speech, Lisa didn't answer.

"Well, take care of him," Tory continued. "He's a nice guy. And my kids . . . be good to them. I'll want to spend time with them, to keep trying to get to know them again. I mean, I *am* their mother."

Tory gazed at Lisa for a long time, then lifted her hand to wave. " 'Bye." She shook her head. "It's just *too* weird. There's something about you . . . " Her words drifted off as she slowly drove away.

Dumbstruck, Val and Lisa silently watched the van's departure.

"What do you think that was about?" Lisa finally asked.

"I don't have a clue. Maybe Tory has finally snapped."

Lisa glanced at her watch. "It's time for me to go to work. Can you follow her? What if she does something crazy? That's my body she's walking around in!"

Chapter Sixteen

Michael cradled his head in his hands. *A separation*. Lisa had picked him up for lunch and told him she wanted to live apart for a while. There'd been no avoiding the subject. This time she hadn't given him the chance. She didn't hesitate to tell him what was on her mind, nor did she give him a clue beforehand that something major was in the works. She simply stated her intention, as if she was telling him she'd decided to resign from the PTA.

He'd been angry at first. He'd told her that running away from their current situation was a guaranteed route to divorce. If anyone left, it would have to be her. He wasn't about to move out. And there'd be no compromises, no debate. The children would remain with him.

Michael had thought his terms would put an

end to her insane plans for a separation, but incredibly, Lisa didn't argue.

He pulled his hair until his scalp hurt. Why should her complacency surprise him? Everything about his wife lately seemed out of character. Though the old Lisa wasn't always as assertive as he might like, she would've fought tooth and nail for the children. For that matter, the old Lisa would've fought to save their marriage. Now, it appeared she'd given up on the two of them, that she was content to surrender their relationship without waging battle to try to save it first.

Michael stared down at a pile of work he knew wouldn't be tackled today. Maybe Lisa was doing the right thing. He missed the way things used to be between them, but those days were obviously over. Though he wanted nothing more than to lash out at her, he knew that in all honesty their rift was as much his own fault as hers. He'd taken their marriage for granted. It was that simple.

Caught up in his own anguish, Michael almost didn't hear the knock at his door. "Come in," he finally snapped, his voice gruff even to his own ears.

When Tory stepped inside, the knot in his stomach tightened. She was one more problem he didn't want to face at the moment.

"I need to talk to you," she said, closing the door behind her.

The sight of her brought back memories of their shared kiss, renewed his hunger for her, tormented him with clashing emotions. He wanted to hold her, shower her with tender kisses. At the same time, he wanted to deny the unwanted feelings she roused in him.

Michael swallowed, then drew a shallow breath. "I want to talk to you, too. Didn't we have a tutoring session scheduled for tonight?" Before she could answer he continued, "I want to cancel it."

Lisa's legs felt rubbery as she neared his desk. "Okay. I'd like to apologize for the other night."

"No need." He picked up a pencil and, staring past her, tapped it against the desktop.

She noticed the tensed muscle along his jaw, heard the curtness in his tone. "I don't blame you for being upset. What happened between us . . . well, I wanted it. I wanted you to kiss me, and I can't explain why I slapped you. Things have just been crazy."

"Tory . . . " Michael closed his eyes, then slowly opened them and looked at her. "You don't have to do this. I'm not mad at you." He tossed the pencil across the room. It hit the wall with a thump and fell to the floor. "My wife's leaving me."

"I see." She pressed her lips together, finally understanding the one-sided conversation with Tory in the parking lot. "Is it because of me?"

"If you mean, did she see me kiss you, yes, she did. But don't worry; there's a lot more to it than that." He gave a humorless snort. "In fact, my indiscretion didn't seem to bother her much at all."

"Where will she go?" When he didn't answer right away, Lisa added, "I know it's none of my business, but—"

"She didn't tell me where she plans to stay," he interrupted. "I don't think she knows."

Lisa prayed Val had caught up to Tory in time. If not, she would have to search for the girl herself. But for now, the look on Michael's face kept her from pursuing the issue of Tory's whereabouts.

217

She crossed the room and sat in the chair across from him. God, how she ached to touch him, comfort him, but her time as Tory was almost up. She couldn't risk drawing him to her more than he already was. "I know you're hurting. I can't imagine that your wife won't come around. Give her a couple of days."

He averted his eyes. His jaw twitched once, twice.

"You'll get through this," she said softly. "You have so many people in your life who care about you. They'll help you if you just say the word."

Michael stared at his hands, then looked up. Anger, turmoil, and grief vied for dominance within his eyes. "What do you really want out of life?" he asked. "What's really important to you?"

The question caught her off guard. She stared at him, unsure of how to answer. "Now isn't the time to talk about me," Lisa finally said.

"I want to." He smiled a sad smile. "If you could be anywhere, doing anything you want, without limitations, how would you imagine yourself five or ten years from now? Where would you be? What would you be doing?"

Her heart went out to him. Other than Dillon, who loved Tory, and Harry from The Club, who was old enough to be her father, Michael was the only man she'd crossed paths with in the last eighteen days who'd been able or willing to look beyond her appearance. She bit her lower lip and tilted her head to the side. "It's funny you ask me that question. I've been tossing around ideas about the future a lot lately."

She thought of the college catalog back at her apartment. She'd been invigorated while scanning the available courses. And somewhat overwhelmed. Her future was an unwritten book, and though fate would cowrite the chapters, ultimately the challenge of filling the pages belonged to her.

Feeling wistful, Lisa smiled. "I want to make a positive difference." She shrugged. "Big or small, it doesn't really matter, just so it counts. Isn't that what most people want when it comes right down to it? To know they'll leave their fingerprint behind when they die?"

"Maybe you're right." Michael nodded, staring at her with curious eyes. "How would you like to do it? What would your fingerprint be?"

She shrugged again. "Nothing spectacular, really. I want to love a husband who loves me back. I see a couple of children." Her throat tightened, squeezing her voice to a whisper. "A boy and a girl, maybe, like Jacob and Kat. I can't think of a better imprint to leave behind than two great kids."

Lisa recognized the expression on his face. It was the same one she'd often seen when they'd first fallen in love. When she was on the receiving end of that look, it was easy to forget everything else but the two of them and the moment.

Words bubbled up from deep inside her, the revelations that surfaced surprising her. "And I think if I could, I'd build a business of my own. A business that would force me to be the master of my own destiny. Its success or failure dependent on me and the choices I make."

"A law practice? I thought you hadn't decided about that yet?"

She frowned, knowing she was speaking for herself rather than for Tory, unable to stop herself from sharing with Michael her sudden, exciting realization. "No, not a law practice. I don't know what, exactly, but I picture it as something fun. Fun is important, don't you think? People need more of it in their lives."

Michael smiled at her. "You should see the excitement on your face. Can I ask you a question?"

"Sure."

"Why don't you drop your pre-law classes now, before you waste any more time? You should follow your dream. Don't let it slip away. There's no reason you can't make it reality."

For Tory's sake, Lisa forced herself to keep in mind whose body she occupied. She needed to stop referring to her own ambitions. "I don't know. Maybe I'm letting myself be sidetracked by some problems I'm dealing with. Everything I've done up to now has been geared to being a lawyer someday. Maybe I shouldn't mess that up."

He shook his head. "Follow your heart. I don't have to tell you that, do I? You're your own person. I admire that in you. You'll work your problems out. Deep down, I think you know where you're supposed to be headed. Listen to your instincts."

Funny, Lisa thought. She didn't think of herself as the person Michael described. Maybe she'd changed. Their conversation the other night came to mind. Michael had said that although she reminded him of his wife, they were different in as many ways as they were alike. She didn't think he was referring to her appearance. Obviously, this calamity had transformed her in more ways than one.

"There's one other thing I expect to be doing in the years ahead," she said, hoping to lighten the mood.

"What's that?"

"Playing roller hockey," she told him, amused by Michael's startled expression. "I definitely see a pair of skates in my future."

* * *

Val parked in the same obscure section of the lot as before to avoid the chance of being spotted by Michael when she picked Lisa up after work.

"Did you find Tory?" Lisa asked anxiously as she climbed into the car.

"No. I lost her in traffic. I had to stop at a light and she got away from me."

Troubled by that bit of information, Lisa relayed the news about Tory leaving Michael, and she and Val decided to spend some time searching before dark.

"Where would she go, Val?"

"Someplace familiar, I'd guess. You said she recognized Dillon. Maybe her memory is coming back. Let's go by the apartment first and see if she's there."

She wasn't. They decided to drive into Norman next, thinking Tory might've returned to The Club to confront Dillon. When they failed to find her there, they drove around the university campus, to no avail.

Lisa knew Val had sensed the extent of her distress when she insisted that Lisa come home with her to spend the night. "Call in sick again tomorrow," Val said. "I won't go into work, either. We'll spend the day looking. Tory will turn up somewhere."

"She has to. The spell ends day after tomorrow. If something happens to her before then, I don't know what will become of me."

They weren't any more successful the next day. Val suggested going to Tory's classes to quiz some of her friends, to ask them if a strange woman had been hanging around asking even stranger questions. But most classes were over for the Christ-

221

mas holiday, and other than Dillon, Kathleen, and Allison, Lisa didn't know any of Tory's friends.

Around midnight, Val pulled to a stop in front of the O'Conner house and killed the engine. "Is this really necessary? Wouldn't it be easier to spend the night at my house?"

"I'm not taking any chances." Lisa nodded toward the house. "As soon as the sun comes up, I plan to be banging on that door."

"We could set the alarm for five o'clock and have plenty of time to get over here before sunrise."

Lisa crossed her arms. "The alarm might not go off, or the car might not start, or—"

"Okay, I get your point."

"I can take you home and come back."

Val reclined her seat, settling in. "If you're staying, I'm staying. I want to be here when it happens. I want to see it with my own eyes."

Lisa repositioned her own seat and snuggled into the soft, expensive-smelling leather, pulling her coat tight around her. "Good, because if all goes well, you'll be driving the real Tory home instead of me. I can't be sure what state of mind she'll be in. She might need some help."

"What about you?" Val asked, sounding as anxious as Lisa felt.

"I guess I'll end up wherever Tory is when the switch takes place."

"That's a scary thought. What if no one is around to help you home?"

"Hey, after what I've been through these past days, I can deal with that problem on my own . . . wherever I end up."

Earlier, Lisa had pulled her long, thick hair into a pony tail. Now she tugged the band off and let the wavy locks fall loose around her shoulders.

"Michael will wonder why you're toting Tory around. Especially so early in the morning."

Val made a face. "We're talking body switches here and you're afraid of what Michael will think about that? Don't worry. I'll make something up. If he doesn't need to believe what you tell him for the spell to work, I won't try to convince him. How about I play dumb? I'll say you showed up at my place acting confused. That way, after you and Tory switch, Michael won't think I'm bonkers, which he would if I insisted you're Lisa." She shrugged. "At this point, I don't think it's all that important what I tell him. Things are bound to get pretty strange."

Feeling as though she'd downed three cups of coffee too many, Lisa said, "I'm assuming it'll happen like before, but I don't really *know* that's the case."

Val took hold of her hand and squeezed. "I'm not going anywhere. I'll be with you all the way." She gave a short laugh. "Until you disappear, anyway."

Lisa smiled at Val, relieved and thankful that she didn't have to wait the night out alone. "Get some sleep. I'll take the first stay-awake shift. I'll start the car at intervals so the heater can warm us up."

As Val drifted off, Lisa's thoughts fast-forwarded again to tomorrow. In only a few hours, she'd tell Michael the truth and the spell would transform her—send her back where she belonged. So far, she'd done everything the fortunes had instructed. She'd looked at her life—and seen the shortcomings. She'd opened her heart—and found the answers. She and Michael needed to work through their problems openly, honestly. No more avoidance, unpleasant or not. She loved him more than ever. It was as simple as that.

And as for herself, her own problems separate and apart from her marriage? She knew now that if she didn't pursue her own interests and dreams—nourish them—she'd wilt like a thirsty flower.

Lisa willed herself to relax. Other than Tory's whereabouts, there wasn't a single thing to worry about now, she assured herself.

But other worries tapped her on the shoulder nonetheless, whispering in her ear throughout the night.

What if it doesn't work? What if you did something wrong or left something out? What if you remain in Tory's body forever?

Overcome by anxiety, she cried through the long, lonely hours of the night. There was no need to wake Val. Lisa knew that, for her, sleep wouldn't come.

But just before dawn she did doze, awakening a short time later when a nauseating surge brought bile to her throat. Lisa shoved open the car door and sucked in giant breaths of air. When she lifted her head moments later, a beautiful, welcome sight greeted her. Pale, pink light pricked the eastern horizon. She watched it spread higher—a slowly rising blush on the skyline.

Beside her, Val stirred. "Wake up," Lisa whispered. "It's time."

Lisa slid from the car as Val blinked awake. "What?" Val moaned, rubbing her eyes and stretching.

Without waiting for her, Lisa headed for the door of the house, not pausing until her fingertips met the smooth, cool ivory of the doorbell. "Oh,

God," she whispered, shivering from both the cold and her frazzled nerves.

"Push it," Val said when she came up behind her.

Lisa looked over her shoulder and met Val's anxious eyes. "I'm so afraid," she said. Then she turned . . . and pushed.

For several drawn-out seconds she waited, tapping one foot against the porch, avoiding Val's worry-pale face, slapping a nervous hand against her thigh to the beat of her heart.

Lisa lifted a fist to the door and knocked. More seconds passed. Finally, she heard faint scratching from the other side, followed by Michael's drowsy, "Who's there?"

"It's me," Lisa said, her breath coming in quick, jittery pants.

"Tory?" The lock rattled, squeaked.

"And Val," Val added from behind.

The door opened a crack and Michael's tousled head appeared. "Val?" He blinked at them, scowling.

Lisa stepped closer. "I need to talk to you, Michael."

"Now?"

"I know it's early." She tossed a glance over her shoulder, past Val, to the quickly rising sun. "I need to tell you something, and I need to tell you now."

"I'm not dressed." Exasperation hung heavy in Michael's voice.

"That's okay. You can come out from behind the door. I've seen you in your underwear plenty of times, and Val's family."

"You've what?" Michael shrieked, his eyes instantly alert.

Val sputtered and coughed.

Lisa took a deep breath. "I'm Lisa," she blurted, then closed her eyes, preparing herself for the silent, black, watery tunnel, the pinpoint of light, the disorientation and whopping headache she remembered.

"Has she been drinking, Val?" she heard Michael mutter. "Did you hear what she said? She said she's Lisa, for pete's sake."

His words pried her eyelids apart. He was scanning her face, and his mouth moved in a way that told her he wanted to say more but couldn't find the words.

"Damn," Lisa whispered. The muscles in her arms and legs began to jerk.

"Val?" Michael said again. "Has she lost her mind? Why are you here with her?"

Lisa turned to see Val lift her hands in the air, her eyes wide and clueless.

"She showed up at my place with the same crazy story," Val lied. "I didn't know what else to do, so I brought her here." Val's gaze darted from Michael to Lisa. She leaned forward, squinting, as if trying to determine who resided inside Tory's body.

Panic buzzed around Lisa like a swarm of bloodthirsty mosquitoes. What was happening? What was Val doing? She returned her attention to Michael. "I'm your wife. I'm Lisa," she said quickly. "Almost three weeks ago, Tory and I switched bodies. I don't know how or why it happened, but it did."

She felt light-headed and dizzy. Michael's image faded in and out, in and out, like a faulty picture tube. The switch was happening now, she told herself. Or maybe she was simply experiencing the aftereffects of another sleepless night. Lisa leaned against the bricked wall at the porch's side. Her eyes drifted shut.

"Let's get her inside," she heard Michael say. He sounded far away, but she could still hear the urgent alarm in his tone. "She called in sick yesterday," he continued. "She's obviously in bad shape."

Lisa felt Val's slender hand on her left shoulder, felt Michael's large, sturdy fingers clasp her right arm. "No," she said, trying not to cry. "I'll be okay. Just take me home."

"Are you sure?" Val asked.

She opened her eyes, looked down, and saw that she was still in Tory's clothes. "I'm sure."

"We should get you to the emergency room." Michael's hand remained on her arm, his eyes concerned. He glanced behind him into the house. "The kids . . . I'd take you myself, but I don't want them to wake up and find me gone. I guess you could stay with them, Val, but . . . well they're taking Lisa's leaving pretty hard. I think it's best that I'm here for them right now."

His plea for her understanding wasn't necessary. Lisa understood better than anyone what Jacob and Kat must be going through, and that knowledge left her with an ache, a feeling of utter helplessness. There was no use trying; she couldn't stop her tears from falling now.

"That's okay, Michael," Val said quietly. "I'll see to Tory."

"Take the afternoon off, Tory," Michael said. "Go see a doctor, maybe a therapist while you're at it. Get some rest."

"I'll call you later," Val shouted as she guided Lisa down the walk toward the car.

"Do that," Michael shouted back. "Let me know how she's doing."

Val helped her into the passenger side of the car, ran around to the driver's side, then scooted in and slammed the door. "I'll explain everything, Tory," she said with unconcealed excitement. "You're not going to believe it."

Lisa stared across at her, wishing for a giant shot of novocaine to dull the pain in her heart. "I'm not Tory." She blinked back new tears. "It didn't work, Val. The fortune didn't come true."

Chapter Seventeen

Lisa slept the morning away in one of Val's spare bedrooms. Shortly before noon, she awoke to another bout of nausea. She ran to the bathroom, lunged for the toilet, then proceeded to lose her previous night's dinner.

Afterward, exhausted, she sat on the floor. The cool ceramic tile beneath her bare legs startled away the last, lingering remnants of sleep. When she felt more steady, she attempted to stand, but another surge of sickness sent her back to the floor.

Lisa tried to free her mind of the perceptions that started crowding in, but they refused to budge, so she examined them one by one.

As she leaned against the shower door, the simple movement of her shoulders brushed her shirt across her bare nipples, provoking a tense ache. She lifted a hand to her breasts. They seemed heavier than usual, although with Tory's well-endowed body it was difficult to be sure.

And then there was the matter of her appetite. Nothing filled her up lately. Even now, bowed before the porcelain throne, she was hungry.

What else? Fatigue. She couldn't seem to get enough sleep. And she was overly emotional, though that was unavoidable, considering everything she'd been through these past weeks.

These past weeks. Lisa counted back. Considered. It might mean nothing. Then again . . .

Drawing her legs to her chest, Lisa lowered her face to her kneecaps. "No, God!"

"What's the matter?" Val rushed into the bathroom without knocking. "You're positively gray!"

Lisa lifted her head to look at her friend. "What am I going to do, Val? I'm in trouble. Big trouble."

"Lisa . . . you poor thing." Val kneeled beside her. "Don't give up hope yet. The day's not over."

"I'm sick."

"No wonder. You cried all night."

"No, Val, I mean I'm nauseated."

"What did you expect? You've made yourself ill, you're so upset."

Lisa shook her head. "You don't understand. My breasts . . . I'm aware of them. All the time. They're sore."

"Is that supposed to *mean* something to me?"

"When you consider the fact that I'm also starving and sleepy and emotional every second of the day, yes, I'd say it should tell you something pretty definite."

"Like what?"

"Like the last time I felt this way I was expecting Kat."

* * *

The air reeked of disinfectant. A glaring white light overhead brightened the stark, colorless room. Funny, Lisa thought, how a place dealing with such private matters could feel so cold and impersonal.

Crisp, white paper crackled as she scooted to a sitting position and dangled her bare legs over the side of the examining table. She'd been damn lucky to squeeze in on the college clinic's schedule at the last minute, she told herself, drawing a deep breath to steady her nerves.

Though she knew with dreadful certainty that the home pregnancy test had been accurate, she prayed this doctor might somehow refute it. Looking beyond the haggard lines in his face to his kind, yet disillusioned gray eyes, Lisa asked, "What's the verdict?"

"From the looks of things, I'd say you're about ten weeks along."

On rollers attached to the legs of his stool, the doctor slid across the room to a counter, where he paused to scribble on a prescription pad. "Make an appointment to see me again in six weeks." He rolled back toward Lisa while extending the slip of paper. "Take this to your pharmacist." His smile was sympathetic and tired, the smile of a man who'd been through this same scenario too many times for his liking. "Prenatal vitamins," he said.

Too numb to cry, Lisa dressed behind a screen, then walked out front to schedule an appointment.

Val waited in the lobby. When Lisa appeared, she stood. "Well?"

"Ten weeks," Lisa said, with an emotion-concealed glance toward her friend.

In tense silence, they headed for Tory's apartment. The scenery whizzed by unnoticed. For Lisa, nothing else existed but the chilling realization that Tory's baby grew within a womb that now belonged to her.

When they arrived, Val closed the door behind them and faced her. "What are you going to do?"

Lisa collapsed onto the sofa. "Any suggestions?"

"For the first time in my life, I'm at a loss for advice." Val sank down beside her. "I guess it's the boyfriend's baby?"

Lisa nodded. "I guess."

"What's his name again?"

"Dillon."

"Will you tell him?" Val's gaze darted away from her, then back again. "Of course, I mean if you don't change back. But I believe you will. You know I do."

"Until I figure out what went wrong, I won't change back, Val. I'm sure of that, so I might as well accept it. As for telling Dillon about the baby ..." She paused, hesitant to voice what weighed on her mind. "I won't tell him. At least, not until I come to terms with a few things myself. There's Tory to consider. I don't know what to do about her, but I have to find her and make sure she's okay."

"What about Michael?"

Lisa stared into space, hollowed by the futility of her predicament, the irony. She remembered Val's earlier suggestion that she get close to Michael. Seduce him into falling in love with her in Tory's body. Would being a second wife to her first husband and a stepmother to her own kids be better than nothing? After the scene with Michael this morning, if she was inclined to attempt such a seduction, she doubted he would let her within ten feet of her.

And even if he would, there was a baby's well-being to think about now. Tory's baby. And Dillon's.

She turned to Val, feeling grim but determined. "There must be a way out of this. I should go back to Confucius Says." She thought of the old Chinese man with his mystical, all-knowing eyes. "The answer is there. I know it."

The phone rang, and Lisa reached across the end table to answer it.

"Tory, this is Harry at The Club."

Lisa instantly recognized the manager's high-pitched voice. "Oh, yes. How are you?"

"One of my waitresses quit. I'm looking for a replacement. Would you be interested?"

Michael squinted as he stepped from the school building into the sunlight. The sound of muffled popping drew his attention skyward, where a flag flapped merrily in the breeze.

Not a cloud in sight. Mother Nature had an odd sense of humor. Today should be gray, dreary, and oppressive, to match his mood.

His shoes clicked against the sidewalk as he made his way toward the car. The few words he'd spoken with Katherine's and Jacob's teachers had been agony—the meeting afterward with the principal even worse.

My wife moved out. Simple words, really. Michael never dreamed they'd be so hard to say. He never imagined he'd ever have to say them. But the school staff needed to know. The kids were upset, perplexed over the sudden changes in their lives. The next few weeks would be especially difficult.

Michael climbed into his car, started the engine, and headed for the office. Again, he wondered how Lisa would get by. Where would she live? What would she do for money? Though she didn't have any answers when he asked her, she didn't seem worried, either. So why was he concerned? She'd brought this on herself. The choice to leave was Lisa's, not his.

Yesterday afternoon, he had called his neighbor, Sandy Northrup, and asked if she'd pick the kids up after school. She agreed, and also offered to watch them for the next few days until arrangements could be made for someone to do it on a regular basis. He'd have to make some calls soon.

There were scores of other things to consider. A housekeeper, for instance. Lisa hadn't cleaned much in weeks. Things would be even worse now.

Bitterness filled his throat until he thought he might strangle on it. Housekeepers, baby-sitters. How could he think about such trivial matters at a time like this? Still, like it or not, plans were necessary.

Michael's sigh was a frustrated hiss of hot air. He'd thought he at least had Tory to help with homework and the firm's bookkeeping. But after this morning, he didn't know what to think about her mental stability. What on earth had she meant to achieve with her crazy declaration that she was Lisa? Instead of easing some of his burden, Tory had suddenly become added weight.

After parking in his usual spot in the office parking lot, Michael cut the engine and leaned back against the headrest. He never should've depended so much on Tory in the first place. He should've trusted his wary instincts from the beginning, just as he knew he should trust them now and let her go. Sever all ties. But he couldn't do it. Other than his kids, Tory was the one bright spot in his life, the one thing that felt right.

"That's crazy," Michael muttered under his

breath, exasperated with himself. "She's a big reason everything's screwed up. How can that feel right?"

Still, he was worried about her—almost as much as he was worried about Lisa.

Except for one white van, the Confucius Says parking lot sat empty. A CLOSED sign was propped in one window. Lisa's heart sank when she spotted it. She and Val tried the door and found it unlocked.

A lone workman stood on a ladder inside. He looked down as they entered, then lowered himself a couple of rungs. "Can I help you?"

"Is the owner or one of the staff around?" Lisa asked.

"Nope. They closed up for a while." A toothpick protruded from one corner of his mouth. It bobbed up and down when he spoke. "I'm doing some work on the place while they're away."

"Away? Where are they?" She dreaded his answer. Something told her they hadn't just left for the day.

"They're in Hong Kong, I believe. Said business slows down around the holidays, so it's a good time for them to visit family. Guess folks tastes lean toward ham and turkey this time of year instead of chow mein." He laughed.

Lisa didn't.

"Surely someone who works here is still in town," Val said.

The man shook his head. "The staff's all family, and it's my understanding that they headed east."

"For how long?" Lisa prodded.

He shrugged. "Can't say. A couple of weeks. Maybe three."

Lisa gave him a coaxing smile. "Surely you

have a number where they can be reached," she suggested, unable to disguise the impatience she felt. "If something goes wrong around here while you're working, how do you get hold of them?"

"There's a place here in the city that takes care of that." He looked her over, then did the same to Val, his toothpick waggling. "Guess it wouldn't hurt to give you the number."

Later, back at Val's house, Lisa called the phone number the workman had provided and discovered that it belonged to a property management firm. The woman at the other end of the line assured her that the Confucius Says folks would return to Oklahoma City soon, but she wasn't at liberty to say when or to give out their Hong Kong number.

"I wouldn't bother them unless it was an emergency," she answered when Lisa asked if the woman could call and relay a message. "Is this an emergency?"

"Yes." Lisa nibbled her lower lip as she pondered the best way to phrase her request, deciding, finally, no best way existed. "Could you tell them that it concerns the fortunes in their cookies? I've done everything they instructed and it's not working. I—"

"You want me to call Hong Kong to file a fortune cookie complaint?"

"Well," Lisa said, wincing, "sort of."

"Sorry, ma'am. I'm afraid that doesn't qualify as an emergency."

Lisa hung up the phone. "I was afraid of that."

"Why didn't you stay home?" Nan asked when Lisa arrived for work at one o'clock the next afternoon. "You look terrible."

Though she'd carefully applied makeup in the

car to try and liven up her pale complexion and conceal the dark circles rimming her eyes, the process hadn't helped much. Lisa smiled at Nan's motherly concern. She touched the woman's shoulder as she walked away, headed for her desk. "I may not look it, but I really feel okay. I didn't want to be at the apartment. It's closing in on me."

The thought of staying home to wallow in self-pity had forced her to the office despite her dread of facing Michael. Lisa was concerned about Tory wandering around with no memory. And she and Val had failed to come up with an idea on how to locate the girl.

Earlier she'd called to have the Volkswagen towed away to be fixed. Val insisted on paying for the repairs, and Lisa couldn't think of another alternative. The vehicle was supposed to be ready after work. Val had offered, too, to pick her up again at five, then drive her to the garage.

Glad to see a full basket of work on her desk, Lisa began to sort through the stack. There were several documents to be delivered, the usual deposit to make at the bank, not to mention the bookkeeping entries that needed to be caught up on when she returned from the errands. By staying busy, maybe she could make it through the day without suffering a nervous breakdown.

She heard Michael's voice through the wall that separated them. The familiar inflection and tone filled her with an overwhelming sense of hopelessness. Shaking it off, she forced her mind to the tasks at hand.

Janice spoke over the intercom. "Line one's for you, Tory."

"This is Tory," Lisa said, realizing with a start how easily the name slipped past her lips these days. For a moment, there was only silence on the line.

"It's me. Dillon."

"Hi." A sudden rush of blood heated her cheeks. She'd come to the conclusion that she'd have to give Dillon a chance. She felt certain the baby was his. If the child couldn't have its own mother, the least she could do was try to see that it was raised by its father. If she never changed back, a future with Michael was out of the question. She doubted he'd consider becoming involved with her when he discovered she carried another man's child. If she could only learn to love Dillon . . .

"Did you get the flowers?"

"Yes," she answered, remembering the forgotten daisies she'd received last week. "They were beautiful. Thanks."

"I wish I could've done more. A two-year anniversary deserves to be celebrated. But then, we didn't really make it the full two years, did we?"

She heard the hint of accusation in his low-pitched tone. "I'm sorry, Dillon. I really should've called to thank you earlier."

"How've you been?"

"Okay." Silence again. What could she say to him?

Dillon cleared his throat. "Last time I saw you, I walked off without my guitar again. I thought I'd come by tonight and get it."

"No need. I'll bring it to The Club. Harry called and asked me to work."

"Filling in for Kathleen?"

"No, on a regular basis. Kathleen quit."

"Oh. That's great."

The change in his voice was striking. Hope filtered through his tone, along with some of the spark she'd heard the first time they met.

Lisa only wished she felt as enthusiastic as he sounded. When Harry asked her to work several evenings a week, she'd turned him down immediately, only to call him back a couple of hours later when common sense dictated otherwise.

She desperately needed the money. She needed to stay busy and distract her mind. And, although her heart resisted, she needed to be close to Dillon, to discover if even a remote possibility existed that she could ever involve herself in a relationship with him.

"Harry's scheduling me for Wednesday, Friday, and every other Saturday night." She drew her lower lip between her teeth, then released it, gazing up as Michael stepped from his office. Her heart beat double-time, as it always did when she saw him these days. "I tutor on Monday and Thursday evenings," she said softly to Dillon while holding Michael's gaze. "I'll have Tuesday and Sunday nights free."

"I guess I'll see you at The Club then."

Lisa lowered the phone to its cradle without saying good-bye, her eyes on Michael. He looked completely strung out. She'd never seen him so down, and it worried her. "Are Kat and Jacob okay?" she asked.

"They've been better, but they'll survive." Michael shifted his feet awkwardly. "Did you get a new job? I couldn't help overhearing."

"I'm taking a regular shift at The Club. It won't interfere with my work here. Or with my obligation to Jake."

He leaned against the door frame, tugging his ear.

"If there's anything I can do to help you, Michael, anything at all . . ."

"There is." He straightened, then gestured toward his office. "Will you come inside for a minute? We need to talk."

"If it's about what I said about being Lisa . . . " She was afraid to say more. If she made up an excuse, lied to him, would the fortune backfire? Would she ruin her chances of ever changing back?

The truth will set you free.

Well, she'd told the truth and it hadn't changed a thing. Maybe it never would. How could she continue to insist she was Michael's wife? He'd think she'd gone mad. He'd fire her.

She was stuck. Afraid to lie, afraid to tell the truth.

"Val called and explained about the medication you were taking for your headaches," Michael said, saving her from making a decision. "I hope you're off the stuff now. Sounds like you had some really crazy dreams."

Lisa went limp with relief. She owed Val a favor. A big one. "I'm really embarrassed about the whole thing."

"Forget it. That's not what I want to talk about anyway." Again, he motioned toward his office. "Come on in."

Chapter Eighteen

Michael closed the office door before settling into the chair beside Tory's. *Damn it to hell! Where do I start? How do I say what I have to say?*

He turned to her. "This isn't working out . . . you and I together every afternoon at the office, then a couple of nights each week."

Her gaze burned him like a hot poker. Michael clenched his fists until they hurt. He hoped the discomfort might eventually overwhelm his turmoil.

"Are you saying you don't want me to help Jake anymore, after all?" she asked.

He forced himself to meet her eyes. If he was going to do this, he wouldn't allow himself to wuss out, as Jake would say. He nodded. "Yes, I want you to stop tutoring. And I want . . . " Despite his determination to rid his life of her, he hesitated. "I also want you to quit this job."

She seemed to shrink before his eyes, so he quickly added, "It doesn't have anything to do with that nonsense about being Lisa. I want you to know that."

Visions of an empty future flashed through Lisa's mind. She wet her lips again, but the effort didn't do much good. Her mouth felt parched, as if she'd devoured an entire box of saltine crackers that morning instead of only three. He was asking her to give up everything. Never mind that he didn't realize the consequences they would all suffer, she and Michael and Kat and Jake, because of his decision.

The utter unfairness of the situation spurred fury, dragging her up from the depths of despair. In the blink of an eye, her life had begun to crumble. She'd done everything she was supposed to do, and for nothing. Well, she'd finally had enough. Starting now, she'd have to fight for the remaining shreds of her identity—fortune cookies and everything else be damned.

She lifted her chin. "No, Michael, I won't quit. I need this job. I want it. You'll have to fire me if you want me to leave."

He shook his head and reached out to her. "I can't go on like this. I'm going crazy being around you. Don't you understand? My life's falling apart. I don't blame you for anything that's happened," he said, with a gentle squeeze of her arm. "I just need to put things into perspective . . . my marriage, my family . . . you. I have to sort through a lot of confusion and make some decisions. When we're together, there's no way for me to think straight. Please, Tory, I know it's a lot to ask."

His words fired up the defensive spark inside her. Lisa pulled her arm from Michael's grasp. "Do you think you're the only one hurting? The only one who's confused? You have no idea what I've been through."

She slid from the chair and sank to her knees on the floor in front of him. "Look at me, Michael. Listen to me. Forget about logic and the way things are supposed to be. Listen to what your heart's telling you. Don't you know who I am? Can't you see?"

Michael cradled her face in his palms. "I know who you are. You're a beautiful, intelligent, compassionate woman." His voice faltered and he pressed his lips together. "But before I can be sure you're the one I'm meant to spend my future with, I have to deal with the present . . . and the past." He brushed a kiss across her mouth, then leaned his forehead against hers. "I want you so much," he whispered. "But I can't. Please understand."

Lisa stood and turned her back to him. She told herself that she should be thrilled Michael loved her so much. Two facts made it clear that he did: He couldn't easily walk away from his wife and he couldn't deny his feelings for the young woman who'd recently changed everything. And she was both—the wife he couldn't forget and the girl he'd fallen in love with all over again.

I'm not Tory! She wanted to shout the words, to take Michael by the shoulders and shake him until he came to his senses. Why not? she asked herself. He was pushing her away from her children and from himself. He'd already as much as fired her. What did she have to lose, now?

Lisa swung around. "I'm not . . . " she started, then stopped abruptly, her chest heaving. "I've lied to you, Michael," she blurted. She leaned against the edge of the desk for support. "I tried to correct that when I came to the house the other morning. I tried to tell you that I'm not who you think I am."

Michael slowly stood. "What do you mean? You aren't going to start talking crazy again, are you?"

Squaring her shoulders, Lisa took a deep breath. "I'm—" The intercom buzzed.

"Mr. Timms is here for your one-thirty appointment," Nan said.

With his puzzled eyes fixed on her, Michael blinked once, then glanced at his watch. "Show him in, Nan."

Five and a half hours later, Lisa stood outside her house waiting for someone to answer the doorbell, resisting an impulse to simply walk in. She hoped Michael didn't come to the door. If he did, it would make her plan so much more difficult to carry out.

To her relief, Jake opened the door. The expression on his face was one she'd never seen before, at least not on Jake. It was Michael's stressed-out look, though he, too, had seldom worn it until recently. In the past, anxiety was a malady her calm, cool husband rarely suffered. It broke her heart to see that, at the seasoned old age of nine, Jake had already begun to struggle with the pressures of life.

"Hi, Tory," Jake said, wrinkling his nose, then reaching up to scratch it. "Dad said you can't teach me anymore. I thought you weren't comin' by tonight. I'm glad you came anyway."

Love surged through her—a rush so fierce, she thought she might burst from the power of it. Filled with renewed determination, Lisa grinned. "I wasn't going to come, but I thought things over and realized you deserve some say in the matter."

Jake pulled off his glasses and looked up at her, bug-eyed. "I do?"

Lisa draped an arm around his shoulders and laughed. "There's a first time for everything,

Jake. It's *your* schoolwork we're talking about, isn't it?" He nodded as they stepped into the house side by side. "Then why shouldn't you be in on the decision?"

When they entered the den, Michael stood before the fireplace, his arms loaded with wood. The sleeves of his flannel shirt were rolled up to the elbow. A muscle worked along his forearm, and the veins there bulged as he added wood to the crackling fire.

Warmed more by the feelings he stirred in her than by the fire, Lisa stopped a few feet from him and stared him in the eye. "I'd like to ask Jake a few questions, if you don't mind."

"Why do I get the distinct feeling you'll ask him whether I mind or not?"

Turning to her son, Lisa asked, "Does it help you make better grades when I work with you?"

Jake's eyes made a hesitant shift from her to Michael, then back again. "Yeah," he said, "it helps a lot."

Satisfied with his answer, Lisa continued, "Your dad doesn't think you need me anymore. If you feel the same way and you'd like me to quit, I'll understand. No hard feelings."

This time, Jake didn't bother to assess Michael's reaction. His face flushed, then twisted with grief. "I don't want you to stop helping me. I need you. Especially now that Mom . . . " He rubbed his knuckles across his eyelids, then slid on his glasses. "Well, since she went away for a while."

Heartsick, Lisa pulled Jake against her and held his trembling body until Michael came over and eased him from the circle of her arms.

Michael took Jake by the shoulders and kneeled. "Everything will be okay, son. I talked to Grandma earlier. She's coming to spend some time with us until Mom's back home. She'll be here to help you, to help all of us."

Good grief, not Michael's mother! Lisa made a panicked scan of the room: the filthy baseboards, the cobwebs in the corners of the ceiling. Before her eyes, dust particles grew into dirt clods, smudges became globby smears. *I can't let her see the house like this! What will she think of me? She'll be convinced this family's better off without me, that's what.*

With a consoling pat to Jake's back, Michael stood. "Would you go knock on the bathroom door and ask Kat if she's okay? She's been in the shower for at least fifteen minutes." He ruffled Jake's hair and smiled. "Then you can start on your homework."

Jake sniffed. "Can Tory stay and help?"

Michael's jaw tensed when his eyes darted her way. Lisa braced herself for what she sensed would occur as soon as Jake was out of earshot. Something told her that, for once, Michael wasn't going to avoid the issue between them. Maybe he'd changed as much as she had over these past weeks.

"We'll see," Michael answered Jake. "I need to have a talk with Tory first."

When Jake left the room, Lisa felt Michael's temper rising. Reminding herself to stay calm, she faced him. "I never intended to upset Jake by coming here. This is a difficult time for him. For all of us. I only wanted to—"

"You don't have to explain to me what we're going through! I know better than anyone." Michael shoved a hand through his hair. "You can help us by staying away. I tried to explain that to you this afternoon."

Despite her resolution to remain cool, Lisa's own temper shot up ten degrees. "And I tried to explain some things to you this afternoon, too, but you're too stubborn to listen and too blind to see what's right before your eyes."

"Let's stay on the subject." Michael paced in front of the sofa. "You know how I feel about you, Tory. I understand that none of this is easy for you, either, and I know you mean well. But you're butting in on something that's none of your business."

Eyes wide at the tone of the conversation, Kat entered the room wearing only panties, her hair wet and uncombed. At first sight of her, an intense urgency grabbed hold of Lisa, frightening her more than ever before. *There's still time left with Kat. A short amount of time before she crosses over that elusive line and suddenly becomes too old to hold in my lap—too grown up to share a lullaby.*

When Jake appeared behind his sister, Lisa swallowed the fear, but it only returned twice as strong as before. *God, they're only mine for such a short time. Please send me back. . . .*

"Can we watch TV?" Kat asked. She turned on the television without waiting for a reply.

"No!" Michael yelled over the scream of a siren as a police car sped across the screen. "You two go to your rooms and start on your homework."

"But I don't have any homework," Kat protested.

"Do some anyway! And put some clothes on, Kat."

Lisa stepped toward Michael, her hands on her hips. "None of this is their fault! Don't yell at them!"

"See, that's exactly what I mean! They're *my* kids. Don't tell me how to deal with them!" He turned to the children. "Now, mind me!"

The troubled expressions on Jacob's and Kat's faces squeezed Lisa's heart and made her want to strangle Michael. He must have noticed, too, because he went still, then scrubbed a hand across his face.

"I'm sorry," he said, his voice softer than before. "Just find something to do in your rooms for a while, kids. Please."

When they were alone again, Michael took her measure, his eyes tired and dejected. "What are you trying to do?" he asked.

"I just want you to admit a few things to yourself."

"Such as?"

"Why did you indicate to Jake a few minutes ago that his mother would be coming home at some point in the future?"

Michael tugged his earlobe. "Because she might."

"Then again, she might not. In fact, she probably won't."

"How would you know what Lisa might or might not do?"

"Because *I'm* Lisa," she said, stepping toward him and pressing a hand to her chest. "I'm your wife."

"Not this again! Are you still taking those drugs?"

"I'm not taking anything. I never was. I said I'm your wife, and I meant it. I'm Lisa." This time, she didn't whisper. The deed had been done, the words spoken without fear or hesitation. If the fortune wouldn't change her back, then it was up to her to straighten out this mess the best she could.

Trembling, she waited for Michael's response so she could proceed to argue her case. She'd tell him things, private things, just like she'd told Val. Then the gavel would fall, sentencing her to a future either with or without him.

Chapter Nineteen

The grandfather clock ticked methodically . . . Jake's and Kat's conversation carried from down the hallway . . . suspenseful background music blared from the television set.

Michael stood motionless and silent while frustrated rage built inside him. He stared at Tory. Fidgeting with the strap on her purse, she shifted from foot to foot. "Well? Aren't you going to say something?" she finally asked.

"Get out." Michael was aware of the low, menacing rumble of his own voice and hated it. Kicking her out was one of the hardest tasks he'd ever had to tackle. But things were definitely out of hand here. He had to make the break with her, and he had to do it now.

She stepped backward as he moved toward her. "But I—"

"I want you out of my house." He grabbed her wrist and headed in purposeful strides toward the entry hall. She stumbled along beside him, the purse slung over her shoulder banging against him with every step. When they reached the front door, he opened it. A draft of cold air hit his face as he guided her out onto the porch ahead of him. He joined her there, slamming the door behind him.

"If this is your idea of a joke, I don't think it's very funny!"

Her breath came out fast and shaky. Michael heard each shuddering gasp in the silence that stretched between them. He drew a deep breath of his own, smelling wood smoke and evergreen in the air.

"Michael—"

"I was a fool to let things go as far as they have between us." He paced the small expanse of porch to and fro. "Whatever it is you're trying to do, Tory, it won't work. Did you really think I'd believe you?"

"It's true." She clenched her fists at her sides, and Michael noticed they were trembling. "I'm Lisa," she whispered.

"I'd have to be insane to believe you." He squinted to see beyond the halo of the porch light to where she stood, her face shrouded in twilight shadows. A tremor ran through him, and he suddenly experienced an uneasy need to put as much distance as possible between them.

Michael backed away from her until the door stopped his retreat. "But you're the one who's crazy, aren't you?" he said, knowing he was allowing frustration to make him say things he'd later regret. "You're crazy and manipulative. You know you're on the verge of losing your job at the firm and here with Jake. Is this some demented attempt to hang on? You know Lisa left us and we're vulnerable. Did you assume I'd grasp at anything, even this, to have her back?"

"Think about it, Michael. The woman you consider your wife hasn't been acting like herself lately. She's lost her memory. That's because our souls switched places and she couldn't handle the shock."

He started to interrupt, but she cut him off. "Then I come along. You're drawn to me." She moved into the light. "I remind you of her, don't I?"

"That doesn't prove anything."

"I can tell you things about yourself . . . about Kat and Jacob. Things only your wife and their mother could possibly know."

"It wouldn't matter if you relayed every intimate detail of mine and Lisa's honeymoon." Michael shook his head, his heart pounding at an alarming speed. "Nothing you say will ever convince me that you're her."

The cold evening air seemed to seep through Lisa's skin, chilling the blood in her veins to ice water. Anger and confusion sharpened the prominent angles of Michael's face. Every muscle in his body looked taut and ready to spring. The porch light reflected in his eyes, turning their amber color to gleaming gold. "What can I say to convince you?" she whispered, almost choking on her fear.

The door creaked as he eased it open and slipped inside. "You need help, Tory." His voice cracked when he spoke her name. "I'm sure the university clinic has a psychiatrist on staff. Please . . . for your own sake, make an appointment."

"Listen to me!"

He started to shut the door, then paused and leveled his gaze with hers. Lisa saw tears in his

251

eyes. "I'm sorry to have to do this," he said, "but you've forced me to it. Don't come back here, or to the office."

She couldn't afford to be cautious with him now—couldn't just let him turn his back and walk away. She wouldn't. Only one thing might cloud his certainty and sway him. "Your father," Lisa blurted, grabbing the door's edge. "I know about his affair. He confessed it to you before he died. I haven't told anyone, Michael." She lowered her hand from the door. "Just like we agreed."

Michael flinched as if she'd slapped him. The color drained from his face; she'd never seen him so pale. For one long moment Michael stared at her, and Lisa wasn't sure what to make of the look in his eyes. Shock? Confusion? Betrayal? Fear? Maybe all of those . . . and more. He drew an uneven breath, stepped back, and closed the door.

Lisa lunged forward, pounding her fists against it, knocking the Christmas wreath to the porch. "Let me in, Michael! You have to believe me! Please!"

After several minutes of banging and yelling, she gave up and staggered through a haze of tears toward the driveway. It was over. She'd taken a chance and lost.

Lisa climbed behind the steering wheel of the Volkswagen, tilted the rearview mirror, and peered at her stricken expression. "You're Tory Beecham now," she sobbed. "And there's not a damn thing you can do about it."

"Come in," Michael said wearily, stepping aside to allow his partner into the house.

After tucking the kids into bed, he'd decided to call Jarrod. Though he considered the man to be more of an associate than a friend, he needed someone to confide in. Friends were one more thing he'd let fall by the wayside over the past two years while he worked at building his practice. Enough hours in the day didn't exist anymore for a social life. At least, that's what he'd convinced himself.

"It's about time you invited me over, Mikey," Jarrod said. Six pack in hand, he strutted into the den and made himself comfortable on the couch. He glanced up at Michael and cringed. "Not much in the mood for a party, are you? You look like hell."

"I feel worse." Too keyed up to sit, Michael roamed the room in a restless gait. He accepted the beer Jarrod offered when he passed by him. "I fired Tory tonight."

Jarrod snickered. "Couldn't handle the temptation, huh?"

Ignoring his partner's response, Michael took a swig from the aluminum can, then placed it on the coffee table. "You won't believe what I'm about to tell you."

"Try me. But sit down first; you're making me nervous."

Michael approached the recliner next to Jarrod, then sat. "This is just between you and me, understand? I don't want it getting around."

"You can trust me."

Though Michael had doubts about that, he leaned forward, his forearms across his knees, and lowered his voice. "Tory tried to convince me she was Lisa."

"I don't understand."

"She came over tonight and told me that she's my wife. That she's Lisa inside Tory's body and that Tory's in hers."

Jarrod made a strangled sound—half laugh, half startled gasp. His eyes widened. "No kidding? Man!" He removed his glasses and polished the lenses with his tie. "So you fired her?"

"I threw her out of the house and told her not to come back here or to the office. She obviously has a serious mental problem. If you want to know the truth, I'm worried about her. Maybe I shouldn't have reacted so harshly."

Jarrod squinted. He slid the glasses back onto his nose. "What else did she say?"

"Just that she could tell me things no one but Lisa would know."

"Like what?"

Michael wouldn't even consider telling Jarrod about his father's indiscretion. "I didn't ask," he answered. It was the truth. Tory had volunteered the information. For the life of him, he couldn't figure out how she knew the family secret. His mother didn't even know it; only he and Lisa did. He couldn't imagine Lisa betraying his confidence about this. Especially not with Tory—hell, not even with Val. But nothing else made sense. Lisa must've told Val and, for some unfathomable reason, Val told Tory.

"Why in the hell didn't you ask?" Jarrod scowled at him. "Weren't you the least bit curious?"

"I just wanted her out of here. She gave me the creeps, Wilder. I have to admit, something about Tory *does* remind me of Lisa, at times."

Michael tugged his earlobe, averting his eyes from Jarrod's appraising gaze. There was no way in hell he'd admit his feelings for Tory. He realized now the foolishness of confiding in his partner. The man would offer no sympathy, only bad advice. But now that he'd started talking, he couldn't seem to quit.

"She's trying to move in on me," Michael continued. "And I can't for the life of me figure out why. She even has the kids on her side."

With a cackle, Jarrod reached across and clapped Michael on the shoulder. "Hell, man, you really *are* out of practice. The lady wants in your pants, can't you see that?" He shrugged, the rise of his sandy brows a lurid insinuation. "She knows you're upset over Lisa, so she dreamed up this little wife fantasy, hoping you'd play along. See? I admit it's a far-fetched approach, but she'd get what she wants—namely you—and ease your guilt all at the same time."

Jarrod gestured toward the phone. "Maybe if you apologize, she'll still be willing. Why don't you give her a call?"

"You've got to be kidding!"

"Mikey! Mikey! Don't tell me you're going to let this chance slip through your fingers? Lisa's given you the brush-off, and this ripe young peach is literally falling at your feet, begging you to take a bite. How can you pass that up?"

"Haven't you ever heard of commitment?"

Jarrod laced his fingers behind his neck, his elbows protruding at either side of his head like chicken wings. "Hey, buddy, if you can get the fruit free why buy the tree?"

"Wilder, you're a sick human being."

Jarrod's grin turned wistful as he gazed at the ceiling. "Too bad Tory didn't set her sights on me." He smacked his lips. "I do love peaches."

He refocused on Michael. "What are your plans for Lisa? If you need a good divorce lawyer, Roger Dunaway is the best in town. I'd handle it for you myself, but I try to steer clear of domestic squabble cases." He grimaced, as though the very idea brought a sour taste to his mouth.

"Forget it," Michael said. "I'll find a way to get Lisa back. I won't give up until I do."

Lisa stepped inside the pitch-dark apartment and slammed the door. Closing her eyes, she leaned against it. Fatigue settled in—a bone-deep weariness that sapped all the energy from her mind and body. Though she knew she had plans to make, at the moment, she didn't want to think or feel. She wanted to hide in the comfort of darkness, escape to the oblivion of sleep.

As she made her way toward the bedroom, a lamp came on behind her, flooding the room with a soft, muted glow. An instant surge of adrenaline sharpened Lisa's nerves. She whirled around. "Dillon!"

He sat on the couch, his face impassive, unreadable. Lisa lowered the hand she'd instinctively clutched to her throat. "How did you get in here?"

"I still have my key." He dangled a keyring from his index finger and stared at her.

Lisa lowered her purse to the floor. She motioned toward the guitar propped beside him. "I guess you came for that?" A note of wariness had crept into her tone. Though Dillon's face was a dispassionate mask, his eyes seemed even blacker than usual, a dangerous glint sparking them as they followed her every move.

The keys jangled when he returned them to his pocket. "I would've left sooner but, out of habit, I punched the button on the phone recorder when I noticed the red light blinking." A chord of emotion wavered in his voice. He moved his hand from the lamp to the answering machine beside it and started the messages.

A disembodied woman's voice, high-pitched and whiny, filled the room. "Hello, Tory? This is

Kathleen. Tonight's girls' night out. You're going with us. No arguments. You've got to quit moping over Dillon sooner or later, you know. I'll be in touch. Bye!"

A beep sounded, followed by another woman's voice, this time mature and all business. "Miss Beecham, this is the university clinic. Something has come up and we need to reschedule your pre-natal appointment. Please give us a call when you get home."

The machine clicked to silence. Dillon's eyes fixed on her face. Lisa's knees buckled as she moved toward a beanbag chair and slumped into it. She bowed her head and closed her eyes, then slowly opened them and focused on Dillon. His Adam's apple bobbed convulsively as he swallowed once, then again.

"Is it mine?" he whispered.

God! Don't let him ask me that! I think it is; I'm sure it is, but . . . How much did she really know about Tory Beecham? Though all the signs indicated that Tory was committed to Dillon before she and the girl switched bodies, how could she be certain what happened ten weeks ago in Tory's life? And how could she tell this tormented young man that the baby was his if there was even a slight possibility it wasn't?

She could think of only one way around this predicament. She would tell him exactly what little she knew and let him draw his own conclusions.

Lisa bit down on her lip, oblivious to the pain. "I'm ten weeks along."

He frowned, his eyes shifting back and forth, as if ticking off days on a mental calendar. Abruptly, the grimace softened. A look of relief passed over his face—the first ray of sunshine after a storm.

"Ten weeks ago. That's around the time we spent that weekend at my uncle's cabin in the mountains, remember?" He stood, then crossed the room, bending to his knees in front of her. Releasing a slow breath, he clasped her hands in his own. "I was so afraid. I thought the baby might be your boss's."

Dillon squeezed her hand and grinned. "We're going to have a *baby!* I can't believe it! It's . . . it's *great!*" He lifted a hand to her hair, his thrilled expression sobering a notch. "How do you feel about it, Tory? I know you didn't think you wanted kids, but now . . . "

Lisa recognized the brief but very real streak of alarm sweeping across his features.

"You do want our baby, don't you?" he asked. "You're not thinking of—"

"No." Lisa returned the squeeze to his hand, hoping to reassure him. "Don't worry. Everything is okay. It just hasn't registered yet. I'm still so surprised." *To say the least.*

Dillon pressed a tender kiss to her mouth, trailing the tip of his tongue across her upper lip before he eased back. A jolt of panic, equally as intense as what she'd seen in his eyes only moments before, shot through Lisa.

"We thought we were only generating heat in that cold mountain cabin when all along we were making a baby," he said, his voice low, seductive. He kissed her throat. "I'm so happy, babe. I know I'll never have as much money as that lawyer guy, and I can't give you all the things he could, but we'll make it work."

She heard his intimate words—felt them sail across her skin, felt his face nestled against her neck. Lisa's head swirled. *Good grief, I'm going to faint.* "Dillon, I—"

"We'll get married whenever you want, however you want. I'm game for anything. A big wedding, a small one. Or we can run off and do it secretly." Shifting, he settled beside her on the beanbag. "It's up to you."

"I . . . I need time to think." The amorous look of content on Dillon's face sent her to her feet. She paced the floor, arms folded across her chest.

"Take all the time you need. We don't have to get married right away. I'll move back in and we can plan things." His slanted eyes darkened with desire. "We have some making up to do first, ya know."

As if in answer to a prayer, the doorbell rang. Lisa lunged toward the entry, certain whomever she might confront on the other side would be preferable to dealing with the situation at hand.

Kathleen and Allison swept in when Lisa flung the door wide.

"Thank goodness we caught you home. I thought you might try to avoid us," Kathleen said. "You know, the way you've been doing this hermit act and everything."

Both women were "dressed to kill." Lisa's already sagging spirit hit the ground. *Girls' night out. Great.*

Simultaneously, the girls spotted Dillon. "Oh!" Kathleen backed up a step. "Hi, Dillon." She frowned, shifting her attention to Allison, then to Lisa. "I guess this is a bad time, right?"

"Not at all." Dillon's hair swayed like an ebony curtain as he rose from the floor. "I've gotta leave anyway." He grinned. "I've got some packing to do."

He came up beside Lisa and circled one arm around her shoulders. "Go on out with Kathleen

259

and Allison," he said. "Consider this your bachelorette party."

"What!" Allison shrieked.

"Show her a good time, girls, but no boozing it up." Dillon kissed Lisa's hot cheek. "Tory and I are gonna have a baby!"

Chapter Twenty

The three women walked side by side toward a building covered in gaudy, flashing neon lights. Gravel crunched beneath Lisa's feet. She stared down at the dust that settled on the surface of her shoes. The fine layer thickened with each step across the parking lot.

"Let's go make a memory," Allison said, her voice bubbly.

"It better be a good one, too," Kathleen added. "You getting married is gonna really cramp our social life, Tory. Not to mention having a *baby!* I can't believe it, can you, Allison?"

At the entrance, raucous noise from inside stopped Lisa in her tracks. Feminine shouts and laughter, along with Rod Stewart's, "If You Want My Body and You Think I'm Sexy," had her eardrums throbbing. A short time ago, she might've considered this an adventure. Not anymore. Lisa wasn't up to a second night out like her recent one with Val.

"Can't we go somewhere else?" She cast a hopeful glance at each of her companions. The urge to lose her dinner in the parking lot grew stronger with every pulsating beat of the music.

Kathleen frowned at her. "Why would you want to go anywhere else? It's not as if these guys are in the city every night, you know."

"That's right," Allison agreed, urging Lisa forward with a gentle push. "Honestly, Tory, they're professionals. Not like those sleazy creeps who perform at the dives."

"Oh, well, *that's* certainly a relief," Lisa said sarcastically.

"We'd better hurry." Kathleen swung the door open. "The dancers quit at ten o'clock."

A musty, acrid odor waylaid Lisa when they stepped inside. Cigarette smoke hovered on the air like sooty fog. Lisa coughed and looked around.

Women surrounded her. Screeching, clapping, giggling women. They sat at the tables, stood against the walls, gathered in groups everywhere. The scantily clad dancer strutting like a rooster at center stage was the only male in sight.

Lisa quickly mumbled an excuse, then made her way across the dimly lit room through a maze of scattered tables toward a door that read LADIES. Much to her relief, she found a pay phone on the rest room wall. She called Val and begged her to come to the rescue.

Minutes later, Lisa returned to Tory's friends. She slunk into a chair beside them, intent on becoming invisible.

"Can you believe it? We found a table!" Allison shouted.

Lisa ordered a club soda when the waitress came by, then spent the next thirty minutes checking her watch, waiting for Val to arrive.

She'd given up on her friend when the next act, a guy wearing a Santa outfit, appeared on stage. "Good grief, you two! That song must be at least fifteen years old! Wouldn't it be more fun to go someplace where the music's more . . . progressive?" The last, desperate shred of hope dissipated at the sight of her companions' irritated scowls.

"That's a standard strip tune," Allison said. "They'll get around to the good stuff. They play all kinds of music. Besides, lots of bored, older women show up when the male dancers are here. The management probably thinks they should play the classics to keep them satisfied, too."

"She's right!" Kathleen yelled, fluffing her curls. "See, there's one right over there. That woman must be at least thirty."

Lisa's gaze followed Kathleen's pointing finger and settled on Val. "At least," she said, then laughed.

Allison cupped her hands around her mouth and leaned across the table. "Do you know her?"

"Yes. She's my . . . my aunt."

Kathleen's eyes widened. "Your *aunt!* Does she come here a lot?"

"The old hussy never misses a show." Lisa stood, struggling to see past the dingy haze of smoke. "I'd better go say hello." She headed toward Val. Kathleen and Allison followed.

Val sat alone at a table close to the stage. Her foot tapped to the beat of the music, her gum-chewing jaw keeping pace. Her gaze followed Santa's motions with unconcealed interest. As he slowly removed his coat with a seductive swirl, she blew a bubble, pulled a cigarette from her purse, then balanced it between her fingertips.

Lisa moved nearer and placed a hand on Val's shoulder. "Val?"

Val jumped and whirled around. Her knee hit the underside of the table, upsetting her drink. Amber-colored liquid spread slowly across the tabletop. "Oh! Hi, Li—"

"It's me, Tory. Your niece." Lisa glanced sideways at Allison and Kathleen. "Don't you recognize me? I know it's been a long time."

"Oh . . . yes, of course." Val gave her an awkward smile. "It has been a while. How are you, Tory?"

"I'm fine." Lisa introduced the girls, then turned her attention to the gyrating, oil-slicked Santa on stage. "I've been worried about you, *Auntie*." Refocusing on Val, she grinned. "Can we talk?"

"Sure." Val lowered the unlit cigarette to an ashtray. She peered up at Lisa with a defensive lift of her chin.

"You two go save our table!" Lisa shouted over the noise to the girls at her side. "I'll be there in a minute."

As Allison and Kathleen disappeared into the crowd, Lisa perched on the stool next to Val.

Val mopped at the puddle of liquid on the table with a soggy napkin. "Why are you looking at me like that?"

"Like what?"

"Like I should be embarrassed."

"I'm just surprised to find you so intrigued by the entertainment. I thought we agreed that these places are degrading. They promote reverse sexual harassment."

"I'm only here because you called me. When I couldn't find you, I decided to grab a table. What was I supposed to do? Close my eyes?"

"I would've sworn you were enjoying yourself when I saw you from across the room," Lisa teased.

Val gestured toward the dancer, then around the room. "My only interest in him and all this is the human nature aspect. Such as, what draws women to a place like this? What entices a man to do such a thing?"

"Spare me," Lisa said.

"Okay, I admit it." Val flattened her palms on the table and leaned forward. "I was hoping maybe Michael had hired on with the male revue and I could see him in his tassel." She waggled her brows.

"Very funny."

They both peeked back at Santa. Lisa nibbled the corner of her fingernail. Val drummed her knuckles against the table.

"He doesn't seem to mind being a mere sexual object," Val said with a slant-eyed look at Lisa.

"You're right. In fact, he looks like he enjoys it. Especially when those women stick dollar bills in his G-string." She made a disgusted sound, then burst out laughing.

"God, I need a date," Val mumbled, eyeing the stripper, her expression similar to a ravenous mongrel's that had just spied a steak. "*Really*. If I've stooped to lusting over the likes of him, I know I'm in bad shape. Why won't you ever fix me up with someone? I've asked for your help so many times, I can't keep count."

"You don't need my help to find men. You pass up perfectly acceptable offers all the time. I saw it with my own eyes the other night when we went out. Your Cotton-Eyed Joe partner was very attractive."

Val shrugged. "He was okay."

"You're too picky. Besides, the only guys I know are the old married type."

"That's not true. What about Michael's partner? I've wanted to meet him for ages. You'd think our paths would've crossed by now, even without an introduction from you."

"Not necessarily. You're never at the law firm, and Michael and I don't do much socializing with Jarrod. Anyway, he's not your type. Personally, I can't believe he's *any* woman's type. He's a self-centered, narrow-minded womanizer."

"The sort you might find at a place like this if that were a woman up there on stage instead of a man?"

"Exactly."

"Then I guess you and I are self-centered, narrow-minded men users. See? I'm more Jarrod's type than you thought."

"We're here under duress." Lisa pressed a hand against her chest. "At least *I* am."

"Why are you here?" Val asked. "And who are those girls?"

"It's a long story, but I'll give you the condensed version."

Lisa ordered a tonic water and lime from a passing waitress, then told Val everything that had happened over the course of the evening, omitting the details about the family secret she'd revealed to Michael.

"What are you going to do?" Val asked when Lisa finished.

"Maybe you could talk to Michael for me," she answered. "You'd stand a better chance of convincing him than I ever would."

"Yeah, that I'm every bit as nutty as he thinks you are. Besides, that won't solve your problem with Dillon."

"Talk to him anyway. If nothing else, find out if he knows how to reach Tory." Lisa touched her stomach. "I'm worried about her. In the meantime, I'll figure out how this change occurred and try to reverse the process. I have to. If not, don't be surprised when you receive my wedding invitation, followed shortly thereafter by a birth announcement."

Val winced. "I'll call Michael tomorrow. If he believes me, maybe the three of us can converge on Tory and Dillon together."

Lisa studied the front door, where prowling groups of young men now entered en masse.

"Must be ten o'clock. They're letting the guys in now," Val said. "You can almost see the testosterone radiating from their eager young bodies."

Lisa stood, preparing to weave her way through the chaos to find Tory's friends. "What does the time have to do with anything?"

"On ladies' night the management doesn't allow men inside until ten o'clock. By then, the women are sufficiently drunk and uninhibited, and the guys are anxious to keep them in that condition by buying them even more drinks."

"How do you know all this? Another of your anthropology studies?"

Val didn't respond. Her attention was diverted by the two masculine specimens approaching their table. The men reeked of aftershave and tobacco. Their heavy-lidded eyes moved assessingly over Lisa, then Val.

"This used to be fun," Lisa muttered into Val's ear. "Even the other night it was a real kick. But now I feel like a piece of beef at a cattle auction."

She glared at one of the men when he winked at her. "I don't miss this one bit," she muttered.

Val stuck a cigarette between her lips. "You're the one who wanted to be twenty again."

The next morning, Michael conducted depositions in the firms small library while nursing a pounding hangover. Jarrod had stayed at the house until midnight, intent on persuading him to let Lisa stew with her problems, for the time being, while he played along with Tory.

Now, with the last question finally answered and the opposing attorney and client preparing to leave, Michael hissed a sigh. He showed them to the door, then uttered a few last words to his own client before heading for the sanctuary of his office.

After popping two aspirin and settling back in his chair, the intercom buzzed.

"It's Lisa on line two," Nan said.

Michael bolted upright. "Thanks." He dragged his fingers through his hair, then punched the button on his telephone. "Lisa?"

"Hi, Michael. I wanted to let you know I've found a cute little apartment in Norman, close to the university."

The enthusiastic note in her voice made him flinch. "How do you plan to pay for it?"

"I'm going on a job interview this afternoon. I have a really positive feeling about it."

"Good for you." He started to ask where, then decided it really didn't matter. She'd tell him if she wanted him to know. "Do you have a phone so I can at least contact you if I need to?"

"Not yet. I'll call and give you the number as soon as I do."

"Fine." Michael rubbed his eyes, desperate to keep her on the line. "One of the PTA moms called this morning to remind you that you're supposed to help with the Christmas party in Kat's class this afternoon."

"Michael, I—"

"You signed up to bring cookies. And you're supposed to stay for an hour or so to help the teacher with the kids."

"I don't remember the first thing about how to bake cookies. And watching a roomful of kids, well—"

"Forget it," Michael interrupted. "I'll handle it." He wondered when he'd find the time, then made a mental note to call the bakery.

"Lisa . . . Did you tell Val the family secret?"

"Secret?"

"You know . . . the one about my father."

"I can't even remember last month, Michael. I mean, do you really think I can remember some secret of your dad's?"

She had a point. And if she couldn't remember the secret, she wouldn't remember if she told Val, either.

Though Michael knew only seconds had passed since her answer, the following awkward silence seemed longer than a church sermon on Super Bowl Sunday. He made an effort to shove aside the bitterness he felt toward her. If he was going to salvage his marriage, the time to start was now. "Lisa, Christmas Eve is only ten days from now. Do you realize that?"

"No. I mean, I guess the holidays slipped my mind. How are the kids?"

"Okay, considering." *Nice of you to finally ask.* "They miss you." Michael bit back the urge to add that he missed her, too. As much as he wanted her back, he damned sure wouldn't grovel.

"I hope they understand—"

"They don't. And it'll be even more upsetting if you're not with us Christmas Eve and Christmas Day."

"Well . . . sure, I'll be there. But I can't guarantee how much of a help I'll be. I mean, after my fire episode the other night . . . "

"You won't have to lift a finger. Mom will be here soon. You know how she loves to be in charge." He had to remind himself that she probably didn't remember his mother.

"I'd better go now, Michael. I'll call you."

"One more thing before you hang up. The trip to the Cayman Islands I'd planned for the two of us after Christmas? I mentioned it to you before."

"Maybe you did. I mean, I don't really remember."

"Well, I think we should go."

"I don't know . . . "

"We owe our marriage one last chance."

"Well . . . let's wait and see how things go over Christmas, okay?"

"Can I take that as a tentative yes?"

"I guess so."

A small seed of hope took root in his heart. "Say it."

"Yes." She gave a nervous giggle, then snorted. "Tentatively, I mean."

Tantalizing aromas hovered in the air at The Club. Upbeat music made a perfect backdrop for the noisy laughter and conversation of a relaxed dinner crowd.

As she stood in the kitchen placing platters on a large, round tray, Lisa felt strangely content. Her stomach growled.

Harry chuckled. "Hungry?"

She rubbed her middle and grinned. "You heard." Harry reminded her of a cuddly, stuffed bear—a giant one. She'd taken an immediate liking to him, with his jovial manner and bright-colored attire.

"When things slow down a bit, take a break and grab something to eat. You're doing a great job, Tory." He patted her shoulder. "Glad to have you back on staff."

Lisa hoisted the tray, stifled a yawn, then pushed through the swinging doors leading into the restaurant. As she passed the bar, she caught Dillon's eye. He winked, sending a shiver of foreboding up her spine.

Around midnight the night before, she'd finally convinced Kathleen and Allison to let Val take her home. She slept until Dillon arrived at noon with the first load of boxes containing his personal items. Shocked speechless, Lisa watched him move back into the apartment. It was as though the pregnancy set in motion a sequence of events she didn't know how to stop.

That afternoon, she'd considered showing up at Wilder and O'Conner for work as though the previous evening's incident with Michael had never taken place. But the thought of him making a scene, bodily throwing her out in front of Nan and Jarrod and Janice, had kept her from following through with the idea.

Lisa placed sizzling plates of fajitas in front of her customers. Her previous plan to spend time with Dillon, to get to know him and attempt to muster up some affection for him, was one thing, she decided. But to have him back in the apartment, living with her, was quite another. She tried not to think about what she would do or say tonight after work when they went home . . . together.

The next hour passed in a blur. The hectic pace didn't leave much time for panic over personal

271

problems, and for that much she was thankful. Finally, Harry ordered her to take a break. Since there was a temporary lull in activity, he joined her at the bar.

"How's everything going?" he asked, placing a sandwich in front of her.

"It's exhausting, but I love it." Since she'd figured out the routine, Lisa really did like working at the restaurant. She savored a big bite of stacked ham on rye as she kicked off one shoe to rub the aching sole of her foot.

Dillon sat a tall glass of fizzing soda beside her plate. "Tory's great, isn't she, Harry?"

"Very efficient," Harry agreed. "A real dynamo." He studied her, a curious expression on his face. "Funny, you were an excellent waitress when you worked here before. Not that you aren't now, but I'm somewhat surprised that you were slow getting the hang of things again."

Lisa was thankful her mouth was full so she didn't have to answer. She gave Harry a chipmunk-cheeked grin and shrugged.

Dillon dunked dirty beer glasses in a tub of water behind the counter, then transferred them to a tray to be washed. "Don't run her too hard, Harry. She needs a lot of rest. She's—"

She scowled into Dillon's dark eyes, effectively cutting off what she sensed he was about to reveal. She felt the fewer people who knew about the pregnancy, the simpler her life would be.

"Well," Dillon continued, "Tory doesn't need to wear herself out, that's all."

Harry stared at Dillon for a moment before returning his focus to the girl at his side. He patted her arm. "You'll be a big help to the new assistant manager. I hired her this afternoon. She said she'd drop by tonight to familiarize herself with things. She wants to meet the staff who're working and observe our closing procedure."

Dillon shook his head, laughing. "I hope this one's better than the last."

"I think she'll do fine," Harry said. "She's older and more mature. She has family responsibilities and a business background." He glanced over his shoulder. "Here she is now. Dillon and Tory, meet our new assistant manager, Lisa O'Conner."

Chapter Twenty-one

"She seems to like you," Lisa said to Dillon as Tory, a.k.a. Lisa O'Conner—assistant manager, walked off with Harry.

After the startling introduction of moments before, Lisa had made a hasty, though difficult, effort to disguise her shock over the turn of events. She'd explained that she and Tory already knew one another, and how. Throughout the conversation, Tory only had eyes for Dillon. Even now, she turned and looked over her shoulder, sending a brilliant smile his way.

"Who seems to like me?" Dillon asked. "That O'Conner lady? No way. She's just being friendly." He scanned the order a passing waitress handed him, then reached beneath the counter for two mugs.

Lisa forged ahead, unsure of what provoked her to pursue this particular line of conversation. "Don't be so sure. She can't quit looking at you."

"You're wrong. But even if she did have a thing for me, she'd be crazy to believe I'm interested. Lisa O'Conner's way too old."

"She's not *that* old. Besides, I think she's kind of pretty, don't you?"

Dillon shrugged, then, turning his back to her, filled the mugs with beer.

"As a matter of fact," Lisa snapped, "I think she's damn attractive!"

"Okay! Okay!" Dillon swung around to face her, one arm outstretched, palm forward. "She's a good-looking lady. What's with you, babe? You're acting like you *want* me to be turned on by her or something."

Embarrassed, Lisa slumped, balancing her forearms on the counter for support. "Sorry."

With a nod at an impatient customer who sat on a stool down the way, Dillon brushed Lisa's cheek with his fingertip. "You're sure acting strange these days. Must be the baby." He nudged her plate. "You're even eating meat."

He skimmed a finger down her palm to her wrist, tracing circles around the sensitive area. Lisa's fingertips tingled and throbbed. She looked into his hooded eyes, her breath catching when she recognized the glowing love there. Love combined with a healthy dose of lust. Her stomach turned a cartwheel, then landed with a thud.

"You know you're the only one for me," Dillon said, his voice a low croon. "I can't wait to get back to the apartment and show you."

275

* * *

"You're as crazy as *she* is," Michael said. He shoved his plate to the center of the table, leaving the fried chicken Val had brought untouched.

"I had a feeling you'd say that."

"What did you expect?" Despite an intense urge to yell and make a scene, Michael kept his tone quiet so he wouldn't alarm Kat or Jacob. "Damn it to hell, Val, am I the only sane person left in the world? You can't possibly believe what you're saying. Did you plant this idea in Tory's head to try and break Lisa and me up?"

"To break you up?" Val echoed. "How can you even think such a thing? You know me better than that!"

Michael dropped his chin to his chest. "I'm sorry. You're right."

"I know it sounds absurd. When Lisa came to me with this story, I threw her out of my house just like you did."

His head came up. "I threw *Tory* out, Val, not Lisa." He stood and began to clear the table. "If you insist on backing up her nonsense, I won't think twice about placing the imprint of my foot on your behind, too."

Bitterness rose to Michael's throat. "Lisa told you about my dad, didn't she?"

Val frowned. "Your dad? I don't know what you're talking about."

"Damn it, Val, do you think I'm stupid?"

"Of course I don't think you're stupid, Michael. But I don't have a clue here. I can't recall Lisa ever saying anything much to me about your father."

Michael stared at her, wishing to heaven he could read her mind. He suspected that Val was covering for Lisa. She *had* to be. But, just in case, he decided to drop the subject.

From the recesses of her purse, Val retrieved a pack of gum and a pack of cigarettes. She weighed each on separate palms, looking from one to the other. With an expression of regret, she tossed the cigarettes back inside her purse. "In a million years, I would've never believed this could happen, Michael. But it *did* happen. The girl who's been working at your office is really Lisa inside Tory's body, and the woman who's been living in this house with you is Tory Beecham in Lisa's body."

"If such a thing was possible, which it isn't, why wouldn't Lisa tell me the truth from the beginning? Why would she play out this charade for so long?"

"At first, she thought the spell would only last a short time. Until the quarter moon, or something like that. She wanted to follow the fortune to the letter, just to be sure, so she waited. But she was also afraid you'd think she was insane. Afraid you'd cut all ties with her and she wouldn't have any contact with you or the kids."

Michael tossed the last take-out carton into the trash and made a conscious effort to still the quivering muscle in his jaw. "I'll say one thing for Tory, she's not stupid. I *do* think she's crazy. How could you, of all people, fall for such a story?"

"Five minutes, Michael. Come with me to see Lisa. Give us five minutes of your time and you'll be as sure as I am that she's your wife."

He felt alone. Alone and, strangely, betrayed. Were the three of them—Tory, Lisa, and Val—plotting some sort of conspiracy against him? "No, Val. You've lost it," he said. "Tory's lost it. Lisa's on the verge of losing it. I have to believe in someone, and I'm beginning to think I'm the only person whose sanity's intact. If I even considered the possibility that what you're telling me is true,

I'd be as bad off as you are."

"Please—"

"I won't! I'm going to work things out with Lisa. The woman who's been living with me these past few weeks and every week since we married. My mother's coming on Monday for the holidays and to help with Kat and Jacob. Lisa's as much as said she'll go to the Cayman Islands after Christmas to give our marriage a second chance. That's exactly what we're going to do."

Dizzy with panic, Lisa trailed behind Dillon as he made his way across the shadowed restaurant parking lot toward his Jeep. When she heard Harry and Tory and the remaining staff locking up behind them, she grabbed Dillon's arm. "I need to talk to Lisa O'Conner before we leave. It won't take long."

She recognized the old suspicions that flashed across his face, hardening his features into a defensive mask. "About her husband?" he asked. "I thought you were finished with him since you quit your job and everything."

By telling Dillon that she'd resigned from Wilder and O'Conner instead of that Michael had fired her, she'd hoped to avoid further questions and thus, further lies. Now she found herself groping for another distortion of the truth. "It's not about Mi . . . Mr. O'Conner. It's about . . . their son . . . Jake. I tutored him in math for a while, and there are some things I think his mother should be made aware of."

"You helped the kid with *math*?" Dillon's eyes grew wide with disbelief. "No offense, Tory, but you and I both know you're *terrible* in math. You can't even balance your checkbook."

"I can't? Oh, uh, I realize that," Lisa stammered. "But Jake's only nine." For effect, she lifted her chin in defiance. "Believe it or not, fourth-grade math isn't beyond my comprehension. Besides, it was a welcome challenge."

Dillon huffed. "Or an excuse to be around O'Conner."

"We've been over all that."

Across the parking lot, Tory waved at Harry with one hand while unlocking the minivan with the other.

Lisa gave Dillon what she hoped was a reassuring smile. No other choice remained but to tell Tory the truth. Returning to the apartment with Dillon tonight would only deepen the hole she was already having trouble climbing out of.

"I'll only be a second," she said, backing away from him.

She jogged the short distance to the minivan. "Lisa! Wait!"

Already inside the van, Tory rolled down the window. "Is something wrong?"

"Can I talk to you for a minute?"

"Sure. Come around and climb in. It's cold out there."

Lisa didn't hesitate to accept the offer. She quickly made her way to the passenger door, then slid onto the seat next to Tory. Nerves and exertion had her taking short, quick breaths that exited her lungs in misty puffs of condensation. There was no easy way to build up to what she had to say, and no time to waste trying to find one. She'd simply tell Tory everything and hope for the best—the return of the girl's memory.

"Dillon's waiting for me, so I have to make this quick." She looked into Tory's concerned blue eyes—*her* concerned blue eyes—and swallowed hard. "I have something to tell you. I'm afraid you'll find it difficult to believe. But if you'll hear me out, I think I can explain a lot of what's been going on in your life these past few weeks."

"What is it?"

"I know what caused you to lose your memory. I was there when it happened. You suffered a major shock and your mind couldn't accept it."

"Did I have an accident or something?"

"I guess you could call it that, but not in the way you mean." Lisa placed one hand on top of Tory's in the seat between them. "I don't know how it happened . . . it seems impossible. But somehow, someway, my soul switched places with yours."

Tory's fingers tensed, drew back slightly beneath her own. "What?"

"My soul . . . my essence . . . my spirit . . . whatever you want to call it, left my body and went into yours. At the same time, your spirit left your body and came into mine." The expression on Tory's face clearly conveyed her fear that the woman beside her might be an escaped patient from a nearby mental institution.

Tory laughed—a jittery chuckle that failed to disguise her apprehension. "This is a joke, right? I mean, what you're saying doesn't happen." She scooted closer to the door. With her left hand she reached for the handle.

"I realize that, Tory. I'm not crazy, I promise you. I'm every bit as confused over this whole incident as you are."

"Tory? You called me Tory."

"That's what I'm trying to tell you. *You* are Tory Beecham in Lisa O'Conner's body—*my* body. *I'm* Lisa in *your* body. That's why everything has seemed so foreign to you lately. The house . . . the children . . . Michael."

At the mention of Michael's name, Tory's

expression shifted from anxiety to consideration to realization. The tension that had her poised to bolt from the van dissolved before Lisa's eyes. Relieved, Lisa released a pent-up breath. *She believes me. She remembers!*

Tory smiled. Her eyes filled with pity. "You didn't need to go to all the trouble of making up such a wild story to get Michael away from me." She giggled as she patted Lisa's hand. "I know the two of you have a thing for each other, Tory, and it's okay. I understand."

She peered toward Dillon's Jeep and said, "I mean, some things are meant to be, and some things aren't." The smile faded, leaving behind only sadness. "Like my marriage. I'm pretty sure it's over. I just, like, feel really bad about the kids, you know? As crazy as they've made me lately, I really miss them. And I feel so guilty. I'm supposed to be a mother . . . but I don't *feel* like a mother."

Tears filled Tory's eyes. She shrugged. "I hope you can understand this. I don't think I'm a threat to you and Michael. Whatever used to be between my husband and me . . . well, I'm like, pretty sure it's gone. But for his sake, and especially for Kat and Jacob, I have to be a hundred percent certain." She took a deep breath, then exhaled noisily. "So I'm pretty sure I'm going with him to the Cayman Islands on the twenty-seventh."

Lisa's heart dropped. "You are?"

"I think I have to. I mean, it's only fair. And maybe while we're gone, you should take the time to see if you have any feelings left for Dillon." Her attention moved beyond Lisa's shoulder to the window.

Looking back, Lisa felt faint when she saw Dillon standing there.

Chapter Twenty-two

The sound of the apartment door closing behind them conjured images in Lisa's mind of a jail door slamming shut, trapping her and Dillon inside . . . alone. She stood in the center of the living room and imagined the clanging of keys against metal bars as the warden locked up.

There's a way out of this. If I calm down, I'll think of it. A miracle. That's what she needed. An accomplice smuggling a cake with a baked-in file.

Dillon switched on a lamp, spreading a warm, inviting glow throughout the room. He shrugged free of his coat and hung it on a rack beside the door, then yawned and stretched in one long, lazy movement. "It's good to be back. I've missed this place." He moved toward her. "I've missed you."

Panic took hold with a not-so-gentle squeeze. Lisa's brain scrambled to come up with a tactic, a diversion, anything to stall the inevitable.

282

Dillon toyed with a strand of her hair, then tucked it behind her ear. His eyes remained on her face as he lowered his hand, his fingers flexed, and placed it protectively against her stomach.

Everything stopped. Lisa couldn't move, couldn't breathe, couldn't speak. Her heart tapped out an urgent SOS against the wall of her chest. Then, suddenly, miraculously, the phone rang. "I'll get it!" She guessed she should be embarrassed that her voice sounded high-pitched and nervous, but she didn't care. She'd been granted a moment's reprieve; that was all that mattered. Heading for the telephone, Lisa said a silent prayer of thanks.

"Hello?"

"Lisa? It's Val."

Lisa went limp with relief. She sat on the floor. "I was hoping you'd call." Aware of Dillon's scrutiny, she averted her eyes. "What's up?"

"Are you alone?"

"I wish."

"Oops. Is Dillon there?"

"In the flesh." She heard a muffled pop. *Val's gum.*

"If this is bad timing, I can call back tomorrow."

"No!" At her exclamation, Dillon frowned. He walked past her into the kitchen, where he pulled open the refrigerator and peered inside.

She lowered her voice. "It's not a problem."

"I spoke with Michael tonight," Val said. "I backed up everything you told him, but he didn't buy a word of it. I'm sorry, Lisa."

"I guess I should've expected it. Thanks for trying."

"There's more. I think he talked Tory into going with him on a trip right after Christmas. Just the two of them."

"I know."

"You do? How?"

Dillon walked to the couch, sat down, and stared at her, a tall glass of milk clasped between his palms. Lisa quickly summed up his demeanor and labeled it impatience. "I'll explain later," she told Val.

"Will you be okay?"

"No, but I'll survive." She no longer felt desperate to keep Val on the line. She was tired of fighting a no-win battle. Her mother once said you play the cards you're dealt. And though the deck was stacked against her, maybe the time had come to accept—to put the past behind her and proceed with her new life.

Weary and defeated, Lisa lowered the receiver to its cradle without saying good-bye.

"Was that someone from the law firm?" Dillon asked.

"No. What makes you ask?"

"Just a guess." He chugged the milk in several silent gulps, then set the glass on the table beside the couch. "We need to talk."

The glittering pain returned to his eyes. If there was one thing Lisa had learned about Dillon Todd, it was that he was an impulsive young man. Quick to tease, equally quick to accuse. He didn't pull punches or avoid conflict, but easily spoke whatever weighed on his mind.

She wasn't accustomed to such a man. She was used to Michael's calm, slow temper, his tendency to shy away from conflict if at all possible. She'd always considered that a strange trait for an attorney, but it didn't seem to apply to his work. She'd seen him in action. Michael had no trouble at all speaking his mind in a courtroom.

Standing, Lisa crossed the room and sat on the opposite end of the couch from Dillon. "I agree. We do need to talk. We have a lot to work out."

"I've gotta get some things out in the open before we take this relationship any further." Dillon pressed his long, slender fingers against his eyelids, then lowered his hands to his lap. "You've changed, Tory. Everything about you. The way you talk, your mannerisms, your likes and dislikes, your clothes. You've even quit going to classes, and you've always been such a serious student."

Lisa thought of the call she'd received a while back from the university's Dean of Students concerning Tory's extended absence. "I plan to start back after Christmas."

"It's more than all that. There's another difference in you that worries me most of all. I don't like the way it makes me feel."

"Dillon, I—"

"Let me explain," he interrupted. "I've never been the jealous type. Oh, sure, when we first started going out I got bent out of shape sometimes." His gaze skimmed her again, head to toe. "Look at you. Guys are gonna notice. It's only natural." He shrugged. "That might've bothered me some at first. But you always made it clear I was the one you wanted, so after a while when men stared, I felt proud instead of resentful."

He blew out a long, slow breath. "I guess I sound kinda chauvinistic, but that's the way it is."

When she didn't respond, he picked at a frayed spot on the knee of his jeans, staring down at his fingers self-consciously. "But I don't feel that way anymore, and I don't like myself very much because of it."

285

"I'm not sure I understand."

"Lately, when it comes to you . . . I'm jealous . . . suspicious. It eats at me 'til I think I'll go crazy."

His tone was deep, more hurt-filled than angry. Still, Lisa's pulse increased its rate. "Have I done something to make you feel this way?"

He frowned, speculating. "It's not so much what you've done, it's more the way you act around me. We've been together a long time, Tory. The major change I sense in you is in your feelings for me."

"Then why did you come back?"

"The truth?"

"Yes."

"Because of the baby. And because I can't seem to stop loving you."

Her heart melted. He was young . . . so full of expectations and overflowing emotion. Lisa didn't shrink away when he scooted toward her. He was a beautiful, caring man who'd be easy to learn to love. And she would learn to love him, for his sake as well as her own. And for the baby's.

Dillon moved closer to her. He traced the outline of her face, her mouth, with his fingertip. "I want things to be the way they used to be between us." His lips brushed hers gently, yearning. "I want you to love me as much as you did."

"Dillon . . . " She yielded to the kiss, to the sensations coursing through her. She wanted to be held and touched, to thrill to the urgency that sent her heart racing. Hesitantly, her arms circled his neck. She pulled the rubber band from his hair and ran her fingers through the silky, dark strands as they fell about his shoulders.

It was a kiss that made her remember and, at the same time, forget. As his hands moved over her, rough and greedy in his haste to possess, she forgot all the reasons she should end the growing heat between them before it burst into flame. Instead, she remembered how it was to lose herself in another person, to surrender to desire with a shiver and a sigh.

He grasped her hips, pulled her onto his lap.

"I want you, Michael," she whispered.

Lisa's eyes sprang open. Beneath her fingers, Dillon's shoulders tensed. He almost dumped her to the floor in his haste to stand. Then he stared down at her, his face raw with pain.

Lisa touched her lips. "Oh, no!" She reached out to him as he backed toward the door. "Please, Dillon, let me explain—"

The icy look he shot in her direction froze her heart as much as her words.

"Don't say anything." He reached for his coat. "I'm through listening."

Monday morning, Michael glanced at his watch, then reached for the phone. Nan answered on the second ring. "It's me," he said. "I wanted to remind you that I won't be in until sometime after lunch. Should be around one. Mother's plane is due to arrive in about thirty minutes. The kids and I are on our way to pick her up now." And it wasn't a minute too soon, he thought as he hung up the phone. School was out. Today was the first day of the Christmas vacation.

After hustling Kat and Jacob to the car, Michael pulled out of the drive and headed for the airport. Morning sunlight sparkled on scattered patches of snow alongside the highway. More snowfall was due by the weekend. Until then, he'd welcome the brief respite in frosty weather. During the past couple of weeks, slick, slushy streets, along with anxiety-crazed holiday shoppers, had made for unbearable traffic conditions.

The plane arrived on time. Helen O'Conner's smile was ripe with grandmotherly—and motherly—concern when she spotted Michael, Kat, and Jacob amid the scattered crowd of people gathered in the terminal. With a pat to her varnished bubble of frosted hair, she bustled toward them, an oversized, multicolored shoulder bag clutched against her body.

As he welcomed his mother with a hug, Michael felt the burden he'd been carrying around lift a fraction. "Thanks for coming, Mom," he muttered into her ear before ending the embrace.

She took his chin between the thumb and forefinger of one hand as she'd done ever since he was a child. "No need for thanks," she said, scanning his face. "You look tired."

She turned her attention to Kat and Jake. "Just look at these children! They're growing up." In turn, she cupped each of their chins, studying their faces. "Jacob, I swear you'll be as tall as me come summer. And you, Katherine!"

Michael noticed the falter in his mother's smile as she took in Kat's ball cap and the scraggly hair poking out from underneath.

"You've lost a tooth since I last saw you," she finished.

They waited at the luggage claim until her bags appeared. Then they loaded the car and headed for home.

"How long are you gonna stay, Gramma?" Jake asked from the backseat, where he sat alongside Kat.

She grinned back at him, then glanced across at Michael. "As long as you all need me."

Michael heard the suppressed emotion in his mother's voice. To his relief, Kat and Jacob began a conversation of their own, leaving him more comfortable to discuss his plans. "If you could help out until Lisa and I return from Cayman, I'd really appreciate it, Mom. Afterward, I have a feeling things will get back to normal."

Helen cast a quick glance over her shoulder at the children before once again facing Michael. "How can you be so sure?" she asked, her voice guarded. "I swear, son, I don't understand why you even want to take *her* on this trip. *She* doesn't deserve a second chance after what she's done to this family."

"Mom—"

"I'm serious, Michael. A devoted mother and wife would never dream of deserting her family. Why, Billy Prescott's wife, Karla—remember Billy? You went through school together. Well, Karla flew the coop, like Lisa, a couple of years ago. Everybody in town said she was flitting around the nightclubs like a regular bar fly. Billy didn't give *her* a second chance. He found him another, more deserving woman."

Michael had a sudden flashback of a snot-nosed Billy Prescott on his back beneath the swings in second grade, leering up at all the little girls' panties above him. He experienced a twinge of pity for the "deserving" new Mrs. Prescott.

"If we have to discuss this, could we do it later?" He peeked into the rearview mirror. The kids seemed caught up in an alphabet game they often played on family trips. They both searched signs along the roadside for the next letter.

"They're not listening," Helen whispered.

"They pick up on more than you think they do."

"I've seen this coming in Lisa for years, son. She's never taken pride in the beautiful home you've given her."

"That's not true."

"Take my word for it. A woman knows these things. I've grown to love Lisa, but I don't understand her. There's something missing. She's never invested the time and energy to give your house that," she paused, considering, "that sparkle . . . warmth, that makes a house a home.

"Now, when I was Lisa's age," she continued, without missing a beat, "wives were content to take care of their families. Why, I was so busy scrubbing and polishing and cooking when you and your sister were small, I can't imagine having time for a so-called identity crisis. If you ask me, all that is is the politically correct term for selfishness. Family should come first in every woman's life."

"And in every man's. You're right, Mom. Whether you believe it or not, our family always *has* been Lisa's top priority, as well as mine. But I have other interests in my life, and so can she."

Helen pursed her lips.

"Maybe I could've prevented this predicament we're in. When Lisa tried to return to work last year, I should've offered her a lot more than half-hearted words of encouragement."

"I can't understand why you'd defend her. She put her own supposed needs first when she ran off and left you and the children."

Michael stopped at a red light, leaned back against the headrest, and sighed. "I'm not defending Lisa. True, I'm not happy about what she's done. But you have to realize that Lisa's not herself these days." He reached for his ear. "She's . . .

290

well, there's something wrong with her. She's sick
or something."

"Well, in my day, when a mother came down
with an illness, she certainly never considered
abandoning her family."

"Mom—"

"Your Aunt Louise had four children at home
when she was diagnosed with a terrible case of
the shingles. But did she run away from her
responsibilities? No. Louise toughed it out, difficult as it was. And you know, I never once heard
her mention an urge to take off."

The light turned green. Michael proceeded
across the intersection. "Mother, could we—"

"And then there was the time I came down with
walking pneumonia. You couldn't have been
more than six or seven, so your sister was only
about four. . . . "

Michael groaned.

Turning toward him, Helen abruptly stopped
talking. "Is something wrong, dear?"

Sunlight cut through the crisp air and warmed
Lisa's skin as she took an afternoon walk through
the park. She'd driven by Confucius Says earlier.
The restaurant was still closed up and deserted.
She felt more hopeless than ever.

On a bench overlooking a small pond she sat,
lifting her face skyward to welcome the struggling rays overhead.

With Tory's youthful skin, worries over wrinkles
and the threat of skin cancer could be put off for a
few years. *Big mistake,* she scolded herself. *Do it
right this time. I'll buy a hat and start using that
sunscreen lotion in Tory's medicine chest tomorrow.*

Perhaps there were benefits to changing identi-
ties with Tory that she hadn't considered. She'd

traveled this road once before. The last time at twenty, she'd been naive . . . invincible, or so she'd thought. This time, the wisdom of maturity was on her side. *I've been granted a second chance to do all those things I always thought I'd get around to but never did. I know all the pitfalls to sidestep now.*

Lisa sank lower onto the bench, her shoulders sagging. Except for a woman and a little girl walking a floppy-eared puppy on the other side of the water, the section of park where she sat appeared deserted. She watched the pudgy child toss bread onto the ground. Moments later, two brave ducks approached to snatch up the crumbs. The dog yapped with agitation as he pursued the fleeing birds.

Lisa smiled, remembering when, years before, when they'd first married, she and Michael came to this park to feed the ducks. They'd walked, arm in arm, along the trails, chased after each other and tumbled onto the grass like children. Many a lazy Sunday afternoon had been pleasantly passed making out beneath the trees. Back then, they'd rented an old house nearby and the future was full of possibilities.

At various other times in both their lives the park had also provided a certain solace. Lisa recalled a day, three years ago, when she'd found Michael here, staring into the depths of the pond, lost in thought. He'd just received the news of his father's death.

Despite the sunshine, she shivered. Cayman would be warm, she thought, pulling her jacket more snugly around her. There'd be no nipping winter chill to remind her that it was December.

Though she'd never been to the island, she and Michael had vacationed in Cozumel about seven years earlier, and she assumed Cayman would be similar. There'd be palm trees and endless stretches of smooth, sandy beach. Long, leisurely, golden days kissed by a balmy tropical breeze.

Remembering all the clothes she'd bought before their previous trip, Lisa smiled. She hadn't needed half of them. They'd spent most of their time in bathing suits, occasionally pulling on a pair of shorts to shop or eat in a casual café.

In the evenings, they'd passed up the nightlife, choosing, instead, to drag a beach chair to the ocean's edge where they sat together and gazed up at the stars. Warm, frothy waves lapped against their ankles as they dug their toes into the sand. Lulled by the gentle roar of the ocean, they'd often fallen asleep like that . . . her back against Michael's bare chest . . . his arms around her, fingers clasped atop her stomach . . . his chin resting in her hair.

She remembered waking there, sometime later, then walking back to their bungalow to make love with the windows open, the scent of salt air and hibiscus drifting on the breeze, the ceiling fan whirring softly overhead. There'd been a dream-like slowness to their lovemaking, a savoring of every moment, each sensation.

Even now, thinking of Michael's sunburned skin hot and slick beneath her fingers, the way the muscles worked along his shoulders, the consuming intensity in his eyes, Lisa felt a stirring deep inside her. A flicker of warmth that quickly ignited into full-fledged desire.

"Loving you's the best thing I've ever done," Michael had told her. She'd never forgotten those words, the tenderness that swept through her when he said them. She never would.

Kat was conceived on that trip. Would Michael remember as he strolled the beaches with Tory, searching the sand for pearly pink shells or watching crabs scamper away at their approach? Would he continue to sense something was wrong . . . different? Or would the memories seduce him? Would paradise convince both him and Tory that they could work out their problems despite everything?

The sound of someone coughing brought her thoughts back to the present. Several feet away, a man stood at the edge of the pond tossing pebbles across the water, his back to Lisa.

The girl across the way giggled as she watched her puppy stalk the hungry ducks. The noise caused the man to turn and look toward the child, and Lisa had a clear view of his profile. She instantly recognized the strong angular jaw, the determination in his squared-off chin.

The man was Michael.

Chapter Twenty-three

The chubby little girl and her mother jogged behind the cocker spaniel puppy, their laughter carried by the wind. Michael watched until they rounded a corner and disappeared.

Only minutes ago, he'd left his mother with the kids and started off for the office. Somehow, he'd ended up here instead.

Michael coughed, raising a hand to his throat. *Just what I need—a cold on top of everything else.* He could see his mother now, hovering over him, subjecting him to Vicks VapoRub and massive quantities of chicken noodle soup.

Despite the image, or maybe because of it, he grinned. Between visits, he somehow always managed to forget how annoying his mother could be. As much as Michael loved her, sometimes, no matter how often he tried to shoo her off a subject, she came buzzing back for more—

again and again, until, despite himself, he wanted to swat her like a fly and end the aggravation.

He walked beneath a tree and sat, then stared up at the barren gray branches overhead, their limbs reaching toward the winter sky like gnarled old fingers. *I should've stayed away from here.* Vivid, flashing visions of him and Lisa during happier times streaked through his mind like lightning, blinding and sharp.

Why had he defended her to his mother? *Because, dammit, I can't accept the way she's changed. I can't let go.* He wouldn't give up . . . couldn't . . . until he tried one last time, gave what they'd shared one final chance to revive. *It'll work. I'll make it work.*

He wondered if it was a mistake to take her to Cayman. Maybe they should go back to Mexico and attempt to jog her memory with the past experiences they'd shared. Things had been so easy between them during the time they spent there years ago . . . so right.

He recalled carefree, silly conversations about ditching everything and moving to a similar tropical paradise. He'd buy a boat and spend his days taking tourists on diving excursions. She'd make seashell jewelry and sell it on the beach. Their children would go barefoot to school, have bushy, sun-streaked hair, and sport an endless tan.

There were plenty of quiet times, too, long stretches requiring no words. Picturing their thatch-roofed bungalow—the cool, Mexican-tiled floor, the sprawling bed that never seemed to stay made up for very long—Michael smiled. Lisa had been finely tuned to his touch, responding as though she were an instrument custom-made for his hands alone.

A memory formed in his mind. Lisa wearing a bikini top and a long, full, brightly colored Mexican skirt—him stretched out on a lounge chair toasting the sunset. Except for the two of them, the beach was deserted, the other vacationers having scattered to their rooms and various restaurants for dinner. He'd felt drugged almost, as relaxed and content as a hound dog lying in the shade of a tree on a hot summer day.

And Lisa . . . she'd seemed so free. She'd twirled around before him, the skirt fluttering about her ankles, her usually pale shoulders tinted gold by days in the sun. Laughing, she swung one bare leg across his chair and straddled him, face to face, her thighs pressed tight at either side of his hips.

Charmed by the teasing blue twinkle in her eyes, he'd gone still while she slid one hand slowly down his bare chest and belly. Moments later, he realized, to his delight, that she wore nothing beneath the billowing fabric of the skirt that pooled around them.

If she'd felt uneasy over the prospect of being caught making love on a lounge chair on the beach, Lisa never showed it.

Yearning flowed through Michael with the memory, agonizing and delicious.

No, his first impulse was right, he told himself. They should go someplace else. To Cayman, not Mexico. They were starting over—a new beginning, a chance to discover each other again and recapture the feelings he'd neglected these past years. Given the chance, he wouldn't make the same mistake a second time.

Given the chance. What if Lisa didn't let it happen? What if all the memories were lost to her forever? What if getting away, just the two of them, didn't change anything for her and she still wanted to call it quits?

Michael shook off the negative thoughts. She'd come around. This trip was the answer. It had to be. Because, when he got right down to it, it wasn't times like that night on the beach he couldn't stand the thought of living without. What made his gut wrench, left an aching hollowness inside him, was the possibility of losing the day-to-day things. Things that had once seemed small and insignificant. Things that he now realized meant everything. The countless times he voiced a thought and Lisa announced that she'd been thinking the same thing. The baiting gestures and jokes they laughed hysterically over that meant nothing to anyone else but them. The simple, quiet times together, watching old movies or reading the paper in bed on lazy weekend mornings.

He'd made mistakes; Michael knew that. Throughout their marriage—hell, even before.

A time he'd long since forgotten came to mind. A time before they married, when Michael had lied to her. As usual, he'd let his insecurities get the best of him by convincing himself that Lisa would leave him if she knew the truth. The lie had been the impulsive, irrational act of a desperate kid. And even when Lisa called him on it, he'd done his best to avoid the confrontation, to pretend that everything was as it should be between them.

Standing, Michael brushed dead grass from the seat of his pants. He knew he'd better get back to the office before Nan called the cavalry to track him down.

If something he couldn't put his finger on hadn't enticed him to look over his shoulder for one last scan of the park, he never would've spotted her. Never would've known she'd been watching him.

Tory sat on a bench several yards away, her head turned in his direction. She hugged a jacket close about her body, and even across the distance, Michael noticed the sickly pallor of her skin, the dusky shadows bordering her eyes. When her gaze met his she stood, squaring her shoulders proudly, almost defensively. She lifted her chin as if to say that she refused to be humiliated by their last meeting.

A confused mix of emotions churned inside him. Anger over the possibility that she'd followed him here, admiration of her pride, worry about the fact that she looked ill. And then, there was something else, too. A quickening of his pulse. A sudden urge to cross the space between them and hold Tory close, feel her length pressed against his.

Why couldn't he stop these feelings from stealing over him whenever he saw her? Michael wondered, hating himself for not having better control. How could he love his wife so much and also love Tory?

Half tempted to turn and walk away, to leave and escape a confrontation, Michael stood motionless and stared.

He wouldn't run away. He'd face Tory . . . and himself.

Moments later, Michael crammed his fists into the pockets of his jacket as he stood facing Tory.

"You think I followed you here, don't you?" she asked.

When he didn't answer, she continued, "Well, I didn't. I used to spend a lot of time at this park with someone I loved very much. Someone I still love."

"So did I. A long time ago." He scanned the desolate surroundings and felt a terrible pang of sorrow, as if he was saying good-bye to a dear old friend, an integral part of his soul. "Right now, it seems like another lifetime."

She nodded and bit her lip, her face disturbingly white. "I know what you mean."

Michael glanced down at the brown grass, then lifted his gaze to hers. "About the other night—"

She held out her hand. "Don't worry. I won't bring it up again. I'm through with all that."

Michael was through with it, too. He'd lost sleep trying to figure out how Tory could know what she did about his family without Lisa having betrayed his confidence. But he wouldn't ask her now. He couldn't bear another conversation about souls and bodies trading places.

"I want you to know something," he said. "Maybe it was silly, what you did . . . what you told me, but I think I understand your motives."

He searched the sky, as though there were answers in the clouds. "Sometimes," he said, "you want something so badly that you'll do anything to get it, or to keep it, whatever the case may be. And it doesn't matter what anyone thinks, if they tell you that you're nuts, if they laugh or turn away in disgust. Because if you could only grasp hold of that one thing, you'd hang on tight and never let go. Nothing else matters."

When he looked at her again, a single tear had started down her cheek.

"You're not just talking about me and the story I told you," she said. "You're talking about yourself. About Lisa."

"I love her." Michael lifted his shoulders. "Before, I would've said it wasn't possible for a man to love two women. Since you came along, I know that's not true."

He stooped to pick up a rock, turned, and tossed it toward the water. How could he explain what he didn't understand himself? There were times when he almost believed Tory's insane fable. In many ways, she actually seemed more like Lisa than Lisa did herself.

He couldn't deny his feelings for Tory. God knew he'd tried. But shouldn't she claim a separate part of his heart than his wife did? The simple, confusing truth was, they seemed to share the same space, as though they were one and the same person.

"I know it was harsh of me to fire you, but I would've had to do it eventually anyway. Your story about being Lisa only provided me with an excuse." An uncomfortable pressure built at the back of Michael's eyes. He wanted to touch her so badly he almost couldn't stand it. "You're better off not seeing me again. I'd only end up hurting you worse if you stayed."

"You'd never hurt anyone," she whispered. "Why are you really afraid to be near me, Michael? What is it you're afraid you'll say?" Her voice sounded hurt, confused. "That if I stayed around, you'd always blame me for enticing you? That you'd never be able to forgive yourself for being a middle-aged man in love with a younger woman, a woman with a younger, more appealing face and body than your wife's?"

He took a step toward her. "If I were a blind man, I'd still fall in love with you. And that's exactly why I would only end up hurting you. Because this has nothing to do with your face or your body. I'm afraid it doesn't have anything to do with you at all. It has to do with Lisa, don't you see that? It's like I'm falling in love with *her* all over again *through* you. You're like her in so

301

many ways. Your mannerisms, the things you say, the way you make me feel when we're together. But you're different, too. You're like Lisa could have been if I'd opened up to her. If I'd given her the support and encouragement she needed . . . if only I'd let her—"

"No, Michael." Her voice was firm, thick with emotion. "If only *she* would've let *herself*. You mentioned roadblocks once, remember? About Lisa being too cautious at times?" When he nodded, she continued, "Lisa set up her own roadblocks."

"Maybe we both did." Michael's chest felt too heavy for him to breathe. The last thing he wanted to do was hurt Tory. But there seemed no way past it. "Lisa and I have a history," he said. "I can't turn away from our past and forget it all, though God knows it seems like it might be easier than trying to win her back."

Somehow, he managed to smile. "I'm not a quitter. I won't give up without a fight. Whatever it takes, I want Lisa back in my life. If there's a way, I'll find it. I'll compromise, make whatever changes need to be made to right the wrong between us."

Lisa's heart turned over. It took every ounce of self-control she could muster not to reach out and touch him one last time, feel the stubble on his chin beneath her fingertips, smooth those unruly tufts of auburn hair into place as she'd done without thinking a thousand times before. She needed to cry, but her well of tears had been emptied by recent events. "You might not believe this, but I'm proud to hear you say that, Michael. I fell in love with a wonderful man. The best."

"You'll get over this," Michael said. "Some lucky guy will come into your life before you know it. Or the boyfriend who sent you those flowers at the office—you'll realize what a mistake you made breaking off with him. One day the two of you will laugh over the crush you had on an older man."

"Don't—"

"I'm sorry. I shouldn't have said that."

Lisa stared into Michael's eyes. "Good-bye, Michael," she whispered.

It took only two strides for him to cross the distance between them. Michael crushed her against him . . . then quickly let her go.

Chapter Twenty-four

"I don't think she likes me very much."

Michael followed his wife's scowl to the kitchen, where his mother twittered about like a nervous sparrow preparing a nest for her young.

"You know my mother." He pulled a tissue from his pocket and sneezed into it. "It's just her way. Her intentions are good."

"You mean I *knew* your mother. Now I, like, don't have a clue how to handle the woman."

More than slightly exasperated by Lisa's defeated tone, Michael reached for her elbow. He led her into the den, where Jake and Kat scrutinized the haul they'd raked in after opening presents earlier that morning. "Relax and let Mom take charge. She's in her element, believe me."

"Are you sure? I mean, this is supposed to be my house and everything. She's the guest and I'm the hostess. Shouldn't *she* be the one relaxing? I feel so inadequate."

"She knows you're having some problems. She understands. And not only does she like you, Lisa, she loves you and always has."

"Then why is it that every time she smiles at me it looks more like a snarl?"

Lisa sounded like she might cry at any minute. Michael wasn't sure he could handle another outbreak of hysteria. He had a desperate urge to crawl back into bed, pull the covers over his head, and hide out for the rest of the day. Maybe longer.

Why did he expect this to be like every other Christmas? So what if it was Lisa's favorite holiday? Was that any reason for him to assume that she might give him a glimpse of her old self?

In the middle of the room Jake sat on his new mountain bike, a helmet on his head. "This bike is totally awesome! Thanks, Mom! I can't believe you got the exact one I wanted. You said it was too expensive when I showed it to you at the store after Thanksgiving." He grinned. "You were foolin' me so I'd think I wouldn't get it, right?"

Not waiting for an answer, Jake climbed down and started playing with Kat. Michael was glad his son didn't know it was Tory, not Lisa, who had picked out his bicycle. Pretty amazing that she'd chosen exactly the one he wanted. A little spooky, too.

He turned his attention to Lisa, hoping to shut out thoughts of Tory and the realization that he missed her. As always, Lisa looked beautiful to him, but even more so today. She'd lost weight, and beneath the hem of the skirt she wore, her calves appeared more shapely, almost muscular. The result of all her exercise, he guessed. Color bloomed in her cheeks and, for the first time in weeks, he noticed a lively light in her eyes. Obviously, working at the restaurant agreed with Lisa. Or maybe it was more than work, he thought with a touch of resentment. Maybe she enjoyed being on her own.

"You'd think I'd remember all this," she said, scanning the room, the kids' faces. "This kind of Christmas, I mean . . . it seems like I've never experienced one quite like it. Everything smells so good. And Kat and Jacob . . . seeing them so excited when they opened their gifts." She shrugged. "I was, like, so warm inside and everything. That sounds goofy, doesn't it?"

Hope swelled in Michael's heart, and he prayed it was justified. Grasping Lisa's shoulders, he searched her eyes. "Does this mean you'll leave with me day after tomorrow? You'll take the trip?"

She hesitated only a moment. "Yes."

Lisa fumbled with the clock several seconds before realizing that the phone had awakened her instead of the alarm. "Hello," she mumbled into the receiver.

"Merry Christmas!"

It was Val. "Ho, ho, ho," Lisa said.

"Really now, Lisa. Today of all days, you've got to snap out of this funk you're in. I can't stand the thought of you spending Christmas alone. Please come to my folks' house, at least for dinner. Mom and Pop would love to have you."

"Thanks, Val, but I can't face anyone today. I'd rather be by myself." *Who am I kidding? I want to be with Michael, Kat, and Jake. I want my family*.

"Besides," Lisa continued, surprised at the calm tone of her own voice, "how do you know your parents would love to have me? They've never met Tory." The silence from the other end of the line told Lisa that Val hadn't considered how she'd explain her new twenty-year-old best friend to her parents.

"You're the same person you've always been on the inside," Val finally said. "They loved you as Lisa, and they'll feel the same no matter who you've become."

"Thanks, but I'll be okay. I promise. You go on and have a good time. Drink an eggnog for me."

Val sighed. "What about Dillon?"

"I haven't heard a word from him since he walked out of here angry the other night after I called him Michael. He ignores me at work."

"Poor guy."

"Maybe it's just as well."

"Are you sure you won't change your mind? Really, you're just being stubborn. Why don't I pick you up on my way out of town?"

Lisa rolled to her side and hugged the pillow. She thought of the long, empty hours ahead. The cold, barren apartment. The deafening silence.

Then she imagined the Potters' old farmhouse decked out in full holiday splendor. They lived in a small town less than an hour away.

With a huge amount of embarrassment and more than a little bit of sentimentality, Val had described her family's typical Christmas scene to her often enough. The gigantic tree adorned with twinkling white lights and homemade ornaments Val and her five siblings had made themselves throughout their childhood years. A table set for twenty with a banquet of food that swirled tantalizing aromas of turkey and spice through the air. And then, near the end of the festivities, Val's mother picking away on the piano while her father sang "Winter Wonderland" in a booming baritone.

Lisa was tempted, but . . . "No thanks," she finally answered. *It would be worse than being lonely. I'd only miss my own home all the more.*

"I'll worry about you all day," Val said. "I'll call you later, okay?"

"You're a great friend. I'd be lost without you." Lisa hung up.

She forced herself to climb out of bed. She showered and dressed. After a quick breakfast of cold cereal and orange juice, she opened the front door to leave the apartment, almost tripping over the package that sat at her feet on top of the welcome mat.

The large, flat box was covered in shiny green paper and topped with a big red bow. Lisa had never been one to waste time when it came to opening presents. She saw no reason to start now.

Inside, she found a framed collage of photographs—Tory and Dillon dressed in hiking garb, sitting on a cabin porch somewhere in the mountains. Tory and Dillon wearing formal attire, standing among a group of other young couples. Tory and Dillon close-up and cheek to cheek, eyes crossed and tongues sticking out.

There were more, lots more, and Lisa scanned them all before removing the note that was taped to the frame's edge and reading the message.

Are you willing to end all of this? It's up to you, Tory—our baby's future, our future. But I won't share you with anyone. It has to be me and ONLY me you want to spend your life with. You decide. Merry Christmas. Dillon.

Weary, Lisa placed the collage inside the apartment, locked up, then trudged through a fresh blanket of snow toward the Volkswagen.

Other than a few other bedraggled souls with nowhere to belong on Christmas morning, the frosty streets were deserted. *There are hundreds of people worse off than me today. I'll go to the homeless shelter and volunteer. I'll do something worthwhile instead of embarking on a pity trip.*

But before she knew it, she had turned onto her old street. She stopped at the end of the block, staring at her house. The van was parked in the driveway, which meant that Tory was inside. And Helen, Michael's mother, had surely arrived by now. Lisa recalled Tory's lack of finesse in the kitchen, then thought what a perfectionist her mother-in-law was in that domain. *Good grief. I wonder how those two will get along?*

She almost giggled over the imagined scenario but couldn't when another realization crossed her mind. *Day after tomorrow Michael and Tory will probably leave town together. And more than likely they'll come home married in every sense of the word.*

Closing her eyes, she tried to imagine her future. A future without her children. A future without the security of knowing she and Michael would be together through thick and thin. She would miss his sense of humor, which used to coax a laugh from her even in the most tense of situations. She would miss the solid feel of his body beside her at night.

These past weeks as Tory, she'd seen a new side of him, felt new feelings for him . . . stronger ones than she'd ever felt before. Being Tory had made her more assertive. Michael had responded to that trait in her by opening up with his feelings, by sharing bits of what he carried around inside his heart and head. They'd finally discovered the emotional intimacy she'd craved, and now she'd have to learn to live without it.

Unsure if fear or the pregnancy caused her sudden dizziness, Lisa gripped the steering wheel. *Accept it. Tory's Michael's wife now. There's nothing you can do about it.*

And then she heard Michael's voice in her mind, as clear and distinct as if he was sitting beside her.

"I'm not a quitter. I won't give up without a fight. Whatever it takes, I want Lisa back in my life. If there's a way, I'll find it."

"No, you're not a quitter, Michael," Lisa muttered aloud. "I never thought I was either, but maybe that's all I am."

She studied her house for a long time, the oak tree in the yard, the curving walkway leading from the sidewalk to the porch. She pictured every room on the inside, then imagined each member of her family celebrating behind those walls.

The kids had opened their gifts by now. She wondered if they liked everything, if Jake was surprised by the bicycle she'd impulsively splurged Michael's money on.

Could she turn her back and leave it all behind? Tuck Michael, Kat, and Jake away in the attic of her mind like treasured mementos from the past, to be taken out from time to time in years to come, dusted off, reminisced over? Could she really begin a new life with Dillon?

She remembered the hockey game—the heady exhilaration of facing her fear head on and skating down that arena. The dizzying, momentary thrill of scoring was well worth the later humiliation of finding out it was the opposing team's goal. In fact, the humiliation hadn't bothered her much at all. Because she'd stepped beyond her comfort zone, as Val would say, and tried. Maybe that was the ultimate victory.

Lisa started the ignition and put the car in gear. "I am not a quitter," she said, pulling away from the curb, a fierce determination lifting her spirit. "I'm a fighter. Like you are, Michael."

Chapter Twenty-five

"Are you *absolutely sure* you want to change back?" Sprawled in the middle of the living-room floor on the blue beanbag, Val scrutinized Dillon's Christmas gift to Tory. "I wasn't completely aware of all the fringe benefits that go along with being Tory Beecham."

Lisa scowled. "How can you even ask such a thing? Of course I'm sure."

Yesterday, after spending several hours serving Christmas dinner to homeless people at the community shelter, Lisa had called Val and asked her to come over when she returned to the city. This evening, Val arrived at supper time toting Chinese take-out and a large bag of chocolate candy. Food for thought, she'd explained.

"This kid is *gorgeous*." Val tapped her finger against Dillon's photo. "If I were in your shoes, I'm not sure I could pass up the chance to . . . to—"

"Sleep with him?"

"You said it, I didn't. Really, Lisa, it's not as if it would be your body. It's Tory's. And it wouldn't be the first time. They made a baby together, you know."

"Of course I know," Lisa snapped. She placed a palm against her middle. "Who's in a better position to know than me? With the exception of Dillon and Tory, that is. And she doesn't even really know because . . . let's not get into all that again."

She waved a hand in the air and sank deeper into her own beanbag. "Besides, my body or not, it would be me experiencing the whole thing."

"Exactly. Which makes it so perfect. You get all the fun without any of the guilt."

Lisa chose a chocolate kiss from several scattered across the carpet and popped it into her mouth. "If that's not a contrived excuse for cheating, I don't know what is. Anyway, there are certain things a lot more important than a stolen moment of so-called fun."

"Easy for you to say. You don't have the sex life of a nun."

Lisa laughed. "I'll fit into that category soon enough if we don't work out this situation."

Val arched a brow and grinned. "Don't tell me you don't find Dillon the least bit appealing?"

Lisa squared her shoulders; then, despite herself, bit her lower lip and winced.

"I knew it!" Val squealed. "You were tempted!"

"I didn't say that. And even if I was, so what? Yes, I think Dillon is attractive. And he's a nice guy, too. I appreciate that as much as any woman. I'm only human. But, attraction doesn't get people in trouble; acting on it does. And I haven't."

"I'm only kidding," Val said. "I know how you feel about Michael. I'd give my eyeteeth for what the two of you have."

Val looked back at the photos and sighed. "Well, since you dumped him, Dillon probably needs the attention of a nice, single, *mature* woman. You know, a woman who's been through it all before. One who can lovingly mend the pieces of his broken heart."

"Pardon me while I puke." Lisa tossed another chocolate into her mouth, then returned her attention to the three crumpled fortunes on the floor in front of her. "Now back to business. What did I misinterpret?"

"Not so fast. There are other things to consider, here. If you change back, you'll be giving up more than Dillon."

Following Val's teasing gaze, Lisa lowered her chin to her chest. "You mean these?" She pointed toward her breasts and sneered. "You can have 'em."

"What? This from the woman who went in halvsies with me on the cost of a Mark Eden bust developer when we were eighteen?"

"They look good, but mostly they just get in the way. It's too uncomfortable to lay on my stomach, and I can't get a good night's sleep on my back. And speaking of my back, it aches half the time. Then there's running. Believe me, it's a whole new experience." She giggled and shrugged. "In my opinion, they're not all they're hyped up to be."

Looking amazed, Val stared at Lisa's bosom, her fingertips drumming on the floor. "I would never have believed it. Just think, if not for this predicament you're in, I might've spent the rest of my life yearning for cleavage."

"I wish I could say it's been worth all the trouble to find out that enlightening bit of information." Lisa glanced at her watch. "It's almost midnight! We've been at this for hours and we're not any closer to solving my problem than when we started."

Michael snuggled up to the pillow he'd positioned lengthways beside him and closed his eyes. Seconds passed. He wrapped one arm around the feather-filled cushion, then lifted one knee, only to find there was nothing to sling it across.

He rolled to his back to stare, disgruntled, toward the ceiling. *Face it. A lifeless bag of fluff is no substitute for a live body.* He wiggled his toes. His feet felt like two solid blocks of ice without Lisa's legs to warm them against.

Uttering an oath, Michael sat up, sneezed, then glanced at the clock. *Midnight.* Head cold or not, in nine more hours they'd be on the airplane, taxiing down the runway, headed for Cayman and a fresh start. And, hopefully, an end to sleeping alone.

He fumbled through the darkness for the lamp and switched it on, resigning himself to the fact that he wasn't the least bit sleepy. He made his way toward the kitchen. Despite all the food he'd consumed yesterday and today, nervous energy insisted he eat.

Thanks to his mom, the kitchen was spotless. When he pulled open the refrigerator door, light spilled into the darkened room. The shelves were loaded with leftovers from Christmas dinner. The bowl of grapes perched atop a plastic-covered dish of candied sweet potatoes seemed just the thing. He grabbed the bowl, returned to his room, then plopped down on the bed.

Grapes. Looking at the fruit zapped him back in time to an office party long before he'd started his own firm. Lisa wore the same Mexican skirt she'd worn the night they made love on the beach in Cozumel. It was summer, and after the party they drove home with the windows down, both of them relaxed and giddy, laughing over everything and nothing.

The children were sleeping peacefully when they arrived. Michael paid the baby-sitter and sent her on her way, then settled himself on the couch to wind down before going to bed. Lisa sat at the opposite end facing him, her legs stretched out, bare feet resting in his lap.

The kids had left a bowl of grapes on the coffee table. Michael sampled one and found it crisp and cool, deliciously sweet. On impulse, he plucked another from the bunch and placed it between two of Lisa's toes. "I've always wanted to do this," he said, sending her a sly smile while lifting her foot toward his mouth.

Lisa giggled. "What are you doing?"

Michael sucked the grape into his mouth, pleased by Lisa's startled gasp when his tongue touched her skin. After a moment, he pulled away and bit into the fruit, never releasing her ankle. "Having dessert," he mumbled in answer to her question.

"You had plenty to eat at the party." She crumpled with laughter again. "That tickles!"

"They didn't serve anything half this good."

"You're crazy."

"About you." He grinned as her other foot began a slow creep up the inside of his thigh.

Watching her, Michael picked another grape and repeated the process. They were painted bright red—Lisa's toenails, not the grapes. The grapes were pale green. And succulent. Sticky juice trickled over the arch of her foot and down toward her ankle. That part drove Lisa crazy, he knew, because they'd never made it from the couch to the bedroom. As for him . . .

Michael groaned. There was something about that skirt. He picked up the telephone receiver and punched in Lisa's number. The reason why she'd insisted on spending tonight at her apartment evaded him. Because of her newfound, overwhelming need for independence, he'd have to rise at least an hour earlier to make it to the airport on time. At this point, he wasn't about to press the matter. At least she had agreed to go on the trip.

"Hello?"

Her voice sounded gritty. Obviously, *she* wasn't having any trouble getting *him* off her mind. "Were you asleep?"

"Dillon? Is that you?"

Michael suddenly felt sick. "Who's Dillon?"

She yawned. "Dillon who?"

"You called me Dillon."

"I did? That's weird." Another yawn. "Dillon Todd is one of the bartenders at The Club. Why would I think he'd be calling?"

"You tell me."

"Is something wrong, Michael? Are the kids okay?"

"They're fine," he snapped. A long silence followed while Michael fumed over Lisa's current stab to his pride with a dull knife. Did she get some morbid sense of satisfaction in drawing out the mangling of his ego? If he had a choice in the matter, he'd prefer a quick, clean slice.

She cleared her throat. "Well?"

"Well what?"

"Why did you call?"

317

Michael sneered at the receiver. "I was excited about tomorrow. Silly of me to think you might be, too."

"I'm sorry. Of course I'm excited! I'm just so tired. I mean, yesterday was something else! But it wore me out. My eyes feel like sandpaper."

"Twenty straight games of Nintendo will do that to a person."

"Could you believe those scores?"

"Amazing." Recalling Lisa's obsession with an activity she'd never once given a damn about before, Michael frowned. "You used to hate to play video games. Kat and Jake would beg you to challenge them. The few times you obliged, your scores were so pitiful, they felt sorry for you and quit asking."

"Well, they're pretty impressed with me now." She laughed. "I had a blast with those two." After a short hesitation, she quickly added, "With all of you, I mean."

Michael chose to ignore her oversight. After she'd finally adapted to his mother, Lisa did seem to enjoy Christmas. When he stopped to consider her behavior, he realized that she'd acted like a wide-eyed child who'd never participated in the traditional celebration.

What pleased him more than anything was her obvious delight in Kat's and Jacob's excitement. Her satisfaction in spending time around them had been sincere, he was sure of it. In that respect, she was more like the Lisa he'd known before this strange affliction transformed her personality. Maybe Christmas had been the first step toward recovery. Tomorrow, he hoped, she'd take step two.

Michael softened. He stared down at the bowl of grapes. "Lisa . . . um, did you by chance happen to pack a long, multicolored skirt? You bought it when we were in Mexico."

"I don't think so. I might've, like, left it at the house or something when I moved out. Why?"

Michael reached for his earlobe and tugged. "Do grapes mean anything to you?"

"Grapes? You mean, the fruit?"

"Yes."

"Not really. Should they?"

He lifted the bowl, then lowered it to the floor out of his sight. "Forget it. I—" He broke off with a low sigh. "We loved having you here yesterday. All of us. Especially me. I miss you."

The following silence pressed a suffocating weight on his chest. What was Lisa thinking? Was he pushing too hard? Would she change her mind about the trip?

"I'm lonely, Michael," she finally said, a catch in her voice.

The weight lifted. Relief made him dizzy. Michael leaned against the headboard to steady himself. "I know what you mean. Even with Mom and the kids around, the house feels empty. *I* feel empty. Hollow inside. There's something missing. That something is you."

The gentle sobs coming from the other end of the line weren't lost on him. He pushed aside the pillow occupying Lisa's half of the bed and smoothed the cold sheets with his palm. "See you bright and early in the morning?"

"I'll be here." She sniffed. "And Michael?"

"Yes?"

"I can't wait. I really can't."

Lisa awoke with a start. Pearly gray light filtered through the slats of the miniblinds. The vinyl covering on the beanbag chair stuck to her cheek. She sat up and stretched.

A few feet away, Val slept on the food-cluttered floor, curled into the fetal position. Lisa pushed aside Chinese take-out cartons and candy wrappers as she crawled across the carpet toward her friend. "Wake up!" she said, shaking Val's shoulder. She glanced at the kitchen clock. "It's eight."

Val opened one bleary eye. With a moan, she rolled face first into her own beanbag. "Give me a break." She lifted her head and squinted at Lisa. "We've only had about four hours of sleep."

"Michael's plane leaves in an hour. If we don't think of something fast, my life's over." Panicked, Lisa stood and began to pace. Her head felt strangely disconnected from her body. Bright pinpoints of light appeared before her eyes and a cold, clammy sweat coated her skin. Legs buckling, she lowered to the floor and placed her head between her knees.

"Are you okay?"

"I guess I stood up too fast. I need something to eat."

"Crackers, right? Pregnant women always want crackers in the morning."

Lisa swept a hand around the room, indicating the scattered remnants of their binge. "After all we ate last night, what I'm really craving is something light. Like grapes."

"Grapes?"

"Exactly." Lisa looked up suddenly, her eyebrows drawing together in dismay. "Oh, God. What if Michael did something like the grape thing with Tory? I couldn't stand it."

"Grape thing?"

She lifted her index finger to her mouth. "He wouldn't. It was only once, anyway. Even if he did, Tory might be totally turned off. It was fun until all that sticky juice started running down my foot." She shuddered. "Of course, I'd never tell Michael that. He seemed to get such a kick out of the whole thing."

"What on earth are you babbling about?"

Heat rose to Lisa's cheeks when she focused on Val's bewildered face. "Never mind."

"Something tells me there's an entire side to your husband I never imagined existed. You, too, for that matter."

Ignoring the comment, Lisa checked the time again. "I have to think!" She propped both elbows on her knees, then covered her face with her hands.

"Wait a minute," Val said. Lisa lifted her head to find Val searching a white cardboard container. She produced a handful of crunchy noodles and shoved them at Lisa. "Eat these."

Lisa went still inside. "Where did you get this Chinese food?" She grabbed the carton and examined it.

"The food? I don't know. I dropped by my office when I got back into town yesterday. My secretary was working. She placed the order and picked it up for me. You don't think—"

"I think this is the Confucius Says logo," Lisa interrupted, her gaze riveted on the carton. "I've been driving by every day to see if they're back, but I didn't go by Christmas Day, and yesterday I was so depressed, I forgot to check."

Val pulled a fortune cookie from another container and handed it to Lisa. "Look."

Lisa brushed a finger across it, as though the cookie was fragile and precious and might crumble beneath her touch. Then she cracked the wafer in half. With trembling hands, she unfolded the tiny scrap of paper inside and read the message aloud.

"You are not yourself. Your life is in turmoil."

She tossed the paper to the floor. "Tell me something I don't know. Who writes those things anyway?"

"Calm down." Val's bare foot began a rapid, tapping cadence against the carpet. "What time do you think Confucius Says would open?"

"I don't know. Around eleven, I'd guess."

"But some of the employees would be there sooner, wouldn't they? To get everything ready before they open up the place?"

Lisa's heart pummeled the wall of her chest. "Let's go. I'll sit in the parking lot all morning if I have to, until someone shows up."

Val stood and looked around the apartment. "Where's my purse? I don't suppose you'll let me brush my teeth before we leave?" She scrunched up her face. "My mouth tastes like an ashtray."

"There's no time."

A blast of cold air greeted them as they headed out the door. "The plane," Val said. "You know it's too late to stop Michael and Tory from leaving, don't you?"

Lisa walked in determined strides past Tory's Volkswagen toward Val's car. "Don't worry. I have another idea. I'll call Jarrod. He's a pilot. He has his own plane."

Chapter Twenty-six

" 'You are much wiser than your years.' " Lisa tossed the slip of paper onto the table, where it joined the other rejects. "That's number ten and still no luck."

"Order some more." During the previous night, Val's normally well-groomed bob had been transformed into sleep hair. She dipped two fingers into a glass of water, then pressed them against a tuft that stuck straight out from her forehead like a unicorn's horn.

Undeterred by her own disheveled coiffure, Lisa motioned toward the waitress standing behind the counter up front. The young woman had eyed them suspiciously ever since they arrived and Lisa inquired about the elderly Chinese man. The waitress identified him as the restaurant's owner. She told them he wasn't in yet. She didn't know exactly when he'd arrive.

Now, at Lisa's signal, the waitress approached their table, her glossy black hair swaying gracefully about her shoulders.

"More cookies?" she asked.

"Yes. Ten more, please. I really appreciate you letting us do this even though you aren't officially open yet."

"You are more than welcome." The girl blinked, a perplexed wrinkle creasing the porcelain skin between her eyebrows. "I hope you find what you are looking for."

Lisa smiled. "Me, too."

The waitress left, and Lisa turned to Val. "We're wasting our time with these cookies. I need to talk to the owner." She checked her watch. "Surely he'll be here soon."

Moments later, the waitress returned with a small plastic tray stacked with golden crescent-shaped cookies. She placed them on the table between Lisa and Val.

Val sat back and lit a cigarette. "How do you know we're wasting our time? The cookies started the whole thing. You might find your answer in one of them. It's worth a try while we wait."

Val smoked her cigarette down to the filter while Lisa broke open wafer after wafer and read each message aloud.

" 'You will be blessed with children.' 'The road you travel is filled with surprises.' 'You are wiser than your years.' " Lisa tossed aside slip number ten and pounded the table with her fist. "This is useless. Where is that man? He has the answers, not these damn cookies."

"Relax," Val said. "I'll buy every cookie in the restaurant if necessary. If there isn't a clue in any of them, *then* you can fret over the owner. I'll even fret with you."

As reassuring as Val sounded, Lisa sensed her underlying nervousness. Without the usual excuses, Val had started smoking the minute they left the apartment. She'd been at it ever since, chewing gum at the same time.

Val ordered cookies by the bagful, offering double the usual cost so there'd be no complaints about deleting the supply.

Lisa cracked open another one and pulled the white scrap from inside. " 'Accept what you cannot change.' Just what I wanted to hear."

She read message after message. Each and every word seemed to solidify her destiny to live the remaining years of her life as Tory Beecham. She had no idea how much time had passed when she finally balanced the restaurant's last wafer on her palm. "If this doesn't contain my salvation, I'm tempted to give up."

Val flicked her Bic, then held the flame against the quivering tip of a fresh cigarette. "You don't mean that."

The tabletop in front of Lisa was hidden beneath golden piles of discarded cookies. Cookies littered the booth on both sides of her hips. Several lay scattered on the floor at her feet.

A busboy came by and swept the rejects on the floor away with a broom, his questioning eyes sweeping Val and Lisa at the same time.

"Maybe I do mean it," Lisa said. "I haven't found any answers here." She nodded at the departing busboy. "They won't tell me how to contact the owner, and I'm beginning to think he's not coming in today. Michael and Tory are on their way to the Cayman Islands as we speak." She sighed. "Maybe a life sentence in someone else's body is my punishment."

"For what?"

She closed her hand around the cookie. "When Michael and I married," she said, her voice contemplative, "I listened to some of my friends who'd tied the knot before us moan about their marriages. You would've thought their husbands were the enemy rather than men they'd chosen to spend life with. Still, I knew they must've been crazy about them once. Why else would they have married? I wondered why, if the relationship was unsalvageable, they didn't get out? Life's too short to spend it in misery.

"I promised myself, then and there," she continued, "I'd never let Michael and I become two people who shared an address, a past, and nothing more. What could be worse than our love for each other becoming contempt?"

Val exhaled a fragrant stream of smoke. "What are you saying? That you broke your promise? I don't believe it for a minute. Really, Lisa, anyone with eyes can see how perfect you and Michael are together. Even after all this time."

Lisa waved the smoke away. "These past few years changed everything. The kids are older and more independent. Michael and Jarrod opened their own firm. He's preoccupied and overly busy, and I'm floundering . . . wondering what to do with the rest of my life. I guess I resented him a little."

She lifted her eyes to Val's. "Okay, I resented him a lot. I don't know if you can understand this, since you don't have children of your own."

"Try me."

"I love them more than anything. They're the best thing that ever happened to me. But even so, sometimes I find it annoying as hell that Michael's plans for his life and career stayed right on schedule after they were born, while mine . . . "

"I thought that was your choice. I thought you wanted to stay home and devote full-time to raising your children while they were small."

"I did. And I don't regret it for an instant."

"You're contradicting yourself."

"Motherhood is so confusing. It's wonderful and fulfilling. And it's the most frustrating guilt trip I've ever traveled. If I go back to work, I worry I won't have enough time to devote to Kat and Jake. But if I stay home, I feel that I haven't made the most of my own talents."

Lisa laughed. "Pretty silly, right? What's with our generation of women? We think we're obligated to do it all now, don't we? Isn't there a small part of you, deep inside, that insists you're cheating by not having children?"

Val's expression turned sheepish. "How did you know?"

"Because I feel the same way about a career. I can't figure out how to climb back on the ladder. I've been off too long. I'm afraid, Val."

"Have you told Michael how you feel?"

"No. That's the problem. I shut him out on this just like he shuts me out when it comes to his feelings. I tried to muddle through it alone and ended up so exasperated, I started to turn into one of those women I swore, years ago, I'd never become. Now I'm paying the penalty. And so is my family."

She opened her hand and stared at the cookie, afraid to open it, afraid not to. "You know what, Val? I know Michael has always loved me, but I sometimes wonder if he *likes* me. Before all this happened I wasn't sure he even *saw* me anymore. I doubt seriously he even suspected any discontent on my part before this switch occurred. I want Michael to like me, Val. I want him to like me *and* love me."

Val stubbed out her cigarette. "I know what you mean. I went through the same thing with Ray."

"Maybe turning into Tory was a good thing," Lisa continued, her eyes on the cookie in her hand. "Something I never expected came out of it. Something wonderful."

"Such as?"

"I discovered *I* like *Michael*, whether he likes me or not. And I love him—I'm not only talking about old emotions." She pressed a palm to her heart. "Those are still here, but I have new feelings for him, too. Stronger feelings than I've ever felt before." Looking up, Lisa smiled. "I can't stop thinking about him. The way he looks and smells. Things he does and says."

She thought of Michael's down-on-his-luck client and the velvet Elvis. She remembered what he'd told her about why he became a lawyer, the advice he'd given her to follow her dream. "Michael talks to me as Tory. There's an entire side of him I never knew existed. A more soft-hearted one. A more sentimental and emotional one. I *think* he likes me, too, Val." She tapped her chest with her forefinger. "The person inside this body . . . the person I really am. It's a shame I had to jump inside someone else to find that out."

When Lisa lowered her hand to the table, Val covered it with her own. "I haven't seen you this intense . . . this *passionate* since you fell in love with Michael the first time."

"I know." She shook her head. "What if I can't break the spell? What if I lose him now, when I've only just found him again?"

"I don't know what to tell you. I wish I did."

"Stick with me, Val. You're all I have." Lisa clasped the last cookie between the fingers of both hands and gently pressed. It snapped in two.

"Well, this is it." Desperation escalated the beat of her heart and her fingers moved faster to retrieve the paper inside. Once it was freed, Lisa almost ripped it in her haste to smooth the slip and read the words inside.

"Speak what is in your heart to the one you love. The truth will set you free."

Goose bumps scattered across Lisa's skin. She shuddered and looked up. *Snowflakes.* She could have sworn she'd felt them fluttering about her. But the air was clear.

"He's here," Lisa whispered, her eyes darting toward the restaurant entrance.

The old man stood in the doorway watching her, his gaze steady and sure. After a moment, he shuffled toward their table, and Lisa noticed that he was small and sturdy. Not much taller than Jacob.

When he reached her side, he stopped.

"The fortune . . . " Lisa said. "It says basically the same thing as the one before. I told Michael the truth. I told him that I'm Lisa."

His wise, ancient eyes drew her into a place where no one and nothing else existed. Everything suddenly seemed clear and remarkably simple. Comprehension dawned like a brilliant sun, burning away the fog in her mind, the desperation in her heart.

Lisa lowered her gaze to the tiny slip in her hand. *Speak what is in your heart to the one you love.*

Why hadn't she understood before? Why had it been necessary for him to spell it all out for her? She looked up at Val. "The truth that's in my heart," she said, smiling with relief. "I had the answer all along. I just didn't get it."

Wispy clouds hovered outside the airplane window. Oklahoma City was no longer in view below.

Wondering why their problems couldn't disappear as easily, Michael leaned back against the headrest, closed his eyes, and squeezed Lisa's hand. He wouldn't push. He'd take things slowly. And, just in case things worked out the way he hoped, the Mexican skirt he'd found in Lisa's closet this morning was tucked inside his bag. A little wishful thinking never hurt anyone.

Michael peeked through the slit between his eyelids, looking sideways at his wife. She wore a new outfit. A shapeless, gauzy, colorless thing. Lisa's body was lost somewhere inside those yards and yards of fabric. Though it might be the latest fashion trend among the young and faddish, as far as he was concerned, she'd lost her sense of style along with her memory.

Still, she was with him. That was all that mattered. The rest he could handle. Michael trailed one fingertip up Lisa's arm to the inside of her elbow. He felt goose bumps prickle her skin and she shivered. *Or was it a shudder?*

"Tell me some more stuff about the island," she said.

Definitely a shiver, he decided when she placed her hand on his thigh and grinned up at him with an almost childlike anticipation.

"I've never been there, but Jarrod describes it as paradise," he told her. "No television in the rooms where we're staying, not much nightlife, no bustling city streets. Nothing to do but relax and enjoy the water, the scenery and . . . " He imagined the rest and responded physically, despite his determination to take things slowly. Weeks of abstinence had definitely taken their toll.

Two bright, pink spots appeared high on her cheekbones. Still, she didn't glance away. "I'll try my best to make this work out," she said. "Christmas made me realize how important marriage and a family really are to me." She offered a shaky smile, then rested her head on his shoulder.

Michael stroked her hair. "I love you, Lisa."

"Where could he be?" Lisa looked impatiently around the airport waiting area. "Jarrod said to meet him here."

"Relax," Val said. "I'm sure last-minute arrangements like these take time. At the very least, he'll have to file a flight plan. Who knows what else is involved?"

Lisa paced in front of a large glass window that offered a view of the runway. She'd called Jarrod from Confucius Says. Why couldn't he hurry?

Michael needed to know the truth about her feelings before she could change back. Why hadn't she figured that out sooner? Their lack of communication had separated them long before the switch with Tory physically pulled them apart.

"Jarrod wasn't too happy about all this," Lisa said to Val. "I guess that's understandable, considering he believes he barely knows me and thinks I'm an ex-employee his partner fired."

"How did you convince him to go through with it?"

"I promised I'd make it worth the trouble."

Val's eyes widened. "How?"

"We didn't discuss specifics." Lisa sighed. "Knowing Jarrod like I do, I can imagine what he expects. I'll worry about it when I have to. Right now, all I can concentrate on is reaching Michael."

"Poor Tory. If you're successful and you do switch back, she'll be left to deal with Jarrod."

"I've already thought of that. Don't worry. I'll come up with something to get Tory off the hook.

I won't leave her holding the bag." Lisa laughed. "Or maybe I should say 'bag of hot air,' since it's Jarrod we're talking about."

Seated in a chair alongside the suitcases they'd hurriedly ran to their respective homes to pack, Val tapped her foot against the floor. "I can't wait to finally meet Michael's partner."

"Well, your waiting's over." Lisa strode toward the hallway. "Here he comes now."

Val stood, walked up behind Lisa, and gasped. "Good God! It's him!"

Jarrod's features froze in an expression of surprise. Then, just as quickly, the surprise melted into a broad, lusty grin. "Hello, beautiful," he said to Val. "So, we finally meet again."

Chapter Twenty-seven

Val stared out the window, her lips set in a thin, unyielding line. Only the rapping of her fingers against the armrest revealed her agitation.

"Out with it," Lisa said, cupping her hands around her mouth and leaning toward Val to be heard over the plane's roaring engines.

Like a punctured balloon, tension seeped from Val's shoulders. "Jarrod Wilder is the man I met in the Cayman Islands on vacation."

Lisa swallowed the snicker that spiraled toward her throat.

"We never told each other our real names," Val continued.

They were airborne now, and the noise from the engines had lessened to a tolerable hum. Thankful they could end all the shouting, Lisa eased back in her seat. "What did you call him?"

"Never mind."

Lisa giggled. "I'm sorry. But it's difficult to believe Jarrod is the affair you've been telling me about all these months."

"And why is that?"

"He's just so . . . so—"

"Maybe I know a side of him you've never seen." Val's flustered glance shot toward the cockpit where, occasionally, they caught glimpses of Jarrod with the co-pilot he'd brought along.

Lisa cleared her throat; then, with an effort, assumed a facade of composure. "Obviously so. Well, at least you've solved my problem of how to make this trip worth Jarrod's trouble."

"Wait just a minute—" Val started, breaking off abruptly when she spotted Jarrod making his way toward them.

He stopped next to Lisa. "Now, Miss Beecham, are you going to tell me what this trip is all about?"

Jarrod's use of Tory's surname took Lisa by surprise. She braced herself for a thorough interrogation. "As I explained on the telephone," she said, pausing to work her lower lip between her teeth, "it's about life and death." *Or to be more precise, the death of my former life, if things don't go as planned.*

"Some details would be nice," Jarrod said, as he unabashedly gave Val the once-over. "Specifics."

"Right. Um, well, it's about Michael."

Jarrod hooted. "No kidding."

As soon as his laughter stopped, a no-nonsense glare that left Lisa cold replaced his amused expression. "Mikey's not going to be very pleased with me for flying you ladies to Cayman in the first place," he said. "But if your intention is to waylay his and Lisa's vacation, he'll have my butt in a sling."

Val, who'd been contemplating a button on the sleeve of her jacket as if it were an object of great fascination, looked up at Jarrod. "Then why did you agree to do it?"

"I'm a sucker for an adventure." He winked. "Besides, I'm probably doing Mikey a big favor by flying the two of you there. I can keep an eye on you. If another pilot without a vested interest in the outcome of all this were to bring you, who knows what havoc you might wreak?"

After a moment, he dismissed Val to resume his interrogation of the main conspirator. "Now, Miss Beecham, you have some explaining to do. This impromptu journey is going to cost you big bucks." He swept an arm through the air, indicating the cabin of the plane. "The rent on this Navajo Chief isn't exactly pocket change, not to mention the cost of the fuel."

"Rent?" Lisa squeaked. "But I thought you owned this plane."

Jarrod barked out a laugh. "I wouldn't fly you to the Cayman Islands in my plane if you promised me a lifetime supply of naked college coeds. When you're traveling out over the ocean as far as we are, it's a good idea to have two engines."

Lisa gulped.

"You said to get you to the island today, no matter what it took," he continued, shrugging. "You're going to a lot of trouble simply because you've been jilted. Or is there more to it?"

His gaze lowered, settling on her stomach. "The baby . . . is it Michael's? Is that what this is all about?"

Amazed, Lisa followed his eyes. Could she really be showing already? Though she'd noticed a change in herself, she didn't think anyone else could. But there it was—a small yet undeniable pooch.

"The baby isn't Michael's," she finally said after a long, tense silence.

"Thank God." Jarrod exhaled noisily. "I was afraid he'd been holding out on me. He's got all the classic symptoms of a midlife crisis. It wouldn't have surprised me to find out that he knew you long before you ever came to work for us."

He pointed a finger toward her like a scolding parent. "If you're scheming to get your hooks in my partner, I want to know, and I want to know now. His marriage and family mean a lot to him. I won't take part in helping you screw up his life."

Surprised by Jarrod's loyalty, Lisa grinned. "Actually, Jarrod," she said, "my reason for going to Cayman is to save Michael's marriage, not to destroy it. There's a lot that's happened that you're not aware of; a lot I can't begin to explain now. When this is all over, Val has my permission to tell you everything, though I doubt you'll believe it."

Jarrod removed his glasses and polished them with his tie. His eyes narrowed as his attention shifted from one woman to the other, then back again. "How do you figure into this, Val?"

"Lisa's my best friend," Val explained. "We've known each other for years."

He frowned. "You know Lisa, too?"

Val nodded.

"That doesn't explain you and Tory."

Crossing her legs, Val began to swing her dangling foot, taking small slices up and down in the space between the edge of her seat and the chair in front of her. "You might say Tory and I have become close over the past few weeks, as well."

"Interesting." Jarrod returned his glasses to the bridge of his nose. He leaned across Lisa to grin at Val. "How about dinner tonight at that little place on the beach? Remember?"

Val's foot paused in midair. She looked past Lisa at Jarrod, her eyes wide and luminous. Lisa watched her friend's hard-edged, solid-as-a-rock image dissolve into a quivering bowl of Jell-O.

"Of course I remember," Val said in a breathless voice. "That sounds wonderful."

Jarrod winked, adjusted the waistband of his pants, then sauntered off down the aisle toward the cockpit.

Lisa scrunched up her nose. "That cologne . . ."

"I know," Val said dreamily. "Doesn't it drive you wild?"

A gull squawked. Down the way, another answered. Palm trees swished overhead. Above the constant rise and fall of the surf's applause, faint notes from a calypso band could be heard in the distance.

From his lounge chair, Michael peered through dark lenses at his wife. She strolled the turquoise water's edge wearing a wide-brimmed, floppy straw hat and a hot-pink string bikini. The bikini surprised him. Not that she hadn't worn one before. Just never one so . . . how could he describe it? So *stringy*, he finally decided, taking in the thin strip of fabric across her back and the ones at either side of her hips. Though he'd never understood why, Lisa had always been self-conscious about her body. He grinned. Not anymore.

As she turned to walk toward him, Michael propped himself up on one elbow. Lisa looked great. He shifted to observe two men who lounged several feet away from him. It was obvious to Michael that, like him, they were watching his wife. From the looks passing between the two, they agreed with his opinion of her attributes.

She sat down in the sand beside his chair. "We haven't even been here one day and I've already ruined your vacation. I mean, because of me, you aren't snorkeling or anything."

"You haven't ruined my vacation," Michael said. "I'm having a great time just watching you."

She smiled, pushing her sunglasses to the top of her head. "Look at this place. I mean, the sand is as white as flour and almost as soft. The water is so blue, I can't tell where it stops and the sky starts. I'd, like, be really, really happy to sit right here all week and not do anything at all."

"Then do it. That's why we're here. To relax. To be happy."

"But you'd rather be in the water snorkeling. I'm such a big baby."

"Don't worry about it. If you don't want to try snorkeling again, that's fine. It doesn't matter."

"You could go without me."

"I'm here to be with you." And he was. Though he'd looked forward to experiencing firsthand what was touted to be some of the best snorkeling and diving in the world, he could survive without it. Still, she confused him. Wouldn't a woman who'd always loved the water with a passion, always been a strong swimmer, instinctively pick up where she'd left off when she got in over her head?

Earlier, Lisa had floundered around like a two-year-old child, a beginner, when they made their way into the ocean with their snorkeling gear. Clinging to him in hysteria, she'd screamed and sputtered and splashed . . . and swallowed a belly-ful of water. Then she'd thrown up when he finally dragged her to shore.

"Well," she said, "maybe toward the end of the week you'll be tired of me. You could go out on your own then or something."

"I might spend some time snorkeling later in the week, but it won't be because I'm tired of you." He leaned down and kissed her softly, tasting the ocean salt on her lips. "I guarantee it."

She giggled, ending with the gentle snort that still made him do a double-take whenever he heard it. Replacing the sunglasses on the bridge of her nose, she turned away from him.

Michael eased back in his chair. How could he make Lisa a guarantee he wasn't sure was true? Something was wrong. Here he was in paradise, alone with his beautiful wife, who was wearing practically nothing. Lisa was as laid-back as he'd seen her in weeks. She even seemed to enjoy his company. But something wasn't right. Something that was, at the moment, twisting his stomach into a ropy knot of anxiety.

It's Lisa. She's still not the same. She's a stranger. And although a week alone in paradise with a beautiful, sexy stranger might be every man's fantasy—though it had been his own fantasy from time to time—it was *only* a fantasy.

This week was meant to be about reality. About reviving his and Lisa's relationship. But the woman he had always loved no longer seemed to reside within the body he knew so intimately.

A child laughed, and Michael opened his eyes to watch two little red-haired girls down the beach shovel sand into a green plastic bucket. Lisa stood and went to watch them.

Maybe he'd been trying to hang on to something that no longer existed, Michael thought as he watched her go. But he couldn't give up yet. He had the week ahead, though he felt certain he'd know the truth before then. Tonight would provide the answers, one way or the other.

The cab pulled to a stop in front of a neat stucco building. Red-flowered hibiscus adorned the walkway leading to the entrance. A light over the front door shone through the darkness on a sign that read OFFICE.

"Is this the place?" Lisa asked.

"This is it," Jarrod answered. He glanced at Val, who glanced back at him.

"Yes," Val said, her voice a tad breathless. "This is it."

They climbed from the taxi and unloaded their bags; then Lisa paid the driver.

Inside, an ebony-skinned woman greeted them with a pleasant, friendly smile, then informed the trio that only one room was available, and only for the night.

"How many bedrooms?" Lisa asked.

"One," the woman answered.

"We'll take it," Lisa quickly responded.

The woman seemed uncomfortable as her gaze darted between the two women and Jarrod.

"My friend and I will share the room." Lisa pointed at Wilder. "He'll try the hotel next door."

"Hold on," Jarrod interjected. "I'll stay here. The two of you can try next door. Better yet," he continued, offering Val a meaningful grin, "you, Miss Beecham, can bunk by yourself."

Val elbowed him in the ribs.

"We'll argue about this later." Lisa turned to the proprietor. "We'll take the room for the night."

The woman wrote Val's name in a ledger and accepted a deposit, then led the way outside. Every few feet along the wooden walkway, two-foot-high poles, topped by oval glowing bulbs, protruded from the sand, lighting their way.

Lisa mentioned the name of Michael's resort to the woman. "Do you happen to know where it is? We're supposed to meet some friends of mine who checked in there earlier today. We'd hoped to stay there ourselves, but when we called from the airport they said they didn't have any rooms available."

The woman informed them that Michael's resort was down the beach, within walking distance. Then she stopped in front of a door and reached for the knob.

Lisa's knees went weak. *Michael and Tory are close by.* Her heart thumped impatiently while she toured the suite. A tiny kitchen, living area, and large airy bedroom opening directly onto the beach made up the place.

After assuring herself of her guests' comfort, the woman stepped outside. "We do not use keys at our hotel. Most establishments on the island do not. There is no crime in Cayman." She lifted a sign from a holder on the inside of the door and handed it to Lisa. It read DO NOT DISTURB. "For if you do not wish the maid to enter," she said.

"Imagine," Lisa said to Val and Jarrod when they were finally alone. "No crime."

"Don't believe everything you're told," Jarrod muttered. "Now, about the sleeping arrangements: I don't do sofas."

Waving a hand through the air distractedly, Lisa dismissed his comment. "We'll work something out. Right now, I need to speak to Michael." She headed for the door.

"What?" Jarrod gawked at her. "Now?"

"You heard me."

"Then I'm going, too."

"Me, too," Val echoed.

"Suit yourselves." On a deep breath, Lisa reached inside her pocket and retrieved the folded scrap of paper she'd placed there earlier. Silently, she reread the fortune.

Ignoring the questions in Jarrod's eyes when she finally looked up, she turned to Val and lifted one hand, fingers crossed. "This is it. Wish me luck. Better yet, wish me good fortune."

Chapter Twenty-eight

The sea air seemed to have miraculously cured Michael's head cold, allowing him to breathe easily for the first time in days. Yet his mind was far from his nose while he paced the bedroom floor, replaying the previous few hours again and again in his mind.

The mood during dinner had been even better than he'd hoped it might be. They dined at a table outside and watched the sun set. Conversation centered around the trip: what they'd seen and done so far, what they planned for the days ahead.

Often throughout the evening, Michael sensed that Lisa was watching him, searching for something, anything, in his features or expressions that might spark a memory. And though he never glimpsed even a hint of recognition in her eyes, she seemed content to be with him.

He scratched his head. Contentment. Not exactly a negative quality in a marriage. Not exactly anything to get enthused about, either. He'd learned that lesson the hard way.

After dinner, they'd carried their shoes and walked hand in hand along the beach. Waves teased their feet, rushing forward at breakneck speed only to recede as quickly after a gentle caress of their ankles.

She was quiet at first, then slowly the questions began. Questions about the past, about Kat and Jacob. Michael answered them all, one by one, his uneasiness building with each tale of their history he recounted. The stories rekindled dormant recollections of the Lisa he'd fallen in love with years ago. The recollections, in turn, fanned an ember of suspicion that the person at his side tonight was not that woman.

Someone couldn't possibly change so much in the course of a few weeks, Michael told himself. Which only left one possibility. One he didn't much care for. The transformation must've occurred slowly over time, but he'd been too wrapped up in his work, in himself, to notice. Unless . . .

An outrageous idea taunted him as he strolled the beach alongside his wife. *Tory's claims might hold credence.*

Back in his room, Michael assured himself that the idea was ridiculous. But if Tory spoke the truth, if what she'd suggested was even remotely possible, then everything else made sense. His love for Tory, and the fact that he yearned for her, even now; her similarities to Lisa in expressions, gestures, personality; the abrupt, bizarre behavior of his wife.

The sound of spraying water came to a halt in the adjoining bath. He heard the shower door click open, then close again. Michael stopped pacing. His heart seemed to halt for a moment, as well, resuming with a beat so erratic, yet so strong, he feared his chest might explode.

She stepped into the room. Like him, she'd draped a bathrobe around herself. Lifting an arm, she reached out to him.

With a wariness he couldn't explain, Michael walked toward her.

She stood on tiptoe, then placed both arms around his neck and kissed him. Moisture trickled from the tips of her hair onto his chest. Michael closed his eyes and let her take control, silently pondering each unfamiliar movement of her lips.

He slipped his fingers beneath the terry-cloth fabric covering her shoulders, then slid them across her back. When he felt the slight ripple of muscle there, he opened his eyes and drew back to look into hers. They were as blue as the sky, as clear as the Caribbean water. Lisa's eyes . . . but a stranger lived behind them.

"I'm sorry," Michael said, his voice low. "I can't do this."

Lisa knocked on the door to room 310, then lowered her trembling fist and waited. "They're not answering."

"They haven't had a chance," Val insisted. "Give them time."

The corner of Jarrod's mouth lifted. "They're probably in bed. We're interrupting." He reached for Val's hand. "Let's leave."

Lisa gripped the doorknob more tightly. "I'm going inside."

"You can't." Jarrod's squinting eyes issued a warning. "You'll be guilty of breaking and entering."

"Surely the door is locked," Val added.

Lisa shook her head. "Remember? Most hotels don't use keys here." To prove her point, she twisted the knob and pushed the door open. "And I can't be breaking and entering. There is no crime in Cayman."

She stepped inside a small living area with an adjoining kitchen, noting, in the back of her mind, that this wasn't exactly the plush resort the Carribean Tour Company had promised. "Michael!" she yelled, heading nonstop toward a doorway to her left.

"I don't believe this," Jarrod muttered as he trailed at her heels, dragging Val along with him. "Tory!"

"Leave her alone." Val tugged at his arm. "Lisa has every right to do what she's doing."

"Lisa? Who said anything about Lisa?"

The threesome entered a dimly lit bedroom. Lisa came to a dead halt. Michael and Tory stood framed beneath the doorway of the adjoining bath, eyes wide, arms around each other, wearing only robes.

"What the hell . . . ?" Michael stepped back, looking at each of them in turn. "What are all of you doing here?"

"Michael," Lisa said, inching toward him. "You won't believe this, but just hear me out. I love you."

Michael groaned. "Please. This isn't the time or the place."

"But it is," Lisa insisted. "Like it or not, the three of us are here together, and I'm going to make you see the truth if it's the last thing I do. I know our marriage isn't perfect. We have problems that need working out, problems you're probably not even aware of. We share fault for that, Michael, because we don't communicate. I never tell you how I feel or what I need. And you don't tell me what's going on inside your head, either."

"Marriage?" Jarrod shrieked, flattening his perm with the hand he slapped to his head. "Has Tory lost her mind?"

Val jabbed him in the side. "Shhhh!"

"I need you to be there for me," Lisa continued. "Emotionally as well as physically. You haven't been, really, for a long time. I need you to listen and try to understand."

Tears streamed down her face. Unashamed, she let them flow. "Because without you, without Kat and Jake, there's an emptiness in my life that can never be filled. I know that now. I guess I've always known it. We've taken each other for granted, but if there's one thing I've learned from this crazy mix-up, it's that the three of you may not be the only things I need, but you're the best . . . the most important."

She took another step forward. "I've learned something else, too. Even if you weren't my husband, even if we didn't share two children, I couldn't let you slip away from me now because I've fallen in love with you all over again."

Except for the muscle quivering along his jaw, Michael stood completely motionless, gaping in amazement at her as she poured out her heart to him.

"I'm screwing this up!" Lisa sobbed. She looked at Val. "I'm not making sense."

"It's okay," Val said, her voice soothing. "You're doing fine, Lisa. Tell him how you feel. Tell Michael the truth. That's all you have to do."

"Look at me, Michael," Lisa cried. "For once in your life, really look at me." She smoothed both hands over her face, down her body, then grabbed a handful of her copper-colored hair. "Can't you see beyond all this? Please . . . look inside and see who I really am."

For several seconds, the only thing Michael heard was the gentle sound of her weeping. Goose bumps scattered across his skin when he realized he recognized the sound, recognized the way it tugged at his heart. With sudden clarity, he realized, too, that he knew the woman inside the trembling young body. She was a part of him, someone he'd loved for as long as he'd known her . . . and he'd known her for years, not weeks.

"My God!" Michael took a step toward her, then another. "Lisa," he whispered.

She sniffed, then drew a deep breath. "There's a lot we need to discuss when we don't have an audience. You see, I may not have everything I want, Michael, but I do want everything I have—or had. I love you. I love Kat and Jake. I want to be your wife and their mother again more than anything. Please . . . " She reached out a hand to him. "Please believe me."

Like a puppet whose strings had gone slack, she crumpled to the floor. Michael's heart jumped up to his throat. He heard a moan beside him. Turning, he caught the woman he'd traveled to Cayman with just as she collapsed.

Silence. Weightless, Lisa struggled through the darkness toward a light shining above her. As she neared her destination, an intense ringing pierced the tranquility.

Sounds swirled around her, intermingled voices from an old record album playing at a speed much too slow. She tried to concentrate on the sluggish words, to recognize someone, anyone, calling out to her.

One voice broke through the others. She embraced its comforting tone, latched on and allowed it to guide her to the surface, then pull her into reality.

With an effort, she opened her heavy lids and gazed at the reflection in Michael's amber eyes.

Chapter Twenty-nine

Lisa blinked. The image remained the same. Or so she thought. Maybe she only imagined her own reflection, the shape of her face, the familiar straight hair. Could she be dreaming? Or merely visualizing what she wanted to be true?

One thing was certain—Michael held her, his face only inches from her own, one arm beneath her legs, the other cradling her neck. She had no idea how she'd wound up in his arms. Lisa touched his cheek. "Michael."

"Are you okay? Can you stand?"

She nodded, and he lowered her feet to the floor. Then, turning, he looked toward the center of the room. Lisa followed his gaze, her breath catching when she saw Val and Jarrod crouched over Tory.

Lightheaded and giddy with excitement, she extended both arms and inspected her hands, glanced down at her body, her legs and feet, then tugged a strand of hair in front of her eyes to check the color. *Mousy.* "It's me! It's really me!"

Throwing both arms around Michael's neck, Lisa crumpled her fingers in his hair, rained frantic kisses across his face. "I'm back!"

Michael stepped away from her and stared. His hair stood up in disarrayed tufts, reminding Lisa of Kat. She laughed. "Well? Say something."

"Listen to you," Michael whispered. "Your laugh." He shifted his attention to Tory, then back to her. "This can't be happening." Cradling her face between his palms, he peered down into her eyes, uncertainty clouding his own. "Kiss me."

"What?" Lisa asked, surprised by his sudden request.

He didn't take time to explain. Instead, Michael pulled her to him, then lowered his mouth to hers. His lips moved hesitantly at first, tasting, testing.

In contrast, Lisa responded eagerly, pressing against him, rejoicing in the perfect fit of their bodies. A mold cast by time, she thought, by years of loving. It occurred to her then, as their breaths met and mingled, that with him life might be chaotic and sometimes frustrating, but without him it merely existed. A cake without icing, a movie without the soundtrack.

Michael's hands slid up the sides of her face, into her hair, then slowly down her neck. "It is you. You weren't there a minute ago, but now you are. I can see you. I can feel you." He kissed her again. And again.

A moan drew Lisa's attention to the center of the room.

"Oh . . . my head!" Tory pushed herself up to a sitting position on the floor. Her eyes were closed and she rubbed her temples with her fingertips. "I just had the weirdest dream." She was facing Jarrod, and when she opened her eyes she asked, "Who are you?" Then she glanced at Val, Michael, and Lisa. "Oh, God! It wasn't a dream, was it?"

"Lisa?" Val looked at Lisa and blinked. "Is that you?"

Lisa gave Val the thumbs-up sign and grinned. "It worked."

"What worked?" Jarrod stood, pulling Tory to her feet. "Is someone going to tell me what the hell is going on?"

"I'll explain it all later," Val assured him. "You, Tory, and I will have a long talk over a late dinner."

"But I thought we'd have dinner alone," Jarrod said.

Val glared at him. "*Really*, Jarrod! Tory's not in any condition to be by herself at the moment."

Lisa had a liplock on Michael, but she heard the conversation going on across the room.

"Those two obviously need some private time together," Val said.

"That's what I tried to tell you both before we barged in here," Jarrod told her.

From the corner of her eye, Lisa saw Tory rub her head.

"I'm so confused."

Val placed an arm around the girl's shoulder. "You remember me, don't you?" When Tory nodded, Val steered her toward the door of the bedroom. "Why don't you come along with Jarrod and me?"

Lisa stopped kissing Michael long enough to say hurried good-byes to their guests.

Frowning, Tory stared long and hard at Michael. "Thanks for everything. I think." She started off again, then paused in the doorway.

"Would it be okay if I borrowed the bathroom for a minute?"

"Sure, go ahead," Lisa said. She and Michael stepped aside to let Tory pass.

Tory paused to stretch before closing the bathroom door. "My back aches as much as my head." She yawned. "And I feel like I haven't slept at all in the last twenty-four hours."

"You haven't," Lisa told her.

"That explains it," Tory said, rubbing her lower spine as she closed the bathroom door.

Lisa exchanged a knowing glance with Val. "I don't think her back aches from sleep deprivation," Lisa mumbled.

"What?" Michael asked.

"Nothing."

"Will she be okay?"

"I think so. But she's in for a shock or two."

"I'll break the news to her gently," Val said. Jarrod stood beside her scratching his head, his expression growing more and more perplexed with each passing minute.

A shrill scream from the interior of the bathroom instantly turned all four heads in that direction. Lisa bit her finger and winced. Her eyes fused with Val's. "I think you're too late."

Hours later, Lisa twirled in front of a full-length mirror, causing the multicolored skirt to flutter around her calves. "I can't believe you brought this." She cast a coy look over her shoulder at Michael. He was lying naked across the foot of the bed, propped up on one elbow, watching her.

Earlier, they'd had a long talk about their past. Not an easy discussion for either of them, but well worth the discomfort. Old insecurities and painful regrets were exposed, uprooted, then tossed aside.

"I wish . . ." Michael said now, looking at her in the mirror.

Lisa flinched. "Please . . . don't mention wishes."

Michael grinned. "Good idea."

She inspected her reflection. "I've never been in such great shape. Tory did wonderful things for my body. This is every woman's dream come true. All the benefits with none of the work."

She lifted one arm and flexed the muscle. "Poor Tory. All that effort and she's back to square one. I'm sorry to say I didn't take as good care of her body as she did mine. I couldn't seem to eat enough chocolate. I didn't sleep much, either." She threw a hand to her mouth. "Oh, no!"

"What's wrong?"

"I'm afraid I got a little drunk one night before I knew about the pregnancy. Tory must have a low alcohol tolerance, because I didn't really drink all that much. I hope I didn't harm the baby."

"It's not your fault. How could you have known she was pregnant?"

"That doesn't make me feel any better. I'll have to tell her, so she can talk to her doctor about it. I'm glad she didn't faint when she saw herself in the bathroom mirror. The pregnancy came as quite a shock."

Michael scooted to the edge of the bed. "Let's talk about you for a minute instead of Tory," he said. "When we spoke the other day about your future, you said you wanted to start a business—something fun."

She turned to him, tilting her head in that way he loved so much. "How would you feel about that, Michael?"

"I think it sounds exciting. When I said you should follow your dream, I meant it. I loved seeing you so enthused about the prospect of your own business." He smiled. "Go for it, honey. I'll be behind you this time, with more than just words."

As remarkable as Lisa's story was, Michael didn't want to discuss it any longer. He didn't want to think about the future right now or about anyone or anything but the two of them and the moment.

What he wanted was to show Lisa what she meant to him. To make up for his past neglect. To make her remember all they'd been to each other, enjoyed together, despite any imperfections in their relationship.

He wanted to show her that he could give her more, much more than they'd shared in the past. Because the love he was experiencing now, Michael realized, went beyond the rekindling of a dying flame. It was fresh and vibrant, pure and unexplored. "I've always been crazy about the way you look in that skirt," he said.

"I know. As I recall, it's gotten me into trouble more than once."

"It's about to again. I find it especially attractive when you wear it without a blouse." He reached out to her. "Get over here."

She was nervous. Ridiculous, she told herself, considering that they'd started this years ago. They were children then, really, with no second thoughts, no money, nothing between them but limitless dreams and each other.

Still, her legs were shaky as she crossed the room to stand beside him. Tonight was a new beginning. The start of a forever she desperately wanted, a forever she'd almost carelessly forsaken. She realized now the enormity of their love, the precious power it held, the beauty, and wanted to weep with relief that she'd found it again. That it hadn't been lost to her.

"It's about time," Lisa teased, as his fingers flicked open the button at the back of her waist. The skirt rippled down her hips, her legs, a splash of vibrant paint at her feet.

Michael stared openly. "Do you have any idea what you do to me? Each time I look at you, it's like the first time. I fall in love all over again." He looked up, and their eyes met. "I have fallen in love all over again. With you."

"Prove it." Breathless, dizzy with wanting him, she sat on the edge of the bed.

"My pleasure," he said. When he trailed a finger from the hollow of her neck to the tip of one breast, her shudder brought a smile to his lips.

Earlier, after everyone had left them alone in the bungalow, all the desire, all the intense and possessive needs had overpowered everything else. Their lovemaking had been feverish, frenzied, an urgent quest to reclaim what had almost been taken away. He wanted more now, to give as well as take, and he sensed that she wanted the same.

"You need to know something," Michael murmured. "Tory and I . . . we never—"

"You don't have to tell me. It's okay."

Despite her words, he saw questions and uncertainty in Lisa's eyes. When she looked away from him, he turned her face toward him with the touch of his thumb. "Even if she'd been willing, it wouldn't have worked. This evening, before you walked in, I told her I couldn't go through with it. She wasn't you, and somehow, though my mind denied the possibility, my heart knew it was true."

There was a welcome sweep of familiarity as his mouth covered hers. His scent, the texture of his skin, the tug of anticipation that set her on a path toward mindlessness. But there was a difference, too. A jolt of fresh awareness in the urgency flickering in his eyes when he drew back to look at her. Needs surged undisguised through his touch.

"You're the only one." She leaned against him, and he brushed the tears from her cheeks. "My past, my future."

The scent of passion hung heavy in the room, drifting on the sultry night air that sighed through the open window. He lowered her onto the bed, his mouth again tasting, savoring, hands gentle and enticing. She wanted to absorb every sensation, memorize every movement, melt into him so that nothing could ever separate them again.

Surrendering to the tangled desires growing inside her, she clung to him as they moved across the bed, the words he whispered against her lips the only sound audible beyond the rush of ocean waves to shore.

He couldn't get close enough. He wanted to climb inside her, to claim every inch of her at once with his hands, his mouth, his body. Her flesh was as slick as his own, her breath hot and maddening where it touched him.

When she strained against him, demanding more, offering everything, it took all his restraint not to give into his need. Instead, he rolled to his back and found satisfaction in watching her. She was wildly abandoned, bold in her enjoyment of his body.

She felt his eyes on her and loved that he watched her, loved knowing that she caused the ragged sound of his breathing, the reckless beat of his heart. When he reached for her again, she closed her eyes and lost herself in sensation as he repaid every exquisite pleasure she'd just bestowed on him. His hands and mouth roamed, lingered, tormented.

Power came with experience, and no one had more than he in pleasing her. He knew exactly what to do to send her over the edge, how to stroke, and where. "Now," she said. "I want you now."

Those few simple words, her greedy mouth and hands, defeated his control. He allowed her to guide him to her, her touch stealing the breath from his lungs.

The heartaches and fears of the previous weeks slipped away. Her body arched. She sobbed his name. He let himself go, driving them both to fulfillment, claiming and being claimed, sealing his destiny and her own.

Epilogue

5 Months Later

'Mom!" Kat ran into the building, dodging paint cans and ladders, sawhorses and buckets. Jacob and Michael trailed behind her.

Lisa lowered her paint brush and looked over her shoulder. "Hi, guys. What do you think?" She stepped away from the wall to admire her handiwork.

Michael narrowed his eyes. "I don't know. It might be a little too pink."

"It looks like Pepto Bismol," Jake added.

A groan rumbled from the other side of the room. A big, burly painter, his white hat and overalls splattered the same shade as the wall, glared down at them from the top of his ladder. "Don't tell her that. We're almost finished here. She'll have us repainting the whole dad-gum place."

Echoes of agreement bounced around the room as two other workmen contributed their opinions.

Lisa placed the paintbrush crossways atop a bucket and shook her head. "Spare me. You guys make me sound like the worst boss in history. I'm as ready to get this show on the road as the rest of you. More so." She winked at Kat while motioning toward the wall. "Learn to love it. We'll call it bubblegum blush."

"Are we gonna keep talking about paint or are you gonna tell her?" Jake asked Michael, grinning.

"Tell me what?" Lisa eyed each member of her family but received no response. She settled her fists on her hips. "Somebody speak up before you all explode."

"You tell her, Dad," Kat said.

"Do you really think I should?"

Lisa shifted from foot to foot. "Out with it already."

"Okay, you win. Your future assistant manager is the father of a beautiful, dark-haired baby girl with big hazel eyes."

"No kidding!" Lisa clapped her hands together. "Why didn't someone call me when Tory went into labor?"

"Apparently, it all happened pretty fast. Mother and daughter are doing great. As for Dillon, I'm not sure. Last time I saw him, his feet weren't quite touching the ground."

"You saw them?"

Michael shrugged, his grin a tad guilty. "We stopped by the hospital on the way here. Sorry; we couldn't wait."

"I'll go tonight. I'm so thrilled for them. Tory deserves to be happy. So does Dillon." *After all I put him through,* she thought to herself. He'd had a tough time accepting the truth when she and Tory broke it to him on their return from Cayman. Lisa wasn't sure he believed them even now. Nevertheless, he'd swallowed his pride and welcomed Tory back into his life with open arms, marrying her only days later.

Much to Lisa's relief and delight, after adjusting to the shock, Tory had joyously accepted her pregnancy. She'd marveled at each new stage, eagerly anticipating the baby's arrival. Lisa felt certain Kat and Jacob had a lot to do with Tory's change of heart about being a mother.

"Well, I hope Dillon will come down to earth in a couple of months," Lisa said. "I've put myself on a deadline. Wishful Thinking will open its doors to the public two months from today, come rain or shine."

As Michael looked skeptically around him, she added, "I know, I know. There's a lot left to do. There are waitresses and busboys to hire, menus to print, and a hundred other things I probably haven't even thought of yet. But with your help and Dillon's, I'll make it."

Michael looked into her eyes and smiled. "I'm sure you will."

His smile faded quickly. Too quickly. "So, what's wrong?" Lisa asked.

"I've been thinking about Tory and Dillon." He shook his head. "They're so young. Tory will probably end up dropping out of school, now. Dillon will be lucky to finish himself. I just hope they can make things work."

Lisa poked Michael in the side. "They won't drop out of school. Tory's job is secure at the law firm, isn't it?"

"Of course it is."

"Well, then, I had a talk with her the other day. She hasn't given up on becoming a lawyer. It may take longer than she planned; she and Dillon know that. They realize it won't be easy. But if they work together, they can raise their child and both keep their dreams intact."

A smile teased the corner of Lisa's mouth. "We're doing it, aren't we?"

"We sure are." When Michael winced, Lisa followed his gaze down to the finger he'd nicked with a knife while helping her prepare dinner the night before. The skin on his hands looked scaly and red. *A lawyer with dishpan hands.* She grinned.

Michael grabbed her arm and tugged her toward a nearby doorway.

"Where are we going?" she asked.

"Show me what you've done to the kitchen."

"It's the same as the last time you saw it," Lisa protested.

Michael turned to her, raising and lowering his brows. "Show me anyway." He glanced at the kids. "You two grab brushes and help the painters."

As they passed through the swinging doors into the unoccupied kitchen, Lisa said, "They'll make a mess."

With determined strides, Michael led her past a room that would soon be her office. He smiled when he spotted the red velvet Elvis portrait hanging on the wall.

When they came to the walk-in freezer, he stepped inside and pulled the heavy door to, making certain it didn't latch. "This thing isn't hooked up yet, is it?" He maneuvered Lisa into a corner, then flattened his palms against the wall at either side of her shoulders.

"No. Would it make any difference if it was?"

"None at all." He lowered one hand and slipped it beneath her T-shirt. "We'd just have to heat up the place."

A flush spread across her cheeks. "I have no doubt we could do it." She grabbed hold of his tie and tugged, bringing his mouth close to hers. "You're making me crazy."

"Complaining?" he murmured against her lips.

"Not on your life."

As he pulled Lisa into the circle of his arms, Michael scanned the small space around them. "Have I told you how proud of you I am? You've made this happen. Your wish has finally come true."

"Yes. All but my latest one."

Michael felt the blood drain from his face. "Tell me you're not about to ask me to take up a new sport. My tailbone's still sore from busting it on those damn hockey skates."

"Don't worry, it's not another sport."

He wasn't sure what to make of the teasing look in her eyes. "You're not considering a tattoo again, are you?"

Lisa laughed. "I was kidding about that. I do miss my butterfly, though."

"If you want me to help get Val and Jarrod back together, forget it. I think I like them better apart."

"Sorry to disappoint you, but they got back together on their own . . . again."

She raised a finger to his lips, and he felt his frown dissolve beneath her touch. "Relax," Lisa said. "You'll find out tonight about my newest wish."

Her grin filled Michael's mind with all kinds of interesting possibilities.

Lisa wiggled her brows. "I've already bought the grapes."

Dear Reader,

I hope you enjoyed reading *Body & Soul* as much as I enjoyed writing it! I was happy to have the opportunity to continue Tory's and Dillon's story in a novella entitled *Blame It On The Baby* included in the *New Year's Babies* anthology, available in November 1999 from Love Spell.

I love hearing from readers. Write to me at Dept. 243, Box 8100, Amarillo, TX 79114, or email <u>jarcher@arn.net</u>.

Jennifer Archer

LOVE ME TENDER — SANDRA HILL

Once upon a time, in the magic kingdom of Manhattan, there lived a handsome designer-shoe magnate named Prince Charming, and a beautiful stockbroker named Cinderella. And as the story goes, these two are destined to live happily ever after, at least according to a rhinestone-studded fairy godfather named Elmer Presley.

___4457-9 $5.99 US/$6.99 CAN

STRANGER ON THE MOUNTAIN
Linda O. Johnston

The mountain lion disappeared from Eskaway Mountain over a hundred years ago; according to legend, the cat disappeared when an Indian princess lost her only love to cruel fate. According to myth, love will not come to her descendants until the mountain lion returns. Dawn Perry has lived all her life at the foot of Eskaway Mountain, and although she has not been lucky in love, she refuses to believe in myths and legends—or in the mountain lion that lately the townsfolk claim to have seen. So when she finds herself drawn to newcomer Jonah Campion, she takes to the mountain trails to clear her head and close her heart. Only she isn't alone, for watching her with gold-green eyes is the stranger on the mountain.

__52301-9 $4.99 US/$5.99 CAN

Dorchester Publishing Co., Inc.
P.O. Box 6640
Wayne, PA 19087-8640

Please add $1.75 for shipping and handling for the first book and $.50 for each book thereafter. NY, NYC, and PA residents, please add appropriate sales tax. No cash, stamps, or C.O.D.s. All orders shipped within 6 weeks via postal service book rate. Canadian orders require $2.00 extra postage and must be paid in U.S. dollars through a U.S. banking facility.

Name_____
Address_____
City_____State_____Zip_____
I have enclosed $_____ in payment for the checked book(s).
Payment __must__ accompany all orders. ❑ Please send a free catalog
CHECK OUT OUR WEBSITE! www.dorchesterpub.com

HIGH ENERGY DARA JOY

Zanita Masterson knows nothing about physics, until a reporting job leads her to Tyberius Evans. The rogue scientist is six feet of piercing blue eyes, rock-hard muscles and maverick ideas—with his own masterful equation for sizzling ecstasy and high energy.

___4438-2 $4.99 US/$5.99 CAN